Heaven's Doorway

Heaven's Doorway

Mary Alice Baluck

Independently published

Editing, print layout, e–book conversion, and cover design by
DLD Books Editing and Self–Publishing Services

www.dldbooks.com

Cover painting:
A Young Woman With Her Parasol on the Beach
Paul Gustav Fischer (1860–1934)

ISBN: 9798652093655

Dedication

I dedicate this book to my dear friend Kathy Sabol, who has constantly encouraged me to write and pursue publication. I acknowledge the remarkable staff at The Blackburn Home, especially Michelle Rudge, Administrator, for giving me access to all of the technology and for being there for me when I needed her.

Table of Contents

PROLOGUE

The solemn funeral procession dispersed into small groups. Quietly, they ambled back through the shaded cemetery toward the house, where they would eat and search to find the right words of consolation for the grieving family.

A lone figure remained at the open grave. Looking up through the trees to a patch of blue sky, he released the flood of tears that had been welling in him for three days. His shoulders shook. His chest heaved with deep sobs.

Jack Mahoney couldn't make sense of the senseless. They had found her body on the beach, her neck broken, covered in filth. Perhaps things would have been different if only he'd made more effort. His grief was riddled with the guilt of good intentions ignored because of his absence.

Emotions spent, he became aware of the oppressive September heat. The sound of droning locusts permeated the still air with a monotonous mantra that reached heavenward, like a petition of prayer for the entombed bodies that surrounded him. From beyond the tall oak trees, he could hear the surf washing the strand of rocky beach where they had found her body.

He removed his jacket, wiped sweat and tears from his face with a handkerchief, and walked slowly back toward the house. He and the children would spend the night, and then, early in the morning, they would board *The Mariner* and sail back to Buffalo.

CHAPTER ONE

Sunday, April 22, 1906

It was unseasonably warm that April. For seven gray days, ominous dark clouds had spread a blanket of gloom over the countryside as a strong warm front tenaciously bullied the cold Arctic air along the Canadian coast, pushing it further north. Lake Erie reflected the mood, churning and roiling up mountainous waves that smacked and pounded each other and collapsed into thunderous sheets of white foam. Torrents of rain soaked the land, washing away the last vestiges of soot–covered snow. Winter's legacy was gone.

Sometime between dusk and dawn, the rain had stopped. Sunday morning's arrival was washed in color. Dark, webbed tree branches and shrubs were now dressed in patterns of chartreuse budded lace. Yellow forsythia peeked bashfully around corners, and crocuses popped up in pastel patches everywhere. The past week's raging furor had finally exhausted itself into submissive serenity as the sun, still low in the east, wove gold and silver threads through calm, azure water that mirrored a cloudless blue sky. The day had the sweet smell of spring. Life at Herron's Point went on.

Maggie Mahoney, up since dawn, had milked and fed old Nellie, fed the chickens, brought in the eggs, brought the vegetables and apples up from the root cellar, then pared and sliced the apples. She cleaned herself up in plenty of time for eight o'clock Mass and decided to wait for her mam on the front porch.

Leaning against the pillar next to the steps, she could see beyond the rooftops of Commerce Street to the vast lake beyond. Its moods were no stranger to her. There, gulls turned and swooped along the shoreline, competing with a dozen or so herons and a single hawk, all of them hungry and in search of fish and carrion washed ashore by the past week's storms. Their raucous competition mingled with the tolling of the only church bell in Herron's Point, at Saint John's Lutheran Church, announcing the Sabbath. The familiar sounds of a town rising from slumber filled Maggie with the expectant wonder of the secrets the day would unfold.

"How beautiful," she whispered to no one.

She gazed at the horizon, veiled and mysterious, water and sky blended into an indefinable curtain that obscured her vision of the other side. Nostalgic fragrances aroused her senses with a profound melancholy that she didn't quite understand. One day, she'd go through that curtain, because somewhere beyond it was a city called Buffalo. Jack was there.

May 4, 1900

It had been almost six years since she'd seen him racing

down the hill toward Water Street, all his belongings in one small satchel. How often she had searched that horizon those days after he'd gone—long, lonesome days, watching and waiting for a ship to bring him back home. None ever came. She still missed him desperately.

Standing there waiting for Mam, her mind was flooded with the memory of her brother and the way he and Mam had been at it all that afternoon so long ago. These very porch steps had become her refuge from the yelling and haranguing, harsh words racing down the hall and through the screen to assail her ears.

"And she'll not be dirtyin' up me threshold with her wanton ways!" she'd heard Mam scream above banging pots and pans as she prepared dinner.

Then Jack, slamming the screen door, had come to sit beside her on the step, his handsome face all red and bothered. He told her he was going away, but she didn't understand. He promised to write. She still didn't understand. Then, with a kiss, he was gone. Confused, she'd watched him sprint down the steps and out of her life.

She was ten at the time. She wasn't expected to understand.

Back then, Jack and Mam were always at it for some reason or another. Lots of times they fought about her. Jack would yell, "She's only a little girl! You work her too hard." And Mam would go into a tirade.

After Jack left, she began to wonder if perhaps it was her fault; she knew better, now that she was almost sixteen. But back then, when she asked why Jack had gone, Mam always snapped, "We won't be speakin' his name in this house agin. Nivver."

And so it was. Brigid Mahoney, in her own inexorable way, had spoken. Maggie obeyed.

But the boarders who dwelt under Brigid's roof at 7 Erie Street heeded not a word of it. Whispers at the table would suddenly stop as Maggie served them roast beef or took away their dinner plates. Her curious young mind needed to know why Jack had gone.

One evening, she deliberately listened to a conversation out on the front porch as the boarders sat, rocking away, enjoying the evening air after a good meal and doing what they did best, gossiping. How could they know she was just on the other side of the screen door, listening?

"It's just a shame," she heard Agnes Carter say in her soft, kind voice. "I miss him and his bounding energy around the house. How he loved to play his little jokes. Mind how he used to sing at the top of his lungs? He had the voice of an angel." She paused, looking out toward the lake as though talking to herself. "I suppose the real problem was he was just too darned good-looking for his own good."

Zebadiah Chadwick walked over to the edge of the porch and spit a stream of brown tobacco juice into the bushes, turned, and faced the group. Zeb had been hired to take Jack's place, doing all the odd jobs around the house, tending to the grounds and outbuildings, stoking the furnace, or whatever else Brigid had in mind. In exchange, he was given Jack's small room at the top of the back stairs. He did pay a very small amount for his meals, given the fact that he still worked over at the shipping yards during the day, doing maintenance there.

"I didn't know the young feller in his growin' up days," he drawled, "but I used to see him lots a times 'round town. Always one or two girls fawnin' over him, hangin' on his arm. No doubt he was a poplar one."

He sat back down, rocking away, all ears for whatever would come next.

Agnes's sister, Clara, nodded at her knitting, then looked up at the group over wire-rimmed spectacles. Her schoolmarm ways were always with her, she having taught the greater population of Herron's Point over the past thirty years. She analyzed things objectively, always trying to understand behavior, then thought or acted accordingly—so unlike her sister, who saw life with such deep compassion and emotion.

She said, "I agree with you, sister. And I miss him, too. But with human nature being what it is, it was bound to happen sooner or later. Seems every girl in town had their sights set on him. Just happened that Martha Laughton outflanked them all. She knew what it'd take to make him hers. Trouble is, she didn't bank on what it'd be like to come up against his mam."

Kurt Baughman gave a nod of agreement. His jowls and chin flapped when he spoke. "Not too many people 'round these parts have come out on the top end of one of Brigid Mahoney's arguments. I'll grant you that. Just goes to show that little missy wasn't quite as smart as she thought she was."

"Yes," Agnes added, having difficulty understanding how any unkindness could be justified. "But it doesn't mean that Brigid should've thrown her own son out like yesterday's garbage. She'll miss him, you'll see. He was a hard worker. Imagine! Her own flesh and blood!"

"You're wrong." Kurt puffed as the others watched the smoke from his pipe billow around his head, waiting for the inevitable promulgation of Bauchman wisdom they knew was coming. "Good riddance, I say. I don't know what this younger generation is coming to these days. No respect for morals."

A dose of Kurt was like a heavy meal, leaving one with a feeling of uncomfortable spiritual indigestion.

"Yep," Zeb agreed, stuffing another chaw in his mouth.

Kurt dragged on his pipe, then pointed its stem at the faces of the listeners in a superior, all–knowing gesture. "His mam did right by tossing him out. What was she supposed to do? How could she welcome that harlot into her house? No siree, she done the right thing. Aint that right, Mama?"

Elsa Baughman put her needlepoint down in her lap and looked into her husband's fat face. Elsa was tall and square. Her skin's healthy, pink glow reddened quickly when she was spoken to. She was shy and reticent, always bowing to her husband's insufferable wisdom.

"If you say so, Mr. Baughman."

Elsa never called her husband by his Christian name. Where she came from, it just wasn't done. She also never disagreed with him. That wasn't done, either.

The couple owned Baughman's Emporium, down on Commerce Street. At one time they'd lived above the store, but as business grew and prospered, they took on more and more merchandise, and it soon became apparent that additional space was needed, so they turned their second–floor rooms into the furniture and large appliance department. Since most of their time was spent at the business, they felt that the care of a house would be too burdensome, and the accommodations at 7 Erie Street suited their needs perfectly. Both were quite comfortable with the arrangement, and no meal was ever missed. Kurt Baughman saw to that.

Maggie went back to the kitchen to finish her chores, completely baffled by the boarders' conversation.

What was a harlot? she wondered. What had Jack done so wrong that Mam would send him away? Why would he leave her forever?

It was sweet Agnes Carter who finally put Maggie's young mind to rest. As postmistress of Herron's Point, there wasn't much that missed her attention. Most folks appreciated the fact that their secrets were safe where Agnes was concerned, considering that some of their most intimate transactions passed through her office. Little as she was, Maggie became one of those folks.

It was late in July, almost two months after Jack had gone. Maggie had just finished washing the dinner dishes. Even though tall for her age, she still had to use a stool to reach some of the shelves. She was stretching up on tiptoe, putting the last of the plates away, when Agnes Carter came down the back stairway into the kitchen. "Where's your mam?" she whispered.

Maggie, taken by surprise, got off her stool and looked questioningly with wide, green eyes into the face of this plain, thin lady with the sweet smile. It was a rare thing to see one of the boarders entering Mam's domain.

"She's in her room. Said she wanted to prop her feet up and read a bit. Her feet have been bothering her something fierce. Do you want me to get her?"

"No, dear. I want to talk to you. Would you mind coming out on the front porch and sitting with me for a while?"

Maggie smiled. "I guess I could," she answered shyly. No one had paid much mind to her comings and goings since Jack had left. This special attention was a welcome embrace.

Maggie hung up her apron, and the two of them went out to the porch swing.

Agnes looked gently into curious eyes that began to widen as she dug into the deep pocket of her calico dress and produced an envelope.

"Maggie, I have a letter here from your brother, Jack."

Maggie's heart raced.

"Now, Maggie, you must listen to me very carefully." Agnes's face was solemn. "It's very important that your mam doesn't know I have this. She's made it quite clear she wants no mention of Jack." She held Maggie's face with both hands and then chucked her chin with her finger. "About a month ago, he wrote a letter to your mam. But when I brought it home and gave it to her, she wouldn't open it. Just threw it in the stove to burn without so much as a blink of an eye. I thought it only fitting that he should know why there would be no response from her, so I wrote to him myself. I asked him to be patient; given enough time, she would probably come around to seeing things in a different light. Then yesterday I got this letter in another envelope addressed to me. He wants you to keep in touch with him. He misses you very much. So now you can see, can't you, that if your mam found out he was writing to you, I think she would be very angry."

Maggie's eyes filled with fear as she glanced furtively at the screen door. What if Mam was listening! What if she came out on the porch and snatched the coveted letter out of Agnes's hand!

"But he's my big brother. He always paid attention and made me laugh. I miss his singing and...and his funny stories...and...I just miss him so much," she said between sobs.

Tears splashed down her cheeks.

Agnes comforted her. "Shoosh, shoosh, sweet child. It'll be all right. If I give you the letter, that means we're going to have to keep this little secret to ourselves. Can we do that?"

"Uh huh." Maggie let out a hopeful sniffle, rubbing her eyes.

Agnes stroked Maggie's hair and wiped her tearstained face with a handkerchief. "Such a pretty little face shouldn't cry like that. I think we should take a walk down to the corner by that big old oak tree. Shall we? Everything is going to be just fine. You'll see."

Maggie took Agnes's hand and followed obediently, her long auburn pigtails bobbing up and down as they walked slowly to the corner. She looked up at this plain, thin woman and wondered why Mam couldn't be like that sometimes.

"My goodness but you're getting tall," Agnes said, smiling down at the girl beside her. "I remember when I used to hold you on my lap and tell you stories."

At the corner, Agnes knelt down, looking into Maggie's bewildered face. "All right now, Maggie, here's what we're going to do. Every time I get a letter, I'll wait for the right time to give it to you. You bring it up here, sit yourself down under this old tree, and read. When you're done with the letter, put it back in the envelope—it has my name on it—and slip it under my door upstairs. Do you think you can remember to do all that?"

"Yes'm." She nodded soberly. Her heart was pounding with excitement.

"Now I'm going to leave you to have a nice visit with your brother." She cupped Maggie's happy face in her hands again. "You won't forget to do everything I told you, will you?"

Maggie smiled lovingly into the face of her benefactor. "No,

Miss Carter, I won't forget."

"There's my good girl."

Jack's letters helped Maggie fill in the missing pieces. He had wanted to marry Martha Laughton, but Mam wouldn't hear of it—Martha being a barmaid at Kelly's Bar and all. When Martha found out she was pregnant, Jack tried to get Mam to see things his way. That's the day the walls rattled. That's the day Jack and Martha went down to the Alexandre & Arnaud Shipping Company and booked passage on a freighter leaving Herron's Point for Buffalo. They were married in a place called the Chapel of Hope. Patrick John Mahoney was born six months later—February 3, 1901.

Each letter Maggie received was precious to her. Even in the dead of winter, she'd manage to get out of the house and up to the oak tree, just like Agnes Carter had said. Agnes not only disposed of Jack's letters, but also saw to it that the letters Maggie wrote to him were posted. Brother and sister had been reunited.

Sunday, April 22

She was still waiting for Mam, but Maggie was comforted as she gazed across the lake. Wherever that city of Buffalo was, she now knew Jack was there and doing very well. He and Martha had bought a nice house so that little Johnny, who had just turned five in February, could have a proper home. With every letter Jack sent, he included at least five American dollars, so that someday, Maggie would be able to afford to go to Buffalo and visit him and Martha. She couldn't know that plans for that trip would be made much sooner than expected.

Sighing, she shifted her feet. It was getting tiresome standing on the porch waiting for Mam. She wanted to sit on the step, but the porch was layered with filthy winter soot.

Mam won't like it if I get my new green cape dirty, she thought. Tomorrow being washday, I'll bet she has me scrub the porch with the warm, sudsy washwater, now that the weather's turned so mild. There's not much dirt that escapes Mam's sharp eyes.

Brigid Mahoney took the apple pies out of the oven and put them on the sideboard next to the baked bread. She looked around. The large kitchen was spotless, full of good smells. She was done—for now, at least. Besides her bedroom, this was the only place in the house she was happy.

She loved to cook. It was *why* she cooked that bothered her. Never had she believed her life would come to this, cooking and tending to six boarders, sometimes seven. She was a bitter woman. It had been ten years since Patrick Mahoney had been killed; she still couldn't accept the fact that he had left her almost penniless. Him, with all his means. She'd never forgive him for that.

Brigid Mahoney could latch onto a grudge, nurse it, entertain it, caress and wallow in it, inviting it to sprout strong roots in her soul. Life was cruel, as she querulously attested if there was a willing ear to listen. There wasn't too much good come out of it—except for Mary Margaret. At first, she had set her hopes on Jack, but that had all turned to naught—the shameless heathen.

Mary Margaret, with her good looks, would marry well. Brigid would see to that. What precious extra money she had was spent to dress her in a fashion befitting any lady. Those long trips to the best department stores in Toronto would not be wasted. All eyes were meant to turn and look when Mary Margaret Mahoney stepped out of the house for any social occasion. Brigid didn't mind including herself in that bit of attention; she was the girl's mother, for gawd's sake. Already, she'd noticed the boys Mary Margaret's age turning red and stuttering—or strutting, showing off just to gain her attention. But Mary Margaret, having known them all her life, was completely unaware of their motives. That was good, because it wouldn't be the likes of them that would be suitable for her Mary Margaret.

Brigid had her plan. Next fall, she'd send her daughter off to that fancy private school in Toronto that her friend Rosemarie went to. Even though Mary Margaret hadn't attended school since the fourth grade, Brigid's boarder, Clara, had kept the girl up on all her studies. Clara loved tutoring Mary Margaret. She was so quick and bright. Clara had said so. So there'd be no problem with her passing the entrance exams; Brigid had no doubt of that. And there she'd meet the proper people, find the right man suitable for marrying. Yes, Mary Margaret would be the one to take Brigid out of this life of servitude. She would see to it.

Brigid's pragmatic and selfish nature did not possess a modicum of compassion or understanding for others—unless, of course, it didn't interfere with her own wants and needs. One of those needs was to receive the adulation of others, as it had been doled out to her in such large measure by her mam and da and four strapping brothers back in Ireland. And Patrick Mahoney, of course.

Her slippered feet thumped on the dark hardwood floor,

worn shiny in front of the big iron stove. With deliberate steps, she hung her apron on the hook next to the hall, went into the bathroom under the steps to wash her face and hands, then crossed the hall to her bedroom to change for church.

Brigid's bedroom had originally been the library, but that had been at a time when Carl Herron still owned the house. It now contained the massive oak bedroom set she and Patrick had bought when they were first married. A high headboard carved with trailing ivy and roses graced a double bed covered in a maroon velvet spread. The carvings on the dresser and armoire matched the headboard, and the draperies on the east window matched the bedspread. An impressive stone fireplace took up most of the south wall, and the shelves of books that had once lined the other walls had been removed. The walls were now covered in a heavy maroon and gray floral paper. A gray, overstuffed mohair chair and footstool were placed in the righthand corner of the room, next to a large window. A full-length mirror rested on its stand to the left of the window. Absent the morning sunlight, which now streamed through a spotless window, it was quite a dreary room. Brigid loved every bit of it.

She took off her shift and observed herself in the mirror. Her reflection revealed a slender, petite woman not possessing the full, rounded figure so much admired these days, but at forty-five, she took great pride in her still girlish figure—style or not. She did not intend to become the frump of a woman her mam had been, all rolls and bulges. However, she would concede that the years had changed her somewhat.

With subjective eyes, she perceived the beauty that had once been hers as a young colleen in Ireland. Her raven hair was now sprinkled with streaks of silver, and she no longer wore it piled on top of her head with soft ringlets around her face. It was much more practical to keep it pulled back into a bun. Her skin was still smooth and supple except for the few lines she saw on her forehead and around her mouth. But after all the suffering she'd had to endure, she accepted them as her due.

This was not the Brigid perceived by others. Her face told it all. Lips that had once been full and sensuous were now set in a firm, thin line, warning that she was capable of snapping at any time. Two fine furrows were set in her forehead above black eyebrows and lashes that had once framed eyes the shade of spring violets. They were now like blue agate, piercing and cold. Occasionally, if she was caught off guard reflecting upon a youthful memory, her face would soften and one could observe the vestige of a beauty that once had been.

Brigid decided to forgo her corset today. After all, she would be wearing her long coat. No reason to be all trussed up. As much as she liked the fashion of the day, she enjoyed comfort better. And besides, the way the rest of those cows in town dressed for church, they'd never know the difference. She put on a starched white shirt with a high lace collar and ballooned sleeves that fitted tightly from the elbow to the wrist. Her beige skirt matched a bolero jacket with capped sleeves. The hem of the skirt and the edges of the sleeves were embroidered in an intricate brown and rose design. Her high–heeled shoes were dark brown suede with gold buckles. She put on a dark brown spring coat of the softest cashmere and a new, large–brimmed straw hat topped with a mound of huge pink and beige flowers. This she fastened on top of her head with two pearl–tipped hatpins. Easter had been the previous Sunday, but with the torrents of rain, she hadn't been able to wear the hat. Surveying her reflection in the mirror once again, she liked what she saw.

No one in church will equal me—not even Mary Murphy, she thought.

With short, quick steps she walked down the long hall, through the foyer, out the door, across the porch, and down the steps. Looking back over her shoulder, she snapped, "Come on, Mary Margaret. Don't dawdle. We don't want ta be late fer Mass now, do we?"

Sunday Mass at Saint Michael's Church

Saint Michael's was a small, gray-weathered clapboard church with nothing to distinguish it but the two stained-glass windows on either side of a large oak door with shining brass knobs. The land had been donated by Patrick Mahoney when the church was built. Past the entranceway, there was a tall, slender, hand-carved oak confessional in the left corner, dark and intimidating. Its latticed windows were draped in dark red velvet. A black potbellied stove sat in the corner on the right— not fired up today because the weather had turned so mild.

The body of the church was a long rectangle, with ten pews on either side of the center aisle. Each pew easily held six adults, but with a congregation of thirty-six families, mostly proliferating Irish farmers, these pews could sometimes be crammed with as many as eight or nine from a family, with the overflow sitting in the next pew. This year's census, done by Father Charles, had brought the number of the congregation up to one hundred and forty-nine souls in all.

The assembly of eight o'clock worshipers was usually made

up of townsfolk who walked from all directions. Comfortable. Never a worry about finding a seat. It was the ten o'clock Mass that seemed to pack the church to overflowing, the empty lot next to the church always filled with tethered horses attached to wagons and carts of all sorts and sizes. The ten o'clock was a real convenience for the families of farmers from over the ridge, who spent the early part of the morning tending to livestock and doing other chores.

Father Charles Scanlon came out of his back door onto the small portico situated on the second floor of Saint Michael's Church. He leaned against the railing, stretched, and breathed in the delicious nectar of spring.

Paul and Tom Murphy, who had been sitting on the bottom step pitching pebbles at a line drawn in the dirt, immediately stood up, removed their caps, and watched as he descended the steep stairway.

"Good mornin' to ya, lads."

"Good morning, Father Charles," they answered in unison.

"God's hand has certainly touched this day, I'm thinkin'. New life's poppin' up all over."

Both boys nodded solemnly.

Father Charles, as he was affectionately called by most, unlocked the back door, and the three went into the sacristy.

One wall was lined with cupboards and drawers that held the vestments and other accoutrements needed for the various services held in the church. The fragrance of candle wax and incense still lingered, tweaking their nostrils. The boys proceeded to dress, donning black cassocks and the immaculately white starched surplices Brigid Mahoney had generously volunteered to have her daughter tend to—these and all of the altar cloths. Maggie Mahoney obediently spent tedious hours washing, starching, and ironing them.

Tom, the older of the two brothers, opened the door to the main body of the church and proceeded out to the altar to light the candles on the white marble altar table, intricately carved with the Pieta as its base. Accustomed as he was to serving Mass, this was the part he liked best. He never ceased being awed by the mystical silence in this holy place. Dust motes, caught in shafts of golden sunshine filtering through the stained-glass windows, bathed the church in ethereal gold dust. He was aware of his mother and father sitting in the front pew, watching him as he somberly went about lighting the candles and checking to see if the readings for the day were properly marked in the large missal on the lectern. That done, he looked down where they sat, gave them a saintly half smile, and returned to the sacristy.

Mary and Tom Murphy always delivered their two boys for Mass thirty minutes early, so they could serve as altar boys. This meant that Mary and her husband had time for extra prayer before the service. It also meant that Mary Murphy got to sit in the front pew.

Maggie quickly fell in step, making Brigid do double time to keep pace with her long, easy strides. They were a handsome pair, mother and daughter, lifting their skirts to avoid puddles as they walked to the corner and up Center Street to Saint Michael's Church.

The day was becoming quite balmy, and Maggie threw the front of her green cape over her shoulders, revealing a tall, slender figure in a green tartan skirt and white blouse. Thick auburn hair, topped with a yellow straw sailor hat, cascaded down her back. Her fine features had a soft, gentle quality, especially around the mouth, for her lips were full and quick to smile, showing even white teeth. But it was her eyes, revealing an open innocence, that kept one riveted by their striking green color.

She raced a few steps ahead and turned around, welcoming the warm breeze that wafted lazily up from the lake. "Oh, Mam, isn't this a glorious day?" Her face was radiant as she opened her arms to the sky.

"Watch where yer walkin', Mary Margaret. You'll be fallin' fer sure and dirtyin' up that beautiful cape in all this mud, I'm thinkin'. I don't need ta be worryin' about somethin' that doesn't have ta be."

"Yes'm," Maggie replied. She turned and walked on ahead, hoping to meet up with her friend Rosemarie before going into church.

Tim Ryan washed up in the big blue basin on the stand next to his bed. The water was as cold as the room. Shivering, he lathered his body with strong soap. The cracked mirror hanging above the washbasin revealed a handsome young face: strong, rugged features, cleft chin, clear blue eyes, and a mass of dark brown curls that he diligently tried to tame with a brush. The fire had gone out sometime last night, but there hadn't been time to restart it, because he'd overslept. He would barely make it to Mass on time as it was.

He put on his cleanest shirt (only worn once) and the one good pair of trousers he owned. One look at his shoes told him he'd best get rid of yesterday's mud. A dirty sock served to give them a quick swipe.

Throwing his tweed jacket over his arm and shoving his cap on his head, he raced out of the one-room house and headed up Frontier Street. He was going to see Maggie. His heart skipped a beat at the thought of it.

Rosemarie Stuart walked down from Superior Avenue, hoping to meet up with Maggie. They had lived next door to each other and been best friends since early childhood, had gone to school together and played at each other's houses. But Maggie had moved and then left school after the fourth grade, and all of that had changed. Rosemarie's parents thought it best to send her to a private secondary school in Toronto, so it was difficult for them to see each other during the school year. The holidays were about the only chance Rosemarie had to visit her good friend, but even that depended on the weather.

She was happy to recognize Maggie's familiar figure walking up the hill. She waved and gave a yell. "Hey, Maggie, hold up!"

Maggie waited at the corner of Saint Michael's. The two girls met and hugged

"Gee, Maggie, isn't this just too grand?" Rosemarie sighed, unbuttoning her coat and pushing it back on her shoulders, imitating Maggie's posture. "Poppa says it looks like it will be a very warm day. But Mum made me wear this heavy winter coat, since my lighter one is still in a box somewhere back at school. Says this is the kind of weather that makes folks sick. I'm about to roast. That's a beautiful cape," she said, admiration in her eyes. "Your mam sure does have an eye for style."

"I know," Maggie sighed, "but I've been wanting to take it off since I started up the hill. I wouldn't dare, though. Mam would have a fit." She gave Rosemarie a questioning look. "Where's your mum and poppa?"

"Oh, they said they wouldn't be able to make it till the ten o'clock. Today's Florence's day off, and Mum decided to bake a cake. You know how she loves to putter in the kitchen when she knows she won't be in Florence's way. Anyhow, the cake wasn't done, so she said we'd have to be going to the ten o'clock. But I told her I didn't want to miss you. It's such a gorgeous day, I thought maybe we could do something this afternoon. I'll have to be leaving for school in the morning. Do you think you could get away? Seems we haven't done anything together for ages."

"I probably could. But it'd have to be after our main meal at one."

"That's grand. Why don't I just meet you down at the pier? That way, you won't have to worry about time. I can always find something to do until you get there."

"Sounds good to me."

The two of them held hands and followed the rest of the parade going into the church.

"Will your mam get mad if we sit in the back?" Rosemarie whispered as they entered the dim church. She knew Brigid's temperament only too well.

"I don't think so. She met up with Mrs. Flannery at the corner, so it won't be like she'll be sitting alone. They both like to sit way up front. I hate that."

Maggie and Rosemarie walked into church, blessed themselves with holy water from the oak–pedestaled font next to the door, genuflected, and sat in the last pew. Rosemarie pulled her coat back around her. The church was cold.

Shuffling feet, intermittent coughs, and the whimpering of a baby broke the silence as people knelt in prayer or gawked around to check out their neighbors.

Molly Flannery and Brigid sat in the second pew, behind Mary Murphy.

The sight of the back of Mary's head made Brigid seethe. Her loathing for this woman knew no bounds. Not only was Mary ten years younger, but the Murphys now lived in the old Mahoney homestead. And Tom, her husband, had taken over the sawmill that had once belonged to the Mahoneys. Life had dealt Brigid a low blow, but she would not be cowed. She took every opportunity to flaunt her superiority in Mary Murphy's face. Her pleasure today would be showing off her new spring hat.

That Mary Murphy! How plain and ordinary and dull she is. Look at her. Dressed like a frump. And where did she dig up that hat? These were the loving thoughts of Brigid Mahoney as she knelt in prayer.

Maggie could see her mother's hat standing out like a peacock in the middle of a dull field of dark felts and cracked straws, limp feathers, and wilting bouquets, each taken down from shelves to weather another season.

How many years had she seen them? She knew fashion was not a priority for most of the women in this congregation, not when their children needed coats and shoes, and their little girls needed pretty little ribbons and bonnets. And then there was the countrified selection at Baughman's Emporium that would leave any searching woman empty of inspiration. Better just to keep the old hat. They seemed to have compromised their dreams of fashion by drifting from winter dreary to spring drab, waiting for that day when they would have more time and money for themselves.

But even Mrs. Murphy's new straw bonnet with those red cherries hanging over to one side couldn't compare with Mam's headpiece. Leave it to Mam.

Maggie wondered why her mother had to be that way. Why did she have to outdo everyone else? What could it possibly benefit her to preen and strut in front of these kind, gentle folks? After all, she was only coming to church. Maggie couldn't know that her mother's only motivation was her complete and all-consuming envy of Mary Murphy. She didn't care a whit about the others.

Within minutes, the sacristy door opened. There was a tinkling of bells as Father Charles and the two angelic altar boys entered—eyes down, thumbs crossed, and fingers pointing heavenward. Everyone stood for the opening prayer.

Tim ran up the steps. Quietly, he opened the big oak door and entered. His ears told him he wasn't too late. He stood inside the door catching his breath, cap in hand, waiting for his eyes to adjust to the dim light. Then his heart quickened at the recognition of the two redheads in the back pew—Rosemarie's hair copper-gold, Maggie's auburn.

He stood in the aisle and nudged Rosemarie, who nudged Maggie to slide over. Maggie leaned forward to see who was pushing in; Tim gave her a sweet grin. She hoped he didn't notice her quivering lip as she returned a coy smile. Suddenly the service became more meaningful. He was there, almost next to her.

After the gospel, everyone sat down for the homily. Because of his small stature, Father Charles' head was barely visible above the lectern. He usually dispensed with formality and came down and stood in the aisle. Today was no different. What he had to say fit in perfectly with Paul's message of charity in Corinthians.

"As you all know, we buried our brother James Conroy this past week. God rest his soul. And his darlin' wife, Kathleen, bein' with child, could use all the help she can get. I know her other nine youngsters are a comfort ta her grievin' heart, and 'tis true the four oldest are fit ta take over a great deal of the farm work, but if ya could just be findin' it in yer hearts ta take a visit there and help out where needed, I'm thinkin' God would bless ya the more fer it."

Maggie was touched. She knew the older Conroy children and remembered being out at the farm the previous fall during cider–making time. Half the town had shown up for the festivities, and Mr. Conroy had taken all the children on a hayride. The Conroys were a happy lot. Mrs. Conroy laughed all the time, passing out cookies and little hugs as the children all gathered together to sip on the sweet cider. Maggie would have to see to it that she got up there to do what she could to help.

When Mass was over, Father Charles greeted everyone at the door as they exited. Tim and the two girls managed to get out ahead of him and walked to the corner.

Rosemarie's poppa had been right. It was turning into a gloriously warm day. Coats were now shed as the girls talked about their plans for the afternoon. The girls invited Tim to join them, which he quickly agreed to as he and Maggie exchanged shy glances.

Maggie watched as he headed toward Frontier Street.

"Maggie, I do believe you're smitten," Rosemarie teased.

Maggie's face turned pink. "You must admit, Rosemarie, he is handsome. And so polite."

"Oh, indeed. And I think he's kinda potty over you, too."

"Do you really think so?" She grinned, pleased that it could possibly be true. Then two small wrinkles of doubt crossed her forehead. "Oh, how could that be? He's nineteen. I must seem like a silly little girl to him."

"Think what you like, but I know what I see. His eyes are for you. And I can't say I blame him," she continued as she backed up the hill. "Have you looked in a mirror lately? You're anything but a little girl. Well, I'd best get home. Mum has things for me to do before dinner. Don't forget, now. See you at the pier."

Maggie headed down Center Street.

Brigid gave Mary and Tom Murphy a cool nod as they turned to leave the church. She and Molly Flannery walked ahead and out the door to greet Father Charles.

I'll make that Mary wait, Brigid thought. "Good mornin' ta ya, Father. And isn't this day one of God's best?"

"Mornin', Bridie. Ta be sure. And isn't it mighty grand you're lookin'?"

"Oh, get on with ya, Father." She slapped him on the arm with one gloved hand and touched her hat with the other.

Knowing how much she enjoyed flattery, he was only too happy to oblige. "And would that be a new hat you're wearin', Bridie Mahoney?"

"Just somethin' I picked up in Toronto when I took Mary Margaret shoppin' fer clothes." Surely Mary noticed. "Growin' like a weed, she is. That was a heart–rendin' sermon you gave today. I'll be doin' what I can to help the poor soul. Now, don't be fergettin', dinner's at one. I've made your favorite, apple pie."

His grin revealed imperfect white teeth as he patted his flat stomach. "Not a chance atall, atall. Sure and there's no better cook in all of Herron's Point. And none in Canada ta equal that apple pie of yours. Can't wait."

And what da ya think of that, Mary Murphy! Brigid thought.

She and Molly walked down the steps, leaving Mary and Tom Murphy alone with Father Charles Scanlon.

CHAPTER TWO

The Dinner

Brigid walked smugly down the hill, quite pleased with herself as she bid Molly goodbye at Huron Street. When she got to Ontario Street, she could have easily gone into the house through the back gate, but she always made it a point to go in the front door. To her way of thinking, back entrances had always been meant for the hired help.

By the time she got inside, Maggie had already set out the oatmeal, fresh milk, stewed prunes, and soda bread on the sideboard in the dining room for the boarders' breakfast. It was just a little past nine. She could hear the murmur of voices and the clinking of silver against china drifting into the center hall as she passed the doorway and continued to the kitchen. Zeb had killed two chickens, just as she had ordered. They were in the sink, waiting to be cleaned.

She put water on to boil. There was work to be done.

Sunday breakfast was always late and light. The Baughmans were members of Saint John's Lutheran Church on Commerce Street, and the Carter sisters went to the

Presbyterian church at the end of Huron Street. Chester Deidrick joined the Carter sisters whenever he was in port, which wasn't often. Both had services at eleven o'clock, so on Sundays, the boarders slept later than usual.

Zeb didn't go to any church. His feeling, which he didn't keep to himself, was that all churchgoers were hypocrites, even though he'd never really given too much thought to the spiritual side of it all. He found it mighty convenient to think that way, since he hated to get dressed up for church—or any other occasion, for that matter.

This arrangement worked out perfectly for both Brigid and the boarders. Knowing that dinner was at one, the boarders ate lightly, not expecting the usual large morning meals of fried potatoes, bacon, eggs, and sausages, not to mention the pots of tea or coffee and Brigid's hearty homemade breads, slathered with freshly churned butter and blackberry or cherry preserves.

Sunday dinner was always promptly at one, and Father Charles had arrived fifteen minutes early. He let himself in the back door and went into the kitchen to talk with Brigid as she prepared the meal, surreptitiously picking at whatever crumbs he could get in his hands and up to his mouth.

"You know, Bridie, I don't think I'll ever get used ta Sunday fasting. Tis a long wait from twelve midnight on Saturday till one o'clock Sunday afternoon."

"Surely you had a crust of bread after the ten o'clock ta fill that hollow of yours?" she asked, looking at him curiously.

"And spoil one of your wonderful banquets? Not a bit of it. He quickly crammed some dressing in his mouth as Brigid stood with her back to him, stirring the gravy and pretending not to notice, aware that he had little to eat other than meals the parishioners provided. His was a life of real poverty.

Maggie moved back and forth from kitchen to dining room, carrying water and food as it was prepared.

The formal dining room was quite large. Two long windows faced the front of the house, and there were two more on either side of a marble fireplace. It was a beautiful room. The large, gold–framed mirror over the fireplace picked up the light from the five–tiered crystal chandelier suspended over a long table, casting its light into the room. Two tall, matching jade ginger jars, encrusted with pink roses and trailing ivy, graced either side of the mantel, and a tall brass clock under a glass dome sat in the middle, its intricate workings quietly marking the progression of time. The walls were covered in a light gray and silver striped paper, and the draperies and cornices were a slightly darker gray.

The linens on the table were white, and a long, low centerpiece of evergreens and pine cones dressed its center. Waterford crystal, Belleek china, and the good silver, all treasures Brigid had brought with her from Ireland, completed the table setting. After dinner, these would all go back into the china cupboard that sat on the back wall, only to be used on Sundays and special occasions.

This room was made to entertain aristocracy. But then, this was not just any boarding house; it belonged to Brigid Mahoney. Having once belonged to Carl Herron, it still contained the furnishings that had been part of its original elegance. Brigid had purchased it that way. And those who chose paid handsomely for the privilege of dwelling in such luxurious surroundings.

The boarders began sauntering into the dining room

around five minutes to one. The Carter sisters entered from the large front foyer, giggling like two schoolgirls—something about a joke the minister had told that morning during his sermon. Agnes Carter, thin as a pencil in a dark brown wool dress with soft lace at the edge of the neck and wrists, entered first. Chubby Clara wore black, broken only by a large pearl pin at her bosom. Despite their ages, they effused a youthfulness that brightened rooms and uplifted hearts. They were totally devoted to each other.

Elsa and Kurt Baughman, who occupied the entire third floor, followed a few minutes later. Kurt was expounding on the disgraceful behavior of the Ritter children during church services, Elsa following, nodding agreement to his insufferable blustering.

"Their parents ought to cuff their ears, teach them some manners," he spouted. "I never saw the likes of it. Whispering and giggling. Disreputable behavior. And all the while the choir was singing." He flung up his arms and rolled his eyes, yanked out a chair, and parked himself.

Elsa sat down quietly next to him.

Kurt was obtrusive and loud, spouting whatever thoughts he had into the air. Fortunately, the Carter sisters buffered his presence.

Agnes, always one to champion the cause of the underdog, spoke up. "Now, Kurt, surely you must remember when you were a lad. Those Ritter children are truly as sweet as they can be. You can't blame them for getting a little bored and restless sometimes."

Kurt grumbled, "Never in my born days will I understand these younguns today."

By the time Zeb shuffled in with his usual hound dog look, the rest of the boarders were seated. Maggie was putting food on the table as he plunked himself next to Clara. Although usually unkempt and slightly dirty, he'd managed to wash his face and hands for dinner. The Carter sisters had set him straight on that a while back. A shock of salt and pepper hair hung over one eye, which prompted him to occasionally jerk his head so he could see.

He said, "Did hear 'bout Bert and Marabelle Swanson up on Ontario Street?" He flicked the hair out of his eyes and looked around, hoping he'd caught everyone's ear. Dirt was not just for digging up; it was always nice to spread some of it around. Satisfied he'd grabbed their attention, he continued. "I don't like to be the bearer of tales, but it aint no secret that Bert Swanson has always had an eye fer the ladies. Not that any harm ever come of it, 'cause Marabelle always had her eye on Bert."

Everyone looked at him in silence, waiting to hear something they didn't already know.

"Anyway, Widow Barnes—you know, the one with the yeller dyed hair, the one that lives over by the quarry?"

Everyone nodded.

"Well, do you recall she lost her husband, Fred, to that pneumonia a few months back?"

He leaned back in his chair, giving them time to do their recollecting, looked around, then leaned forward to take them into his complete confidence, saying almost in a whisper, "Now I know you ain't gonna believe this, but his body 'twern't hardly cold when she took up with Bert."

He paused once again to make sure he had their curiosity completely piqued. Satisfied, he continued. "Seems he and Fred had been great pals, workin' together at the quarry and all. Then after poor Fred got the pneumonia and died, Bert felt it his Christian duty to spend some time consolin' the poor widder. Which was purely understandable to Marabelle under the circumstances, them bein' such friends and all. Now, as far as she was concerned, that was the extent of it, 'cause she understood how it would be if she lost her Bert. She'd be needin' some consolin' herself. She had no idea what was going on.

"But then Bert comes home one day and says he's movin' out. Goin' to live with the widder, he says. Now, he ought never told her that while she was ironin' them clothes. Beat him unmerciful with that hot iron, she did. And you know what a little fella he is. Marabelle must have forty pounds on him. 'Twern't never a fair fight. So now he's over to the widder's house. Healin', I guess. They're plannin' to move over to the States soon as some of them burns and bruises go away. I'm thinkin' they'd better git movin' pretty quick, before Marabelle gits her temper up again and does the both of 'em in."

The faces around the table sat gaping. Clara let out a long "Ohhh, my!" just as Brigid and Father Charles came in.

It was exactly one o'clock.

Only on Sundays did Brigid grace the dining room table with her presence, and only because of Father Charles. Otherwise, she and Maggie ate in the kitchen after Maggie was done serving the boarders.

Maggie hung her apron on the hook in the kitchen next to the hall and went in to join them, taking a seat next to Elsa. The good father said grace, and food was passed around, family style. Conversation began with a discussion of the unseasonably warm weather, much welcomed and appreciated by everyone except Kurt.

"Too hot for this time of year. Won't last. If we get a freeze, it'll ruin the fruit crop, and we don't want that. Do we, Mama?"

Elsa looked up. "No, Mr. Baughman. We don't want that." She turned back to the platter of chicken in her hand, took a large helping, and passed it on.

Zeb grunted, "Pass the mashed potatoes. And I sure would like some more of them there pickled beets. Best I ever et."

The two Carter sisters sat opposite the Baughmans, daintily eating. Clara said, "Sister, why don't you tell the others the joke Pastor Roberts told at church today? He had everyone laughing."

"No, I think it best if you tell it, Clara. I'm just not as good at telling stories as you are."

"Well, all right, then." She looked around to see if she had everyone's attention.

Zeb was lapping up his food. Kurt raised his eyes from his plate for a second as if to say, "Go ahead. I can listen and eat."

"Well, first of all, Pastor Roberts was talking about how we should love one another and how we should help those in need. Then he told us about poor Kathleen Conroy being left with her brood of children and one on the way, and as to how we should make an effort to help. From that he went on to say how blessed we all are to live in this wonderful country, with such freedom and opportunity. And then, out of the blue, he said that it reminded him of a little joke. He said, seems his friend's grandfather had come to this country seeking freedom. But that freedom didn't last long. His wife came over on the very next boat."

Everyone laughed politely. Zeb grunted, "More stuffing, if ya don't mind."

Father Charles was quite pleased with the story. Said he'd have to be rememberin' it for a later time.

"Oh, Pastor Roberts wasn't finished," Clara continued. "He seemed quite taken up with the congregation's laughter. So much so, he continued with another joke that had absolutely nothing at all to do with the subject at hand."

She looked around at the smiling faces and went on. "It seems this very successful businessman went to church to pray for a hundred thousand dollars. He desperately needed it to close an important business deal. As luck would have it, he knelt down next to another man fervently praying for one hundred dollars that would save him from losing his home. This poor man was so intent in prayer he didn't realize he was actually talking out loud. The businessman became quite distracted and impatient, and in order to silence the man's disturbing prattling, he reached into his pocket, took out a hundred–dollar bill, and pressed it into the other man's hand. The man was so surprised and elated at the quick response to his prayers that, after thanking the stranger profusely, he got up and ran out of the church. Now alone, the businessman turned back to his prayer. 'And now, Lord, that I have your undivided attention...'"

Everyone laughed out loud. Zeb, who had actually quit eating to listen, let out a belly laugh, revealing a shiny–gold front tooth. Brigid covered her mouth to keep from spitting out her carrots. Clara had put everyone in high spirits.

They continued to enjoy good company and good food. Praises, the real sustenance that nourished her soul, were heaped on Brigid for the delicious meal.

After dinner, the boarders crossed the foyer and went into the comfortable elegance of the parlor to read or rest and digest—all but Agnes, who sat at a small spinet and began playing a Beethoven sonata. Father Charles and Brigid took themselves for a walk while Maggie cleaned up and did the dishes, humming the whole while.

Warm sunshine streamed through the kitchen windows. She opened them and the pantry door to let the refreshing outside air cool down the room. There'd be no need for a coat that afternoon.

After finishing the last of the pots and pans, she went into the bathroom and stood at the mirror to brush her hair. Never having considered her looks one way or the other, she stared at her reflection and wondered what Rosemarie had meant. It was the same familiar face. She saw nothing special there, although she was quite proud of her long, thick auburn hair and found great pleasure in brushing it until it fell down her back in silky waves. And while it was pleasing to know that her skin was clear and unblemished, unlike so many of the boys and girls her age, she was oblivious to the fact that she was truly becoming a desirable young woman.

Satisfied that she looked presentable, she left by the back door and walked around the house, feeling alive and carefree. The rest of the afternoon was hers. Tim would be there at the pier.

CHAPTER THREE

The Pier

When Maggie reached the front of the house, she saw Tim, his back and elbows braced against the fence as he stood gazing out at the lake. Her heart leapt.

He's come to walk me down to the pier! she thought.

Her silent footsteps cut across the lawn, and she caught him by surprise.

"Hi, Tim," she said shyly.

Startled, he turned. "Boy, you sure know how to sneak up on a fella." His smile gave her that same queasy feeling she'd experienced in church. "I expected to hear you coming out the front door."

"You're kinda a surprise yourself. I was expecting to see you down at the pier."

Never having called on her before, he realized that his unannounced appearance probably did seem a little strange to her, and his face reddened with embarrassment. He wanted to tell her he'd been looking forward to seeing her ever since he'd left church that morning.

He should just blurt it right out, he knew. Tell her how he'd felt every time he'd seen her in town this past year, ever since the last July 1st picnic on Canada Day, when she'd looked up at him with those beautiful green eyes, breathtaking, filling his dreams, haunting him.

She couldn't know how many times he'd walked by her house, hoping to catch a glimpse of her out in the yard, longing for the chance to get to know her better. Then there was that day he'd seen her pegging up the wash on the line, but his heart had begun to race so fast all he could do was wave and say Hi as he raced on by, fearing he'd trip over his own tongue if he stopped to say more.

No, he couldn't tell her those things. Not yet. But walking her down to the pier was a way to spend some time alone with her before they met up with Rosemarie.

"I just came from the Thurstons', up on Huron Street," he said, using it as his excuse, covering his uneasiness with an insouciant grin.

He continued talking as they fell into step, walking to the corner of Erie. "Charlie Thurston works with me down at the quarry. He used to love to fish, but now, with his four kids and all, his time's pretty well tied up. He's always asking me to bring him up some bass if I have a good catch. Pays me good for them, too. Anyway, I just took him two beauties. Caught them right after Mass this morning. Had enough to fry up for my dinner, with two to spare. Delicious. That's why I was up this way. So I figured I might as well wait around and walk down to the pier with you—since it was around that time, anyway."

At the corner of Erie and Center Streets, they could see the lake, a canvas of watercolor in tints and hues of all shades.

Sailboats and small fishing craft dotted the water. To the right of them, the Point reached out like a mother's arm, embracing large ships under its wing. Its artistry was not lost on them as they strolled down the hill in silence.

Never had that walk down Center Street been so beautiful. Maggie was ebullient. She couldn't remember ever feeling this happy and alive.

Still, she'd never thought of herself as unhappy. No. Life had always been whatever Mam wanted it to be. And she dutifully obeyed day by day, content with knowing it ran smoother that way—although there was a restless longing she had noticed in herself, lately, a sense of elusive mystery that caught her off guard sometimes when she was the busiest, when she found herself wondering about life in general and her future in particular. If Mam happened to catch her dreaming or staring into space, she would yell, "Mary Margaret, quit your dawdlin'! There's work ta be done." "Dawdlin'" seemed to be one of her favorite words.

More and more, Maggie was beginning to question Mam and her ways. Not that she could ever thwart her. But today— today was different. Today was new and exciting, and Mam had no share in it. Today was hers.

She considered the strange twists that life seemed to turn. Life was just about as predictable as the lake's moods. She'd known Tim ever since she could remember. In school, he was one of the older boys. And she'd had a crush on him ever since that time in the second grade, when he'd retrieved her jump rope from the three nasty tormentors who were holding it over her head, teasing her. His size made it no contest as they quickly dropped the rope and ran away. "Don't worry about them none," he'd said as he wiped her tears with his handkerchief and handed her the rope. "They don't mean no real harm. You're such a pretty little thing. Just trying to get your attention, I figure."

But then life seemed to go on without another notice from him. There were times when they'd see each other around town and would speak quite cordially. That was all. She'd been so young, then, looking at him from afar with adoring eyes, but as with so many other things, that was her little secret.

Then, this past year, he'd begun behaving in a much more affable manner. Probably because of what she'd done for him at the July 1st picnic, when she'd cleaned and wrapped that terrible gash he got on his leg. He'd been running to catch a ball and tripped over a horseshoe spike sticking out of the ground just as she was passing by. She immediately ran to get the iodine and bandages from Mr. Clarkins, the chemist, who always came prepared for the usual July 1st accidents, and she saw to it that the cut was cleaned and bandaged. That had finished the picnic for him; his leg was really hurting, so he took himself home.

Whenever she'd see him after that, he was especially friendly, but she interpreted this amiable behavior as his gratitude for helping him that day. And now, here he was beside her. How extraordinary life could be.

She wished she could think of something interesting to say as they walked the few short blocks to the pier. The only thing that came to mind was the weather.

At the bottom of the hill, Center Street divided into two short walkways that surrounded a green. In the center of the green was a large bronze statue of Carl Herron, founder of the town. On either side of that statue was a wrought–iron bench.

Both walkways took you to Water Street, where a narrow cobblestone path led up the center to the statue. Each year, a border of perennials grew on either side of the path. Maggie could see the green tips of tulips forcing their way out of the soft, soggy ground. Two tall, ornamental lampposts, each with three large, glass globes, guarded the entrance. If you crossed Water Street, you would enter the pier.

Almost all of the shoreline along the coast of Water Street was rocky. A wide strip of grass had been planted to border the shoreline to prevent erosion. A long pier at the bottom of Center Street extended a hundred feet out into the water. Today this entire shoreline was littered with driftwood and other debris washed up from the past week's storms.

Kelly's Bar and Marina were located at the far east end of Water Street, right before the entrance to Alexandre & Arnaud Shipping and the Point harbor. Sailors coming into port could wander over and quench their thirst at Kelly's. The east end of Water Street ended at Division Street. The west end of Water Street stopped at Frontier Street. The north side of Water Street was also divided at Center Street. The east side was grassy and wooded, filled with four apple, four peach, and four cherry trees. Four dogwoods bordered Center Street, and four bordered Division Street. Tall arborvitae bordered the entire back of the property, dividing it from the buildings on Commerce Street.

The west end of Center Street was a park. It was also grassy. There were swings, slides, teeter totters, a maypole, and picnic tables, and the back of that property that bordered Commerce Street was also graced with arborvitae. There were maple and oak trees for shade, as well as four dogwood trees bordering Water Street and four bordering Frontier Street.

Benches were nestled intermittently beside each of the lampposts that lined Water Street's boardwalk. The entire quarter–mile area that was maintained as a park was where the town's celebrations were held, and its inhabitants could come to shed the burdens of their days while refreshing themselves with nature's beauty and the soothing rhythm of the lake. Children came to play, accepting it all as part of their estate in life, questioning nothing.

Maggie and Tim were not alone in their desire to enjoy this beautiful day. The entire area buzzed with activity: squealing, running children; barking dogs; babes in prams pushed along by doting mothers wanting to give their cherubs the benefit of warm sunshine; people on benches enjoying the view; and fishermen, big and small, out on the pier with their poles extended, staring into the water, mesmerized by the invisible activity of marine life below.

Rosemarie had managed to get there ahead of them and find a spot at the far end of the pier. She was lying belly down, head hanging over the edge, one arm dangling in the cold water, when she heard the clattering vibration of footsteps on the weathered planks. She rolled over and sat up, waving. "Hey, you two." Her impish smile revealed freckles that had been tucked away by winter's gloom. The water's mist had created a halo of golden ringlets around her cute, snub–nosed face.

"Hey, yourself," Maggie said as she and Tim joined her.

The trio sat on the edge of the pier, removing their shoes, swinging their legs over the side of the pier with their bare feet in the water, soaking up sunshine and watching in silence as the water dipped and rose, lapping against the rocking boats moored alongside.

A freighter moved slowly away from one of the docks over at the Point, its huge hulk dwarfing the other crafts bobbing up and down at Kelly's Marina. Insatiable gulls flew in circles overhead, begging for crumbs. None were offered.

Almost in unison, the three lay back to look up at a sky now filled with puffy white clouds. The game began as the sun moved slowly westward.

"I see a castle with two turrets," Maggie said.

Where?" Tim asked.

"See it? Over there on the right." She pointed.

"Oh, I see it," Rosemarie answered.

"I still can't see it," Tim puzzled. "But I see a horse with a rider on its back. Look straight ahead."

"That doesn't look like a horse. It looks more like a camel to me," Rosemary retorted.

They all laughed.

The game went on. An hour passed, an hour of giggly, laughing fantasy. Maggie was the first to sit up.

"My, it's warm." She wiped glistening beads of perspiration off her brow.

Tim and Rosemarie sat up and agreed.

"What shall we do now?" Rosemarie asked, standing, smoothing her long skirt. Those freckles had truly blossomed.

"We could go back to my place, get my dinghy, and go fishing. I've got enough poles and plenty of bait. How's that sound?" Tim offered. He glanced at Maggie's face for approval.

Maggie looked at Rosemarie. "Shall we? I haven't been fishing in so long." She saw Rosemarie's grin; she approved. "That sounds like great fun, Tim."

Tim lived at the bottom of Frontier Street and the end of

Water Street, about a quarter of a mile west of the pier. His house was one of a number of one–room plank houses built during the early development of Herron's Point. His was the only one left. The thick, wide boards of the house were set in a vertical position, unlike the conventional horizontal method of building. There was a small window in each of the two side walls of the house and plank doors in the front and back. Most homes of this type had one large fireplace for cooking and heating. In Tim's house, there was a big, black iron stove used for heating and cooking. The grassy stretch that ran about fifty feet from the back of the house led to a small dock on the waterfront, where Tim kept his boat. Several outbuildings were on the far side of the house.

At one time, Frontier Street had been the western boundary of the town. Then the discovery of limestone a few miles further to the west resulted in the establishment of the Harrison Mining Company. With a demand for labor to work the quarry, more people had settled, and the town had begun to spread westward. Water Street had not been extended, as the other streets had, to accommodate the need for homes. All of this new territory had been incorporated with Herron's Point.

The short walk from the pier took only a few minutes, the three friends walking barefoot, swinging their shoes as they skipped and jumped along the cobblestones.

Maggie and Rosemarie ran down to the dock as Tim disappeared around the far side of the house and returned with poles and a tackle box.

He handed each of the girls a pole. "Now, be careful. I put the hook in the cork bobbin so you won't get yourselves all snarled up. Later, if you need help putting the bait on, I'll give you a hand," he said with the expertise of a seasoned fisherman.

Maggie stood the long pole in front of her and surveyed it with curiosity. "Do you really think I'll catch something with this thing?" Her green eyes flashed with excitement.

"Never can tell. I went out early this morning and had great luck. Maybe it'll be the same this afternoon. Maybe not. The one thing about fishing is, you gotta have patience."

Tim helped each of the girls climb into the boat. "Rosemarie, you sit at the far end. Maggie, you're at this end," he directed.

The boat teetered and the girls squealed, precariously making their way, settling themselves on the wooden seats at each end of the dinghy. Tim climbed into the middle and took hold of the oars.

Maggie covertly watched as he dipped and pulled at the oars, pushing them out into the lake. His muscular arms worked with familiar ease. She thought, I love that dimple in his chin.

Stretching her legs, she could feel the warmth of the sun through her skirt, her body alive with an excitement completely unfamiliar to her. Dismal days filled with work and responsibility seemed to fade.

Sighing with contentment, she looked toward the diminishing shore and the picturesque town with its welcoming park and gently sloping hill where houses nestled, one row after another, clear up to the ridge, where tall pines offered protection from the world beyond—so peaceful. Then she looked at Tim—so handsome.

"The last time I was in a boat, I was with my brother, Jack. That was such a long time ago," she said wistfully. "He'd take me out fishing every once in a while, but I always got my line tangled up. And he'd laugh at me. I loved his laugh. One time, I caught a really big fish. I don't know what kind it was, but we took it home and had it for supper. Mam can really cook up a delicious fish."

Tim gave her a quizzical look. "How is your brother? Do you ever hear from him?"

"He's fine. Living in Buffalo and doing right well for himself—or so I've been told." She wasn't sure it was safe to say more. She'd never told anyone about Jack's letters.

"Look! Look over there!" Rosemarie shouted, pointing toward the shore. She started to laugh and clap her hands. "Can you see that bunch of otters playing? Do you believe it? They're sliding down the muddy bank into the water."

Tim pulled up the oars as the three of them watched, fascinated by the childish play of five otters splashing into the water, then climbing out and back up the hill to do it all over again.

Soon tiring of the sport, the otters swam along the shore, diving for fish, bobbing up and down like small logs floating upstream, oblivious to the three observers who watched until they were out of sight.

Tim realized they had drifted out quite a way. "I think this is as good a spot as any to put our poles in. Don't want to go too far out." He turned. "Rosemarie, there's a large can filled with cement back there. Would you drop it over the side? That way, we won't drift too much."

She began to struggle with the heavy can under her seat.

"Can you handle it?"

"Don't know why not," she said indignantly. "I have to carry my mum's basket of wet laundry outside sometimes. It's sure

Mary Alice Baluck

heavier than this can." The boat rocked as she heaved it over the side with a spray of water that sprinkled her face. The can sank.

After the hooks were baited—not an easy task with two squeamish girls—they all remained silent, intent on watching bobbins bob up and down. This was what Tim had said it would take—patience.

"I...I think I have a nibble. Something's on my line!" Maggie said with disbelief.

Tim moved up behind to help her. "Now watch. Wait till he takes it under. There! Now pull."

Maggie yanked on the line. "I think he's hooked."

The fish leapt out of the water, startling her, causing her to almost let go of the pole.

Tim grabbed her hands to hold them steady. "Take it easy, now. You don't want to break the line and lose him."

Maggie's body was electric. Tim's arms were around her, holding her hands, his gentle voice in her ear and a fish on the other end of the pole connecting them. Completely unstrung, she let him take over and watched as he pulled it in.

"Boy, he's a big one. Your mam'll enjoy cooking him up tomorrow," he said as he strung a line through one gill and out the gasping mouth, throwing the fish over the side.

"Yes, but what I want to know is, how do you know it's a he?" Rosemarie asked.

They all laughed.

By the time the sun met the west, they had managed to pull in five good–sized fish. The girls wanted no part of them. It had been fun, but they weren't about to carry those smelly things back home.

The air had taken on a slight chill. It was late afternoon, and

59

as soon as the sun went down, they knew it would probably get cold, since the earth hadn't stored up enough heat, yet.

"I think we'd better be heading in," Tim said. "When we get back, I'll make us a cup of tea."

It wasn't proper for two unchaperoned girls to go into a house alone with a male companion, but neither Rosemarie nor Maggie considered this as Tim opened the door and proudly ushered them into his domain.

The one–room house was as neat as a pin—and warm, even though he hadn't rekindled the fire in the stove after returning from church. There were no curtains on the windows. Instead, green potted plants grew profusely on the sills, allowing the afternoon sunshine to pour in, making the waxed plank floor gleam. The walls and ceiling were whitewashed and clean. To the left of the door, pressed flowers framed under glass were arranged in a wall grouping around the table. The table and four chairs sat on a large, oval braided rug. On either side of the room, two large lanterns hung down from the dark beams bracing the ceiling. Tim's bed, which was covered in a colorful quilt, the washstand, a high chest, and a large easy chair took up the right side of the room. All the furniture had been handmade from honey–colored pine. His clothes were hung neatly on hooks on either side of the window in the front wall. The kitchen area was to the back and left part of the room, with cupboards and the sink on the back wall. The big iron stove seemed to fill up most of the middle of the left wall. The loft above could be reached by pulling a folding ladder down by a rope. This was where Tim had slept as a young boy. Now that he lived alone, he used the space for storage.

Tim offered the girls a seat at the table and went out the

back door to fill the teakettle from the pump that stood on a cement slab by the door. He left the door open, allowing the breeze to come in from the lake.

"It won't take long for the water to boil," he assured them, and then proceeded to adjust the heat on the stove. Gathering cups, saucers, and a plate of chocolate biscuits, he set them on the table.

All the while, Rosemarie and Maggie looked around, amazed that anyone could put a whole house into one cozy room.

"How long have you lived here by yourself, Tim?" Rosemarie asked.

Tim screwed up his face, thinking. "I guess it's been almost four years, now, since Da died."

"You were awful young to have to live by yourself, weren't you?" Maggie commented.

"Naw! Not really. I've been pretty much taking care of myself since I was ten. Ever since Mam died of influenza. She's the one that pressed those flowers hanging on the wall and braided this rug and made me that quilt." He pointed them out proudly. "She put a big piece of her heart into this place. I think of her a lot—even though she's been gone almost ten years, now."

He paused for a moment, his face softening. The mention of her seemed to evoke tender memories.

"Da wasn't much good for anything after that. Took the life right out of him. Like she took part of him with her." He paused as though deep in thought, then continued. "I sort of had to fend for myself after that. Been working ever since."

Both girls knew about Tim's father, Liam Ryan. He'd been

the town drunk for years. Maggie had often seen Mam scowl when they were out somewhere and he would come staggering up the street.

"The good fer nothin'. Been like that ever since his wife died. No backbone in that'n, I tell ya. The shame's fer that young'n of his. I don't envy his lot in life. Probably end up just like his da."

But Tim was made of better stuff. Not only did he take care of himself, but his father as well, dragging him home when he found him asleep in the park or some dark doorway, but mostly from Kelly's Bar. Tim sold fish, chopped wood, delivered parcels from Baughman's—any spare job he could find.

Then there was his kind neighbor, Mrs. Orwell, up on Frontier Street, who made sure there was always a pot of soup or a loaf of freshly baked bread that she wouldn't be needing. Tim would take it with gratitude. It made her heart ache to see a lad so young growing into a man before his time. When he got a job working in the quarry, he was only thirteen.

The steady money solved many problems and created others. Liam Ryan managed to drink a lot of it away.

It was brutally cold the winter Roger Evans found Liam frozen to death in the doorway of his pharmacy. He'd fallen asleep there in a drunken stupor. Tim was almost sixteen at the time. A handful of town folks turned out for the funeral. Brigid sent two loaves of her homemade bread and a large pot roast surrounded by tender onions and carrots to the house. "Fer the livin'," she said.

The tea was brewed and poured. So as not to squander the rest of the day, they decided to go out back and sit on the dock to watch the sunset. Juggling their cups, they sat on the edge of the dock, feet dangling, wiggling their toes, sipping tea, and marveling at the beauty of it all. Just minutes before, the blue sky and drifting clouds had cast a blanket of warm serenity over the countryside. Now it was alive, rife with color. A spectrum of reds and oranges enveloped the heavens in a spectacular display as the setting sun, with fingers of scarlet–crimson fire, saturated the clouds and gilded the lake. An ore ship inched across the horizon, leaving a trail of snaking black smoke to briefly mark where it had been. It was a breathtaking sight, a perfect finish to a marvelous day.

Maggie, overwhelmed at the spectacle, her voice soft and pensive, said, "This reminds me of when I was little. Da would bring me down here sometimes to watch the sunset. He called it Heaven's doorway because it was so beautiful. Said it was God's gift to us, a teasing taste of the glories that would be ours when we got to the other side. I just know he's over there watching."

Had she looked, she would have seen the love in Tim's eyes as she spoke.

The girls knew it was time to head home. It was that time of day when the light was soft and ready to go out. Tim said he would accompany them.

Rosemarie's house was on Superior Avenue, the last street before the ridge. The three decided to race the six blocks up Frontier Street to see who could reach it first.

Tim had given both girls a head start, but before he got too far, he saw Mrs. Orwell on her knees, working in her garden, readying it for the summer season. She straightened her back, waved, and gave a big smile and a yell. "Hello, there, Tim!"

There was always time to talk to this kind lady who had befriended him as a child, and he knew the girls would wait.

Mrs. Orwell, just curious as to how his life was going, asked questions as she continued to pull out the young weeds that aspired to stake an early claim on the garden patch. She commented on the fine weather and remarked about the two pretty young ladies she'd seen with Tim at the pier earlier as she strolled along the boardwalk. Occasionally she'd look up with loving tenderness to listen to the responses of the handsome young man she had taken under her wing so many years before. She had been widowed at the age of thirty–seven, childless, and Tim had become and still was a source of great joy in her life.

Tim responded to her inquiries, told her she shouldn't be working so hard, and promised to come by the following week to give her a hand with the yard work. He couldn't remember how many times he'd sat in her kitchen, drinking tea and eating biscuits as she went about preparing dinner for herself and making sure he had his.

The girls waited. Tim caught up, and the three continued walking toward Rosemarie's house, giggling at the recollection of those silly otters sliding down the hill.

The scent of new life permeated the air; a soft tinkling of piano keys wafted through an open door and danced along the street; lights flicked on behind curtained windows; the sound of squealing children could be heard as they played somewhere in the distance behind one of the houses; a woman's voice, shrill and loud, called out for her son; and somewhere a dog barked.

Completely taken up with laughter and each other's company, they were unaware of absorbing the beauty of the atmosphere that surrounded them, yet they became silent and their steps slowed as though to make the day last just a little longer. At a later time in their lives, these memories would return, unannounced, as a haunting bit of youthful nostalgia, triggered by a fragrance, a sound, or the whisper of a warm spring breeze.

The homes on Superior and Michigan Avenues boasted of affluence, this part of town having been developed last by the wealthy businessmen with establishments down on Commerce Street. Frank Brewster, who ran the shipping yard, and Elmer Harrison, owner of the quarry, had bought up the available land after the town and their fortunes began to multiply. With time, money, and planning, these homes were built on a much grander scale, outshining the clapboard houses clustered as closely as possible to Commerce Street during the laborious birth of the town. Through the years, the people who now lived on these broad avenues became the elite of Herron's Point. That was because, when the town began to spread westward, the demand for most housing came from the common working man and his family. Only the Herron estate on Erie Street, built ten years after the town was founded, remained unequaled by any other in that area.

Maggie had once lived on Superior Avenue, right next door to the Stuarts. Rosemarie's father, Doctor Robert Stuart, a native of Scotland, had established himself down on Commerce Street. Maggie never approached her old neighborhood without experiencing memories of her life here and her da. Nothing had been the same since he'd died.

"Gosh, Maggie, you're going to have a birthday pretty soon," Rosemarie said as they neared her house.

"In two weeks," she replied while concentrating on avoiding the cracks in the sidewalk. "May sixth, in fact."

"I'm sorry I won't be around to wish you happy sixteen.

Remember the great birthday parties we had when we were little?"

"That seems so long ago. But they were fun, weren't they?"

"When's your birthday, Tim?" Rosemarie asked, not wanting to exclude him from the conversation.

"I was nineteen in February," he said.

It was all so peaceful as the three young people stopped in front of the Stuarts' large Victorian house. At first there was an awkward silence as they faced each other, not knowing how to break the spell of happiness they'd all shared.

Finally, Rosemarie looked at her two friends and said, "Well, it's been a wonderful day, you two. I don't know when I've had a better time. But Easter vacation is over, and it's back to school for me. Lucky the boiler at school broke down, or I wouldn't have had today. I'd have been back there already."

She gave Maggie a big hug, wishing her friend could go with her, sadly aware of their different lots in life. "And have a magical birthday. You deserve all the happiness you can get," she said, giving her another misty–eyed hug.

"Thanks, Rosemarie. And you have a safe trip to Toronto."

"I will. Trouble is, I don't know when I'll see you again. After the term's over, I'm going directly to the States to stay with my Aunt Eleanor. She'll be having her fourth baby, and they can't afford much help, so Mum wants me to go over to Buffalo and give her a hand for the summer. But I'll write."

"Be sure you do," Maggie said, tears in her eyes.

Tim watched the two friends part and was touched. He had never spent much time with Rosemarie before, but she'd turned out to be great fun, with a wonderful sense of humor. He leaned forward and shook her hand. "Best of luck to you. It's been grand fun today," he said.

She waved goodbye again as she walked up the gravel driveway toward the house.

Maggie wiped her eyes, slightly embarrassed by her display of emotion. "I'm really going to miss having her around, even though we haven't seen each other much lately. She's always been my very best friend."

"Well, at least you still have me. I'm not going anywhere," Tim said, looking into her troubled green eyes.

It thrilled her to hear him say this, but she didn't know how to answer. Since when did she have him? Today was the first time they'd ever spent any time together. Well, there was last year at the picnic.

As they walked over to Center Street and down to Erie, Tim talked about his work at the quarry. He liked what he did, especially since he'd been made foreman of his own crew, giving orders to some who were twice his age. He'd been there almost from the very beginning, so he had learned just about all there was to know about the job.

At one point, they brushed against each other and their hands touched. Tim took Maggie's hand in his. She didn't object. It felt strong and wonderful, warming her entire body with a thrilling excitement.

They continued on in silence, soaking up the last precious moments of the day. It was a day that would be branded in their minds forever, the sweet ecstasy of first love.

Finally, Tim spoke. "Maggie, I can't tell you how grand today has been. Would it be all right if I came to call next weekend? Say, next Friday?"

Maggie immediately thought of her mam and knew it would

be impossible. "I'm sorry, Tim, but there are the boarders to think of. We serve them dinner at six. By the time the dishes are done, it's already dark. In fact, I'd best be getting in now. We have a cold supper on Sundays because of having our big meal at one. It's just about time I should be setting it out. It won't be long till it stays daylight longer, though. Until then, there's only Sundays. I'm usually free after two. That's about all the time I have for now."

"Then Sunday it will be." He smiled as he gave her hand a squeeze. "I'll meet you at the back gate around the same time as today. How will that be?"

Her face was radiant. "Sunday around two, then."

The dusky part of the day had vanished into darkness and shadows as they walked up to the back gate on Ontario Street, lingering, looking into each other's eyes. They were one with the night, the moon and stars as observers, twinkling their silent approval.

They didn't see Brigid's face at the window, observing them from the unlit kitchen. Her eyes did not twinkle.

Maggie stood and watched until Tim melted into the shadows, then turned to go into the house.

A light went on in the kitchen. Brigid was not happy.

CHAPTER FOUR

The Walk

Brigid and Father Chuck decided to take the high road for their after–dinner walk. Brigid had no desire to mingle with the swarm of town folk she knew would be down at the park today. She had no taste for the mundane small talk of the locals that would be given out in large doses there. She much preferred to walk along side streets, looking at houses, seeing what was new and how folks were keeping things up.

The pair was quite comfortable strolling along in silence, as most good friends are. Finally, Brigid made mention of the freshness in the air, and as to how the people in the neighborhood who still had outside facilities managed to keep them from reekin', unlike some she knew over near the quarry.

As they continued along the other end of Erie Street, Father Chuck spoke up. "Ya know, Bridie, your Maggie's becomin' a fine–lookin' young lass. Such a darlin' girl. I'm hopin' life holds only good things in store fer her."

"Those are me sentiments exactly," Brigid answered, setting her lips in a firm line, nodding her head. "One day, she's goin' to meet up with a real fine gentleman. One that will be deservin' of her refined nature."

Brigid was quite aware of Father Chuck's real opinion of her handling of Mary Margaret. He'd disapproved when she'd taken her out of school at such a young age and had often said as much. At one time, they'd almost come to the point of severing a lifelong friendship, but in order to keep the peace, he finally saw it her way. Still, he couldn't help commenting sometimes, as tactfully as possible, of course, on the fact that such a bonnie young colleen should be out playing with her little friends instead of being stuck in the house all the time. As if she didn't know what he was trying to tell her. What did he know of a woman's world? Men!

Brigid wouldn't acknowledge to Father Chuck, or anyone else, that she had a plan. Her Mary Margaret would marry well, and the house at 7 Erie Street would once again become the center of society for the best of Herron's Point's citizens. Nor would she ever concede that she had begun to expect so much from Maggie at such an early age in order to make that plan work.

In the beginning, when the boarding house was first established, Bernice MacEvers had been hired to do the menial work. And work she did. Maggie was only six back then, but by the time she was ten, Brigid had seen fit to take her out of school and put her alongside Bernice, who could teach her all the finer points of housekeeping. She also used Clara Carter to keep Maggie up on her sums and reading, making sure her education didn't suffer. So where was the harm?

Maggie was an obedient child. She learned to do the serving and cleaning, and slowly, more and more was added to her workload—until, by the time Maggie was twelve, Brigid was able to let Bernice go. To her way of thinking, her Mary Margaret did a much finer job. With the profit Brigid made from the boarders, letting Bernice go only added to the bank account she'd started from the remains of cash that was left after the purchase of the Herron house. Then there was the money John Mahoney had given her, and the few thousand dollars she'd inherited three years ago, after her mother's death.

The twelve thousand dollars she'd managed to save was still growing, a well-kept secret between her and Norman Fisk down at the Citizen's Bank. Not too shabby a sum. Part of it was to be used as a dowry for Mary Margaret if she married well. But in the event that didn't come to pass, Brigid would never be left destitute. She figured that somewhere within the next five years, her life would be restored to some semblance of the privilege she had once known, perhaps even more so.

Father Charles knew nothing of all that. He, like most folks in town, thought she'd been left with only the clothes on her back and the means to resettle in a boarding house to make a living and raise her two children. Somehow, Brigid had managed through the years to convey that message to those she confided in as she would recount the litany of injustices in her life. The extravagant clothes bought for Mary Margaret and herself were considered by others to be foolish squandering. To her it had always been a natural way of life; now it was an investment that would later reap dividends. I'll be one of the important people once again, she often told herself.

"Oh, and was I fergettin' ta mention I'd be gettin' another boarder soon? Comin' to stay for the next two or three months, he is," she said with a satisfied smile.

Father Charles raised his eyebrows and looked at her with interest.

She continued, "Some high muckety–muck from Toronto. Seems he's got work to do over at the shippin' yards, checkin' on the books, or somethin' like it. Frank Brewster stopped over yesterday to make all the arrangements. Says he doesn't want his man stayin' at MacPhearson's Hotel, him bein' such a fine young gentleman and stayin' so long and all. 'Only the best fer him,' he says."

"Sure, and he's right, Bridie. Yourself has done wonders makin' that grand house into the home that it is. There's no one can be denyin' that."

Those words were the kinds of strokes that made Brigid purr—silently, of course.

As they continued up Division Street and over Ontario, Father Charles became nostalgic. "Do ya ever think of the old sod, Bridie?"

She looked at the profile of the man walking beside her. It revealed a deep sadness. "More times than I can count. Why'd ya ask?"

"The divil if I know," he laughed. "Maybe 'tis this beautiful weather that brings out the longin' so strong. But I won't be denyin' it's been eatin' at me a while. I would dearly love ta go back home. Just one more time."

"Don't talk like an old ijit, Chuck Scanlon. Perhaps yer fergettin' the hunger and starvation that was still plaguin' the poor land when ya left. Not that meself did that much sufferin'. Not in me da's house. But it was all around fer me to be seein'. Not a pretty sight atall, atall."

"I'm rememberin' its horror. I'm rememberin'. Young and

old alike dyin' fer lack of a crust of bread, thrown off their land durin' the famine, and wanderin' around searchin' fer work and a place ta rest their weary heads. Sometimes I get the feelin' I should've stayed there, where there was a real need fer spiritual upliftin'. People in these parts don't truly know what it means ta be downtrodden. Poor, maybe, but not so poor their bellies aren't fed or there isn't the hope of farin' better. Especially fer their young'ns."

He raised his arms, then dropped them by his side in futility. "Sometimes of late, it's mighty lonely I'm feelin'. Those long nights this past winter was when I'd get ta recollectin' what grand times your brothers and meself used ta have. That's when me brain got ta rememberin' 'bout the bunch of us goin' down ta Kelly's Pub fer a pint of Guinness and some darts ta while away an evenin'. It was durin' those times of rememberin' that the achin' would get the better of me, and now I'm left with this longin' fer home."

"And would it be doin' ya any good ta be goin' back now?" Brigid asked. "There's none of 'em what's there. Sean's gone off ta some desolate place in Africa ta doctor the sick. Brian's livin' in France, now, married ta some French lass he met while lookin' fer work over there. And ever since young Tom became a doctor, he's after followin' Sean. So that leaves Eddie, who seems ta have dropped off the face of the earth. After me da died, he stayed around, takin' care of me poor, heartbroken mam. Then when she left us all, God rest her soul," Brigid blessed herself silently, "he just ups and disappears. There's no tellin' where he is. We'll be hearin' when he has a mind ta be lettin' us know, I'm thinkin'."

They were nearing Saint Michael's when a sudden gust of

wind arranged a tuft of thin brown hair onto Father Chuck's forehead, giving him a forlorn, disheveled look. He pushed it back and stopped, his face grim as he stared at Brigid. "Now don't be takin' me wrong, Bridie. Yourself and the rest of the ladies in the congregation have done a grand job of seein' ta me meals, makin' sure I have sufficient to eat. And I can't be thankin' ya enough fer it. But it's home I'm missin'. It seems the fainter the memories get, the more longin' there is ta get them back."

"Now yer soundin' like me old homesick mother–in–law, Gracia. If it hadn't been fer her, I'd of nivver met me Patrick. Do ya mind the time himself came over to Ennis with his mam?"

"And how could I be forgettin'? And wasn't it himself who brought me over here?"

"And mighty anxious you was ta come, if I recall."

"That I won't be denyin'. And I've not been sorry fer a day of it. But now that Saint Michael's is growin' up, I'm feelin' someone else can come in and take on the job."

"Now, Chuck Scanlon, that's not talk I want ta be hearin'. What would I be doin' without the likes of ya? If I can't have me brothers, yer the next best I can think of."

"Well, we'd best be talkin' about it another time, Bridie. Right now, I'm a wee bit tired and need me rest, so I won't be keepin' ya company any further. I'll hafta be goin' ta see Paddy Donovan later. He's been ailin' all winter with the rheumatism. Can hardly get around, ya know, and I'm thankin' ya again fer the grand meal ya prepared. It was a sumptuous feast."

It gave Brigid a twinge of unease to see her dear friend slowly drag his feet toward the back of the church, head bowed, shoulders slumped. She watched until he was out of sight, then continued her walk, but his manner had been unsettling, completely out of character. And now her mind was where Father Charles had put it: Ireland. It was not unusual, then, that her wanderings would take her past the house up on Superior Avenue and the memories that were there.

She paused for one agonizing moment. It pained her to think of Mary Murphy living in her house. It had been the selling of this house to the Murphys that was the bitter pill still sticking in Brigid's craw. She'd never liked Mary Murphy, not from the first day she'd met her. Nervous and twitchy, like a little sparrow, she was. She'd always seen to it that Mary never fit in with any of her plans, excluding her from any social gathering at her house. It galled her that Mary Murphy was now accepted into that same group of people she'd spent so many lovely evenings with at dinner parties and dances, a part of her life that no longer existed. Still, the Murphys had been the only ones willing to pay the price she'd asked for the house.

She continued walking slowly back to Erie Street, her blood boiling with anger toward the injustices wrought against her. None of this would have to be, Patrick Mahoney, she thought, if you hadn't gone and got yourself killed.

Well, that would all change. She had her plan.

CHAPTER FIVE

The Trip

July 1880

Patrick Michael Mahoney, the only son of Gracia and John Mahoney, had led a charmed life growing up on Superior Avenue in a beautiful, stately Tudor house in a town that was almost as young as he was.

Herron's Point had been settled in 1848, primarily by German, Scottish, and Irish immigrants who had chosen the coast of Canada and the lure of free farmland rather than one of the many newly developed northern territories in the United States. Carl Herron, who had purchased this large parcel of land, offered free farmland to those who would clear it of the vast, virgin pine forest in return for the lumber. The town, in its laborious birth, soon discovered it had to transcend its petty religious and ethnic differences in order to survive as a community.

Along with Carl Herron, who built the Herron Shipping Line, John Mahoney had made his fortune in lumber by establishing the Mahoney Sawmill, and when Patrick Mahoney was old enough, he went to work at the mill alongside his father. He was a handsome young man, quite tall and slender, with thick auburn hair and a smile that would melt the coldest heart. By the time he was twenty–six, it was a source of wonder to all who knew him that he'd managed to escape marriage by sidestepping the advances of some of the prettiest girls in town.

It was also around this time that his mother, Gracia, became deeply depressed, longing to return to Ireland to see her brother, Mike, and her sister, Fiona. Doting husband that he was, John became quite concerned with her malingering, but with business never being better, he couldn't be spared at the mill, so he asked Patrick to take some time off to accompany his mother back to her homeland. As he readied for the trip, Patrick couldn't begin to imagine the role serendipity would play in his life.

It was a rough, stormy passage, but Gracia's hopes rose with each new day that brought them closer to their destination. Even after they'd docked and she saw the squalor and the stark, vacant eyes of hunger in the faces they encountered on their journey to Ennis, scenes which at another time would have touched her deeply, she hummed and sighed with contentment. She was almost home.

The homecoming was a grand reunion for all family members, so many that at first Patrick couldn't seem to sift them out and tag them right.

They stayed with Gracia's sister, Fiona Harrigan, a short, round woman with wavy black hair and a pleasant, dimpled face. Her husband, Conan, a stocky man not much taller than his wife, had eyes that seemed to dance when he spoke, putting those around him at ease. Patrick was struck by the similarity of their looks, and when he mentioned this at a later time to his mother, she said, "That's the way of it, Patrick. When two people are livin' together so long in harmony, they begin ta take on each other's faces."

Patrick considered this, realizing she must be right. It had never occurred to him before, but he could see now that his parents were also quite similar in appearance. His mother's hair, once black, had turned a beautiful silver when she was quite young, and he'd watched his father's hair change slowly over the years from red to sandy–brown to gray. Now both were silver–haired. They were both tall, and both had green eyes, fine features, and excellent teeth. There were differences, of course, one being his father's small mustache, which gave him quite a dapper appearance. But there was no question that their marriage had been one of harmony. His father adored his mother, and she lavished love on him, as she did on all those she held dear.

Patrick decided that the real similarities weren't primarily physical. It was that mixture of mannerisms assimilated through daily communion with each other that created the illusion of similarity. Patrick couldn't say which of his parents he resembled. Probably both, though most said it was his father, because of his red hair. But unlike either of theirs, his eyes were blue.

The generosity of John and Gracia Mahoney had been instrumental in helping the Harrigans fare better than most during the long recovery following the famine. Conan owned the local grocery and butcher shop, and they lived in a lovely cottage filled with bedrooms enough to sleep their brood of eight.

"Sure, and there's always room for more," Fiona announced the day they arrived. Her dimples grew with the smile on her chubby face as she happily showed them around the house and then to their rooms. "Sure, and won't ya be sharin' a bed with me Sean?" she said, looking up into her handsome nephew's face with pride. "He's not the smallest, and he's not the biggest. That should even itself out somehow, don't ya think? And I won't be mentionin' he's got the biggest bed."

Gracia's room would be with the two older girls, Maureen and Shannon, who had readily agreed to share one bed, giving their Aunt Gracia the other.

The Harrigan children were a happy lot, ranging in ages from one to sixteen, and they attached themselves to Patrick immediately. This kept him amused for several days, but he soon found himself restless, wanting something to do. Gracia was quite taken up with family and visiting, which he understood, and he tried to accompany her most of the time, but a body could only take so much of it all. Unlike for his mother, the local gossip of so many relatives held little interest for him.

Early mornings, he took to walking into town by himself, intrigued by the antiquity of the stone buildings, stopping off to pray at the Ennis Abbey on Francis Street, strolling down to O'Connel's Square, and exploring the quaint shops crowded together along the narrow cobblestone streets.

But soon the town of Ennis lost its novelty. He was drawn to the countryside, taking long hikes along the River Fergus or down nameless dusty lanes, marveling at the neatly stacked stone walls dripping with scarlet fuchsia that bordered the roadways.

Sometimes a donkey cart would pass him by, carrying

hopeless faces: large, hungry eyes of children, inheritors of the poverty a famine had left behind. They haunted him. Still, their spirit was not lacking. They would nod and greet him. "How ya keepin'?" Or, "And 'tisn't it a day we're havin'?" in acknowledgment of the misty rain so often experienced in those parts. It was difficult for him to imagine the plight of these plucky people still recovering from those dark days—and the little he could do to help.

Sometimes he roamed into green fields cut through by streams of crystal water, with meandering sheep and cows lazily grazing in pastures dotted with bright red poppies. Fields were clearly defined by low stone walls that rolled down valleys, wrapping themselves around pristine lakes and up the other side as far as the eye could see, like a patchwork of someone's ingenious design. Occasionally, whitewashed cottages with thatched roofs popped into view, pigs and chickens roaming the area freely, wash hanging on the line and flapping in the breeze, giggly children playing in the yard. Obviously, there was food for some. Then his path would cross others that had not fared so well: cottages in disrepair with sagging roofs, no signs of life or livestock, some burned to the ground. But wherever he went, there were flowers: heather and roses, snapdragons, pinks and the like: mixtures of bright, vibrant color dotting the countryside, climbing around cottage doors.

One morning, his journey took him outside of Ennis to a place called Quinn and a structure named Quinn Abbey, a 15th–century Franciscan friary. He was fascinated by its history, it having grown out of the ruins of a Norman castle, and he marveled that most of it had survived the centuries almost perfectly intact except for the roof. About three miles beyond the friary, he discovered the ruins of Knappogue Castle and again was taken with the antiquity of it all. In the world he came from, the white man's history was still in its infancy.

But the sight that particularly piqued his interest that day was further down the road, where a man up on the roof of his cottage was raking the thatch. It would have pleased him to stay longer to watch, but he'd used up the morning. He'd promised to take his mam to see Uncle Mike that afternoon. Seeing his precious mother so happy was what truly pleased him, the color returning to her cheeks day by day. The trip had been a good thing.

That same evening, Uncle Conan asked Patrick if he'd like to go to Kelly's Pub on Carmody Street for a pint of Guinness and a game of darts. This sparked his interest immensely and set him to wondering if the Kelly that owned the pub in Herron's Point was somehow related.

It was a grand evening, unusually clear, as they strolled the few blocks to the old pub filled with blue smoke, music, and laughter. Conan ordered two pints and proudly introduced his nephew from over the seas to everyone in the place. They were a congenial lot, asking questions, curious about the New World.

Then Conan's old friend, Dr. Tom Walsh, a tall, portly man in a gray suit and beautifully starched white shirt, approached, asking if they would like to join in a game of darts. He and his four strapping sons had just finished a round. Dr. Walsh, taking Conan aside, said, "If the truth be told, these lads are wearin' me out. Why don't the two of us old jockos sit back and enjoy the watchin'? We're beyond needin' ta compete with this young lot, I'm thinkin'."

Patrick took an instant liking to the oldest Walsh son, Sean, also a doctor, a big, burly man with a constant grin and a fantastic sense of humor, the source of many laughs that evening. Later, he told Patrick he'd been practicing medicine in Killarney for the past six years, and now, having left his practice, he was home for a two–month stay before departing for a remote village in the Congo.

As the evening wore on, Patrick (who, for reasons he didn't understand, became Paddy) found he was quite adept at hitting the bullseye, ingratiating himself to everyone there. Music permeated the atmosphere, creating a propensity for singing at the top of one's lungs—a kind of camaraderie he'd never experienced before. It was something he knew he would never forget. By evening's end, he found himself invited to a party at the Walshes' cottage the following night. Their baby sister, Bridie, was celebrating her twentieth birthday.

Gracia and her sister, Fiona, took most of the Harrigan brood off to visit brother Mike the following evening, and a slightly nervous Patrick came into the parlor. Uncle Conan looked up from his evening paper and smiled, giving a nod of approval. "And isn't it mighty grand yer lookin', Paddy Mahoney? You'll be turnin' the heads of all the colleens at the party with such good looks and those fine clothes of yours. Not often they get ta be meetin' anyone other than the clods 'round here."

Patrick liked his Uncle Conan immensely, accepting his praises as he would from his own mam, considering them exaggerated compliments bestowed upon him through the blind eyes of love. Patrick Mahoney was completely without guile.

"I went to Farley's bookstore in town today and got a book of poetry by Keats. Do you think that's a proper gift for the young girl, Uncle Conan?"

"Sure, and why wouldn't it be? But I'll be tellin' ya this. If it's not, she'll be lettin' it be known. She's a spoiled one, she is. And it's those brothers of hers who've made her so. Pamperin' her from the day she was born. Now, ya know where the cottage is, don't ya? It's just a wee walk from here."

Patrick nodded.

Uncle Conan gave Patrick a pat on the back as he escorted him to the door. "Well, run along with ya, then, and don't be fergittin' ta have a good time."

Patrick was quite impressed with the Walsh cottage. It was much larger than any around it. In his part of the world, it would fit in nicely on Superior Avenue.

The cottage was set on a corner at the edge of town. He could hear the music and singing as he entered the gate and walked up the flagstone path to the front door. Mrs. Walsh, a short, round woman with crinkly laugh lines at the corners of her eyes and a very sweet smile, welcomed him with such enthusiasm that he felt immediately at home.

The house was filled with young people. Sean came over to greet him, happy that he'd come, and took him around to make him known to everyone there. For Patrick, it was almost as confusing as meeting his mother's relatives. Maybe by the end of the evening he would actually remember some of their names, but names or not, he knew he was in good company as they quickly fitted him into their conversations.

When Sean introduced him to his sister, Bridie, Patrick was quite taken with her beauty. She was exquisite, the most beautiful girl he'd ever seen. Her eyes, a deep violet, were framed with thick, black lashes. Raven hair haloed her face in ringlets. Her skin was a creamy alabaster. She welcomed him graciously, accepted her gift as though it was her due, and after a few words, went about enjoying the attention given by so many other admirers, keeping this tall, handsome redhead in her sights at all times, watching. If on occasion their eyes did lock, she would quickly look away as though preoccupied, but not before giving him a coy smile.

Patrick was quite taken up himself with trying to entertain a host of young, fawning female admirers. I must seem a curiosity to all of them, he thought.

Mrs. Walsh brought in a huge platter of salad sandwiches, some ham and some tomato, on the best homemade bread Patrick had ever eaten. Then Brigid cut a scrumptious chocolate cake.

Everyone had their fill as they watched her open her gifts. Then all gathered around the piano as Mrs. Walsh played requests. Patrick enjoyed the familiar ones he'd heard his mother singing around the house and joined right in. But many, like "Finnegan's Wake," were unfamiliar to him. He was quite entertained by the humorous stories with lilting melodies.

When the crowd sang "Green Fields," the festive mood of the room became serious. Patrick wondered about that and was later told that many songs, such as "Green Fields," were written about Ireland and its struggles. This kind of music preserved their Irish history. Somehow, Bridie had managed to stand next to him, her petite figure diminished by his height. When the party was over, and he said his goodbyes to all, Bridie stood at the doorway and shook his hand.

He thought, Was that just a hint of a squeeze?

She said, "Sure and we're hopin' ta be seein' ya agin, Patrick

Mahoney."

He smiled and floated out the door.

The enchantment of the balmy summer evening surrounded him despite the light mist that brushed his skin. The hour was late, yet the night was barely dusk in this part of the world, not like the midnight blue sky he'd be walking under if he were back home. Still, a large wedge of yellow moon was up there, at times eclipsed by drifting, shadowy clouds. And Bridie's face was in it all—laughing, teasing, and beautiful. He couldn't remember ever having had a better time.

The next day, Sean stopped by the Harrigans' to see Patrick. "Mam asked me to come over and invite ya ta dinner this evenin'. And wasn't she sayin' we have so much food left over from the party, it'd be shameful not ta be sharin' it?"

He wouldn't dare tell Patrick he'd been sent over by direct orders from his baby sister, Bridie.

Patrick's heart leapt. He'd wondered how he was going to manage to see Bridie again. He no longer needed to wonder.

"So what are ya sayin', lad? Think ya can make it?"

"I see no reason why not. Mam has plenty here to keep her busy. I'm sure she won't mind. What time?"

"We'll be eatin' around seven, but come over whenever you're havin' a mind ta. Another lad, Charles Scanlon, is home from the seminary, and you'll be enjoyin' meetin' himself. Salt o' the earth, ol' Chucko."

Brigid Walsh had set her cap for Patrick Mahoney the night of the party, and she was not to be denied. Before the next two weeks had passed, he'd found himself completely captivated. When his mother began talking about going home—"It's your da I'm missin'," she said—Patrick knew he couldn't leave his Bridie behind.

Following the three weeks for the banns, a small family wedding took place at the cathedral, officiated by newly ordained Father Charles Scanlon. One hundred and twelve in all joined the celebration at the Walshes' home, and that party lasted until the wee hours. Brigid and Patrick spent a blissful two days in Galway, at the end of which, Gracia Mahoney, with an enamored bridegroom and his perfectly contented bride in tow, set sail for Canada.

John Mahoney met the trio at the depot upon their arrival. It pleased him to see his wife in such good spirits, and he was quite taken with Brigid's charm and beauty.

When he reined the dray around the corner of Division Street onto Superior Avenue, Brigid, who had been snuggling next to Patrick, sat upright to peer over the edge of the carriage, extremely impressed with the beautiful neighborhood. As they clip–clopped their way up the driveway to the imposing Tudor house that would be her new home, the many windows of diamond–shaped leaded glass sparkled in the sunlight, beckoning her in to enjoy the view from the other side.

She had made the right choice. This would be her home. She adored Patrick Mahoney all the more for it.

Within a month of their homecoming, Gracia decided to hold a grand reception for her son and his new bride. She'd never been much for entertaining except for the occasional small dinner party; she was quite concerned about invitations and choosing a menu for such a large crowd. Mildred Rankin, the Mahoneys' cook for the past thirteen years, was also hard put to come up with a satisfactory solution. When Brigid heard of their dilemma, she immediately jumped in and took over.

"Now, Mother Mahoney, how many people are we thinkin' about, and what time of day do ya have in mind?"

"Well, I'm not sure, Bridie, but I suppose afternoon. Perhaps a Saturday would be fine. And as ta the number, I haven't actually figured that out yet."

"Why don't we do that right now?" Brigid said, and within minutes, Gracia found herself at the dining room table, her daughter–in–law across from her with pad and pencil. Invitations to the families of the workers at the sawmill were the easiest, because John would just pass them out at work. The others would have to be addressed and mailed.

With almost every name, Gracia had a comment or two, such as, "The Bakers just had their seventh child, a darling boy. Hank Rosin is our plumber. Carl Herron and his pretty wife, Emily, are back from their trip to Italy, so they'll be here. You'll enjoy Emily, dear."

With invitations out of the way, Brigid concentrated on the menu.

"Since your guests will come in the afternoon, you will simply have a tea, with small sandwiches, cookies, and cake. I'll see ta the cake, and surely Mildred can make an assortment of decent cookies."

Gracia was aware of Brigid's thoughts on Mildred's culinary skills. Brigid let her thoughts on everything be known.

The day of the reception, Brigid was in her element, the center of attention. She found herself drawn to Emily Herron, the young wife of aging Carl Herron. Although thirty–six, Emily was without a doubt the most stylish, influential woman in town. It wasn't beyond Brigid to be charming, even delightful, to those she chose to endear herself to, and the two developed a strong friendship that lasted over the years, until after Carl Herron's death.

Brigid settled into her new surroundings easily. Her wishes were happily fulfilled by Patrick, so proud of his beautiful wife, and not so happily by the servants, who were expected to jump at her every command.

She loved to cook, and little by little took over the kitchen as her domain. Mildred Rankin, having cooked for the Mahoneys for thirteen years, found herself gradually reduced to peeling vegetables, washing pots, and tears. When she saw what she vehemently referred to as "the writin' on the wall," she put in her notice, along with a few choice words directed toward the new lady of the house, making sure the door was sufficiently slammed as she left.

Gracia was distressed, but she kept her tongue and the peace. Kitty Eggers was then hired to do the menial scullery chores.

On August 23, 1881, John Charles Mahoney II was born. The entire household staff was thrilled with the presence of an infant in the house and fell to doting on him as they had his father, Patrick. Surrounded by love, he thrived, growing into a noisy, active young boy who filled the house with singing and laughter. He was a miniature image of Brigid, quite a handsome lad, but the servants overlooked this flaw. His disposition made up for any physical characteristics he'd been unfortunate enough to inherit from his mother. Everyone called him Jack.

More and more, Brigid took over the running of the house. She was not pleased with the casual way her mother–in–law handled the hired help and overlooked the neglected dirt in corners.

Gracia was no match for her strong-willed daughter-in-law, and allowing that she was much more capable at overseeing things and that the meals had never been better, she relinquished her hold and began spending most of her time with her grandson, whom she adored. Brigid now had full reign.

It was about two years after his return from Ireland that Patrick wrote to Charles Scanlon and asked him to get permission to come over to Canada and pastor a church at Herron's Point, explaining that the Catholic population had only sporadic visits from various priests sent by the diocese in Toronto. There was a dire need for someone to minister to their faith. He promised him a church would be waiting if he would only come and fill this need.

It took almost six months of red tape before Chucko got permission from his superiors and was released from his duties in Ireland. Then the building of Saint Michael's began. The Mahoney Lumber Yard donated all the supplies, and Patrick donated four exquisite stained-glass windows and a prime piece of property on the corner of Michigan Avenue and Center Street that he had once intended as the building site for a small home for his family. Brigid had no intention of leaving the house she was in.

The work on the church was a labor of love by the members of the congregation, who saw to every detail of its construction, including living facilities above the church (there were no funds for a separate rectory) for the good father. Father Charles Scanlon arrived three weeks after its completion and proudly took over as pastor. Representatives from the Diocese of Toronto came in to help concelebrate the first High Mass at Saint Michael's Church on August 5, 1883. The church was packed to overflowing.

In 1887, news of Conan Harrigan's illness came across the water. Gracia became inconsolable. With young Jack now spending his days in school, she was left with too much idle time, feeling in the way, always underfoot as her daughter–in–law spent busy days running the house, planning teas and dinner parties. Once again, she found herself languishing over home and family.

John, who had been aware of his wife's unhappiness for quite some time, decided it would be best if they signed the house over to Patrick and both returned to Ireland to live out the rest of their days. Being eight years older than Gracia, and not in the best of health as he approached his sixtieth year, John felt he was ready to step down and let Patrick take over the sawmill. He did not relinquish ownership, however. Although he was quite a wealthy man, the income the sawmill generated monthly could be put aside, so that in the event of his death, there would be an income for Gracia for as long as she lived. He made sure Patrick would be compensated handsomely for his work at the mill, giving him to understand that it would someday be his. Thus, having provided for all of his loved ones, John Mahoney was ready to move on.

Gracia bid a teary farewell to her son and grandson. Her efforts to mollify her goodbyes to Brigid were sincere, knowing that, despite her own dislike for her daughter–in–law, Brigid would take good care of Patrick and her grandson. She felt her presence would not be missed. It was her baby sister, Fiona, who would need her now. As hard as she'd tried, in all the years she'd lived in her lovely home on Superior Avenue, she'd never been able to reconcile to the beautiful land she'd come to be part of. She was finally going back home.

In 1890, several months before Jack turned nine, Mary Margaret came into the world, with a head full of red hair. Unlike Jack in both looks and manner, she was quiet and unassuming. Patrick immediately dubbed her his little Maggie, and the name stuck, much to Brigid's chagrin. She would always be Mary Margaret to her.

When he wasn't at work, Patrick's days were filled with the joy of satisfying Brigid's every whim and playing with his two children. Jack was so proud of his little sister, hauling her all over Herron's Point in his red wagon to show her off. Their next-door neighbors, the Stuarts, had a little girl, Rosemarie, the same age as Maggie. They grew up spending their days playing together.

CHAPTER SIX
Patrick
1854–1896

It was a bitter, cold day in February when Brigid got the news that Patrick had been killed in an accident at the sawmill. He'd been overseeing the unloading of lumber from a wagon when a chain hoisting a large trunk snapped, the trunk hitting him in the head, crushing his skull.

Although John Mahoney couldn't make it in time for his son's funeral, he did return as quickly as possible to see to the affairs of his family and business. Gracia, suffering from the loss of her son and also a severe bout of arthritis, couldn't make the trip. John felt he had no choice but to give the running of the sawmill over to Robert Murphy, a capable man who had been Patrick's foreman, giving him an option to buy him out after five years. To Brigid, he gave five thousand dollars, which he considered to be more than generous, to see to her needs. "And whatever else you'll be needin' after this is gone, I'll be sendin' to ya. Just keep me informed of your wants. You know that whatever is left after Gracia and I are gone, which could be quite considerable, will be goin' to your children."

In the dark days that followed, Brigid was consumed with grief and a brooding anger. She was aware that her in-laws didn't care for her, but for the life of her, she could never figure out why. Hadn't she worked like a dog running a proper house for them all? Unlike Patrick, and her family before him, they'd never made the effort to make her feel important or appreciated.

Five thousand dollars won't be keepin' me in this house ferever, she thought, not with payin' fer the help and maintainin' these grounds. And like a beggar, I'm supposed to ask! It's meself that'll be needin' the money. Now! Not me children. It'll be a cold day in Hell when I'll be askin' fer any of their handouts. And if I know Gracia Mahoney, there won't be much left fer me children by the time she gets done spendin' it on that enormous family of hers over there.

That's when she devised her plan. She'd make her way in the world. She wouldn't be cast aside like an old boot. She wrote to John and Gracia only once, assuring them she'd not be needing their help. Never responding to Gracia's pleading letters for news of her grandchildren gave her a sense of vindictive satisfaction.

I'll be lettin' them suffer like I've had to do, she said to herself.

Emily Herron came back for Patrick's funeral. Carl Herron had died three years earlier, and she'd gone to live in Toronto to be nearer her three children, who had found nothing in Herron's Point to keep them there. "If there's anything I can do, Bridie, anything at all, you just let me know," she said.

And Brigid remembered.

Brigid loved her home on Superior Avenue. The important people lived there. The ones who counted. But the house at 7 Erie Street would be a much better location for what she had in mind. The Herron house had been up for sale for the past three years, ever since Carl's death, but there was little demand for such a large, expensive house in a town so small. And anyone who would want one would surely choose to locate on Michigan or Superior Avenue.

She took a train to Toronto. Brigid had no qualms about taking advantage. Not with all of Emily's millions.

And so, after Brigid told Emily there would also be electricity, plumbing, and central heating needed, which should be taken into consideration—that is, if she decided to take the white elephant off her hands—Emily quickly conceded, and the deal was set. She was more than generous selling the house with all its furnishings for less than the price the house on Superior Avenue brought.

The Herron property at 7 Erie Street took up an entire block, surrounded by a decorative, four-foot, black iron fence that could be entered through the front gate on Erie Street or the back gate on Ontario Street. The outbuildings consisted of a chicken coop, an outhouse, a tool shed, and a small carriage house with second-floor accommodations, which at one time had been occupied by Elmer Stokey, the caretaker, and his wife, Flora, the Herrons' cook. These buildings were located to the left and back of the house. To the right of the house, there had been a beautiful flower garden surrounding an octagonal gazebo, which had since gone to seed. During the past three years of neglect, all had fallen into disrepair.

The house itself was a large Georgian structure, three

stories high, painted white, with long, green–shuttered windows on the first two floors and a row of narrow windows along the third level. A widow's walk was perched in the middle of a green slate roof.

The grand furnishings throughout the house had been brought in from all parts of the world. Other than her own precious mementos and a few valuable paintings, Emily left them all. With more money than she could use in her lifetime, she was quite settled and content in her fashionable redbrick townhouse in Toronto. Brigid had taken a large burden off her hands.

When the house was built, Carl Herron had insisted on a porch that spanned the front of the house. It was here he spent his later years, sitting in a rocking chair, looking out over the lake, greeting people as they walked by, affording him a means of keeping his finger on the pulse of the town he had built. When he was found dead in his rocking chair at sunset one Saturday in May, his eyes were open, and there was a smile of satisfaction on his face. People took it as a sign he'd gone to his Maker pleased that his dreams and hard work had come to fruition.

After Brigid took over, she put Jack and his friend Stephen Hargrove to work outside, while she and Bernice MacEvers threw open windows and doors to air out the musty smell of abandonment—beating rugs, washing windows, and scrubbing and polishing each of the thirteen large rooms.

Jack and his friend gave the outside of the buildings and the fence a new coat of paint, rejuvenated the garden, and finished up their work by demolishing the outhouse. The second floor had five bedrooms, and the largest bedroom in the back had been divided, so that the plumbing for the bathroom could be installed. All wall lamps and chandeliers had been wired for electricity.

Chickens and a rooster were now established in the hen house. Nellie, their cow, was bedded quite comfortably in the carriage house, grazing on the wide lawn on the side of the house during the day, chewing contentedly as her big brown eyes watched with interest the flurry of activity around her.

Since she was only six, and likely to be in the way, Maggie remained with her friend Rosemarie during the day.

Before this work was ever completed, Brigid had recruited her boarders. With Patrick dead only seven months, she had embarked on a new life. The boarders moved in on September 3, 1896, two days before her thirty–fifth birthday.

CHAPTER SEVEN

A New Arrival

Saturday, May 5, 1906

The train pulled into the depot on time, squealing and wheezing, then puffing and snorting like a pent–up bull. Princess shied, jerking the wagon, throwing Zeb off balance.

"Gosh–dern skittery animal," he mumbled, pulling himself erect and calming the dappled–gray mare. He climbed down onto the platform and waited. "Shouldn't be hard to recognize one of them fancy city folks," he continued mumbling to himself.

He was right. Robert Arnaud alighted, shading his eyes from the glaring noonday sun with his hands—the only one to get off the train.

He was much younger than what Zeb had expected. Zeb's heavy–lidded eyes took in all of Arnaud, and he speculated. Another one of them rich man's brats come to show us poor country folks how things is done, Zeb thought. Certainly gentleman material in his fine, tailored suit and spats.

Zeb approached, skillfully avoiding the platform as he spit a stream of brown tobacco.

"Mr. Arnaud?" he said, grinning. A gold tooth glinted in the sunlight.

"That's right."

"I'm Zeb Chadwick, come to fetch ya fer Mr. Brewster down at the shipping line."

Robert extended his soft, manicured hand, accepting Zeb's grubby paw, heartily shaking it with a friendly smile.

"Nice to meet you, Zeb. Frank told me I'd be well taken care of when I arrived."

Quite disconcerted by the unexpected commensurate greeting, Zeb clumsily pointed an arm toward Princess. "If ya care to take a seat on the wagon, I'll collect yer luggage and take ya to the boardin' house where you'll be stayin'."

Robert climbed onto the buckboard, watching Zeb as he lumbered over to the baggage car and loaded his trunks on a dolly. With the luggage secured in the back of the buckboard, Zeb settled in his seat, spit out of one side of his mouth, and gave a clicking "gee–yup" out of the other.

They left the small gray and red depot behind and trotted off toward an expanse of open farmland that extended far to the west and north, a patchwork of greens and browns intersected by a lattice of train tracks. Shortly, Zeb turned left, heading south onto a wide, cobblestone road.

"Beautiful country," Robert commented.

"Yup. Surely is. And mighty peaceful. Farmers got an early start this year, too, with the weather bein' so mild and all. Most spring plantin's been done."

Within minutes, they were at the top of the ridge. Wide ribbons of tall, stately pines on either side of the road stood like imperial sentinels guarding the town below, protecting it from the onslaught of wind and snow that swooped down unmercifully from the north in the winter. Lake Erie loomed up ahead at the foot of the sloping hill, an enormous green emerald glinting with facets of golden sunlight, spilling over the far horizon and hugging the rocky shoreline of the sleepy town tucked neatly between it and the ridge.

"Now, there's another pretty sight," Robert commented, leaning back to enjoy the view.

On the left, a deeply rutted dirt road wove its way through stands of oaks and maples. Somewhere beyond, a buzz of activity could be heard.

"What's going on back in there?" Robert asked.

"That'd be the sawmill over by Osaga Falls," Zeb drawled. "You probably noticed the train trestle passin' over the river 'bout a mile or so back when you was comin' here."

Shifting the bulge in his jaw from one side to the other, he spit over the side of the buggy. Brown tobacco stains at the corners of his mouth hyphenated his lips.

"In the early years, when the farmers was clearin' the land of all them pine trees, they used that road to haul lumber over to the sawmill. Then, after they was cut and made ready fer shippin' and marketin', the sawmill'd haul the lumber back over here to Broad Street, that bein' where we are now, and straight down to the shippin' yard or up to the railway depot. There's still some occasion to use the road, but not much. Nowadays, most of the lumberin's done upriver and sent on down. And ever since them railroad folks put in them side rails off to the other side of these woods, the sawmill don't have much need fer that road no more."

"Interesting," Robert commented, looking curiously at the

unflappable face sitting next to him.

"Have you always lived in Herron's Point?"

"Yup. Forty-one years, now. My pap came here when the town was bein' built. Worked at the sawmill fer ol' John Mahoney, he did. Lost him and my ma to the influenza epidemic back in '57. Died within two weeks of each other. I was growed by then. Been on my own ever since."

"Unfortunate. Do you have any other family here?"

"Naw. Just me," Zeb answered. Then his doleful face nodded toward the right. "Town folks all live over here to the right side of Broad Street that's separatin' the harbor, shippin' yards, and sawmill from the town. Carl Herron planned it that way when he built the town. And exceptin' fer Water and Commerce Streets, which just seemed to sprout when the town was first built, he named all the east-west streets after the Great Lakes, him who spent a great part of his life sailin' on 'em. These last two streets we're passin' right now, Michigan and Superior, are where all the swells live. They don't call 'em streets. Too good fer that. They call 'em avenues." He stuck his nose up in the air, giving Robert a sardonic grin.

Robert smiled. "So that's why the town is named Herron's Point? This Carl Herron fella started it?"

"Yup. Bought up a mighty parcel of this land here after his ship was sunk durin' a terrible storm. It was young Johnny Mahoney what saved ol' Carl's life, and they ended up on this here very shore. Them poor immigrants he was haulin' up to Minnesota all got drowned."

"Interesting. It's always fascinating to learn the history of how people and places got together."

"Hard to get lost in a place like this. Comin' from a big city like Toronto, I suppose you'll find it kinda slow movin'."

"So far, I've found it quite appealing. Actually, I'm looking forward to my time here. I intend to learn all I can about the shipping business and this town. By the way, Zeb, you mentioned earlier that you'd be taking me to my lodgings. If you don't mind, I'd prefer to stop off at the shipyard and see Frank Brewster first. I'm anxious to get myself established there. Just give me the directions, and I'll walk over to the boarding house later."

"Suits me. 'Twon't be hard to find," Zeb replied.

Princess slowly clip–clopped down the hil.

"Ya know, Mr. Arnaud, it's not for me to question, but would ya be any kind of relation to the Arnaud that owns the shippin' yards?"

"As a matter of fact, I am. And I don't mind your asking. My father is Pierre Arnaud. One of the owners. We have an import–export business back in Toronto. That's where I'll be working when I go back home. But my father feels I should learn all aspects of the business, so that's why I'm here. We also have another shipping line near Quebec City, along the Saint Lawrence. That's the one my grandfather and his friend Henri Alexandre started back in 1836. Father married Henri's daughter, Antoinette, and it's been the family business ever since.

"When Carl Herron put his shipping line up for sale fifteen years ago, my father jumped on it. 'Lake Erie's where all the action is, son,' I remember him saying to me. What did I know? I was six at the time, and just starting school. Turned out he was right, though. With all the immigrants coming in and filling up the land, and with such a supply of raw materials to be had, the

Great Lakes have turned into a beehive of activity. Best investment he ever made."

"That's mighty interestin'."

Princess, anticipating being put back in the barn, knew exactly where she was headed, and without any coaxing from Zeb, turned left into a wide, semicircular cinder driveway leading up to the short end of a long, T–shaped building. A large sign ran along the length of the roof:

ALEXANDRE & ARNAUD SHIPPING

A smaller sign over a door, indicating Offices, faced the driveway. The lake–side stem of the T–shaped building was lined with loading docks facing the ships at the Point. Another rectangular building facing the loading docks was divided into garages for machinery and stalls for horses on one side and loading docks on the other, facing the railroad tracks.

The entire shipping yard was filled with men busily loading or unloading. Some supplies were coming in from the ships; those were destined for boxcars at the railroad tracks beyond the far end of the building. Other supplies were being unloaded from boxcars; these were targeted for shipment at some point along the Great Lakes. The long strand of land, better known by the natives as the Point, jutted out onto the lake and made up the harbor.

Muscular men familiar with the daily activity of strenuous lifting steered their horsedrawn wagons to and from the four large freighters moored at their docks. Cranes emptied the ships' holds or filled them with cargo. The entire area was alive with cacophonous sounds of activity. There was a burst of laughter as someone at the docks bellowed an off–key version of "Roamin' in the Gloamin.'"

"Well, here ya be, Mr. Arnaud. Ya won't have no trouble findin' your way to the boardin' house. You can see the top of it from here." Zeb pointed. "That big green roof up there with the widow's walk. That'd be 7 Erie Street. I'll be takin' yer luggage over to the house now and bringin' Princess back here to her stall. But I'll be seein' ya agin at supper. Yer in fer some real good eatin'.'"

Robert could hear Zeb's 'gee–yup' as he climbed the steps and opened the office door.

Can't be much of a place if that old coot lives there, he thought. How'd I ever get myself exiled to a place like this? It's going to be a long few months.

When Zeb delivered the luggage that Saturday afternoon, Maggie realized the new guest must be a man of means. The trunks were covered with labels from exotic places: Paris, Rome, Budapest, even Cairo. Mam had told her someone important would be coming, and she'd spent all day Friday getting his room ready. She'd just finished dusting the parlor and was passing through the foyer, heading toward the kitchen to help Mam with dinner, when the screen door began to rattle, a man rapping.

She hadn't expected anyone so young. And so good–looking. And beautifully dressed.

"I'm sure I must be at the right place," Robert smiled through the screen. "Something smells delicious. And since I was told there was no better cook than Mrs. Mahoney anywhere around these parts, I just followed my nose right up to this front door."

Maggie laughed as she opened the door to welcome him. "You must be Mr. Arnaud. Please come in."

She watched as the handsome young man stepped into the foyer, looking around at the fine surroundings. "This is truly an elegant home. Much more than I expected from such a small town as this."

She smiled. "I suppose you'll be wanting to freshen up and rest a bit before dinner. I'll just show you to your room."

Maggie led him up the stairway. She pointed out the bathroom at the top of the stairs, explaining the schedule for bathing as they continued down the hall to the front of the house.

"This is your room." She nodded toward the windows as she walked over to raise the shades and pull back the lace curtains. "There's a lovely view of the lake. I do hope you'll be comfortable here." She pointed with pride to the beautiful room.

She walked over and took the large ewer off the washstand in the corner. "I'll just get you some warm water, and you can freshen up. If you'd like, I'll unpack your trunks for you after dinner."

"That's very thoughtful of you, miss. I don't even know your name."

"Just call me Maggie." She smiled shyly.

"Well, Maggie, I thank you for putting me so at ease. And there's no doubt I'll enjoy the comfort of this wonderful room."

Robert took advantage of the view while he waited for Maggie to return with the water.

"Now you can just relax. Dinner's at six. You'll be meeting the other boarders then." Once again, she smiled and left him.

Robert watched her move across the hall and disappear down a back stairway.

My God, he thought, what beautiful eyes. What a stunning creature.

He washed his face and hands. Restless and aroused by his new surroundings, especially Maggie, he strolled back over to the windows.

She's right. This view is outstanding.

He'd seen much of the world, purely for pleasure, of course, and thought of each new place as an adventure. He loved to travel. But he hadn't relished being exiled to this backwater town and put to work. Still, with a little female companionship of the nature he'd just met, it wouldn't be so bad. He decided to go down to the kitchen to meet the lady of the house. Maybe Maggie would be there.

Brigid was leaning over the oven door, basting the leg of lamb. His voice startled her.

"Hello, madam, I'm your new boarder, Robert Arnaud," he said, entering the kitchen that rarely saw a visitor. "Just thought I'd come in and meet the lady everyone's been telling me about." He extended his hand.

She closed the oven door, gave him a quizzical look, wiped her hands on her apron, and accepted his handshake. "And just what might ya be meanin' by that?"

"Only that you're the best cook around these parts, I'm told. And if your dinner tastes as good as it smells, I'll know it must be true."

"Go 'long with ya," she grinned.

Brigid's kitchen was quite large. A huge black stove sat in the center of the west wall, flanked by oak cupboards and countertops that wrapped around to the left for about four feet, then stopped at the swinging doors leading to the dining room. On the right side of the stove were more cupboards and countertops that wrapped around that corner to meet a large sink and four more feet of cupboards and countertop. Two windows sat above the sink, dressed in green–checked, tie–back gingham curtains.

The door next to that led to a mud room and out the door, with a four–by–six–foot pantry on the side. On the other side of that door were three windows in the same dressing as the others. A welcoming window seat was underneath the windows. It was padded with a dark green cushion and scattered with colorful pillows. A large, round oak table on a dark green and gray braided rug was in that section of the kitchen.

On the other side of the swinging doors was a fairly tall icebox and a strip of hooks for aprons and sweaters, then a doorway that led down the center hall. Next to that was a large stone fireplace. Two rockers rested on either side across from the oak table. Another door next to the fireplace led up the back stairway.

At the end of the room was Maggie's bedroom. This room was the coziest and most desirable room in the house. Not only did Brigid love it, but Maggie did as well.

Another doorway next to it led up the back stairway to the second floor. With the exception of necessary dinner preparations, the kitchen was immaculate.

Robert made himself at home, sitting at the kitchen table, chatting as Brigid busied herself at the stove, stirring a vanilla pudding.

It was a pleasant visit in a pleasant room, just long enough for him to ingratiate himself with the lady of the house and find out more about his surroundings. Maggie was nowhere to be seen, but he'd detected movement in the dining room. Probably setting the table. He'd check it out.

After he left, Brigid was quite elated.

Now there's a boarder worth havin', she thought. What a charmin' gentleman.

Robert Arnaud was a hit with everyone. He charmed the Carter sisters with flattery; listened with rapt interest, nodding intently, as Kurt Baughman expounded on the plight of the country's invasion of foreigners; complimented Zeb on the fine landscaping around the house, especially the flower garden on the east side; and showed genuine regard for Chester Deidrick's experiences as captain of the *Herriot*.

All the while, Maggie moved in and out of the kitchen, serving dinner. Robert was aware of her presence, of the fragrance of lavender soap as she leaned over to serve him generous portions of lamb.

If he'd ever had any reservations about this trip, he now discarded them. He was going to enjoy his stay here. She would be worth it all.

Sunday—May 6, 1906

It had been decided that Robert would accompany them to the eight o'clock Mass on Sunday.

Maggie knew this could create a problem. She was already aware of her mam's strong disapproval of Tim. They'd had it out that evening two weeks before, after she'd spent the day with him and Rosemarie. "He's just not yer sort," Brigid had said, sticking her chin out doggedly. "You should be expectin' better fer yourself."

But Maggie had held her ground. She and Tim sat together at church the following Sunday, and he'd called on her that same afternoon. They'd walked up to the Conroys' farm, giving Mrs. Conroy a hand with the chores in the barn while the three older Conroy boys were in the fields doing the spring plowing. It had been a wonderful day.

But today she knew Mam would insist she sit with her and that new boarder—right up front. How would she explain that to Tim? And why should she have to? Today was her birthday. Shouldn't she have what she wanted?

Brigid preened and strutted all the way up the hill, a handsome gentleman on one side and Maggie on the other. A matching pair if she ever saw one. They met up with Brigid's friend Molly Flannery at the corner of Huron Street, and Brigid proudly introduced her to Robert.

He bowed, plying Molly with compliments, "What a lovely complexion, Mrs. Flannery. And such beautiful eyes. Blue as cornflowers, Mrs. Flannery," which flustered and delighted her completely.

Brigid swelled, ready to burst with pride. He would fit quite nicely in her plans. They continued on to Michigan Avenue—Molly and Brigid, Maggie and Robert.

Tim was waiting on the corner, watching, slightly nonplussed at seeing the handsome young stranger beside Maggie as they came up the hill.

Brigid brushed right on by, expecting Maggie and Robert to follow. But when she reached the church door, she could see the three standing on the corner, talking. Seething, she followed

Molly inside.

When Maggie introduced Robert to Tim, Robert sensed the affection between the pair immediately. He said, "I'd best go sit with your mother, Maggie. I think she's expecting that I do."

When it came to women, Robert's instincts were keen. They told him he would make a better impression if he joined up with the two older ladies, knowing from experience that they always made great allies.

"It was very nice meeting you, Tim," Robert said, shaking his hand again. "I'm sure we'll be seeing more of each other."

Tim nodded.

I'll bide my time, Robert thought. This fella isn't bad to look at. Certainly no real competition, though. When it comes right down to it, Maggie will come around my way.

Maggie smiled with relief as he walked up the steps and into the church. This was not as difficult as she'd feared.

It'll be a good birthday, she thought.

She and Tim sat in the back.

After Mass was over, Tim walked Maggie back to the house. They both commented on how tired Father Charles looked.

"I think he works too hard," Maggie said. "He's so dedicated. He walks everywhere, visiting up over the ridge and in the town, making sure there's never a want or need. Concerned about everyone but himself."

Tim fully agreed. "It must be an awfully lonely life. I noticed your mam sees to it he doesn't go hungry, though. I was down at Fellerman's market one day and heard her talking to some of the ladies shopping there, telling them what days they should be having him in for dinner. What does she do, set up a dinner schedule for him?"

"Actually, she does. She's head of the Altar Guild and makes it her duty to see that he has a place to eat every day. He really has just one big room over the church, you know. No one to take care of his needs there. Someone's always inviting him to come and eat or sending him something—soups, stews, homemade breads or cakes, knowing that if he had to look after himself, he'd probably starve."

They stood at the back gate touching hands, lingering.

Tim could look into Maggie's eyes forever; they swallowed him up. Finally, he broke the spell, saying, "Since today is your birthday, would you like to go sailing this afternoon? Fred Jacobs said I could use his skiff for the day. Perfect weather for it."

"Sounds wonderful." She would have liked it if he'd asked her to go to the moon.

Brigid was furious. How could Maggie choose to sit with that good–fer–nothin' Liam Ryan's son in preference to a gentleman like Robert? But it was her daughter's birthday. She'd best hold her tongue. There would be a wonderful coconut cake for dessert after dinner, with sixteen candles. Perhaps Robert would ask Maggie to go walking later. She could already see he'd taken an interest in her.

If Robert had taken notice of her, Maggie wasn't aware of it. She did, however, notice the small pile of gifts that had gathered on the sideboard in the dining room. She was truly excited about the whole idea of being sixteen, feeling quite grown up with her hair piled on top of her head and wearing her peppermint–pink striped dress with the huge puffed sleeves, the one Mam had picked out the last time they were in Toronto. Tim had even commented on how pretty she looked.

It had taken her the best part of thirty minutes to do up her hair that morning, and she had to admit it looked nice, much more womanly, like Mam said, but all the fussing and primping were really just too much trouble. She wouldn't wear it that way very often, she decided.

After dinner, Maggie cleared the table, and Brigid brought in the cake. Everyone oohed and aahed. Birthdays had not been much of an occasion since she was a little girl, but this one was special, because it marked her passage from youth into womanhood.

Unaccustomed to such attention, Maggie blew out the candles and began to blush.

Everyone laughed and clapped.

"Open your presents," Clara said. "It isn't every day a girl has her sixteenth birthday."

Agnes got up, took the packages off the sideboard, and placed the gifts in front of Maggie. "I hope you like what we got you," she said excitedly. "I think it's something you could have used this morning." She handed her the package with the pink bow. "Here. Open this one first."

Maggie was aware of all eyes watching her hands shaking slightly as she slowly untied the bow. It was a pair of tortoise–shell combs with small, crystal–green stones resembling emeralds inlaid along the edges.

Maggie gasped, "How beautiful! Thank you so much, Agnes, Clara." Her eyes misted.

Agnes smiled with satisfaction at seeing Maggie so pleased. "When we came across them down at Baughman's, Sister said, 'Now won't these look just perfect with Maggie's beautiful hair and green eyes,' and I couldn't help but agree. We're so happy you like them, dear."

"You deserve beautiful things," Clara added matter-of-factly.

"The one in blue wrapping paper is from us," Elsa Baughman said, blushing.

"Picked it out myself," Kurt bellowed. "Soon as I saw it, I said, 'Now, that's the perfect thing for our Maggie.' Didn't I, Mama?"

Elsa nodded and turned red.

Maggie smiled at them both as she tore away the blue tissue. "Oh, what a lovely apron. I certainly can use this." She held it up for all to see. "Look at the nice patch pockets. And isn't that a pretty pattern? Thank you, Kurt and Elsa."

Elsa's blush deepened. "You're welcome, Maggie," she said, almost in a whisper.

"Open mine," Zeb said. "I didn't have any pretty wrapping, so I just used some butcher paper. Figured s'what's inside that counts."

Maggie ran her hands over the smooth leather binding of a book of poems by Emily Dickinson. "My goodness, Zeb! This is wonderful. I just love poetry. How did you know?"

Zeb squirmed slightly. "I asked Clara to pick somethin' out fer me, not having any notion as to what to buy fer a young girl myself. I'm glad you like it."

"I love it. Thank you, Zeb."

The next package was a box of three linen handkerchiefs from Father Charles.

"They're just what I need, Father Charles. Look at the beautiful lace around the edges, everyone. Aren't they pretty?"

"I'm wishin' it could'a been more," Father Charles said

wistfully.

"I love them. Especially because they're from you." Maggie got up, went over to his chair, and gave him a kiss on the cheek. "Thank you, Father." He truly was the only father she had.

"You still have one more," Clara said. "Hurry and open it. I can't wait to eat a piece of that delicious–looking cake."

Maggie figured it was from Mam. She tore away the tissue, opened the box, and saw an exquisite crystal bottle of perfume.

"On such quick notice, I wasn't sure what to get you," Robert said as he anxiously watched her open it. "I know most young ladies love perfumes." He looked for a sign of her approval.

When Brigid had told him of Maggie's birthday the day before in the kitchen, he knew he'd been given an opportunity to quickly gain her favor. Kurt had been more than obliging to walk over and open the store for him after dinner. What better way to captivate her? Females were easily swayed by extravagant gifts.

Maggie was overwhelmed, never having had such a grown-up gift before, and so expensive. She lifted the diamond–shaped crystal stopper from the vial and sniffed. "Oh, it's wonderful. Like a field of carnations. Thank you so much, Mr. Arnaud. But you really shouldn't have gone to so much trouble. With you being new in town and all, I can't imagine where you even found the time."

"It was no trouble. And please call me Robert. I love birthdays. It's as much fun watching someone open gifts as it is getting them."

Brigid came over and handed Maggie an envelope. "I'll be wantin' ta give ya this," she said, standing there, waiting for Maggie to open it.

Maggie was completely puzzled as she looked at the sheet of paper she'd taken out of the long white envelope. "What is it, Mam?"

"'Tis yer registration to Saint Cecilia's in Toronto. You'll be needin' to go there this June to take an entrance exam. But that'll be no problem fer you, I'm thinkin'." And ya won't be cavortin' around with that Tim Ryan. I'll see to that.

"Mam! I can't believe this. You mean I'm actually going away...to school? Oh!" Now she was truly overwhelmed. "This is so exciting. I can't wait to write and tell Rosemarie. This has to be the very best birthday I've ever had." She jumped up and hugged her mother, lifting her right off the floor.

"Go 'long with ya, Mary Margaret."

Unaccustomed to displays of affection, completely flustered, Brigid turned to the others. "How many will be wantin' cake?"

Robert did ask Maggie to take a walk with him. She'd cleared the table and was busy in the kitchen when he came in, escaping Kurt Baughman's request to play gin.

"It's such a beautiful day for a walk. Perhaps you could show me the town, Maggie?"

"I'm so sorry, Mr. Arnaud, but I'm to go sailing with my friend Tim as soon as I finish the dishes. Perhaps the Carter sisters or the Baughmans could oblige you."

Brigid, who was preparing to take her usual Sunday walk with Father Charles, overheard and immediately stepped in. "And can't that Tim Ryan be takin' ya sailin' any day? What with Mr. Arnaud needin' to learn his way around, I'm thinkin' it would be an act of kindness to show him the town. Tim won't be mindin' atall, atall."

"But I can't disappoint him, Mam. He borrowed a skiff just for today." Maggie was not to be dissuaded. She looked at Robert. "What I will do, Mr. Arnaud, since the days are getting so much longer, is take you around the town after supper. It's always lovely that time of day. We can walk down by the lake. You'll just have to see one of our beautiful sunsets."

"That sounds like a fine idea, Maggie. I'll look forward to it. And please, I'll ask you again, call me Robert," he said with a broad smile that hid his feeling of rejection, something he wasn't accustomed to—worse yet, knowing full well he would be exiled to the parlor for an afternoon of gin with Kurt Baughman.

She'll be worth the wait, he thought.

Brigid held her tongue in Robert's presence, but when he left, she turned on Maggie. "How can ya be thinkin' to turn down such a fine gentleman as that?" she snapped. "And fer the likes of Tim Ryan."

"Mam, I didn't turn him down. Really. I just feel I should keep my promise to Tim." She had no desire to upset her mam. Not after that wonderful gift she had just given her. "But I will go walking with Mr. Arnaud this evening. Now, isn't that fair?"

"Hmph!" Brigid stamped out of the kitchen. She wasn't used to being thwarted.

CHAPTER EIGHT

Young Love

They were up at the Conroys' farm the Sunday after her birthday when Maggie told Tim about going away to school. She didn't know why she'd waited so long. Perhaps it was because a part of her didn't really want to go.

She had always missed being at school with her friends, especially Rosemarie. And now they would be together, at least for the next two years. She was thrilled at the prospect of her new life; there was no question things would be different. Still, it was hard to imagine her future away from the boarding house, especially since Tim had come into her life—a life that was quickly becoming very confusing. It had been much simpler when no one seemed to pay attention, moving through days doing whatever Mam said needed to be done. But she did have to admit it was much more exciting this way.

Tim and three of the older Conroy boys were removing stumps from a field they were planning to plant with wheat the following year. Five stumps had already succumbed to the strength of their young, muscular bodies as they chopped and dug under the heat of a blazing sun. Wiping away the sticky sweat dripping off his nose and chin, Tim looked up to see Maggie walking across the field with a pitcher of fresh, cold water and a large wicker basket. After a morning of back-breaking work, all four young men welcomed the food Mrs. Conroy had so thoughtfully provided. They sat in a circle, passing around sandwiches of chicken between thick slices of homemade bread and oatmeal biscuits still warm from the oven.

Though it was only the middle of May, the noon sun was extremely hot, so when they'd had their fill, Seamus, the oldest brother, suggested they all head for the water hole in the adjacent meadow to take a swim and cool off. Tim refused the tempting invitation, saying he'd rather just sit back and rest. The three brothers gave each other a knowing look.

Tim and Maggie watched the long, lanky bodies race toward the stand of maple trees near the fence. Cattle grazing contentedly on the other side looked up to see what the ruckus was. The welcoming shade and the water hole, fed by a natural spring, were a source of refreshment for man and beast alike.

The pair lay back in the soft spring grass, looking up at a flawless blue sky as whoops and hollers echoed through the adjoining field. The fresh scent of clover permeated the air. That's when she told him.

Tim sat up, resting his elbows on his knees, his chin in his hands, and gazed toward the invisible swimmers in the meadow beyond. Try as he might, he couldn't hide his disappointment. These past few weeks had been the happiest of his life. There was still the summer ahead, he knew, but then she'd be gone, and he would miss her desperately.

Hesitating, searching for the right words, he finally leaned down, taking his callused hand to brush a wisp of hair from her face, and smiling, leaned over to kiss her softly, his eyes filled with love. He said, "I'll certainly miss seeing you, Maggie, but I know how much this means to you, so if it makes you happy, then how can I help but be happy for you?"

For one perfect moment, her heart soared. Nothing else existed but his love. How could she bear to leave? But they were young, and hopefully two years of school, with a whole summer of being together in between, would pass quickly. Then they could build a life together.

Between washing and ironing clothes, cleaning, and serving meals, Maggie managed to spend every free moment during the rest of May and the first part of June studying for her entrance exam, the exception being her Sundays with Tim. Those she refused to give up. Their relationship had grown so much more intimate this past month.

And now, with her need to concentrate on her approaching test, several evenings a week, Tim would stroll by and sit with her in the gazebo, drilling her from the lists of questions Clara had said would probably be important. This way they were surrounded by the beauty and privacy of the garden, avoiding the boarders' prying eyes and endless gossip on the front porch. Clara, just beginning summer break away from her students, also had ample time to help out with tutoring, constantly encouraging and assuring her she was quite ready. Maggie went around the house, reciting capitals of the world or defining long lists of scientific vocabulary as she made beds or washed dishes, wishing she had Clara's confidence. In less than a week, she'd be heading for Toronto.

"Mrs. Mahoney, I will be only too happy to go along with

Maggie and see that she doesn't get lost," Robert volunteered as he sat at the kitchen table watching dinner preparations. "I could use a break from the shipping yard, and having lived in Toronto all my life, I could even show her a few of the sights. Toronto's a wonderful city. So much to see."

Brigid was elated. She and Maggie had been to Toronto many times on shopping trips, but her knowledge of the town consisted of going from Union Station on Front Street, then walking the three blocks up York to King Street, where most of the stores she was interested in were concentrated within a four-block area. In and out of the shops she'd go, Maggie in tow from the time she was a small child, doggedly searching up one side and down the other for the latest fashions with the best prices. Her favorite store was Eaton's, but if she couldn't find what she was searching for on King Street, she'd drag an exhausted Maggie up Yonge Street to the Toronto Arcade, where there were three stories of shops. After making all her comparisons, she might end up back on King Street, sometimes at the first shop she'd entered (usually Eaton's) and make her purchase there.

Then they would have lunch at Monique's Tea Room, around the corner of King, on Bay Street. Through all the years, this ritual had never varied. The minute they'd walk in, the delicious aroma of cinnamon and other spices would capture their senses. The tearoom was done up in shades of pink and white: pink organdy curtains, small round tables covered in deep rose cloths with little white vases of pink rosebuds in the center. Even the waitresses wore pink dresses, with white lace caps and little white lace-edged aprons.

Of course Maggie was a young woman, now, but from the

time she was little, she would always act so grown up, very ladylike, sitting on a tall white chair with its round, pink–velvet seat, holding her white gloved hands in her lap, feet dangling. She always got a cup of hot chocolate with a watercress sandwich or a slice of quiche, then a dish of chocolate ice cream. Brigid never knew that this and the train rides were the only parts Maggie enjoyed. She hated those shopping trips and was always relieved when the day was over, so they could head back to the station and go home.

Brigid couldn't help but appreciate Robert's offer and the fact that Maggie would be free of the worry of finding her way through the large city. Tim Ryan had become a thorn in Brigid's side, but Maggie would be spending the day with Robert. That really lifted Brigid's spirits. What better opportunity for Maggie to experience a day out with a real gentleman, the kind she would become accustomed to after she went away to school and attended some of the social gatherings in Toronto? And since Toronto was Robert's home, Brigid had high hopes he would keep in touch with Maggie while she was in school there.

It was settled. On June 22, Robert would accompany Maggie to Toronto. They would catch the six o'clock train in the morning and arrive somewhere around nine. The test was scheduled for ten and was expected to take about two hours. That would give them the rest of the day before catching the eight o'clock train back to Herron's Point.

The thought of spending the day with Maggie aroused Robert. For the past month, he'd tried in every way possible to get her attention, but she'd proven to be a real disappointment. She was always pleasant, ready to accommodate his requests for a second helping at the table or some extra starch in his shirts, even an occasional walk down to the park when he'd catch her at an odd moment, reading in the garden. But that wasn't the kind of accommodating he was seeking.

In Toronto, there'd never been that problem. He always had his choice of any number of young women who seemed only too happy to pander to his needs. And his needs came often.

Obviously, Maggie was not impressed by his social standing, his money, or even himself. To her, he was just another boarder. Still, she was a delightful diversion in this dull town. A real challenge. Her indifference only whetted his appetite for her favor. He would have her, feel her soft, full breasts against him, kiss that delicious, sensuous mouth. He'd never known such a delectable creature—and he'd known many. This trip to Toronto should do the trick.

By the time the day is over, he thought, I'll make her forget all about that Tim fella.

The night before they were to leave, Maggie had difficulty falling asleep, tossing and turning, her mind fretting over the next day's exam. She couldn't believe it was actually going to happen. It was Mam who had taken her out of school when she was ten, and Mam who was putting her back in at sixteen. But Mam had never really let her neglect her education. She'd always had Clara see to it that she kept up with her studies at home. There'd been days when she was younger when she would be so tired after cleaning and working all day, but Clara made sure she didn't fall behind. She really hoped the exam wouldn't be too hard.

What if I don't pass? she thought.

She began to think of Tim. He was always her last thought before she fell asleep. She wondered what it would be like to have him next to her in bed, holding her, loving her. Pleasurable sensations filled her body with desire. In these few short months, she had fallen deeply in love with Tim. And she knew he loved her, too. He'd told her so the Sunday they'd hiked over to Osaga Falls. That was the day he'd kissed her hard and fiercely, holding her so tightly, and yet so tenderly. Her whole body went limp with loving him.

Mam had been so angry again that day when she'd returned, and was determined that she shouldn't see Tim, going on and on about Robert Arnaud. She couldn't say enough about what a fine gentleman he was, and how Maggie should be nicer and pay more attention to someone who knew how to appreciate a lady.

Maggie liked Robert well enough, but there were times when she thought he was quite bothersome with all his compliments and fawning, always popping up when she least expected him, hanging around in the kitchen when she did dishes. There'd never been anyone, outside of Mam and herself, who'd spent so much time in that kitchen.

She quietly held her ground that day, as she'd done so many times before when Tim Ryan's name came up. It wasn't like her to argue with Mam about anything. Always doing whatever Mam said. But Mam would not have her way in this. She had no right to even try. Tim was wonderful. Why couldn't she see that? Tomorrow she would be spending the day with Robert. That should make Mam hap... She was asleep.

From the time she was a small child, Maggie had always enjoyed riding the train to Toronto, looking out the window, watching the countryside roll by.

Although Robert hated trains, today he relished the thought of it and made all the right moves, keeping the conversation light and adventuresome while attempting to wash away some of the dread Maggie felt for the impending test.

They arrived at Union Station right on schedule. Robert was happy to see that Gregory had received his message and was waiting as they exited the terminal and approached Front Street. He'd written ahead, asking that the family carriage meet them when they arrived. He knew his mother would never fail him.

From the time they first got off the train, he was quite aware of heads turning to look at the beautiful redhead on his arm. There wasn't another around that could match her beauty. His ego was completely sated as they approached the carriage.

Gregory climbed down from his perch. He was dressed in a black cutaway jacket and tapered pants (both tailored perfectly), a white shirt and large gray cravat, black leather boots, gray suede gloves, and a gray top hat banded in black, with a small green feather sticking out of the left side.

As Robert introduced him to Maggie, he watched her face. He could see from those dancing eyes that she was thoroughly impressed. Gregory gave a small bow from the waist and took her elbow to assist her up into the open carriage, where she adjusted the large, bustle–like flounce in the back of her skirt and sank into the luxury of soft leather.

From her vantage point, Maggie could see the masses of people scurrying to and from the busy terminal that faced the Toronto harbor. The hustle and bustle intrigued her as stylish ladies and well–dressed gentlemen got into carriages or those new machines they called automobiles. Others were running to catch the trolley, but most were just walking. The rhythm of activity was intense and so stimulating, giving her a sense of excitement at being part of the mainstream of life.

She felt quite grown up, almost pampered, in the pink and white, peppermint–striped dress that Mam had picked out early in the spring, on their most recent shopping trip in Toronto. She remembered her saying, "Sure, and isn't this a dress suitable for any young lady about ta be sixteen?" She'd worn it on her birthday, but today was an occasion that suited it perfectly. Of course she'd added a pair of white gloves, dabbed a bit of the perfume Robert had given her behind her ears and on her wrists, and taken the time to pile her hair on top of her head, fastening it in place with the two tortoise–shell combs, the gift from the Carter sisters.

She'd refused to wear the hat Mam had insisted on, saying it was just too much. She didn't want to be worrying about messing up her hair taking it off when she'd be taking her test. Though Mam said it was only proper for a lady to wear a hat in public, she finally relented. Maggie had had her way. She really was growing up.

Gregory turned up York Street and continued as far as West Queen Street, then took a left for one block and turned right again on University Avenue, a wide boulevard lined down the center with lush, green chestnut trees. Robert took delight in pointing out the sights of interest along the way: the Parliament buildings, Osgoode Hall, the Armouries. It delighted him to see Maggie hanging on his every word, sitting up as tall as she could, not wanting to miss a thing as they continued through Queen's Park, with its campus atmosphere, surrounding Toronto College.

Soon they were at the city limits. Gregory took what seemed to be a country road, but within minutes they approached an iron gate supported by red–brick columns on either side. The brass plate on the left column read "Saint Cecilia's Academy, Est. 1876." The entire property appeared to be surrounded by a high, wrought–iron fence. There was a small, charming brick gatekeeper's cottage inside the fence, reminding Maggie of a large doll's house, and a long, gravel driveway lined with tall poplars that wound toward an ivy–covered brick structure almost completely hidden from view.

The gatekeeper, a wizened old man disturbed from his nap, grudgingly yawned and admitted them after Robert stated their purpose. Summers were not usually taken up with much traffic in and out. He continued to stare after them with sleepy eyes as they trotted up the driveway, wondering if it was worth his while to go back to his nap. Probably not. Dern fools'd just want out again.

"You're going to do just fine, Maggie," Robert said as they approached the cluster of ivy–covered brick buildings. Taking her hands in his and giving her a quick, brotherly peck on the cheek, he continued, "Anyone can tell you're an intelligent young woman just by the way you conduct yourself. And when you're finished, I'll be right here waiting. Then we'll have lunch and celebrate your success. I know just the place. After that, I'll be anxious to show you around Toronto."

Robert remained in the carriage as Maggie entered the main building. She was greeted at the door by Sister Felicitous and taken into a room off the main hall next to the office. Sister Felicitous was young, with the most beautiful ivory skin and rosy cheeks Maggie had ever seen. She was kind and reassuring as she explained that the test would be timed and supervised by her.

"You have nothing to fear, dear," she said. "I will be with you at all times, and if you have any questions, feel free to ask."

The test was not as difficult as she had anticipated. Either that, or Clara had done her job well. It took all of the two hours to complete, but there had been a small break in between when Sister had given her a cup of tea and offered her some chocolate biscuits.

They casually chatted about the school, and Sister said yes, she knew Rosemarie Stuart well, lovely girl. Then they resumed the business at hand. When Maggie finally filled in her last answer and handed in her papers, Sister Felicitous walked her to the door, shook her hand, and gave her a friendly smile. "We'll notify you of the results within the next week or so."

I'm sure I passed, Maggie thought.

Robert was there, waiting. Once again, they were delayed as the old man slowly stirred himself to open the gate, muttering to himself that he could have had a good nap if he'd known they were going to be so long.

The rest of the day was theirs.

Maggie had never imagined Toronto to be so large, or so full of such beautiful homes and such impressive buildings. All she'd ever seen were the shops near Union Station.

Robert had gone out of his way to show her the best the city had to offer, beginning with a picnic lunch by a beautiful fountain near the entrance of Queen's Park. Robert said his mother had had it prepared just for the occasion. He didn't mention that it had been at his request.

Then Gregory drove them all around the city, occasionally stopping as they got out to walk up and down a busy street in the business district Robert seemed to be so familiar with. He cut such a handsome figure and seemed to be well known wherever they went. She couldn't know how much it pleased him to display the beautiful girl he had clinging to his arm.

Toward the end of the day, he took her to an exclusive china shop on King Street, insistent on buying her a memento of their day in Toronto. She politely refused his offer, completely content to just browse. Never had she seen so many beautiful articles of china, porcelain, crystal, silver, and pewter.

His persistence won out when they got back in the carriage and he handed her a gift box wrapped in shiny silver paper. It was the Dresden music box she had so admired when they'd first entered the shop.

The most wonderful part he had saved for the end of the day, when Gregory took them down to a large marina on the bay, once again solicitously assisting her out of the carriage. This time, he escorted her from the dock onto a bright red sloop.

That was the last she saw of Gregory. Robert immediately took over, skillfully sailing them out to the Royal Canadian Yacht Club on Toronto Island, where he was a member.

It was a marvelous place, much like an enormous estate, with magnificent gardens and lawns, tennis courts, and an impressive clubhouse. The two–and–a–half–story structure was supported in the front by huge white pillars, with cooling verandas on two levels, quite resembling a mansion in the antebellum South.

All of the staff seemed to know and welcome Robert, anxious to be of service. In one of the several elegantly appointed dining rooms of the clubhouse, they dined leisurely on lobster and a wonderful wine that tickled Maggie's nose. Gaping with naiveté, she looked around in wonder at the genteel ambience—shining crystal, the gentle clink of fine silver against delicate china, and a soft murmuring of voices.

By the time they returned to the marina and walked back to Union Station, Maggie found herself completely enchanted by the entire day, the city—and Robert. She had to admit that he was every bit the gentleman Mam had claimed him to be. Even the long train ride home was exciting. There was so much to talk about, and Robert had been such a gentleman, making sure she had a pillow to rest her head, although she was too keyed up to use it.

Robert was completely pleased with her response to the day's events. Things couldn't have turned out more perfectly.

It was almost eleven o'clock when the train pulled into the depot. Robert had purposely not arranged to have anyone meet them, knowing the walk was not that far, a good half mile at the most, relishing this intimate time with Maggie. Just the two of them.

It was a beautiful starlit night as they walked in silence, making their way down Broad Street, listening to the gentle lapping of waves washing against the shore as they approached Erie Street. Robert held Maggie's hand to ensure she wouldn't trip. She didn't object, considering that the night was dark and she was quite exhausted.

Erie Street was almost completely dark when they arrived at the front door and went into the foyer. Brigid had kept a small lamp burning in the parlor.

Maggie turned to say goodnight, covering her mouth to hold back a yawn. "Robert, I can't thank you enough for showing me such a wonderful day." She leaned up and kissed him on the cheek.

He could no longer contain himself. Doing what he'd wanted to do all day, he grabbed her in his arms, kissed her hard on the lips, and began fondling her breasts.

Maggie pulled away, mortified. "Robert, please! Don't spoil things. It was such a lovely day, and I do so appreciate the fact that it was because of you I had such a wonderful time. I thank you for every minute of it. Can't we let it go at that?"

Realizing he'd mistaken her gratitude for desire, he backed away. "I'm so sorry, Maggie. I don't know what got into me. But you're so beautiful. I just couldn't help myself."

"Please, Robert. Don't apologize. I just want us to remain friends. That's all. Now, if you don't mind, would you put out the lamp before you go upstairs? I must get some sleep. I have to be up by five."

She turned on her heels and disappeared down the hallway.

Robert stood alone, filled with self-recrimination.

What is it going to take to win her over? Why couldn't I have waited? I pushed too fast. I should have given her more time to think about me and the wonderful time we had today.

But then his self-abasement was replaced by anger.

Who does she think she is? All I did was kiss her. Why should I have to apologize for something she's wanted me to do all along? She's a tease with that coy smile of hers—and those eyes! Surely I didn't mistake the passion I saw in them during dinner. Surely I didn't imagine it. My instincts about women are better than that.

Disgusted, he turned out the light in the parlor and made his way up the stairs in darkness.

Agnes Carter always made it a practice to bring the mail home with her at the end of the day. And that particular day, June 28, was one for celebrating.

Maggie had been on tenterhooks waiting for the news. When Agnes came into the kitchen and handed her the long white envelope, she immediately tore it open and read the letter from Saint Cecilia's, congratulating her on her high marks and welcoming her as a new student. She couldn't contain her excitement.

Robert, who'd become a permanent fixture in the kitchen before dinner, was closest to her. She threw her arms around him and began to dance, twirling him about, then raced over to the stove and grabbed Mam, then Clara, who was standing in the doorway anticipating the good news, giving each a hug and a kiss on the cheek.

It was obvious that they were all happy for her, but Robert had once again been aroused by her approval of him as a dancing partner. He took it as a sign she had forgiven him. Ever since that incident in the hallway, Maggie had been polite but quite aloof.

Perhaps this letter will rekindle her memory of the wonderful time we had in Toronto, he thought.

All the boarders offered Maggie their congratulations, especially Clara, who felt she'd had a personal stake in the entire venture. Maggie couldn't thank her enough.

Tim came over that evening after supper, and they took a walk down by the lake. Maggie had been much more relaxed since she'd taken the test. This past week or so had been wonderful. She and Tim were even closer than before. She'd told him what a wonderful day she'd spent in Toronto, describing in detail her dinner with Robert at the yacht club. She hadn't mentioned the incident with Robert after they'd come home, however; she wasn't quite sure why, except that she saw no reason to upset him.

She'd saved her good news until after they strolled out to the end of the pier to sit and watch the sun slowly dip toward the western horizon. Sky and lake became a kaleidoscope of color. Staring at its peaceful beauty, she said softly, "Tim, I got the best news today. I passed my entrance exam. I can't thank you enough for helping me study for it."

Tim put his arm around her, pulling her close. He didn't want to lose her, but he was truly happy that she was going to get something she'd wanted for so long. After years of drudgery, she was being given a chance to escape it all and broaden her life. There would be time for the two of them after she'd finished her schooling.

He turned her face toward him with his free hand and stroked her cheek. "I'm so happy for you, Maggie. You know how much I love you—how much I'll miss you."

Their eyes locked. It was all Tim could do to restrain himself from pulling her to him, kissing her, but there were others on the pier. Those things just weren't done in public.

Maggie rested her head on his shoulder as they watched the final setting of the sun.

It was not unusual for Robert to watch surreptitiously as Maggie and Tim walked away from 7 Erie Street, hand in hand. How many evenings had he done it of late? It galled him to see Tim take that liberty. But then, hadn't Maggie allowed him to hold her hand on the way back from the train depot that night? Still, she had kept her distance and immediately let go when she was assured of her own footing. How many nights had she come to him in his dreams, smiling, calling to him, fondling him, loving him, giving herself over to him as he ravished her until he was completely spent? Why was it so difficult to get her to see him as the better man of the two? He had so much more to offer.

In order to avoid Kurt Baughman on the front porch, he decided to go out the back gate and down to Kelly's Pub to spend his evening. The day had been hot and humid; it would be cooler by the water. And there were a couple of older women he'd seen on the few occasions he'd been down there with Frank Brewster after working late at the shipyard. They'd noticed him, too. Perhaps he'd get lucky.

Kelly's was smoky and noisy. The two women he'd counted on seeing (Betsy and Virginia, he later found out) were sitting at a table out on the crowded deck that ran the length of the building, overlooking the marina. He saw them through an open doorway as he approached the bar and immediately changed his course toward them.

They looked up as he strolled out and politely nodded in their direction. "Lovely evening, ladies. And where in God's world could you find a more beautiful sunset?" he commented as he continued toward the railing.

Knowing he'd caught their attention, he took a deep breath of moist evening air, so much cooler than back at the house, and leaned on the railing to gaze out over the lake. The sun had just made its exit below the horizon, and twilight left the blue sky and water drenched in soft shades of pink and mauve.

In the distance, he could see a young couple sitting at the end of the Center Street pier. He was sure it was Tim and Maggie. His blood boiled.

Lightbulbs strung above the deck railing winked on. From

the corner of his eye, he could see the two older women watching him. Still leaning on the rail, he turned to look over his shoulder in their direction. Then, smiling, he said, "I see your glasses are almost empty. May I offer to buy you ladies something cool to drink?"

The ladies returned his smile and accepted coyly, just as he'd known they would. That was all it took to be invited to join them at their table and become better acquainted.

Throughout the evening, he was informed of many things. He learned that both Betsy and Virginia were married. Their sailor husbands were out of port at the time, so they spent several evenings a week at Kelly's, in need of some diversion and a few laughs. Of course most of the ladies in the town thought them too loose in their ways, but they were young and didn't mind being snubbed by the "old biddies." A little fun at Kelly's Pub helped to make their lonely nights just a little more tolerable.

When Robert realized that that was all he was, a diversion, he was disappointed. Still, the evening wasn't a total loss. He was quite surprised to find he actually enjoyed their company immensely. They were fun.

The moon sat low in the east, casting a streak of silver across the midnight–black water. The clouds held the heat of the day close to the earth, occasionally passing over the moon to blanket the night in complete darkness. Tall–masted sailboats, a houseboat, rowboats, and even a canoe joined dancing lightbulbs, undulating like shadowy creatures threatening to climb up over the deck. The wash of waves lapping against the boats in the marina, along with an occasional warm lake breeze, gave Robert a sense of being adrift at sea. Along with the pints of ale and abundance of laughter, it all proved to be quite an intoxicating evening. Robert loved this fuzzy feeling of contentment.

As the evening came to a close, Betsy, the bolder of the two, insisted he have one last drink before he left. He obliged her with a toast to a wonderful, fun-filled evening, in spite of knowing from past experience that one more drink could possibly take him beyond his limit to a place of no return. Then he might not be responsible for his actions. At some point, past fuzzy and silly, he knew he would have no memory of what he'd done. Blacking out, they called it.

It had happened to him twice in Toronto. With each incident, his father had had to come to the rescue, bailing him out of jail for indecent behavior and disturbing the peace one time. Fortunately, because of his wealth and long-reaching influence, Pierre Arnaud was able to pay off the offended parties and protect his son from the law, but that didn't protect Robert from his father's fury when they got home—where, after the second fall from grace, Pierre made it quite clear that it would be absolutely unthinkable to disgrace the Arnaud name. The mention of dispossession did come up.

On those two occasions, as with so many other falls from grace, Robert's mother, Antoinette, who had spoiled and pampered him from childhood, stepped in to protect her son from what she referred to as her husband's tyrannical ravings. "He's just sowing his wild oats," she snapped.

But the second offense really had been quite serious—involving a married woman. He'd supposedly remained after a party, surprising the hostess, Angela Walters, in her bedroom as she readied for bed. She was shocked and frightened at his appearance, but was quick-witted enough to grab a lamp from the night stand, and as he staggered toward her, she knocked him unconscious.

Fortunately for him, Steven Walters was escorting his old mother safely to her home and was not present in the house. Had he been there, Robert might not have survived the ordeal. As it was, the husband returned to find his wife sitting on the floor in a state of hysteria, not knowing what to do, with Robert's unconscious head in her lap as she waited for the police to arrive.

She didn't confide to her husband that she felt somewhat to blame, remembering she had been a bit of a tease that evening. Robert was so young and handsome—and unconscious.

Later, after Robert had been taken into custody, Angela spoke to Robert's father, who calmed her down. With a bit of cajoling, she finally agreed that no real harm had been done. She also preferred to let the entire incident drop, not wanting the notoriety.

Her husband was of another mind altogether. "The drunken bastard needs to be taught a lesson."

Pierre and Steven Walters had a little chat.

Robert slowly opened his eyes, rubbing his head in a stupor, incognizant of the events that had just taken place, barely aware he had been taken into custody. The whole affair took less than two hours. The argument at home took a little longer.

Pierre had been silent on the way back to the house, but as soon as Hubert, their butler, let them into the huge marbled foyer and all the servants were out of earshot, he began.

Antoinette was waiting for them in the library. As they

entered, she walked over, put her arm around her tall son's waist, and looked up lovingly into his bloodshot eyes, tenderly touching the knot on his forehead.

Somehow, she saw Robert as the victim. "It's not his fault that women make fools of themselves over him. If I know Angela Walters, she probably encouraged him."

Robert's foggy recollection of the evening led him to believe she was right.

"He's only reacting like any normal, healthy male."

In her eyes, Robert could do no wrong. This kind of scene was not uncommon in the Arnaud household. Robert had developed his convoluted ideas of what he considered to be principles through the twenty-one years of haranguing and contradiction between bickering parents over what they considered best for him. He'd learned there were no hard and fast rules; it simply depended on whom he was dealing with at any given moment.

From his father, strict and unyielding, but far from the tyrant his wife depicted him to be, he'd learned the value of honesty and integrity, hard work, and respect for his fellow man.

From his mother, he'd discovered that all these values could easily be manipulated, if need be, with the opposite sex. And he'd found that many times there was that need. Appearances were what mattered. His good looks and charm, especially where women were concerned—and in particular his mother—could easily erase an occasional indiscretion.

He counted on his charismatic appeal to do the trick. Not so easily done, however, if one was not in control of one's actions. That was his dilemma. That last episode had made him acutely aware that his capacity for alcohol was limited. In spite of his mother's protection, he knew that his father, a man of his word, meant every word he'd uttered about dispossessing him. He had to be careful.

Maggie had just finished getting ready for bed and turned out the kitchen light. It had been an extremely hot, humid day, so she decided to leave her bedroom door open to catch any waft of breeze that might come through the open windows and screen door in the kitchen. Doors had never been locked, and none of the boarders ever came in through the back. Even so, it hadn't occurred to her that any of them were still out.

The household had been quite still when she'd shut the front door and turned out the lights in the parlor and foyer. She stripped off her nightgown and got into bed, exhausted from the heat. No one would ever know. She was always the first one up.

Robert could see the light in the back of the house as he weaved his way over Erie Street. He wasn't quite drunk, still in control, but he had to admit he was feeling pretty mellow.

Maggie must still be up, he thought. He would go around to Ontario Street and in the back gate. Perhaps she would come out and sit with him in the gazebo, where it was cooler and they could talk.

By the time he reached the back gate, the kitchen was in darkness. Disappointed for the second time that evening, he quietly entered the house, hoping not to disturb anyone. He stood for a moment to get his bearings, his eyes adjusting to the shadowy forms in the kitchen as moonlight cast its light across the room: the table, the swinging door to the dining room, the entrance to the hallway leading to the front of the house, the back stairway next to the fireplace, and... Maggie's bedroom door was open.

She couldn't be asleep, yet, his muddled mind reasoned. I'll just take a peek. If she's still awake, I'll ask her to sit in the garden with me. The air's really quite stuffy in here.

He approached her door and stood looking down as moonbeams filtered through the bedroom window, revealing her naked body, her beautiful face, her hair spread around her like a silk veil.

As the blood in his groin heated up, he could feel his erection. He knelt down beside the bed and whispered her name.

She appeared to be in a deep sleep. He reached over to touch her cheek.

She stretched her legs and moaned softly, then awakened and screamed, startling him.

He immediately put his hand over her mouth. "Shhh. Don't be frightened. It's only me. I don't want you to wake your mam."

Maggie grabbed the quilt beside her, covering herself. "What do you think you're doing? You have no right to be here. So help me, Robert, if you don't get away from me, I will call my mam, and she'll throw you out of here, bag and baggage!"

Robert became quite contrite and apologetic. "Maggie, please. I didn't intend for this to happen. I—I've had a little too much to drink. Your door was open, and I came over to ask you to sit out in the garden with me. When I saw you there, so beautiful, I couldn't help myself."

"Just get away from me!" she said with fury. "Go away. Now!"

"Please, Maggie, don't be angry. I know I was wrong. But surely you must be aware of how much I'm attracted to you. I—I don't know what gets into me sometimes. I would never deliberately hurt you. Say you forgive me. Please."

Maggie could see his face—frightened and confused, not the usual self–centered, confident, charming Robert. That person would never grovel. This Robert was a whimpering child. There was no question a few drinks had altered him. However, that couldn't begin to excuse his behavior.

"Just go, Robert. You're tired. We'll talk about this another time."

Like a beaten puppy, he backed out of the room, mumbling to himself, "So sorry...sorry."

By the time he'd gone down the hall and was ascending the front stairs, the reality of the last few sobering moments struck him, clearing his head of the alcohol he had tried so carefully to monitor.

He was thankful he hadn't been really drunk. No telling what might have happened. He was grateful he still had enough control of his faculties and enough presence of mind to quiet an incident that could have brought the whole household down on his head.

The clearer his thinking became, the angrier he got and the more he began to wonder why he should have had to apologize at all. She was a tease, always smiling and obliging, brushing against him when she leaned over to take his plate or pour his coffee. She wanted him. It was like his mother always said. Women couldn't resist him. Hadn't she invited his advances?

CHAPTER NINE

Going Away

Chester Deidrick was the only boarder missing from the breakfast table to say his farewells. But then, he wasn't around much. As captain of one of the freighters that came in and out of the harbor, he paid for his room and board in advance—and full price, at that—because he wanted to be assured of good meals and a pleasant place to rest his head when he got into port. To him, it was well worth the price. He could be gone for as long as three weeks at a time.

"Won't ya be havin' just a wee bit more of these fried potatoes, Mr. Arnaud?" Brigid asked.

"No, no. Not another thing, Mrs. Mahoney."

"Perhaps just a bit more of this ham, then?" she said, making it her personal obligation to see to it that Robert Arnaud should want for nothing his last day with them.

"No, truly, it was a delicious breakfast," Robert said, waving the plate away, placing his hand, palm down, under his chin, gesturing. "I'm filled up to here. I have no place to put it. I'm just hoping I'll find some room for the farewell luncheon the gentlemen at the shipping yards are throwing for me down at MacPhearson's Hotel this noon. Not that any of it'll begin to compare to one of your fabulous meals. I declare, Mrs. Mahoney, you've spoiled me completely. I'll be hard pressed to find another like you in Toronto."

"Go 'long with ya," Brigid cooed coyly, slapping him on the shoulder with her free hand. She returned to the kitchen, brandishing her platter of potatoes and ham through the swinging doors with a flourish.

A guttural, rasping sound came out of Kurt Baughman as he not so cleverly concealed a belch by clearing his throat. "We'll be missing your company around here, Robert," he blustered. "Probably me more than most," he puffed, "seeing as how I'm always surrounded by a brood of clucking females. It's been mighty refreshing having another male around and some intelligent conversation. Ain't that right, Mama?"

Elsa Baughman's cheeks turned pink as she nodded. "Yes, Mr. Baughman."

Zebadiah Chadwick showed obvious affront at having been excluded from the male population that gathered around the dining room table daily. "Yup, we've had some real intelligent conversation around here fer a change." Zeb glared into Kurt's face as turned back to Robert and continued. "It'll be sorely missed. That can't be denied. And we'll be missin' all those lively stories 'bout the city life back there in Toronto, too."

Zeb took one last swig of coffee and pulled his lanky bones out of his chair. "I'll be seein' to your luggage now, Mr. Arnaud. You say it's all in the foyer?"

Robert nodded.

"Then I best be gettin' it up to the depot. It'll be waitin' fer ya when yer train's ready to leave."

Zeb shuffled out of the room, mumbling. To the discerning ear, the last word heard before he disappeared into the foyer could have been interpreted as "windbag." Kurt got up, peered over his fat belly at his pocket watch, and motioned to Elsa. "C'mon, Mama. Best we get down to the store."

Elsa quickly stood, waiting beside her chair as Kurt lumbered over to Robert and shook his hand.

"Best of luck to ya, young fella. If we ever get to Toronto, we'll be sure to look you up."

Robert graciously smiled as Kurt pumped away. "Now, see that you do that," he replied, hoping such a thing would never come to pass. He'd had just about enough of this crowing braggart.

Elsa gave a quick, pink-faced nod in his direction as they left the room.

Agnes Carter daintily set her coffee cup back in its saucer. "I'd best be saying my goodbyes now, too," she said softly. "I'm due at the Post Office in ten minutes." Her eyes rested on the composed, aristocratic face of the young man sitting across from her. "It has been a pleasure having such a fine young gentleman in our company these past few months. I wish you well in Toronto, Mr. Arnaud."

Robert stood as Agnes and Clara made ready to leave.

"My sister's sentiments are also mine," Clara said. "And please, if you are ever back here in Herron's Point, do come to see us."

Each sister in turn walked around the table and kissed him on the cheek.

Robert knew how to be charming. Hadn't he captivated the

entire town with his charismatic personality? Why hadn't it worked on Maggie?

He stood, taking the hand of each woman, holding them at arm's length, looking at the gentle, open faces of the aging sisters. "It has been my pleasure to have spent so much time in the company of two such lovely ladies." This time, he truly meant it.

Now that the others were gone, Maggie came into the dining room to clear away the remains of the breakfast dishes.

She knew she'd have to face Robert before he left. It had been all she could do to stay clear of him these past two weeks. Awkward, to be sure, but in her own way, she would say her goodbyes. Then he'd be gone.

Robert leaned against his chair, watching Maggie's beautiful face as she stacked the dishes on a large tray. She looked so young and vulnerable with her long, auburn hair tied back in a pink bow that way.

Clinking china smothered the silence between them. He finally broke through it. "Maggie, I'm going to miss you. I know you've been avoiding me these past few weeks, and I'm truly sorry if I've offended you. But you must believe me when I say I meant you no harm. My heart rules my head sometimes, and I act like an emotional fool. I hope we can part as friends."

Maggie had listened to these contrite words before. Each time she'd thwarted his advances, she'd heard them. But two weeks ago in her bedroom, he had gone too far. He wouldn't fool her with his shallow, puerile words, the way he'd won over Mam—and everyone else, for that matter.

When Maggie looked up, her green eyes pierced him, filling him with desire. He'd never known such craving for a woman, not even Helena, who would become his wife within the month—but no one in Herron's Point need know about that. It was difficult to be near this ravishing creature without wanting to possess every part of her; unthinkable that he would never see her again. Still, it must be. Life must go on as it had been planned out for him: a good marriage between two influential families. There was no turning away from that.

"I think it best we forget the whole incident," Maggie said, half smiling. "I do want to wish you a safe journey—and a good life."

She looked at the young man facing her. He had used just the right amount of pomade to keep every light-brown hair in its proper place. He was the picture of refinement in his gray morning coat and black-striped trousers. A burgundy cravat and diamond stickpin set off his immaculate white shirt—every inch a gentleman. At least, that's what she'd once thought until that incident two weeks before. The word "gentleman" no longer applied.

"I still have some loose ends to tie up at the shipyard this morning," he said, "so I'll have to be leaving, now. I find it difficult to accept that I won't be seeing you again." His face was doleful as he approached her. "Do you think we could kiss goodbye and part as friends?"

"I think a simple handshake will do," she said coolly, extending her arm to halt his advances.

The warmth of her hand was more than he could bear, heating him with a burning desire to grab her in his arms.

It was at just that moment Brigid chose to come through the door. Entering from the kitchen and realizing that Robert was about to leave, she rushed over and took his face in her hands, kissing him soundly on the cheek.

"I'd not be wantin' ta miss givin' ya that before ya take yer leave," she said. "And don't be fergettin' to stay in touch. You'll be rememberin', you're invited to spend any part of the Christmas holidays as our guest?"

Brigid could say goodbye, but she had no intention of letting go, and she felt that anyone would be a fool if they didn't see that Robert was crazy about her Mary Margaret. Things couldn't have worked out better if she'd planned it herself. He'd be back.

"We're goin' to be sorely missin' havin' ya around," she sighed.

Unlike his usual self–assured manner, his diffidence was obvious as he backed away toward the foyer. "I...won't be forgetting any part of my stay here." He glanced quickly at Maggie's dispassionate stare. "Everyone has been more than kind." For one awkward moment he was at a loss for words, then smiled at them both. "I'll keep in touch."

Maggie heard the screen door slam behind him. It had the sweet sound of gone.

Equipped with rags, cleaning supplies, and a bucket of hot, soapy water, Maggie went upstairs to the guest room he had occupied for the past two months. It was a large, gracious room in need of airing and a good cleaning to ready it for the next occupant.

She opened the two windows at the front of the house. A cool morning breeze wafted in, engaging the delicate lace curtains in a gentle dance. The windows afforded a wonderful view of the lake as she stood for a few moments gazing over the rooftops of Commerce and Water Streets. Lake Erie was calm, playful waves bouncing golden splinters of sunlight into the air. Far to the east, she could see the Point, with its long arm jutting out into the water; three freighters rested in its harbor. Straight ahead was the long pier at the bottom of Center Street, occupied by some fishermen intent on catching tonight's dinner. If she stretched high enough on her toes, she could see the roof of Tim's house at the far western end of Water Street. Her days were always happier when she knew she'd be seeing him. He'd be coming tonight at seven.

Okay, Mary Margaret, quit your dawdlin'. There's work to be done, she told herself, mimicking Mam's words, knowing this is what she would hear if Mam were around to catch her standing there. How many times had she heard her use that expression? Thousands, maybe?

She immediately got to work, stripping the bed so it could air out the last remains of Robert Arnaud.

It took the entire morning to dust and scrub, wax and polish. When she was done, she stood back to admire the beautiful room. The windows and mirrors gleamed. The washstand, with its white china bowl and pitcher, had been scoured of any remains of Robert's facial hair. It was time for lunch.

When she returned to the room to make the bed, the day had become quite hot. She immediately put down the windows and drew the shades to block out the heat of the day and protect the carpet from disastrous fading. The room had the clean smell of furniture polish and strong pine soap.

She was just smoothing the sheet when she heard the screen door slam. At first, she thought it was Clara, coming back early from visiting her sick uncle up over the ridge. But hadn't she said she'd be gone most of the day? The rest of the boarders were off working, and Mam was gone with Father Chuck for the afternoon on some errand of mercy.

Muffled footsteps climbed the thick burgundy runner on the staircase. Her heart quickened when she recognized his heavy step coming down the hallway toward the room that had been his.

She hid her apprehension and turned to greet him. "My goodness, Robert, you're a surprise. I expected you'd be on your way to the railway station by now. Zeb took your luggage up there hours ago. Did you forget something?"

His tall frame filled the doorway. A lock of his fine hair hung on his forehead, totally out of character. His mouth was twisted in a simpering grin, and his eyes were glazed over, staring right through her. The strong odor of alcohol assaulted her senses.

Why is he looking at me like that? My God, he's drunk.

Instinctively, she felt fear. "Did...did you have a nice farewell luncheon?" she asked, trying to humor him.

"Oh, it was jush fine," he grinned, slurring his words. "In fact, it was so mush fun, I thought I'd come back here one more time. I found myshelf mish...mish...missing you already."

"Aren't you worried you'll miss your train?" she asked. The blood had drained from her face, but she managed a weak smile.

"Hell, no. Got plenty'a time. An hour at least."

His eyes covered her body like an obscene thought. His intense tone became less garbled. "Just thought I'd come back and keep you company for a bit. Couldn't get those green eyes of yours out of my mind. Kept thinking about them all through lunch."

He looked like he was going to cry. "You know I'm going to

miss you, Maggie. I just want us to be friends."

It was difficult for Maggie to comprehend him this way. He'd probably had too much to drink at the farewell luncheon. Maybe far too much, but he was no longer slurring his words. He didn't talk like he was drunk, just weird.

She had to get him downstairs and out on the porch, into the fresh air.

"Well, I'm pretty busy right now, Robert." She leaned down and picked up the sheets from the floor. "I've got to get this linen down to the laundry. Why don't you wait for me on the porch? It'll just take a few minutes to finish with my work here. Then we can sit on the swing and talk."

"All I want is just one kiss goodbye," he said, making a move toward her. "Honest, Maggie, just one little teensy–weensy kiss."

He grabbed her arm and yanked her to him. She clung to the laundry as she would a metal shield, but he was strong. His hands were all over her. His stinking mouth came down hard on hers, hurting her lips. His tongue was in her mouth, sickening and vile. She couldn't breathe. She felt she was going to throw up.

Finally, he released her, staggering toward the bed. "I have to sit down before I fall down," he giggled. "Guess I just had too much to drink." He put his head in his hands. "I don't seem to do anything right where you're concerned. Seems I'm always telling you I'm sorry for something."

Remembering his past lamenting over bad behavior, she was hoping that would be the extent of it. She turned and faced him, collecting enough breath to speak. "Robert, you really do have to go. Aren't you worried you're going to miss your train?"

If she didn't know better, she could almost feel sorry for

him sitting there, so forlorn and dejected.

He tried to get up and began to teeter. She reached over to help him keep his balance, then froze with terror.

His face was wild. Spittle formed at the corners of his twisted mouth. Snatching the laundry from her arms, he pushed her to the bed.

She let out a yell.

He was on her, heavy, strong, tearing at her clothes as she kicked and clawed. He struck her hard on the face, making her ears ring and her head reel with pain. Grabbing her two hands in his one strong one, he put his forearm across her throat to keep her head down. She could barely breathe.

"You little bitch," he snarled into her ear. "You've been wanting this from the first day I came. Always smiling. Teasing. Butter wouldn't melt in your mouth. So anxious to please. I'll bet you know how to make that beau of yours happy. I've watched the two of you. Now it's my turn."

His panting voice was cruel. The weight of his body was intense as he used his leg as a wedge to push her legs apart. Holding her down, he groped and fumbled with one hand until he had torn away her cotton dress. He was pawing her breasts, kissing her, then prying and probing with his fingers, groaning obscenities. He was like a madman, intent on satisfying an appetite that had obviously not been assuaged by eating, but intensified by drinking his lunch.

Maggie was helpless. With his arm across her neck, her screams came out as whimpers.

He forced her legs apart with his knee, and she could feel the hardness of him as he entered her. Using both hands to hold her down, he arched his back, thrusting as hard as he could, his face distorted with the ecstasy of animal passion.

The ripping, searing pain was excruciating. Only the empty rooms in the house heard her screams. She passed out.

Except for the ticking of the alarm clock on the nightstand, there was no movement. The house was silent. She opened her eyes and knew he was gone.

Her whole body ached and burned; she moaned in an effort to get up. There was blood on the clean sheet she had put on the bed not thirty minutes before. She ripped it off.

It hurt to walk. Dazed and bewildered, she made her way to the downstairs bathroom to wash out the stained sheet. Somehow, she knew she could never let Mam or anyone else see it.

Soaking the sheet in the washbowl, she filled the tub with hot water, stripped off her tattered, blood–stained clothes, and got in. The water burned her tender skin, torn and bleeding, her breasts bruised and bitten, yet somehow the water soothed her.

She scrubbed with soap, hoping to wash away the memory, the filth, the painful, sacrilegious horror. She crawled out of the tub and dried herself. She must hurry before anyone came home. They shouldn't find her this way.

The mirror revealed a dark purple bruise emerging on the left side of her face. This was a nightmare, but unlike some others she'd had, she knew this one would not go away. She would tell no one of her shame. Tim must never know.

Wrapped in a towel, she went into her own small room to dress in clean, fresh clothes. She wanted to get under the covers and hide, stay in bed, but she knew that was impossible. She must finish her work.

She took her tattered clothes and burned them in the

fireplace in the kitchen, making sure only ashes remained. Everything must appear as it always did. She didn't know how, but she would have to see to that.

Whimpering like a wounded animal, she forced herself back upstairs and into the bedroom she had so lovingly cleaned. It took all that was in her to finish making the bed.

When all was in order, she went outside to escape the cold, ominous silence of the house. She needed the warmth of the sun.

The abhorrent, shameful pain she felt overshadowed any physical discomfort she was experiencing as she leaned against the pillar on the front porch. As she gazed blindly at the lake, a strong shudder overwhelmed her. It wasn't the kind of shudder caused by exposure to a cold gust of wind, or even the shudder of fear when one is threatened by the unknown. This shudder began at the very core of her being, its tremors invading every corpuscle, every living fiber, as though trying to unloosen and rid her of the self–loathing and disgust that were so deep inside.

She had been defiled, but she must have done something wrong. Why else would this have happened?

The only existing reality was that horrible, filthy memory. There was nothing else. Impulsively she wanted to run down and plunge into the lake, cover herself again with cool, sweet, cleansing water, and wash it all away.

She could barely walk down the steps. Sitting down, she put her head on her knees, wrapping her arms over her to hide from the light. She was desolate, lost, alone. The only Maggie she had ever known was gone.

When Mam returned home later that day and saw the terrible bruise on her face, Maggie explained it away as an accident.

She'd tripped over the laundry she was carrying to the basement and had fallen down a whole flight of stairs. True to her character, Mam scolded her for being careless and clumsy.

Maggie had to excuse herself immediately after dinner. She could go no further.

"Mam, I don't think I can do the dishes. Would you mind, just this one time? I must have hit my head really hard, and I'm beginning to feel sick all over. I really have to lie down. If Tim comes to call, please tell him I don't feel well."

She didn't wait for an answer, bolted into the bathroom to throw up, then dragged herself to her room, shut the door, and threw herself on her bed.

Blessed sleep came, but not for long.

The nightmares soon began.

CHAPTER TEN

The Discovery

Until that horrible afternoon in July, Maggie's life had been like the unfolding of delicate petals, blossoming day by day into full flower. But the bloom had been nipped, cut away; the beauty and mystery of life were gone. In sunlight, darkness seemed to surround her.

Tim noticed. He'd understood why she couldn't see him the day she'd had that terrible fall down the steps. The same day, Robert had gone back to Toronto.

They still saw each other often, and part of her seemed to welcome him with a need for his company, but something was terribly wrong. She was sullen and silent, no longer smiling or laughing with wonder at the world they'd begun to share together. She'd distanced herself from his gentle advances, avoiding his touch. Why? Was it possible she was missing Robert? He tried dismissing the thought, but it kept creeping back, like a nagging itch under the stiff collar of his Sunday shirt.

Brigid also noticed the change in her daughter. However, she accepted Maggie's churlish moods as a resentment of her constant disapproval of Tim. There was also a slight chance that she was also missing Robert. She could only hope.

Had it not been for Tim, Maggie felt she would have lost her mind altogether. Every day was a dark tunnel with no sign of light. At least when she was with him, she could take heart that there was some possibility of overcoming this deep depression, this feeling of self–loathing. He was so gentle and patient with her melancholy. When would it end?

Brigid hired Claire Conroy to take over the boarding house chores during the time Maggie would be in school, and Claire was thrilled at the prospect of earning some money in town in order to help out at home. She'd started the first week of August, working just a few hours each day, returning home at night. This arrangement would last until the day Maggie was to leave for school, after which Claire would move into Maggie's room and take over the entire job. Brigid had planned that the first week of September, Maggie should be free to pack and get ready for school, which would begin on the tenth of the month.

Claire was a wonderful diversion for Maggie, whose job was to teach her to take over her duties. Claire was a happy, talkative fourteen–year–old, a bit plump (just baby fat, Maggie surmised), with a sweet singing voice that seemed to keep her company as she tackled each chore with great enthusiasm. The pleasure of working with such a happy youngster took Maggie's mind off herself, and she looked forward to her coming each day.

She also anticipated going off to school, knowing the demands made on her academically would prove challenging. There would be no time to dwell on unwelcome memories. Perhaps the nightmares would go away. She must move forward.

With Claire doing so much of her work, Maggie now had the luxury of extra time, so when Rosemarie arrived back home on the fourth of September, she was free to go and welcome her.

It was with mixed emotions she walked up the hill. She couldn't wait to see her good friend, yet she knew that what she was about to reveal to her would distress Rosemarie greatly. Strange that just when she'd been given so much to look forward to, so much had been taken away.

She could hear Rosemarie's talkative voice before she ever reached the Stuarts' back porch. "Hey, Rosemarie," she yelled mockingly, "can you come out and play with me?" remembering the many times she had done that when they were little.

There was a flurry of footsteps, the screen door flew open, and Rosemarie raced down the steps, laughing, throwing her arms around her friend. They hugged and kissed, dispensing with the usual small talk that initiates a first meeting after a long separation.

Maggie's face grew somber. "Rosemarie, do you think we could take a walk over to Osaga Falls?"

A look of concern crossed Rosemarie's face. This was not the Maggie she had left last April. Her gorgeous eyes were vacant of their usual fire and light.

"Sure. Just let me go tell Mum. We've been unpacking my summer things and repacking for fall. That can always wait."

The blazing sun cut through a pale blue sky almost gray with haze, causing the air to be heavy with sticky heat. They made their way across Superior Avenue, holding hands, swinging their arms, Rosemarie chattering about her new nephew, Raymond, and her summer in Buffalo. Milkweed, goldenrod, and Queen Anne's lace abounded in the tall, wild grass along the top of Broad Street, and grasshoppers shot out like bottle rockets, targeting juicy morsels below.

They turned off Broad Street and walked along the rutted road leading to the sawmill, then entered the shadowy path winding to the falls. A pungent, earthy sweetness greeted them with cooling relief under the thick canopy of trees, recapturing some of their earliest memories of happy childhood days.

Strolling in silence, one behind the other, they became immersed in nature's symphony. A crescendo of locusts was accompanied by the swell of droning honeybees; brassy and reedy bird calls were given accent by the percussion of a woodpecker; the distant sawmills' wailing tenor joined in the chorus, along with the tympani of thumping lumber. The constant accompaniment was the roar of water rushing over the falls.

As they exited the shelter of trees, they could see the long, narrow sawmill to the north of them, alongside the Osaga River. Crossing over the railroad tracks, they approached the basin of the falls, cautiously clinging to branches and slender tree trunks along the slippery, mossy path leading down to the bottom. Once there, they had their choice of the many huge, flat rocks scattered along the shore, perfect front-and-center seating available to climb up on and rest while being soothed by the mesmerizing constancy of cascading water.

This particular bank of the river had always been a favorite picnic spot for the young people in Herron's Point, especially young lovers like Maggie and Tim, who sought to escape the prying eyes of adults in a small town that knew all. Maggie and Tim had not been here lately.

The two girls climbed a large, dry rock far enough away

from the misty spray, yet close enough to enjoy a colorful rainbow that arched above the waterfall. Rosemarie stretched out and pulled her long, blue–striped skirt up to her thighs, took off her shoes and stockings, and leaned back, arms bracing her sides, tilting her face to the sky to catch the golden shafts of sunlight that pierced through the ceiling of green foliage.

"Remember the first time we were old enough to come down here all by ourselves?" Rosemarie asked dreamily.

No response.

Rosemarie glanced over at Maggie, who was sitting with her chin on her knees, her arms hugging her legs, staring into space.

"Maggie, what's the matter? Something's wrong."

Tears rolled down Maggie's cheeks, soaking into her gingham skirt. "Oh, Rosemarie," she sighed. "I have to tell someone. I don't know...what I'm..." She began to sob, hiding her face in her knees.

Rosemarie slid over and put her arm around Maggie's shoulders. "Maggie, it's okay. I'm here. Please tell me what's bothering you."

Keeping her head down for the most part, between sobs and moans, sniffling and blowing her nose in a handkerchief, Maggie recounted the events of July 12.

By the time she was finished, Rosemarie's face was as red as the checked gingham in Maggie's dress. She was furious. If Robert Arnaud had been in front of her at that moment, she would have killed him happily.

"You mean you've kept this all to yourself for all this time?" She was incredulous.

"Uh uh." Maggie nodded into her skirt.

"My dear friend." Rosemarie patted Maggie's back consolingly. Her stomach was in knots. "That bastard. Well, it's good you told me. You should talk about it. Clear your head and rid yourself of that horrible memory. You know you can talk to me about anything, anytime. Anyway, we'll be off to school next week, and soon you'll be so busy, it will just fade away like a bad dream."

Maggie let out a long, anguished wail. "But that's not all!"

"What do you mean?"

"I mean, I—I won't be going to school with you. After what happened, I was so overwrought, I didn't realize I'd missed my monthly on the twenty-first of July. But when I missed it again in August, I thought—in fact, by now I'm almost sure—I'm—I'm—oh, what am I going to do?"

"Oh, mercy!"

For a time, there was nothing but the roar of water cascading over the falls.

"Rosemarie, I'm scared." She lifted her head and looked at her friend with the face of a suffering Madonna.

"Oh, dear, sweet Maggie! You're the best person I've ever known. You don't deserve this. But you're going to have to tell your mam. She'll be able to figure out a solution. After all, she is your mam. Maybe she could send you over to stay with your grandparents in Ireland for a time."

"I suppose I should have told her from the beginning. But you know what she's like. She probably would have thought I did something to encourage him. According to Mam, Robert is a prince among clods."

"I know how hard your mam can be sometimes, but you're her daughter. She would never want anyone to hurt you."

"I suppose you're right. And there's no way I can avoid telling her now, anyway," she sighed, sucking in short, quick gasps that brought on another flood of tears. "But what am I going to tell Tim?" She sobbed inconsolably.

Tears streamed down Rosemarie's face at the sight of her friend's pain, and she threw her arms around her and cried, "Oh, Maggie, I don't know! I wish I could take all this away from you."

They were joined by the water's tearful outcry at the injustice of it all.

Rosemarie offered to go with her when she told Brigid, but Maggie refused her help.

"I have to do this myself."

The aroma wafting through the kitchen screen left no question as to the evening meal: corned beef and cabbage.

The screen door creaked as she entered. Her mother was at the stove, stirring the contents of a large pot with a wooden spoon. Old habits die hard, and Maggie went to the dining room to check the table, ready to set things in order for the boarders. Happily, Claire had already taken care to set the table before she went home.

Using every ounce of courage she could dredge up, Maggie decided this was as good a time as any to broach the problem.

"Mam," she said softly as she returned to the kitchen.

Brigid turned, her face red from the stove's heat. A wisp of hair hung in her face and she blew it back, insuring its proper place by pushing it with the side of her arm, immediately becoming aware of the distress in Maggie's bloated face. Her first thought was that she'd fought with Tim. Good.

"What seems to be troublin' ya, child?"

"Mam, I—I have to tell you something I should've told you a while back."

A quizzical look crossed Brigid's face.

"Mam, do you remember the day Robert Arnaud left?"

"Sure and how would I be fergettin' that? There hasn't been a day since that himself and his charmin' ways haven't been missed."

"But Mam, he's not what you think."

Why was her mother so blind? She felt her anger rise.

"That same afternoon, after you left with Father Charles and everybody else was out of the house, he came back. I was up in the bedroom cleaning when he came in. He was really drunk. He—he—raped me, Mam."

Her face became distorted at the words she'd finally released, and she began to cry.

"And now I think I'm going to have his child."

She sat at the kitchen table, her head down, unable to look at her mam—completely drained, yet relieved that she'd finally bared her shame.

Brigid stood frozen. This couldn't be what she heard. She hissed through her teeth, "What's that yer sayin'?"

"I know I should've told you when it happened, Mam, but I was so ashamed. I didn't really fall down the steps that day. Robert did that to me."

She sobbed, tears streaming down her cheeks, her tortured eyes looked up into her mother's face, searching for some kind of understanding.

Dead silence.

Twisting a sodden handkerchief in her hand, she continued. "I don't know why I felt the way I did, not telling anyone. But I haven't had my monthly since that day and I..." She couldn't control the tears.

Brigid's face turned from red to purple rage. What she had just heard was incomprehensible. Impossible. "Yer lyin', Mary Margaret," she spit out. "If any part of this is true, 'tis that Tim fella that had a part in it. Why do ya have to besmirch the name of a good man just to cover yer own wanton ways? How many times have I warned ya? I knew no good could come from that Liam Ryan's son!"

Maggie looked at her mother in disbelief. "Why would I lie, Mam?" she said between sobs. "Tim knows nothing about this. I told no one until today."

"I know yer lyin' because Zeb himself told me Frank Brewster came back ta the shippin' yard after that luncheon and said fer him ta get over to the hotel and pick up Robert. He said the whole party'd got ta drinkin' too much. When he picked Robert up, he was at the corner by the hotel, wanderin' around like a lost pup. Himself delivered Robert up ta the depot and put him on the train personal."

"I don't care what Zeb said, Mam. All I know is, Robert came back to the house drunk. I tried to get him downstairs, but he grabbed me and raped me. That's how I got all those bruises. Mam, please believe me," she pleaded.

Brigid had been so blinded by Robert's charm that this news was impossible for her to accept. In her mind, he was incapable of such an act. If Maggie was pregnant, her logic told her it had to be Tim who was the father.

"Why should I be believin' ya when ya been ignorin' me wishes all the way? Yer just coverin' up fer that Tim Ryan. That's what yer doin'." Her voice rose with every word. She pointed the wooden spoon at Maggie's face. "And don't be thinkin' I don't know what's been goin' on between the two of ya. Herbert told me about seein' ya down at the pier. Himself with his hands all over ya. And Willa Bobsey and Veronica Pitts both told me they saw ya goin' into Tim's house together more than once. I've been warnin' ya about him, and now ya got yourself in trouble and everyone'll be talkin' to boot."

By now Brigid was in a screaming rage. "Robert was nothin' but a gentleman in this house, to meself and everyone else. If he'd be wantin' to do harm to ya, he could have done it when he took ya off to Toronto, or any other time durin' his stay here. Yourself told me what a wonderful day ya had in Toronto. And wasn't it yourself who said what a fine gentleman Robert was? And now yer expectin' me to be believin' he'd be comin' back here to do such a horrible thing. I'm thinkin' not."

Maggie slumped in her chair and laid her head on the table, completely exhausted with grief. "Please believe me, Mam. Please. I don't know what I'm going to do," she whimpered.

Brigid turned back to the stove to stir the cabbage, then whirled around, pointing her wooden spoon at the door, unleashing her fury. "Out of me house!" she screamed. "Yer just like yer brother—bringin' shame on this house. Out of it, I say. Pack yer things and go to yer precious Tim."

She stamped across the room and went down the hall to her bedroom, slamming the door.

CHAPTER ELEVEN

Banished

Maggie was glad it was the dinner hour as she blindly made her way down to the lake. With the exception of a few diehard fishermen out on their boats, shoulders stooped in the expectation of pulling in just a few more before the storm hit, there wasn't a soul around to interrupt or question her heart–wrenching sobs. She couldn't imagine where all the tears were coming from. It seemed she'd spent the day releasing a deep well that had been filling up since that terrible day in July. When would it end?

It was strange that her thoughts should turn to the boarders, picturing them sitting around the table, eating everything in sight, relishing any new, choice morsel of gossip to fill up their hungry minds. Wondering where she was—that would give them plenty of food for thought.

Who would be doing the serving? And the dishes? Well, Claire would be there in the morning. No sense worrying about any of them. The boarders would be taken care of. But what about Mam? Surely she would think things over and have a change of heart.

Maggie became aware of an almost invisible sunset. Patches of silver and crimson poked through the tattered sheet of gray sky. Heat lightning danced along the horizon, announcing an imminent storm. She sat on the bench next to Carl Herron's statue and looked out across the murky lake that was calmly lapping against the wooden pier, not yet agitated by the approaching tempest.

She wished her brother Jack would somehow appear from across the water to tell her what to do. He'd be the one to help her. She hadn't realized until this moment that she hadn't heard from him for quite a spell. Perhaps that was because she hadn't been in touch, what with all that had happened. She just hadn't had the heart to write.

The beaded handbag hanging from a braided cord on her wrist contained the three hundred and twenty dollars she'd saved from the letters Jack had been sending her for the past six years. Hadn't he said the money was to be used to come and visit him? But it would be dark in an hour or so. Where would she spend the night?

Rosemarie! She knew she could always spend the night at her house. And surely there'd be a boat leaving for Buffalo tomorrow. But she'd best hurry, or soon the heavens would open up to weep along with her.

Hope as she might, she knew her mother would never relent.

The day's heat had drained the life out of Tim, and he'd left the front and back doors open to catch a bit of the air that had been stirred up by the threat of rain. He warmed up the last of the stew he'd been eating for the past three days. Mrs. Orwell's peach cobbler sat on the countertop, but he really wasn't hungry for it. Perhaps later, before he went to bed. Today's heat and the accident down at the quarry had taken away his appetite.

Shutting his eyes released a vivid picture of Charley Straub's body falling like a meteor out of the sky. Scaffolding had given way. It was lucky Tim had been there to pull him away from the huge chunk of limestone that followed him down into the pit. It had taken four of them to get his dead weight back up onto level ground.

Trying to avoid causing Charley more pain had been the worst of it. The memory of those screams as the wagon carried him away to the clinic on Frontier Street, hitting every rut and chuckhole, made Tim shudder. He was glad he'd stopped on the way home from work to check on him, relieved to see old Charley lying there under clean white sheets, a big smile on his swollen, bruised face, contentedly sipping a glass of milk. They had set his broken arm and leg, stitched and bandaged the cuts on his forehead and chin, and tightly wrapped his broken ribs.

"I'm a lucky man," he'd said. "Got to learn to be more careful."

Tim took his dishes to the sink, poured hot water from the kettle on the stove into the dishpan, and quickly washed them. He was anxious to get going—hoping, as he did every time he saw Maggie, now, that somehow this evening would be different.

There was definitely something wrong, something deeply troubling her. How could he help but think it was connected to Robert Arnaud? Wasn't it the day after Robert had gone back to Toronto that he'd noticed the change?

He knew he was losing her. He didn't want to accept why,

but how could he blame her? A man like Robert Arnaud—not only handsome, but with so much to offer any woman. Yes, it had been the day after Robert left. That was when she'd changed.

Still, he could see that a part of her welcomed, almost clung, to his company, even though her passion and joy were gone. She pulled away from his touch, but her eyes seemed to linger almost pleadingly on his face.

Last spring and the first part of the summer had been so wonderful. He'd fallen deeply in love and thought Maggie felt the same about him. When they were together, she'd responded to his embraces with a passionate desire so strong that his wanting to possess all of her forced him to pull back, realizing she wouldn't try to stop him if he went further.

That day at the Conroys' farm, when she told him about going away to school, he wanted to ask her to marry him right then, but this was something that seemed to be very important to her. Even more so for her mam. Soon, she'd be going away.

Tim carried his soap and towel down to a copse of mulberry bushes at the water's edge that protected him from the view of curious eyes walking along Water Street. As he stripped down and dove into the warm lake to lather his body and wash away the day's sweat, his thoughts were of Maggie, wishing she were next to him, their naked bodies touching, fondling, loving each other. He reached an ecstatic climax.

Spent to the point of complete exhaustion, Maggie dried her eyes, blew her nose, and hoped she had the energy to carry her damask traveling bag the six blocks up the hill to Rosemarie's house. Fortunately, it wasn't too heavy. She'd just taken a few necessities and the money she'd saved from Jack's letters. There would be no need to burden herself with the fancy clothes her mam thought were so important.

Tim wasn't sure, but the closer he got to Center Street, the more the figure on the bench looked like Maggie. How odd. What was she doing there at this hour?

He approached just as she let out a deep sigh, bent to pick up the bag next to her, and turned to get up.

"Maggie! What—?"

She burst into tears the instant she saw him and ran crying into his arms. He felt the warm, damp sensation of tears soaking through his shirt as her shoulders heaved with sobs. He was at a complete loss. What was happening?

"Oh, Tim!" she wailed.

He held her, stroking her hair, soothing her until he felt her body go quiet and limp, then led her back to the bench to sit down. Glad he'd remembered a handkerchief, he began dabbing at her wet, blotchy cheeks. His heart ached seeing the pain in her tortured eyes as he held her face in his hands and asked, "What's wrong, Maggie? Has something happened to your mam?"

The absurdity of the question almost made her laugh. But there was no humor in her. "Oh, Tim, it's not Mam. It's me."

She began all over again, sobbing uncontrollably, hiding her face in his shoulder. She couldn't look at him. Not just now.

He comforted her and waited.

When she finally began to recount the events that had led her to this very spot, Tim experienced a gamut of emotions. Rage engulfed him as he listened to Maggie painfully unravel that July afternoon.

I'll kill him! he thought.

He was relieved that Maggie still loved him, yet disappointed that she hadn't turned to him for comfort when she needed him so much.

All those days I doubted her love for me! Why couldn't she have trusted my love for her? He was overcome by a feeling of helplessness. She had suffered so much pain.

I should have been there to protect her, he thought.

He felt an intense anger at her unbelieving, hard–hearted mother. What kind of mother was she?

It began to sprinkle, but neither of them seemed to notice, staring across the roiling water, both lost in their inner storms.

A loud clap of thunder shook the sky. They both jumped. Tim grabbed Maggie's bag, and the two raced down Water Street toward his house, the rain pelting them as it drenched the countryside.

Once inside the cabin, Maggie began to shiver uncontrollably, her hair dripping like a wet mop. Tim's was a mass of glistening ringlets. He grabbed a towel and began to dry her head and face, then took the quilt off his bed and wrapped it around her shoulders, leading her over to the chair he'd set next to the stove, which was still warm from supper.

"If you'll just slip out of your wet clothes," he said, "I'll give you one of my shirts and some trousers. You're soaked to the skin." He hovered, forgetting she had her own clothes in the bag next to the door.

Maggie gave him a blank look, empty of emotion. It didn't matter—wet or dry, it didn't matter. She just wanted to sleep.

"I'm fine, Tim. Really I am," she said, unaware of her chattering teeth. "The rain shouldn't last too long. Then I'll go to Rosemarie's for the night. I plan to go to Buffalo to my brother,

Jack, tomorrow."

Her voice, perfunctory, faded away as she stared blankly at the pictures on the wall in front of her.

He knelt down next to her chair, took her hands in his, and looked pleadingly into her face. "Please don't do that, Maggie. I already felt like I lost you once. I don't want to lose you again. I'll figure something out. It's not like you've done anything wrong. There's no reason for you to run away."

She sat like a stone, heavy and unfeeling, too tired to respond. Tim sat on the floor and rested his head in her lap.

They were silent, listening to the drumming rain on the shingled roof.

Finally, he stirred and stood up. "I just had a thought."

Maggie's eyes followed him as he walked to the window and looked out.

"Looks like it's letting up a bit," he said.

He walked back and knelt in front of her again. His face was tender, his eyes filled with love. "Maggie, I'm not going to let you go. What's happened can't be undone, but none of it was your doing. I want to marry you. Please say you'll stay."

His words stirred a small spark, touching her deeply. He was such a fine person, so gentle and kind, everything Robert Arnaud was not. How could her mam be so blind as to not see it? She sighed deeply to hold back the tears of gratitude for his love. How could she burden him any more than she already had?

She spoke up lethargically. "I can't stay here, Tim. It's bad enough, the things people will be saying about me. I can't bring that shame on you, too."

"But no one need know. Not if we get married right away. I'm sure Father Scanlon will see things our way."

"Not if I stay in this house, he won't."

"But that's what I was just thinking. I could take you to Mrs. Orwell's. She's got lots of room in that big house of hers. And she's all alone. She loves company. I'm sure she'd be only too happy to take you in until we get married. I just know it."

Suddenly the spark became just the tiniest bit of a flame, lighting a darkness that had engulfed her for so long.

"Oh, Tim, do you really think so?"

If there was some hope, then perhaps this nightmare could end and she could have the life she so wanted with Tim. And the child that was growing in her—why couldn't it be theirs?

Penelope Orwell listened, her face revealing her inner revulsion as Tim related Maggie's dilemma.

"Oh, that horrible, horrible man!" she sputtered. "How could he do such a terrible thing? And her mother! It confounds me to think she would turn such a sweet child away."

She shook her head in quiet disbelief, never doubting for a minute the truth of what Tim had told her. "Of course the poor dear can stay here. I don't know the young woman, although I've seen her many times around town. Such a lovely creature. And from all you've told me, I'm sure we'll get along just fine."

A lump formed in Tim's throat as he looked at the woman across from him, the smile on her face effusing a beauty that through the years had become as dear to him as his own mother's.

Tim had asked Maggie to stay at his place and change into some dry clothes while he'd gone to talk to Mrs. Orwell. When he returned, she was still sitting in the chair by the stove, her eyes half closed—as wet as ever. She didn't look up when he came in.

"Rain's gone," he said, ignoring her posture. "Just a quick thundershower. Cooled everything down and turned into a beautiful evening. Mrs. Orwell's really excited about having a houseguest. You two are going to get along famously."

Maggie gave him a disconsolate glance. "I feel like I'm such a bother, Tim. Perhaps I should just go up to Rosemarie's, like I planned."

"Now, don't talk nonsense. It's all been decided. Come on, Maggie," he coaxed. "You'll see. She really does want you to stay."

He took her hand, and heaving a deep sigh, she shrugged off the quilt, obediently following as he picked up her bag and led her out the door.

Penelope Orwell was standing in the open doorway, waiting, as Tim and Maggie came up on the porch.

"My dear, you're soaking wet," she said, smiling benignly at Maggie. "You'll catch your death. Now you just come along with me. I'll show you to your room, and you can take off those sopping clothes."

She immediately hustled her up the stairs to a room at the back of the house. "Now, strip down and put on this nice warm robe, while I fill you a hot tub to take off the chill."

She was out the door.

Maggie, fatigued and disoriented, stood in the middle of the room, unbuttoning her dress.

This wasn't real. It wasn't her room. It was big and pretty. Such lovely colors in the quilt. What was that pattern? Stars?

After dropping her clothes where she stood, she was overcome by a sudden chill. Her head was reeling. Quickly she wrapped the fleecy robe around herself and lay on the bed, shivering. A whirring sound kept spinning in her head. Now softer...softer... She was in darkness.

Rosemarie had spent a sleepless night, tossing and turning with worry over the distressing news Maggie had given her. After bolting down breakfast, she headed for the boarding house to check on Maggie's state of mind.

As she rapped on the back door, she could hear a sweet voice singing softly in the kitchen, then recognized Claire Conroy as she came through the pantry, wiping her hands on a dishtowel. Rosemarie recalled Maggie's last letter, explaining that Claire had been hired to take her place when she went off to school and telling how much she liked working with her. Rosmearie's heart ached with disappointment at the thought that now Maggie would not be going.

"Rosemarie, how nice to see you!" Claire said, opening the screen door. "Come in. I understand you've been away this summer visiting the States."

Rosemarie stepped inside. "Yes. It was a nice summer, but it's certainly good to be back home. My, Claire, you've certainly grown since I last saw you. Minus your pigtails, you look quite the young lady."

Claire blushed as she led her into the kitchen and walked over to continue drying the dishes.

"Is Maggie around?" Rosemarie asked.

Claire gave her a curious look. "No. This morning, when Mrs. Mahoney said she would be gone for a while, I got the idea she'd decided to leave for school early. She never did explain. In fact, I thought she'd be with you."

"Well, that's odd. Where is Mrs. Mahoney? Perhaps she can tell me where Maggie's off to."

"I don't think that's the best idea. She wasn't feeling well when I got here. Kind of snappish like. As soon as the boarders had eaten and gone off, she said she needed to take a headache powder and go lie down. Been in her room the best part of an hour, now."

Rosamarie's stomach churned. "I won't disturb her, then, but thanks anyway, Claire. It's been awfully nice seeing you again." She smiled as she went back through the pantry and out into the sunshine.

At the back gate, she had no idea which way to turn, her head swimming with questions. So Maggie had told her mother and there had been trouble. But why had Maggie left? And why hadn't she come to her, Rosemarie? Where else could she have gone?

Tim! He'd be at work now. But that didn't mean Maggie wouldn't be there.

Rosemarie went to Tim's house to see. Finding no one at home, she decided to try again in the afternoon.

She was sitting on a patch of grass in front of Tim's house when he came strolling toward her, gave her a big grin, and sat down next to her.

"Rosemarie, how grand seeing you again. How's everything with you? You're well, I hope."

"Oh, Tim, I'm so worried about Maggie! I went to see her today, and Claire said she was gone. You wouldn't happen to know where she is, would you?"

Tim's face darkened. "Her mother is a demon. I swear, Roesemarie, I don't know how she could do such a thing to her own daughter, but she put her out of the house."

Rosemarie gasped. "I surmise I won't be telling you anything Maggie hasn't already told you."

"Oh, I know, all right. I only wish she had said something to me when it happened. At least she should have told her mother at the time. But she probably wouldn't have believed her then any more than she did yesterday. She thinks I'm responsible for Maggie's condition. Imagine!"

Rosemarie stared into Tim's face, speechless. She couldn't find words to express the loathing she had for Brigid Mahoney. The woman couldn't be more vile if she'd been an accomplice to Robert Arnaud's deed. In fact, in a sense, she was. Rosemarie finally found her voice to ask, "Where's Maggie now?"

"She's staying with my friend Mrs. Orwell, up on Division Street." He stood. "Why don't you go up and talk to her? Seeing you will do Maggie a world of good. I'll be up in a bit, soon as I wash off this quarry dirt."

Mrs. Orwell was in quite a dither when she opened the door. Rosemarie explained who she was. "Come in, dear. Come in. It's just awful. That dear, sweet thing is so sick. As a matter of fact, I called your father to come see her, but he was up at the Brauer farm delivering their seventh baby. Doc MacQuaid is up there with Maggie right now."

Rosemarie slumped into the wing chair next to the door. Poor Maggie. What else could go wrong?

Penelope Orwell wrung her hands as she explained. "Last night, when Tim brought her here, I sent her upstairs to take off her wet clothes. Land sakes, but she was drenched to the skin. I left her to change into a robe while I drew a hot bath. Figured that would take off the chill, you know. But when I went back, she was wrapped in the robe and all curled up in bed, fast asleep. I covered her up and told Tim a good night's sleep would probably do her more good, so we let her be, and Tim went home. He'll be beside himself when he finds out."

"Finds out what, Mrs. Orwell? What's wrong with Maggie?"

"She's delirious with fever. Doc MacQuaid says she's got pneumonia, and it's just a matter of waiting it out until the fever breaks. But her fever's so high, he can't guarantee which way it's going to go. Her condition's that grave."

Rosemary covered her face with her hands and cried. "Oh, my poor friend! How could these terrible things be happening to her?"

Father Charles didn't ask. He hadn't seen Maggie at Mass that Sunday and had taken it for granted she'd already gone off to school. He took note that Claire served the Sunday dinner quite well, considering the sour faces around the table, barely uttering enough for a civil conversation. It wasn't until he and Brigid took their usual Sunday walk that he was to learn the reason for the solemn atmosphere.

"Me poor heart's been broken, Chuck," Brigid mewed as they walked along Erie Street.

"What's this yer sayin', Brigid Mahoney?" He gave her a surprised look. "And who would be the scoundrel responsible fer such a deed?"

"It's me own Maggie, may God fergive her and the saints preserve her. She got herself in a family way with that Tim. Utterly disgraceful. 'Tis a sad state she's in."

"She's ailin', then? Would that be the reason she wasn't at dinner?"

"How would I be knowin' that, there bein' no other choice but ta put her out of me house?"

She looked into Charles Scanlon's shocked face, her lips pinched, her jaw set, ready for the argument she knew was coming. The same one she'd heard when she'd made Jack leave the house.

"But Bridie, you cannot be doin' that! Not ta our Maggie. Such a love, no matter what she's done. You'd best be thinkin' before you commit ta such a judgment. Remember, there's no problem that love cannot solve. This one especially. Our Lord taught us that."

"Sure and it's yer head that's gone soft. I didn't ask fer this problem. The headstrong girl wouldn't listen ta me. Now she's where she belongs—with that Liam Ryan's son, Tim."

"It's not that I can't be truly understandin' yer quarrel with her. But she's yer own daughter, fer God's sake!"

"Not ta my way of thinkin', she aint. Not anymore."

Father Charles gave Brigid an exasperated look. "I'll be warnin' ya, Bridie. Ya best be thinkin' hard on it."

Brigid became sullen. As they approached Saint Michael's, he said his goodbyes. "I'll be keepin' the both of ya in me prayers."

His voice softened as he gave her a pleading look. "Try ta soften yer heart, Bridie. They're a fine young couple. Things'll work out fer the best. They always do. You'll see."

Brigid continued on without a backward look, anger building up with each step she took, consumed with disappointment that Maggie had destroyed all her plans and expectations. The only consolation she found was in feeding the justification for her own choler.

The ungrateful gombeen, she thought. After all I've done fer her. And I suppose I'll be after losin' me deposit at Saint Cecelia's.

Early on the Monday morning after Father Charles had had his talk with Brigid, Tim showed up at his door.

"Come in, lad. Come in and set yourself down. It's terrible sick yer lookin'. Can I be gettin' ya somethin' to drink? A cold glass of water, perhaps? Or maybe somethin' a wee bit stronger?"

Father Scanlon was reasonably sure he knew the reason for Tim's visit, but he couldn't have guessed at the seriousness of it.

Tim collapsed in the only upholstered chair in the sparsely furnished room. "No, thank you, Father. I can't stay. I have to get over to the quarry soon."

His despair was obvious as he covered his face with his hands.

"It's Maggie, Father. She's—"

"Yes, yes, I think I know what yer about to be tellin' me. I talked with her mother Sunday. It's—"

"No, Father, it's not that. She desperate sick. She's out of her mind with fever. Doc MacQuaid says..." Tim began to sob.

"What's this yer tellin' me, lad? Our Maggie? How could that be?" He pulled up a straightback chair from the kitchen table and straddled it, facing Tim. "Where is the poor child? I must go to her."

"She's staying with Mrs. Orwell over on Division Street," Tim said, blowing his nose and straightening his back to gain composure. "The afternoon her mother put her out, I found her down on Water Street in a terrible state. Then we got caught in that thunderstorm. You remember the one last Thursday? Well, we both got drenched, and she caught a terrible chill. She's been at Mrs. Orwell's place ever since, delirious with fever."

Father Charles looked at Maggie's pale face, beaded with perspiration, her long hair matted and sticking on her neck.

Penelope wiped her brow with a cold cloth, tending to her parched lips with drops of water.

"If ya wouldn't be mindin', Mrs. Orwell, I'd be mighty grateful if yourself would kindly join me in prayer." As he spoke, he knelt down beside the bed and took Maggie's limp hand in his.

Penelope followed suit on the other side of the bed as he began to recite the Our Father.

After anointing her with oil and concluding with a series of prayers unfamiliar to Penelope, he wearily stood up and let out a heavy sigh.

Penelope got to her feet and said, "Would you like a nice cup of hot tea, Father? It's already brewing in the pot."

He was furious. Brigid had told him of Maggie's condition, and Tim had come to tell him of her illness, but it was Penelope Orwell who filled him in on the details going back to last July. He was heartsick; his mind couldn't fathom the pigheadedness of his dear friend Bridie, not recognizing the truth of it all.

Oh, she was a stubborn one, all right. They'd had their go-rounds about many things, like when Jack had left home. That was just one of them. But he'd accepted her right as a mother to act on her strong feelings, right or wrong.

Maggie had always been a sore spot between them, and Father Charles had always bowed to Brigid's decisions, even though he didn't approve. This time, though, he couldn't reconcile with her actions. Not this!

He'd known Maggie since she was an infant. No sweeter child was ever born. Like any proud uncle, he'd watched her grow up, heard her childish, innocent confessions. No, there was no wrong in Maggie. Her life had always been one of simplicity, uncomplicated and without guile.

Not so her mother.

Well, he had to confess that Maggie was no longer a child, but how she must have suffered alone these past months, when she should have been able to turn to her mother from the beginning! Brigid would definitely hear from him on this.

Claire was pegging up the clothes in the back yard when he walked through the back gate that same Monday afternoon. She informed him that Brigid was out doing some shopping.

"Is there a message I can give her, Father Charles?" she asked.

"No, I'm thinkin' I'd best wait till I can talk to her meself."

Claire couldn't help but notice the touch of sadness in his voice, the dejected look on his face, and the slump of his shoulders as he turned to take his leave.

He took ill Tuesday morning and never did get back to Brigid. After he saw Doc Stuart about the pains in his chest, the doctor immediately called Toronto and set up a consultation with Dr. Jonathan Hildenberg, a heart specialist. By Tuesday evening, Father Charles had made the trip to Toronto.

CHAPTER TWELVE

Heartbreak

Monday. Four days without a word. Brigid was definitely concerned.

She'd had time to digest the news Mary Margaret had given her, and she still couldn't accept the claim that Robert could commit such a horrible act. No, it was that Liam Ryan's son, Tim. Surely the blame lay squarely at his feet. But at least she was a wee bit calmer about the matter, and Mary Margaret was her daughter, after all. She was probably staying at her friend Rosemarie's house. Perhaps when she came back for the rest of her things, they would have a long talk and she could suggest she go stay with her grandparents in Ireland. That way the town would not know of her shame. And Brigid would be spared the gossiping tongues.

Tuesday morning, Ray Alberts dropped by to collect Brigid's insurance premium. He knocked at the back door to announce himself, then let himself in.

When Brigid saw him, she went to get her purse.

Once a month, Ray came in, wearing his usual white shirt

and rumpled suit, and sat down at the kitchen table to share a cup of tea, some biscuits, and the town gossip he had gathered from his rounds during the previous month.

Maggie was always in the kitchen because it was ironing day. Brigid knew Maggie was the reason Ray lingered. The three would take a little break, which usually lasted about three quarters of an hour, and then he'd take his leave. Brigid usually enjoyed these little visits, knowing full well why he stayed, but happy to get the latest news.

Maggie was completely oblivious, and Brigid never concerned herself about Ray's motives. At twenty–seven, he had no inclination to spend his hard–earned money courting a woman. He figured that by the time he was forty, he'd have saved up enough to find a suitable wife. His face was as pinched as the pence in his pocket.

This Tuesday, Brigid told him Maggie wasn't there, and he knew why.

"It's a hot one out there," he said pulling at his frayed white collar and wiping the sweat off his forehead with a graying handkerchief. He looked at Brigid, who had her premium money in hand, and said, "I understand your daughter has been quite ill. I hope she's feeling better."

His curiosity about yesterday's incident had to be satisfied.

Brigid's stomach churned as she stared at him. "What is your meanin' of that?" she snapped. Surely the town didn't know of her condition yet! "The last I saw of her, she was in good health."

He was surprised at her response and didn't know if he should pursue the matter. "I was collecting over to Mrs. Orwell's house yesterday, when I passed Father Charles coming down the front steps. I thought this was rather curious because of her being a Presbyterian and all. Then I thought, maybe she was having a spiritual change of heart or something."

He paused for a minute as he watched the blood drain from Brigid's face.

"Yes, yes," she said.

"Well, Mrs. Orwell was quite beside herself when I commented on seeing Father Charles. Said she had a very sick girl staying with her, and he'd come to tend to her spiritual needs."

Once again he paused.

"So, why would you be sayin' she's me Mary Margaret?"

"Because then I went to the MacNamaras' for my next collection. Mrs. MacNamara said that her husband, who works with Tim Ryan over at the quarry, told her that Tim was quite exhausted and concerned about his girlfriend's condition. He'd been spending his nights at her bedside over at Mrs. Orwell's house. Mrs. MacNamara said she couldn't for the life of her understand why Maggie Mahoney would be there when she had a perfectly beautiful house of her own with a mam that was quite capable of tending to her. That's how I know it's your Maggie."

Brigid knew that must have been the reason Father Charles had stopped to see her on Monday. If she'd gotten back to him, she wouldn't have to be listening to this terrible news, standing there like a gaping fool.

Ray realized he'd upset Brigid terribly.

"I do apologize, Mrs. Mahoney. I thought you'd certainly know. I think the world of your Maggie and was really just inquiring about her health. I'm sure she'll be fine. And whatever the problem between the two of you, I'm also sure it will be worked out."

Brigid handed him her premium money, and he left her with the beginnings of another migraine. She went to her bedroom, leaving Claire, who had been ironing and privy to the entire conversation.

That evening, Brigid went to visit Father Charles. He wasn't home.

On Wednesday, Brigid told Claire to pack up all of Mary Margaret's belongings as soon as she finished the remainder of the ironing.

"Tomorrow, you can drop them off at Mrs. Orwell's before you go to Stockwell's for the beef I ordered. Inquire after Mary Margaret, too, but don't be dawdlin' there too long."

Her heart wanted to go and see about her daughter herself. Her pride wouldn't let her.

Claire, still not knowing the cause of the problem between mother and daughter, came back Thursday before the lunch hour all excited. "Oh, missus, Maggie is going to be just fine. I asked Mrs. Orwell what was ailing Maggie, and could I please talk to her, but she said Maggie was sleeping and needed her rest. She seemed very pleased that Maggie had come through the worst of a very bad pneumonia and said it would take some time for her to gain back her strength. She was also surprised you didn't know about her condition, because Father Charles said he would let you know. She also said you were welcome to come and visit her at any time."

They'll not be seein' the likes of me now, Brigid thought. They didn't find it fittin' ta fetch me when she got sick. I've been betrayed completely.

Brigid immediately went to Saint Michael's to speak to her friend. A very tall, good–looking young man in a black shirt and trousers opened the door.

"And who might you be?" she said curtly.

"Why, I'm Father DeSalle, come to take over Father Scanlon's duties. I might ask you the same question."

"Brigid Mahoney. Father Charles' dearest friend."

"Oh, where are my manners? Won't you please come in?" He smiled and stood aside for Brigid to enter.

Brigid brushed past him, looking, expecting to see Father Charles sitting in his old, overstuffed chair.

"And where is himself?" she asked, bewildered.

Father DeSalle's face grew serious. "I'll be making the announcement at the Sunday Masses, but since you are so concerned, I'll tell you that Father Scanlon is seriously ill."

"That can't be. I know he's been slowin' down lately, but that can't be."

"I'm sorry to say he has a heart ailment. From what I understand, he'll be returning from Toronto sometime next week. But he won't be capable of doing much for some time. I'm to take over his duties and tend to his needs in the meantime."

Brigid pinched up her mouth, then said, "If there's any tendin' ta be done, it'll be done by me."

Somehow Father DeSalle knew not to argue.

Brigid was completely overwrought. Between her daughter and her best friend, her migraines increased. Claire was a blessing to her at this time.

Maggie struggled through a dark tunnel toward a voice that kept calling her name. When she opened her eyes, a kind face smiled at her. It took her a few minutes to recognize Penelope Orwell.

"Oh, my dear, it's so good to see you awake," Penelope said. She stroked Maggie's matted hair and wiped her face with a damp cloth. "Tim will be overjoyed when he comes home tonight. He's been beside himself with worry."

Maggie tried to lean up on her elbows and fell back into the pillows. "How long have I been like this?" she asked weakly.

"It's been almost four days, love. Four long, worrisome days. Father Charles was here to see you this morning. What a sweet man! Then, about ten minutes ago, your fever broke. Now I want you to rest while I go and fetch you some vegetable broth."

Maggie smiled. "Thank you for caring for..."

She was no longer fighting demons. She was in a peaceful sleep.

Life was no longer a quagmire now that Maggie was beginning to feel better. Tim spent all his free time with her and Penelope. He'd heard about Father Charles at Sunday mass but hesitated to tell Maggie about it until she was a little stronger. Day by day, he could see the color returning to her beautiful face.

The bond between Penelope and Maggie grew stronger as the days passed. Afternoons, they would sit in the garden knitting blankets and little sweaters and booties for the new arrival. Penelope spoke often of the fact that she'd never been blessed with children and how she so looked forward to meeting the child Maggie carried in her. "No matter how it was conceived," she said, "a child is innocent of wrongdoing."

Aware of Maggie's deep emotional pain, she drew her out, and Maggie found it easy to confide in her, an intimacy she had never experienced with her mother. Penelope knew that Maggie would never forget her emotional trauma, but she delicately whittled away at her pain with tactful questioning. With all the wisdom she possessed, she knew she had to prepare her for her marriage to Tim. He was, after all, almost like her own son.

It was two weeks after Maggie got sick that Father Charles returned to his room above the church. Brigid insisted he come and stay with her for the best care, since Father DeSalle would be occupying his space, but Father DeSalle stood firm.

"He can't have too much fussing right now. What he needs is complete rest. No, it's best he remain in his own surroundings, where he can stay in touch with his parishioners through me."

For once, Brigid had no choice but to back down. She really didn't like this new pastor telling her what she could and couldn't do. She also knew that if she tended to one, she'd have to feed the other, too. She saw to it that another bed was installed.

Zeb collected Father Charles from the train depot and brought the buckboard around to the back of Saint Michael's.

Brigid wasn't prepared for the sight she saw. He had lost weight, his face was drawn and pale, and he wearily made it up the steps, pausing twice to rest. Her heart was heavy.

Tim wanted to see Father Charles the following Sunday after Mass, but Father DeSalle refused to allow any visitors, and parishioners were disappointed. Father DeSalle in turn reported to Father Charles some of the names (there had been so many) of those who had inquired after his welfare.

When Father Charles heard Tim's name, he said, "Let him come and see me next Sunday."

He had already learned from Brigid that Maggie was

recovering. It had been one of the first questions out of his mouth. Relieved that she was doing fine, he didn't pursue the subject further—at least not then. But as the days passed and he gained some strength, he began to express his feelings to Brigid on the matter.

Brigid would stiffen. There was no talking to her, and he didn't have the energy to try. She was his dear friend, but also a source of conflicting emotions.

Doc Stewart said he didn't want Charles going up and down the steps, but since the weather had been so favorable, he did want him outside, getting some sunshine.

He was sitting in a chair on the top landing the Sunday Tim came bounding up the steps. The two shook hands, and Tim concealed his shock at seeing such a change in the man.

"So, how're ya keepin', Tim, lad?"

"Just fine, Father Charles. And yourself?"

"Well, Doc says 'twill be a while. It's me heart, they say."

He looked beyond the railing toward the crest of the hill, then back at Tim. "It's just grand to be home. And I understand Maggie is doing well. Such a love."

"She told me to give you her best. Getting stronger every day. Just like you will. Doc MacQuaid says it will be a few weeks before she should get out and about, but she'll be coming to see you before you know it."

The pair sat in comfortable silence for a few moments, listening to droning beetles, watching leaves fall silently to earth, drinking in the best that autumn had to offer.

Finally, Tim spoke. "Father, Maggie and I want to get married as soon as possible. I know you're not up to it yet, but Maggie says she won't get married unless you perform the ceremony. When do you think that will be?"

Father Charles looked long and solemnly at Tim. "'Tis a good thing you're wantin' ta do, lad. Are you sure you're up ta the doin' of it? It's not fer the fact yer feelin' sorry fer the poor lass?"

That thought had never crossed Tim's mind. "I love her deeply, Father. And she truly needs me right now, what with her mam being the way she is, and all."

"I was thinkin' as much. But I had ta ask."

Once again, there was silence. Then Father Charles looked at Tim with a wisp of a smile and said, "How does the second Saturday in November sound ta ya? That'll give time fer recuperatin' and plenty of time fer the banns ta be announced. That's about six weeks down the road. I know you'd be wantin' it done sooner, but things got in the way fer the three of us, and we can't argue that fact."

Tim's face broke out in a big grin. "Father, whatever you say will make Maggie happy. She loves you like her own, you know. And by that time, the two of you will be hale and hearty, I'd say." He stood to leave and extended his hand. He was shocked by the fragility of the other man's hand.

Maggie was elated at the news and immediately sat down to write a letter to Rosemarie to ask her to be her maid of honor. It took her another week before she felt strong enough to go tell her mother the news and invite her to the wedding.

Brigid was caught unawares when Maggie came walking in through the pantry door.

"And what would ya be wantin' with anyone in this house?" she snarled. "Seems you've been doin' just fine down at that Penelope Orwell's place. Not a word of yer comin's and goin's fer three weeks, and now ya just pop in."

Maggie sighed. "It was you, after all, that asked me to leave, Mam. And I've been sick, or I would have been here sooner. But I'm feeling much better now. I came because you're my mam, I love you, and want to ask you to come to my wedding the second Saturday in November."

Brigid instinctively wanted to go to her daughter and hug her, happy that she was no longer sick, but her pride held her back. She had been deeply wounded, first by Mary Margaret, who had lied to her, then by Penelope Orwell, who seemed to think she had some claim on her daughter's life.

"I'll be thinkin' on it. But I promise ya nothin'."

She turned and clipped down the hall to her bedroom— something she'd have done before, had she seen Maggie coming.

A week later, Maggie received a letter from Rosemarie.

Dearest Maggie,

I was so happy to hear from you and thrilled at the good news, both the fact that you're getting better and that you're to be married. You can't know how much I've worried about you.

Of course I would be honored to stand for you at your wedding. I can't tell you how much it means to me to be asked, and I will definitely make sure I get a long weekend away from school so we can spend some time together.

Your loving friend,
Rosemarie

P.S. Mum and Papa said they will be happy to attend your wedding. They're looking forward to it.

She did not add the fact that her mother had filled her in on the local gossip. Maggie deserved none of it.

Mary Murphy had stepped in to assist the new pastor, Father DeSalle, when Brigid would have no part of him. Mary had heard all the rumors about Maggie after the banns were announced, but she had never been one to pay much mind to gossip of any kind. Many times when Maggie was visiting Rosemarie, Maggie would come next door to visit Mary and talk about the days she had lived in the house, and Mary considered her to be a wonderful young lady. She even hoped that someday her boys would find girls as sweet to bring home as their wives.

It was the day she tried on her navy blue suit with the white braided trim to wear for the wedding that Maggie first felt the life in her move. It was a strange sensation and totally unexpected. Yet she knew that no matter what the circumstances that had brought this life about, she would always love and protect it—and he, or she, would truly belong to her and Tim.

As she viewed herself in the full–length mirror, she realized the suit was slightly snug. Not so much that anyone would notice, but she could feel the jacket pulling on her full breasts, and the skirt waist barely snapped. This in no way deterred her happiness for her approaching wedding day. She loved Tim so much that nothing else mattered.

CHAPTER THIRTEEN

The Wedding

When Rosemarie arrived on Penelope Orwell's doorstep the Friday before the wedding, it was a joyous reunion for the two girls. They spent the day helping Penelope in the kitchen, preparing food for the small reception the next day, talking about Rosemarie's school antics and the new young man she had met at a school dance.

Maggie showed her the beautiful things she and Mrs. Orwell had made for the baby, and they both became pensive as Penelope stood by, watching.

"Gosh, Maggie," Rosemarie said, "I wish things could have been different for you. But you're marrying such a wonderful fellow, and I just know you will be the best mother in the whole world."

Then she turned to Penelope. "Maggie couldn't have found a better friend than you, Mrs. Orwell. You've been just wonderful to her. And I want to thank you for putting up with me and my everlasting chatter. My mum says I yowled the day I was born and haven't stopped making noise ever since. But it's been such a delightful day."

"It is I who should thank you for filling my day with laughter. I enjoyed every minute of your so-called chatter. Somehow the presence of young people in the house has made even the chore of cooking a pleasure. I only wish I had two daughters as lovely as the two of you. I will sorely miss Maggie when she moves in with Tim."

"Oh, but we'll be neighbors," Maggie said, affectionately putting her arm around her. "We'll see each other every day, and when the baby comes, you'll be the other grandmother."

There was an awkward silence with the mention of "other grandmother."

Then Rosemarie spoke up. "Well, Maggie, I'll be here early tomorrow. Isn't this exciting?"

Claire dished out the hot oatmeal. Agnes nonchalantly mentioned she'd be attending Maggie's wedding that morning and asked Claire if Mrs. Mahoney was planning to go.

"Oh, no, ma'am, she isn't. Poor lady's gone back to bed. Seems to have a great many headaches these days. When they hit her, other than preparing the meals, she has to lie down with the shades pulled. They seem to make her fiercely sick, throwin' up and all. With Maggie leaving home and Father Charles being so sick, I think it's all just too much for her," Claire said softly, then added, "Poor thing."

Poor thing my Aunt Mable, Agnes thought.

Agnes went upstairs to get ready for the ceremony. She was thrilled when Maggie had stopped by the Post Office to invite her and Clara to the wedding. She had gotten Emiline Watkins to take over her duties at the Post Office and was really looking forward to the wedding.

She thought of what a wonderful young man Tim was, taking on the burden of someone else's child.

During her many visits to see Maggie when she was sick, Penelope Orwell had filled her in about the poor girl's ordeal. She couldn't imagine how that sweet young woman had managed to hold all that inside. But then, whom could she have turned to? She only wished there was something she could have done to ease her burden.

Their Maggie would make a wonderful wife and mother. She certainly deserved the very best. Under the circumstances, things were working out quite well for her.

Penelope Orwell was all adither, giving the house a quick onceover while Maggie was getting dressed, making sure all was perfect for the small brunch she would be having after the ten o' clock ceremony. She felt as though her own daughter was about to be married. Being a Presbyterian, she was not familiar with the way the Catholics did these things, but she would just watch and follow the others at the church.

She watched Maggie come down the steps, radiant in her navy and white suit, wearing a small navy hat surrounded by a cloud of white tulle that Penelope had added.

A lump formed in her throat. It was impossible to keep the tears that were burning behind her eyes from flowing down her cheeks as the two of them embraced and wept. In the few short months they had been together, a strong bond of love had been formed.

Rosemarie, more excited with every step she took, came racing up the porch steps, flung the door open, breathless, threw her arms around Maggie, then stood back and said, "I would have been here sooner, but one of the hooks on my dress came off, and Mum had to sew it back on. Then Sparky hid one of my shoes, and it took me forever to find it. That dog has been playing those games with me ever since he was a pup. It used to be fun, but today I was ready to kill. At least he didn't chew it up, like he used to. My, you look beautiful, Maggie!" Then she plopped in the big, soft chair by the door to gain her composure.

Maggie and Penelope laughed.

"Don't fret yourself, dear. Take a minute to catch your breath, and then we'll be off," Penelope said.

It was a perfect autumn day. The air was crisp and the sunshine bright, with powder puff clouds dotting a deep blue sky. The trio could hear the surf gently washing the shore behind them as they climbed the hill to Saint Michael's in silence. It was as though each was absorbing the gift nature had given them on this very special and solemn occasion.

Tim and his friend Bob Courtney were talking to Father Charles as the three entered the church.

Father Charles gave Maggie a fatherly kiss on the cheek. "Sure, and won't the group of you be going up ta the front pews while I prepare fer the ceremony. Tim and Bob will be sittin' on the right, and Maggie and Rosemarie on the left. I already told yer other guests ta take the pews behind."

Maggie watched as her loving pastor walked toward the front of the church, and her heart ached to see him so thin and frail. She had not seen him since she had left home, had no memory of him coming to see her when she was sick, and it was Father DeSalle who said the Mass on Sundays. She had wanted to visit him, but Tim had said, "No. You can't get past that Father DeSalle. He insists that Father Charles not be bothered with company while he's regaining his strength. I understand your mother is one of the few people who are granted that privilege."

When Maggie glanced over at Tim, her eyes were misty, and he understood.

Father Charles poured all the love he had into the wedding Mass. When it was over, he embraced Maggie and sobbed. "I've loved ya as me own daughter, child. May God be with ya always."

Then he pulled out a large handkerchief, blew his nose, shook Tim's hand, and smiled as the couple turned from the altar and were greeted by a small gathering of well-wishers— one being Mary Murphy.

It was a wonderful reception. Maggie was overwhelmed by the appearance of all the boarders.

Elsa had insisted that Kurt take the morning off, and for some reason, he knew not to argue. He really did have a soft spot for the girl.

Clara had made a last-minute decision to get one of the mothers to come in and sit with her class for a few hours. She just couldn't miss this wedding.

Zeb had even put on a suit for the occasion. Three of Tim's friends were there. And the Stuarts, of course.

But when Mary Murphy walked in with a huge bundle, announcing, "I made this for you myself. You've always been a special young lady to me, and I hope it will bring you warmth and comfort for many years to come," Maggie was speechless. It was an eiderdown comforter.

After all the gifts had been opened and everyone had their fill of ham sandwiches, potato salad, fruit, punch, and cake and said their goodbyes, a heavy silence took over.

Penelope knew she would have to say her goodbyes, too.

Maggie lingered, helping Penelope clean up. Tim pitched in, the both of them making small talk and commenting on how well things had gone. They thanked Penelope over and over for everything she had done, but eventually she knew Maggie and Tim had to leave.

Penelope stood at the front door and watched until they disappeared from view, then shut the door and sat down in the big chair next to it and sobbed.

CHAPTER FOURTEEN

A Very Great Loss

Tim was a happy man. He had known he would need a great deal of patience with Maggie in order to consummate their marriage. This he had plenty of. But he had never anticipated the response he got from her on their wedding night.

Once they were alone, Maggie was pensive—shy, yet she welcomed his embrace and returned his kisses with a fervor he hadn't expected. When it came time to go to bed, he became aware of her embarrassment at getting undressed, for there was nowhere for her to do this except in front of him, so he excused himself to go out and get wood for the stove. On returning, he found her in bed, waiting, welcoming him with open arms. Their night together began with gentle discovery, then tender lovemaking that culminated in fiery passion.

Maggie was happy. Those horrible black days she'd experienced after she was raped were finally behind her. Not that any of them could ever be forgotten, but it was Penelope Orwell who had been instrumental in probing those wounds so deeply imbedded in her memory and exposing them for what they were.

During the early days of Maggie's recovery from pneumonia, Penelope just listened to her talk as they busied themselves around the kitchen or sat under the linden tree in the back yard, sewing or knitting. Maggie's emotional pain was not difficult to detect.

Slowly, Penelope led her to understand that she had done nothing wrong. With a wisdom beyond her forty–five years, she also understood that this experience of Maggie's, if not dealt with properly, could become a problem between Maggie and Tim, so she began to talk about her own husband and their marriage together. She talked of the union of two people and the love they shared. She spoke openly about her own sex life and how gratifying it was, even though these subjects were generally taboo among women. She expressed her concerns about Maggie's innocent love for Tim, for she didn't want to see him hurt. Never preaching or sermonizing, she managed to broach the subject tactfully during their many bits and pieces of conversation, leading Maggie to understand that marriage was not a young girl's notion of Prince Charming and happy ever after, but a decision that must be approached with the maturity of a young woman who understood she was about to embark on a lifetime commitment, with all that it entailed.

At first it had been difficult for Maggie to completely open up to the woman who had befriended her. She and her own mam had never discussed such things. In fact, she and Mam had never really discussed anything concerning feelings—especially Maggie's.

Penelope never pushed or prodded or demanded, and slowly, a bond of trust developed between the two women.

Maggie began to speak with ease about her most deeply felt emotions. And so, by the time the day of her wedding had arrived and she inspected herself in the mirror, she was amazed at the image that looked back at her. This was no longer the obedient young girl trying to please her mam, the girl filled with daydreams and naiveté, but a young woman who had suffered, been to the brink of Hell, and come back. Penelope Orwell had helped heal her both physically and spiritually. As a result, her love for Tim had become stronger because of it.

The weather turned bitterly cold the day after their wedding and remained that way, which kept them indoors for most of the week, talking and making plans for adding on to the one-room house. The cozy confinement gave Maggie a chance to relax and become familiar with her new home. By the third evening, she had no problem disrobing with Tim in the room— all inhibitions now gone.

Maggie was an excellent cook, which Tim grudgingly had to attribute to Brigid's training. They had Penelope over for dinner on their fourth day together. It was obvious to Tim that these two women had formed a very deep bond of affection for each other.

Once back to work, Tim looked forward to going home at night. No longer did he have to face an empty room, for it was now filled with the aroma of good food cooking and the radiant smile of the person he adored.

Maggie found herself at a loss for something to do the first day Tim returned to work. It didn't take much efort to clean one room and plan the evening meal. Tim had helped her wash the clothes the previous Saturday, hauling in the old copper tubs from the shed and boiling the water, and for the rest of that day, they'd walked around dodging sheets and such waiting for them to dry, cuddling together in bed with the damp, pungent smell of soap hanging above their heads. But now she was alone. She decided she would go see Penelope.

After trudging through the snow that had been relentless since the previous Thursday, she spent a wonderful afternoon with her friend, chattering away and exchanging recipes.

The next day, she decided to bake what Penelope called "the cake of all cakes," only to discover that there was no baking soda. Examining the cupboards to check on supplies, she made out a list of things needed, bundled up to face the elements, and went off to the market.

The snow had stopped, but the wind was biting. By the time she arrived at Fullerman's Market, she was half frozen. When she entered the store, the bell above the door sounded a weak little clink to announce her entrance.

Everyone turned to look as she stamped the snow off her boots. Ned Wachter and Buzzy Greenfeld were sitting around the potbellied stove, each eating a dill pickle from the barrel next to the counter. Ben Fullerman was waiting on Wanda Cartwright, while his wife, Flossie, took care of a lady Maggie didn't know.

When Maggie commented on the freezing weather, Buzzy Greenfeld grunted. The rest turned away, ignoring her, and kept on with what they were doing.

As she waited her turn, she looked over the shelves of canned goods and then into the glass case of homemade candies. She decided she would buy some chocolate for Tim as a surprise in his lunch tomorrow.

When Wanda Cartwright was leaving with her bundles,

Maggie held the door open for her and inquired after her daughter Mary Jane, since the two had grown up together.

"Just fine and dandy," was Wanda's icy reply, leaving without so much as a thank you.

Maggie felt rebuffed and nonplussed, but walked over to Ben Fullerman with a smile. "How are you, Ben?" she asked.

"Just fine," he responded curtly. "What can I get for you?"

Maggie felt a keen sense of discomfort, but gave him her order without adding another word, said her goodbyes to all, and left without a response from one of them. Well, that might have been another grunt she'd heard from Buzzy.

As she made her way back home, tears were biting behind her eyes, but she dared not cry for fear they would freeze on her face. She couldn't understand the treatment she'd been given and began to rationalize.

Perhaps there was some kind of confrontation in the store before I got there. Perhaps they were all angry over something and took it out on me. Come to think of it, there wasn't any conversation to speak of after I came in. And certainly Ben Fullerman had no cause to treat me that way; he was always nice to me. When I used to come in to shop for Mam, he would say things like, "How's the prettiest girl in town?" Or, "Your mother doesn't know how lucky she is to have a gem like you." Why would he ever have a reason to be mean to me?

By the time she finished baking the cake, she'd forgotten the incident. When she was packing Tim's lunch for the next day, she realized she had forgotten to buy the chocolate. But that was all right. There was a nice slice of peach delight cake made from Penelope's canned peaches to take its place.

The next day, Maggie decided to go to Baughman's to buy

the flannel that she and Penelope had talked about for making diapers and little nightgowns. It would be nice to see Elsa and Kurt again. After yesterday's incident, she needed a few friendly faces.

The store was quite busy in spite of the nasty, cold weather, but then it was a Wednesday. With the washing and ironing done and the cleaning and baking yet to come, Wednesday was more or less a day that freed most women up from their usual chores.

She spied Kurt first, sitting behind the cash register ringing up a customer, as pompous as ever—king of his domain—and gave him a big smile. "Morning, Kurt. Bitter weather out there."

"I told everyone we'd be in for it. Too much warm weather in the fall. Had to be something bad coming, I told 'em, and I was right."

And when was he not?

Elsa spied Maggie as she came in and went to her immediately. "Maggie, love, what can I do for you?" she said shyly as she put her arm around her and led her away from the front of the store.

Maggie thought this was odd. It was almost as if she wanted to get her away from Kurt.

"I hope you have a good stock of white flannel, Elsa. I'm going to need about twenty yards."

"Certainly, dear. Come this way."

After she made her purchase and inquired about everyone at the boarding house, including her mother, Maggie decided to browse around the store. Everywhere she looked, faces turned away, except for one redeeming few moments when she ran into Mary Murphy, who couldn't say enough about her wonderful wedding reception and to extol the virtues of Penelope Orwell.

When she approached the cash register to pay for the flannel, she asked, "Why is everyone snubbing me, Kurt? What have I done? The same thing happened to me yesterday."

"Don't you know, my dear girl? Everyone in town is talking about you and your marrying that Tim fella. Most of them think it's rather odd, considering your mother put you out and all. What are they supposed to think? Not that I care. But you can't blame them for wondering about the circumstances."

If it hadn't been for Elsa, he would have babbled further.

By the time Elsa got to the front of the store, she realized it was too late. She could see it on Maggie's face. "Never you mind, sweet girl. It will all blow over and be forgotten when folks find the next thing to gossip about."

Once outside, Maggie felt disoriented. It was almost as though this town she had grown up in was a foreign place. Kurt's words had shattered her, and she wanted to just lie down and disappear like melting snow.

This time, there were no tears of hurt to flow. At least not yet. Only anger. Anger at a town that knew nothing of her problem, yet judged her anyway. A burning, furious anger that pulled her back to reality and the only sanctuary she knew—her new home and Tim.

On the way, she thought of Kurt's words, completely oblivious to the cold.

No wonder Elsa tried to get me away from him. She was protecting me. But there's no way she could do that. Better I learn from him, because I was certainly going to find out sooner or later. I was so completely isolated at Penelope Orwell's house. I had no idea what's been going on in this town for the past two months. How simple of me not to realize that people would talk.

Once inside the house, she had more time to think and stew. When Tim came home from work, she ran into his arms, sobbing uncontrollably.

Tim, Maggie, and Penelope discussed the situation. Tim said he'd suspected there was a little talk, just from comments some of the men at work had made. He'd expected a few heads to turn when the marriage banns were announced, but only because of the stand Brigid had taken against him and because Maggie was not living at home, but he hadn't experienced what Maggie had these past few days. Both he and Maggie were so young. They couldn't realize that wagging tongues could be so vicious, especially since they had done nothing wrong.

Penelope said she knew what people were saying, but ignored them for the most part. She didn't tell of the two confrontations she'd had with old friends who told her she was crazy to harbor the likes of a girl like Maggie Mahoney. There really wasn't much she could say, since she couldn't reveal the circumstances that had brought Maggie to her door. She had confided in Father Charles, Agnes, and Clara. But they could be trusted to keep Maggie's secret.

For the most part, things remained the same each time Maggie had to go out for something. Once in a while, she would encounter a friendly face and a cordial greeting, but they were few and far between. In retrospect, she realized it had been that way even when she and Tim went to church on Sundays before they were married. But having just recovered from a serious illness and being with Tim, she hadn't noticed any of it because of the burden she carried with such a heavy heart. If Tim had noticed, he'd never made mention of it.

She did have her loyal friends. When Clara and Agnes occasionally came to call, they filled the little house with laughter, always leaving her with a lighter heart. Even Zeb had stopped by one evening to visit, offering to help Tim sweep the snow off the roof the following Saturday.

"Gettin' pretty heavy up there," he'd said. "Must be at least a foot. Gotta be careful it don't buckle your roof."

Tim had accepted his offer gratefully.

On the first Sunday in December, Tim and Maggie received a big surprise. They had a standing invitation for dinner every Sunday at Penelope's. While they stamped the snow off their boots on the front porch, she greeted them at the door, her face flushed (Maggie thought it must be from the heat of the stove), and were a little taken back when they saw Clifford Benchly sitting as nice as you please, shoes off, feet resting on a footstool, reading *The Point* newspaper.

Penelope became slightly flustered. She said quickly, "Mr. Benchly didn't realize he had a hole in his boot, and by the time he trudged through the snow to get here, his one shoe was soaked. I have it by the stove, hoping it'll dry out."

They needed no introduction, since the young couple had known Clifford since they were children. He owned the Sweet Treats ice cream parlor, where all the young people hung out. But what was he doing here?

Conversation at dinner was a revelation to both Maggie and Tim as they listened and observed. Obviously Penelope and Clifford were quite comfortable with each other—Clifford complimenting Penelope on her cooking, Penelope blushing at one point when he took her hand in his, and looking at them, said, "I don't know when I've met a more gracious woman." He was also a great storyteller—a side of him they'd never seen at the ice cream parlor. There was a lot of laughter, and all in all, it was a very enjoyable afternoon.

Maggie was dying of curiosity. Using the excuse of needing help with the sweater she was knitting Tim for Christmas, she made it a point to go up the following day to find out just what was what with Penelope and her dinner guest. She didn't want to pry, she wouldn't pry, but perhaps her friend would be willing to share some news about the man who seemed so completely at ease in her house.

She wasn't disappointed.

Sitting at the kitchen table drinking tea, Penelope stared at the handkerchief she was twisting and said, "I suppose you're wondering about my friend, Mr. Benchly?" Then she looked directly at Maggie.

"Well...er...yes, I was. I've never heard you mention his name before."

"Actually, Clifford and I have known each other for years. His wife, Sara, and I were the best of friends. Both of us childless and all. But then she took sick—oh, I'd say almost five years ago, now. And in two months, she was gone. The doctor said there was nothing that could be done. Her kidneys failed her, I believe is what he said. Clifford took it quite hard, so I did what I could to help by taking him a pot of soup or some stew once in a while, and we'd just sit and chat. Then, since we both belong to the same church, I talked him into joining the choir. The choirmaster was thrilled to get him, being that he has such a wonderful tenor voice."

She took a long sip of tea as Maggie waited anxiously for the rest.

"Two days after you left, this house seemed so empty. Feeling quite alone and sorry for myself, I would say, I took myself down to Sweet Treats to buy some ice cream to go with that leftover wedding cake. One of the coldest days this year, and I was craving ice cream. Imagine! There were quite a few young people sitting at the tables, drinking sodas and the like, and Clifford was cleaning off the counter when I walked in. He was his usual pleasant self when he greeted me, so we talked a bit. Then—I don't know what possessed me—I invited him to dinner to help me finish the leftovers from the reception. He happily accepted, and we had a wonderful evening together. In fact, he's been coming to dinner at least twice a week ever since. I especially wanted you and Tim to meet him, never thinking you had probably been in his shop many times, so I invited him to our usual Sunday dinner."

Once again she paused and looked at Maggie. "So what do you think of him?"

"Penelope, he seems like a very nice man, and if he makes you happy, then I think the whole idea of you seeing him is wonderful. In my eyes, there is nothing you could ever do wrong, and anyone who is lucky enough to have you as a friend is blessed."

Patches of pink formed on Penelope's cheeks. "Those are sweet words, Maggie. And I do thank you for the many days of happiness you've given me. My life was so empty before that evening you came to my doorstep like a drenched waif. But in the last three months, you have filled my days with purpose."

She seemed to be searching for words, then threw her arms up in the air. "Maggie, I feel...alive again."

Maggie laughed. "I'm so grateful that I wasn't a burden."

"Now, that's just about enough about me. How are you feeling, and how is that little angel you're carrying treating you? It certainly looks like it's thriving."

Once again, Maggie laughed as she put her hands over her rounded belly. "It's doing just fine. Sometimes I resent the fact that I had to start my marriage this way, because there's no question what the people in this town think of me. Yet in my heart of hearts, I know I did nothing wrong, thanks to you, and I will love this child in spite of it all." Her eyes grew misty. "And Tim is such a love. I'm a very lucky girl to have him."

Penelope gave her a smile, stood up, and patted her on the arm. "Let's get to Tim's sweater."

The freezing weather never relented. Winters at Herron's Point were always cold, but this one was fierce. It kept Maggie housebound and isolated from the rebuffs of the townsfolk as she worked on the homemade gifts she would give at Christmas. Tim's sweater had turned out quite well, and she was almost finished with the needlepoint on the linen tablecloth she was making for Penelope.

She stood up and stretched to get the kinks out of her back and examine the work she had just finished when she experienced a dizzy spell.

I need fresh air, she thought. I haven't been out of this house for days.

She bundled up with layers of sweaters and a coat and went out the back door and down to the dock. Clearing a spot as best she could, she sat down and looked out at the expanse of frozen water.

Everything was gray. Hulks of ships stood motionless, imprisoned in the frozen water at the Point. Nothing moved except the puffs of breath that came from her mouth in small clouds.

She looked toward the horizon, as she had done so many times before, and thought about her brother, Jack. That's when a very, very small seed became a kernel of thought in her mind.

If this weather continues, the entire lake will freeze. Tim and I could walk over to the States with very little problem. Well, maybe just a few. But it could be done.

She'd heard of others who'd done it. Why not? The more she thought about it, the more plausible the idea became. She'd have to speak to Tim about it.

What had been truly heavy on her heart these days was the treatment she'd been receiving from her mam and the town. She knew that with Tim's love, she could withstand those obstacles. But what about the baby? There was no question in her mind that this unborn child of hers, once a citizen of the community, would receive the same treatment. This she couldn't bear. They would have to leave.

How fortuitous that Penelope now had Clifford. If they did go away, they would not be leaving her alone.

And her mam? What could be done to change that? Maggie had tried many times to talk to her and recalled the day, shortly after she'd invited her to the wedding, when she'd succeeded in pinning Brigid in her kitchen again. But there was little talking to her. Brigid had made it clear that she was extremely unhappy with the situation.

"You've made yer choices, lass. And wouldn't ya be knowin' ya made a mess of it all. 'Twas Tim ya were wantin', and it's himself ya got. I want no part of it all after the shame ya brought on this house and the humiliation I've had to endure."

Maggie looked forlornly down at her shoes and then pleadingly at Brigid and said, "But Mam, I told you the truth. I've done nothing wrong. I'm sorry if I've hurt you in any way. Won't you believe that?"

There was silence.

Maggie continued. "It's true. I do love Tim. And we will be married."

Brigid stiffened.

"But you're my mam, and I love you, too."

Brigid had missed Maggie desperately. But once again, the stubborn, proud part of her held her back. Her own daughter had thwarted her wishes. And look where it got her! Brigid's loathing for Tim Ryan and the grief he had caused her were reasons enough to wash her hands of the whole affair. For she still felt quite certain that Maggie's condition was his doing. Just the fact that he was marrying her was proof of that.

Maggie's shoulders sagged when she realized there would be no reasoning with her mother. Silent tears rolled down her cheeks as she turned and left through the pantry, rejected and dejected.

A cold wind brought Maggie's thoughts back to the dock with a shiver. When she'd first come out, the air had been exhilarating. Now her only thought was to get back into the house. Tonight she would speak to Tim about her idea.

No one could ever accuse Tim Ryan of being stubborn, but when Maggie first brought up the subject of moving to Buffalo, he balked. The thought of uprooting and moving away from all that was familiar to him did not sit well. He loved this town and the house he had grown up in. It was all so much a part of who he was. Then there was his job. Right now, there wasn't much work at the quarry because of the weather, but there was the refinery, where his crew worked indoors, cutting and stockpiling stone for spring shipments. He had worked many years to achieve the position he now held.

Maggie had written her brother about their plan to move, and he had assured her there would be a job waiting for Tim when they arrived in Buffalo. Even so, as much as he loved Maggie, Tim couldn't say yes to her idea. He also felt that Maggie was overreacting to the people of the town. Not that there wasn't cause for her feelings, but surely by spring, folks would have turned to other things. The baby should come sometime in April. Who could turn their back on a new baby?

Maggie knew she was asking a lot of Tim. She had tried to convince him, but if this was his stand, she would not insist or pursue the matter any further.

The day before Christmas, Brigid saw Maggie coming in the back gate.

"There's no doubtin' the condition she's in," Brigid said aloud. "That coat wasn't made fer an expectin' mother. Oh, Maggie, you've broken me heart," she sighed quietly to no one as she took to her room.

Maggie let herself in the kitchen just as Claire came down the back stairway.

"Well, you're a surprise," Claire said with a smile. "And all laden down with packages, I see. Don't you just love Christmas?"

Maggie was happy to receive the warm welcome and returned the greeting. "I have some gifts for everyone. They're not much, but I made them all. There's one for you, Claire," she said as she put the packages on the kitchen table. "Where's Mam?"

"She was in here just a few minutes ago. I suppose she's off to her bedroom again. I'm sorry, Maggie, but I've been told before not to disturb her there." Claire was embarrassed, knowing full well by now the obvious reason for the rift between mother and daughter. "But please stay and have a piece of the fruit cake your mam made. It's delicious."

Maggie looked around the familiar kitchen with its wonderful aromas, remembering the many years she had lived in this house. It seemed so long ago. Now she was a stranger here.

"No, Claire. I really have to be getting back. I have a turkey that needs tending to. But open your present, please. I hope you can use them."

Claire accepted the package Maggie handed her with the enthusiasm of a small child and ripped away the tissue paper to reveal three linen handkerchiefs trimmed in lace. "Oh, Maggie, they're just lovely. I especially like the violet one. But they're all so pretty. I've never had such nice handkerchiefs." Then she looked at Maggie with a somber face. "But I have nothing for you."

Maggie smiled. "It's my pleasure to give them to you, Claire. The entire time I was crocheting them, I was remembering your beautiful singing voice. I used to listen to you as you worked around the house. You have a wonderful gift, and you shared it with me. Now this is the least I can do."

Once the door closed behind her, Maggie knew she would never enter the house again. But as Penelope had told her so many times, she must move forward with her life. She had a choice of filling it with bitterness or joy. She had been fighting hard to choose the latter. It just seemed so difficult, especially at times like these, when her heart ached for the love and acceptance of her mother and a sense of belonging. Where was the unfettered freedom of youthful innocence? All that had been taken away, as though it had never been. Still, Maggie was determined to make this Christmas a happy one for Tim.

Christmas Eve was unlike any Maggie had experienced before. The happy chatter of boarders sitting around a warm fire in the parlor as they exchanged gifts, Agnes playing Christmas carols as everyone sipped on toddies and joined in singing, the tree sparkling with silver and gold ornaments in the front window—all of this was now a memory as she busied herself dressing the turkey she would take to Penelope in the morning, before Mass.

Tim was in great spirits. Standing behind her as she stood over the counter chopping onions for the dressing, he gave her a hug and kissed the back of her neck, then turned her around and looked intently in her eyes. "Maggie, you are more beautiful now than the day we were married. Have I told you lately how much I love you?"

Maggie laughed and kissed him on the chin. "Not since before dinner. Just let me finish up, here, and you can tell me again under the covers."

Christmas morning brought with it a bright blue sky and freezing temperatures. Icicles glittered on eaves, and the snow crunched under their feet as Maggie and Tim delivered the turkey to Penelope's oven and walked over to Saint Michael's Church for Mass.

When the service was over, Father DeSalle greeted

everyone in the back of the church as they filed out. Maggie said she had a gift for Father Charles and would like to go up and wish him a happy Christmas.

"Please keep your visit brief," Father DeSalle said tersely. "The poor man tires very easily these days."

Maggie resented this cold indifference to her concern for the man she had grown to love as a father. If Father DeSalle hadn't always been so overly protective of him, she would have gladly visited him every day. As it was, she hadn't seen Father Charles for at least a month. What she didn't realize was that her Father Charles was so beloved by all the parishioners that there would have been a parade of congregants going in and out all day, every day, had that been permitted. Father DeSalle, aware of the seriousness of his brother priest's illness, could do no more than protect him from that happening.

Tim and Maggie climbed the back steps and tapped lightly before letting themselves in. Father Charles was sitting in the big armchair, a shawl around his shoulders and a book in his lap. It was obvious he'd been napping.

When Maggie walked over and gave him a hug, she was shocked by the frailness of his body. But the radiance of his smile at seeing her brought a lump to her throat. It took all her strength to hold back her tears.

"It does me heart good ta see the pair of ya," he said. "Maggie, love, yer lookin' radiant. I'm thinkin' yer happy now, are ya? And isn't it the good man ya got there that's makin' ya so?"

He was thrilled with the sweater vest Maggie had knitted for him and declared he would be wearing it under his jacket the entire winter, thanking her over and over for the precious thought she had put into it. They kept their visit brief, as Father DeSalle had suggested, for Father Charles' voice weakened with each word he spoke.

As they walked back to Penelope's to celebrate the day, there was heaviness in Maggie's heart, a grief she had never felt before.

If only he can get through this winter, she thought, perhaps the spring sunshine will put some color in his cheeks, and his appetite will increase.

It was four days later that the news reached Maggie by way of Zeb. He had stopped by in the early afternoon to deliver some firewood Tim had asked for.

When Maggie opened the door, he immediately removed his woolen cap. Twisting it in his hands, he said, "Sorry, missy. Woulda had this wood here this morning before I went to the shippin' yards, like I promised Tim, but it's been a mighty fretful day, what with Father Charles dyin' and your mam wailin' and carryin' on so. 'Twern't none of us got a decent breakfast."

Maggie sucked in her breath and fainted.

She felt cold air on her cheeks when she opened her eyes. Disoriented, she first thought she was outside, then realized that the door was wide open, and somehow she was on the bed.

'Wh...happened?" she moaned.

Instantly recalling Zeb's words, "Father Charles died," she began to weep.

Relieved that Maggie was all right, Zeb began to pace. "I'm so sorry, missy. I thought ya knew. Seems the whole town's already got the news. Didn't ya hear the bell tolling over to Saint John's this morning?'

Maggie continued to weep.

She'd heard the bell toll around ten minutes after seven, just after Tim had left for the quarry. Other than on Sunday mornings, it never tolled unless there was a death in the community, and she had said a little prayer for whoever it was that had died, never thinking it was someone she loved so dearly.

Not knowing what else to do, Zeb found a cloth and soaked it in cold water from the bucket by the sink. He had seen Claire take a cold cloth to Brigid's room and figured it should work.

Placing it on her forehead, he said tenderly, "There, there, little missy. Yer good Father Charles was sick fer such a long spell. It's just the way of things."

Maggie turned on her side and buried her face in the pillow. With muffled sobs, she said, "I'll be fine, Zeb. Thank you for caring. And please shut the door on the way out."

Zeb was pleased to be dismissed. Having been raised by parents who had always taken a stoic approach toward life, he wasn't good at handling other people's problems. Yet he had a deep affection for Maggie and was touched by her grief. Before he closed the door, he turned back toward the bed and sighed. "I'll be leavin' ya now, but if there's anything I can do fer ya, just let me know."

As the door closed, Maggie realized there was nothing anyone could do to take away this pain she felt in her heart. Not even Tim.

Father Charles' body was laid out at the foot of the altar in Saint Michael's Church. For two days, the townspeople paraded past him to show their respect—turning to Brigid, who had planted herself in the first pew for the interim, to give words of consolation. Brigid was inconsolable.

Tim had taken a few days off work so he and Maggie could spend their vigil at the church. It pained him to see her so deeply grieved. As he watched the line of people parade past the coffin, then turn to lavish words of consolation on Brigid, he also became acutely aware of just how badly Maggie was being treated. "Shunned" was probably a better word for it. Covert stares at her swollen belly, whispers and raised eyebrows. Words of consolation for the loss of the man she so dearly loved did not come her way.

How could he have been so stupid, they were thinking. How could he think that just loving Maggie so much would make everything all right?

On the third day, Father DeSalle said a requiem Mass to a church overflowing with mourners. There would be no procession to the cemetery, since there was no way a grave could be prepared. The ground was frozen solid. It had been arranged that Henry Wyath, the mortician, would take the coffin back to his home, to be placed in a shed until the weather allowed a proper burial.

After the service, Father DeSalle announced that all were invited to Brigid Mahoney's for a light repast. Mary Murphy had offered her large and spacious home for the occasion, but Brigid was having none of that. After all, Father Charles was almost kin—her dearest, dearest friend. It would be a reception in his memory, and that privilege did not belong to the likes of Mary Murphy.

Tim and Maggie lingered in the background, ignored for the most part, waiting for a personal invitation from Brigid. It was not forthcoming.

New Year's Day, 1907, came and went with little to celebrate. Maggie seemed to languish in her own thoughts, responding to Tim's affection, but once again, the fire had gone from her eyes, and a smile was rarely seen on her face. Tim knew he would have to take some action.

On the third of January, Maggie was finishing up the dinner dishes when Tim picked up a dishtowel to help and said, "Maggie, I've been thinking about what you said about crossing over to the States. Pete Stokes tells me the lake is frozen solid. Since your brother is willing to help us get settled, I see no reason why we shouldn't go as soon as possible."

Maggie's eyes showed a sparkle he hadn't seen for quite a spell as she turned to face him.

"Do you really think we could do it?" she asked excitedly. "It's been so long since I've seen Jack. And I've never seen little Johnny. Or the new baby! Oh, wouldn't it be wonderful? We could all be a family again."

Then a wrinkle of doubt crossed her forehead. "But could I do it? In this condition, I mean." She put her hands on her stomach. "I'm almost a full six months, now."

Tim put his arms around her and kissed her forehead. "You can do it, Maggie. Actually, you aren't that big at all. Maybe it's because you're so tall. My friend Ephram down at the quarry, his wife is only five months along, and she's three times the size of you." He took his arms away from her and joined his hands together in front of him, forming a circle.

They both laughed.

"Course, she's barely five feet." He picked up the dishtowel again.

The two of them became quiet as they finished the dishes.

Then Maggie sat down at the kitchen table and signaled for Tim. "All right, captain, sit yourself down and tell me the plans. When does this crew get underway?"

It warmed Tim to see Maggie in such good spirits. He had not been wrong to make this decision and only wished he had listened to her in the first place. They could have been settled by now if it hadn't been for his pigheadedness.

Although they had decided they would take nothing with them but necessities, there was still much to consider. Most of their clothing and mementos would be stored at Penelope's until such time as they could send for them. But they'd be needing some things for immediate use, and for that, they'd have to pack a small valise and pull it with them on a sled.

Selling the house was their biggest concern, and Maggie prayed it would not deter them from leaving before the month was up. With the money she'd saved, Tim's modest nest egg, and the money from the sale of the house, she knew they would have more than enough to start afresh. But as far as she was concerned, she would forgo the house being sold, if need be.

Tim's biggest concern was the actual traveling time the trip would take. Once he had calculated the miles to Erie, Pennsylvania, taking into consideration that they would be pulling a small sled, which might slow them down some (it would also serve to allow Maggie to rest occasionally), he decided the trip was quite doable as long as they left at an early hour.

As soon as they reached the Erie shore, they would find lodging for the night and someone to transport them to the train depot, heading on to Buffalo the next day.

Another consideration was the weather. Subzero

temperatures had persisted since the beginning of November. Tim reckoned there would be a thaw sometime in January, and they could wait it out until such indications of weather change.

Selling the house turned out to be much simpler than they could have hoped for. Gunther Klein had been staying with his brother, Otto, since he'd come over from Germany the year before. When Otto, who worked with Tim, heard of Tim's leaving, he immediately told Gunther. One room of his own to call home was all he wanted, and one look at the coziness and comfort of that room was all he needed. The deal was set. Both Tim and Maggie were ecstatic when he offered them three hundred dollars. He would take possession in February.

Tim was becoming as excited as Maggie. He had never been anywhere other than Herron's Point in all his life. This was turning into an adventure he was truly looking forward to. His only real concern now was whether Maggie could withstand the very long walk. But youthful optimism was with him, as it was with Maggie. He never again questioned the obstacles that must be overcome. Those would be faced as they met them. Maggie placed complete credence in Tim's ability to handle things, and he, in turn, was willing to face any challenge as long as Maggie was happy.

Penelope Orwell, on the other hand, was quite concerned.

"Now, stop your fretting, Penelope," Clifford said one evening after listening to her go on about the hazards of Tim and Maggie's plan. "Those two young people are going to be just fine. They've got pluck, is what I'd call it. Their whole life's ahead of them. It seems to me they're using the good sense God gave 'em to leave this town. From what I'm told, people cross over during the winter all the time. Course, it's usually where the boundaries are closer together. But nonetheless, it's been done. So no reason why the two of them can't do the same." Then in a softer tone, he added, "Tim's a sensible fella. He'll see no harm comes to Maggie."

It was January twenty–second that the temperature rose to five degrees above freezing. On the twenty–third, it was a degree higher. As Tim returned from the quarry, where he spent his mornings for something to do, he noticed the icicles on the eaves melting.

"I think we can plan on leaving tomorrow," he announced upon entering the house.

Maggie looked up from her darning in disbelief. "Oh, Tim! I just can't believe that in a few days, I'll be seeing Jack again. This is like some kind of dream."

That same evening, Clifford and Tim hauled the trunks over to Penelope's basement for storage, and the four of them spent their last evening together. Penelope produced a large basket of food for the trip, explaining, "You'll be needing sustenance for such a long walk. And when the basket's empty, just leave it. I also insist that you take these two blankets along, just in case the wind starts acting up. You never know about those things, and it's always good to be prepared. You can just tie them on top of the other things."

There were many hugs, kisses, and tears before Tim and Maggie left for home.

CHAPTER FIFTEEN

Crossing the Ice

January 1907

There was a bone–chilling dampness in the night air created by the previous day's thaw. The sky, completely cloud–covered, contributed to the blackness surrounding Tim as he made his way to the shed to get a lantern, some rope, and the red sled that had delighted him as a child on winter days. He then stopped off at the house to collect the items needed for the trip, so he could put them on the sled and haul them to the icy shore. Occasionally the moon managed to break through and shoot down a few splinters of silver moonbeams, illuminating small patches of snow.

Inside, Maggie was intent on making the one–room house tidy for its new occupant. On the way out the back door, Tim looked over the blankets piled in his arms and said, "Maggie, I'll be back to get you as soon as I tie everything down. It's mighty dark out there, and I don't want you walking to the dock by yourself."

Satisfied that all was in order, Maggie put on her long wool coat, wrapped her scarf around her neck, pulled her cap down over her ears, and doused the lamplight before putting on her mittens. As she stepped outside, she could see Tim coming up the path carrying the hurricane lantern, its flame licking and beating against the glass, casting eerie, dancing shadows into the night; its light was quickly devoured by a jealous darkness waiting to reclaim its space.

As she watched him approach, a thought struck her like a cold, icy hand.

I've asked him to give up his home, his job, his friends.

She had been wrapped up in her own misery, and not until this moment had it occurred to her that what she'd asked of him was pure selfishness on her part. As soon as he reached her side, she threw her arms around him.

"Oh, Tim, I love you so much! How can I ever thank you for all you've done for me?"

This spontaneous display of emotion Tim interpreted as happiness and excitement, relief to finally be freeing herself of a town whose shameful treatment of her had caused her such unhappiness. The fact that she was looking forward to this particular distasteful journey was proof of that, and he was glad he'd finally consented to make it with her.

Although he'd been adamant in his feelings when she'd first brought the idea to his attention, it was the witnessing of the town's behavior toward her at Father Charles' funeral that had won him over to her way of thinking. Lifelong friends and neighbors treating her like some kind of pariah—sweet Maggie, who had never deliberately harmed anyone. And that mother of hers! The only word for her was cruel. Where was her heart?

With all Maggie had been through, first the rape, then her mother's scorn, the pneumonia, the town's rejection, and the death of a man she adored, Tim had become truly concerned for her emotional wellbeing. If this was what it would take to make her a happy woman, then so be it. He would do all in his power to protect her on their journey.

He leaned down and kissed Maggie on the forehead. "It's time to go, my love," he whispered.

They walked down a path bordered on either side by mounds of snow that jumped and danced to the rhythm of light and shadow and arrived at the shoreline, where the sled awaited.

Tim girded the sled's rope around his waist, leaving just enough slack, picked up the lantern, and they started out. Their silent footfall sank into the soft snow, imprinting a pattern of where they had been. It was five–thirty in the morning.

First light came in like a whisper, desperately trying to wash away the darkness. Their world was now colored in shades of gray.

Having walked for about an hour, Tim decided they should stop to rest. They used the sled as a bench and sat looking back to assess their progress.

A dark outline in the distance wrapped itself around the horizon, all tied up with a ribbon of lights. Maggie wondered which one of those lights twinkled from 7 Erie Street.

"Let's go," she said, standing up and turning her back on where they had been.

When the sun made its appearance, they once again stopped and looked toward the east to observe the sunrise performing its majestic golden ritual. The sky, now cleared of gray cloud cover, marked it as one of those rare Canadian winter days. By the time the sun had reached its full omnipotent magnificence, they both instinctively shielded their eyes from the shimmering brightness that surrounded them. The lake was a desert of snow, blanketed overhead by a deep periwinkle blue pillowed with down.

They were distracted by a tick–clicking sound behind them and looked about three hundred yards to the west to discover two young otters chasing each other.

Maggie delighted in their playful antics. It reminded her of the first day she had ever spent with Tim, the day she and Rosemarie had gone out on the lake fishing with him.

The two frolicsome creatures ran in circles, making it difficult to know which one was chasing which. Soon the mother otter poked her head out of an ice hole with a large fish in her mouth. With a swing of her head, she flipped it onto the ice, then disappeared to search for more.

Two greedy little otters screeched to attention and pounced on the fish, each pushing and shoving to get the lion's share, when Tim said, "Look up there, Maggie." He pointed to a dark form soaring on a current of air. "It's an eagle."

It quickly approached the two unsuspecting otters.

"Oh, no!" Maggie shrieked, covering her eyes to avoid witnessing what was about to take place.

Just as the eagle began to circle for the kill, the mother otter poked her head out of the ice, holding another fish in her mouth. She threw it on the ice and spoke in a language her two children understood perfectly. They dove into the hole with her just as the eagle plummeted with an efficiency of motion, scooped up the floundering fish, and flew away.

"It's all right, Maggie. You can uncover your eyes, now. They got away."

"Where'd they go?"

"They're under the ice with their mother."

"But what if the eagle comes back?"

"Otters are pretty smart," he said. "This lake is riddled with holes for ice fishing. That's one of the main reasons I brought the lantern along. Wouldn't want to step in one. She'll likely lead them into shore following a pattern of holes, bringing them up for air at each one. That's probably how they got out this far in the first place."

They continued moving on, taking off hats, mittens, and coats and putting them on the sled as the warmth of the sun permeated their woolen layers of clothing. They had taken on a giddy optimism about what they now called "our big adventure" and talked incessantly about nothing and everything, making strong strides southward.

Tim had put a lot of thought into this trip. Although it had been impossible to pin down a date, he knew that when the right time came, they would be ready.

Everyone he'd spoken to about it had said it was folly. "Wait until spring for the little woman's sake," they'd said. But he knew it was not an impossible undertaking and didn't want to go into any explanations as to why this trip was so imperative for the "little lady" herself.

The weather had certainly cooperated by freezing the lake over, and this break in the weather had given them the perfect opportunity to leave. Their destination was around thirty miles away, directly south, from Herron's Point to Erie, Pennsylvania, which he reckoned would take all of fifteen, maybe sixteen hours if they paced themselves right. That should bring them to the other side about eight o'clock in the evening, he figured.

When the sun was directly overhead, they stopped for lunch. They took both blankets, spread them one on top of the other on the snow, and laid out the banquet of food. Penelope had outdone herself, both with variety and quantity.

"Isn't this wonderful!" Maggie said as she chewed on a piece of fried chicken.

Tim had already consumed a chicken leg. He licked his fingers and reached for a ham sandwich. "I swear, she must have thought she was feeding Napoleon's army. Look at all this food. And all of it delicious." His face grew wistful. "I'll sorely miss her, Maggie."

The same overwhelming sense of guilt Maggie had experienced that morning returned. Tears welled up in her eyes.

"Tim, I hadn't realized until today how much I was asking you to give up. Please forgive me for being so selfish." A tear splashed on the blanket.

It wrenched his heart to see her so. She didn't need this to add to her plate of sorrow.

"Maggie, love, you are my happiness. I said I would miss Penelope, but I'm only happy if you are. We'll make a wonderful life for ourselves in the States. And it's not like we'll never see Penelope and Clifford again. They promised they would come over and visit us this coming summer, remember? Now, how about a big slice of that chocolate cake, and then I think we'd best get moving on."

Tim noticed that Maggie had slowed down considerably after lunch. They'd made their best time in the early hours. He knew the rest of the way would be a lot slower moving, but was quite satisfied with their progress. It would be nightfall within the hour, and soon after that, they should be guided by the lights from the Erie shore.

Completely absorbed in the goal ahead, they hadn't noticed the darkened sky behind them. They did become aware of a definite chill in the air and stopped to put their coats back on. That's when they saw the winter storm approaching.

Soon the wind picked up, and the entire sky was blackened. Snow began to fall, at first in gusts, and then so heavily they could barely see in front of them. Tim was disheartened, but he knew that for Maggie's sake, they had to go on.

With his compass in hand, he assured Maggie that it would be best to continue. She agreed.

They took the blankets Penelope had so wisely insisted they take along to protect themselves from the strong wind that assaulted them unmercifully as it heaped huge drifts of snow in their path. As the darkness of the storm surrounded them, it was difficult for Tim to read the compass. At one point he lifted his hand close to his face to take a reading, and the compass slipped out of his ice–covered mittens and fell, sinking into the deep snow at his feet. After several minutes of futile searching, they decided to go on without it.

The storm alone would slow them down considerably, but Tim knew he had to get Maggie to shelter sometime before this day was over. The storm subsided as quickly as it had come, lasting just long enough for the sun to set.

There were no lights to direct them to the shoreline. It became so difficult to make their way through the new–fallen snow that Maggie's legs began to cramp, and Tim knew they could go no further.

"Maggie, I'm afraid we're lost. I'd put you on the sled and pull you the rest of the way, but I'm not sure what the right way is. I guess we have no choice but to camp here for the night." His voice was filled with concern.

They threw themselves wholeheartedly into rolling up snow, and within minutes, a circle of wall took shape. Leaving a small opening, the pair stepped inside the shoulder–high haven.

Tim turned to Maggie and said, "Welcome to Paradise, my brilliant wife."

Maggie walked to the edge of the wall and looked to the silent, inky night beyond. Tim stood behind her, his arms around her thickened waist, resting his chin on the top of her head. "It's almost like we're the only people in the world. Just the two of us and a frozen lake," she mused.

"Fiercely beautiful," he responded.

Neither was cognizant of the direction they were looking, for the view was the same in any direction they might choose to face.

"I'm starved," Tim said and turned to light the lantern he'd hooked to the sled. "You know, Maggie, Penelope lined the wicker basket with newspaper to keep the food from freezing. We can use it to cover the snow and put the blankets on top. That way, we can cuddle and keep each other warm after we eat, and if need be, we can use some of the items in the valise to help keep us warm."

"I only packed one change of clothes for each of us," Maggie said. "Just a flannel shirt for you and a wool dress for me, along with some personal items. But we're both layered to the skin with wool, and thank goodness the temperature's not too bad. We'll be fine." She flashed the best smile she could muster.

Both were quite hungry, and the selection of food was enough to sustain them for the next three days: pickled eggs, applesauce, baked beans, ham sandwiches, fried chicken, cookies, cake, and a peach pie. They ate with relish and washed it down with small doses of snow.

Overtaken with exhaustion, Maggie fell asleep in Tim's arms immediately after they had cleared the blankets of food. Before sleep overtook Tim, he doused the lantern and looked up through his roofless abode, happy to see that there were no stars. This cloud cover would keep the temperature from going down too far. Protected from the wind, he knew they would survive the night.

When Maggie became aware of Tim stirring, she groaned and stretched her stiff limbs. "Just give me a minute to put this body of mine back together." She stood up and stretched her aching muscles. "I think it will be another cold day in Hell before I attempt to sleep in an igloo," she groaned.

Tim laughed, amazed at the tenacity of a woman six months pregnant with such a will to go on. The depth of Maggie's unhappiness in Herron's Point was such a driving force, she would endure any hardship to escape it.

"It's still dark," Tim said. "I have no idea which direction we should take. But since we put the opening to this wall facing the direction we were headed, I think it best that we keep on moving that way. The temperature's tolerable, and perhaps by dawn, we'll be able to get our true bearings."

Maggie agreed, and they set about packing up the sled, leaving their little snow castle behind. They had no idea how long they'd walked before dawn's first light, but realized at its onset that they had been heading west.

Unlike the previous day's sunrise, this one arrived to bathe ribbons of clouds in orange and silver. There was a stark beauty about the day, and although the temperature was still holding above the freezing level, they knew they wouldn't be shedding their coats.

"Well, Maggie, we've taken a bit of a detour, but I have no doubt, barring another storm, that we should reach land before this day is over. We have to be somewhere fairly close."

They immediately turned south and walked for hours, stopping often to rest. When they had first discussed the trip, they knew it would be necessary to take a sled but feared it would be a real impediment to their progress. Now they realized it was a blessing. Not only had it assured them of food and warmth; it afforded them rest in relative comfort while Tim massaged Maggie's legs to keep them from cramping.

When they first saw the outline of a land formation, they were ecstatic. It took what seemed forever to reach the rugged, deserted shoreline, its rocky beach rising to a crest of bare trees. With a burst of energy, they plowed through the rock–covered snow. Climbing a small hill, they came upon a rutted, snow-covered road bordered by snow–laden evergreens.

"There must be people close by," Tim said. "These sleigh tracks and horse prints are fairly fresh. Looks like someone's been off in the woods collecting firewood."

"Oh, I hope so," Maggie sighed wearily. "Wouldn't a good, hot cup of tea be just about the best thing ever right now?"

They followed the trail of life for about a quarter of a mile. Smoke rose from a small white cottage on their left with a welcoming warmth. Exhausted and spent, they turned into the walk leading to the front door.

CHAPTER SIXTEEN

An Awakening—Herron's Point
Jack Mahoney—Buffalo, New York

She woke up and stared at the ceiling, dreading the thought of facing another day. This past month had been a nightmare of black nothingness, a hole with no bottom and no means to climb out. Brigid spent most of her days languishing in her room, mourning the loss of the only real friend she'd ever had.

Thank goodness for Claire, who, recognizing the depth of her grief, took it upon herself to run the household, patiently waiting for some indication that Brigid was ready to take back her domain. Brigid could hear her in the kitchen singing as she prepared breakfast for the boarders, and for some reason, those soothing notes turned her thoughts to Maggie, then back to Father Charles.

After Father Charles had returned from Toronto, she'd made it quite clear to Father LaSalle that she intended to see to her friend's needs. This she did every day. Father Charles would often bring up Maggie's name in conversation, making his feelings known as to how wrong he felt Brigid's treatment of her daughter had been. He had neither the strength nor desire to argue the point when Brigid would bristle, flailing her arms as she recited the litany of wrongs that her child had wrought against her. Everything was always about Brigid. She seemed incapable of seeing the other side of things—unless it didn't involve her, of course.

But he persisted in his own gentle way, insisting that Maggie had told the truth about her situation, and that Brigid should have reached out in compassion to help. He repeatedly warned her she would rue the day she had not done so.

Willful pride had always been Brigid's stumbling block, but she'd never considered that her own thoughts on the matter of Maggie's situation were intrinsically tied to that defect. Lately, though, that wall of imperfection had been crumbling. The very thought that she had been wrong only added to the devastating grief she felt.

Today she had no doubts. She knew she'd been wrong. It was as though Father Charles were still with her, whispering in her ear, "Make amends. Go to her. Show her you love her." She recalled his words: "Love is the answer to all your problems."

Although it would be one of the most difficult things Brigid had ever done in her life, she resolved to get dressed and make a call on Maggie. She could no longer endure this pain of grief that was incapacitating her. Taking this step might help.

And it certainly will be an act my dear old friend can smile down upon, she thought.

Claire was quite surprised to see Brigid in the kitchen, fully dressed. "My, my, missus, it's so good to see you up and about. I was just readying to bring you your breakfast." Smiling, she pulled a chair out from the table. "But now you can just sit yourself right down here and keep me company while I tend to the boarders."

Her smile faded as she watched Brigid put on her black wool coat.

"I won't be eating just yet," Brigid said curtly. "There's a piece of business I have to tend to first."

With no further explanation, she walked down the hall and out the front door in a flurry, leaving Claire to wonder.

Brigid's heart was racing, and she began to sweat as she approached the small brown house—a stark contrast against the black skeletons of trees and the icy expanse of the snow–covered lake.

No smoke rose from the chimney. She attributed both that and her warm discomfort to the mild weather and her heavy coat. Nervously, she rapped on the door. There was no thought in her mind as to what she would say, but the words would come. She would say what she had to say, and it would all be over. There was never a doubt that Maggie would forgive her.

After rapping several times, she realized there was no one inside.

Where could that girl be off to at this time of the morning? she wondered.

She decided she must be at Penelope Orwell's house. Well, she would go fetch her, and they could come back to this house and have their talk. She would see to it that the mission she'd set out to accomplish would be completed before she returned home.

When Penelope responded to the light tapping and opened the front door, she was quite taken aback by the appearance of Brigid Mahoney.

"I've come ta see me daughter, Maggie, if ya don't mind, Mrs. Orwell."

Penelope detected a slight quiver in Brigid's voice. "So sorry, she's not here—"

Before Penelope could finish, Brigid turned on her heel and started down the steps, muttering, "Well, I won't be keepin' ya, then."

Penelope called out, "Mrs. Mahoney, Maggie's gone."

Brigid swung around. "She's what?"

"She and Tim are crossing the lake to a town called Erie. They're going off to Buffalo to live. They left just this morning."

Brigid stood paralyzed for a second, then shrugged, and said, "Well, it was of no consequence that I needed ta be seein' her," and bolted down the steps.

There is no way I will show that woman how I really feel, she thought.

Brigid scurried back up to Erie Street and over to the front of her house. But before she went in, she looked out at the lake, and her soul silently wailed in pain.

Buffalo, New York

It had begun to snow sometime in the early morning hours. Jack Mahoney awoke around six o'clock and decided he'd best hurry to the lumberyard before the snow piled any higher.

By the time he unlocked the doors to the storefront, there was no doubt in his mind that there would be no business today. This snowstorm promised to be the granddaddy of them all. But that was of little consequence, he thought. Now he had an opportunity to catch up on all the paperwork that invariably eluded him during the constant interruptions of a normal business day.

It was midafternoon when Lincoln Washburn made his appearance.

Jack looked up from his desk as the bell above the door clinked to announce him. "Didn't expect to see you today, Wash," Jack said, staring at the picture of Wash's black face draped in white snow, standing there holding a snow shovel. "There was no reason you had to come to work. No one else has shown a face around here. Not that I've cared, mind you. One of those rare days for catching up on things."

Wash began huffing and stamping off all the snow he'd collected along his way. "Well, Mistah Jack, I be thinkin' 'bout all that snow in front of the store, and how's it be keepin' people away tomorrow, so when it let up a little, I brung myself over here to clear it away."

"What would my family and I do without you and your wife?" Jack sincerely wondered out loud. "It was good of you to let Emiline stay the night, Wash, what with Patsy running a fever and Martha ailing like she is. An act of Providence, I'd say. Otherwise she'd never have made it to the house this morning, and I wouldn't be sitting here. She's a real godsend to Martha and the baby. And me."

"Well, you tell her she best be stayin' again tonight, 'cause this here snow ain't fit for no woman to be walkin' in. Just tell her I fixed me a big ol' pot of them ham hocks and greens. 'Tween me and Brutus, we'll do just fine. That ol' dog is mighty comfortin' on a cold winter night."

Jack reached for his coat. "Get yourself warmed up a bit while I go find a shovel. I'll give you a hand."

By the time Jack Mahoney and Lincoln Washburn finished clearing away the snow from the storefront, it was dark.

It was days like this that made the five–block walk from the lumberyard to his house seem more like a five–mile trek. Jack lifted each leg high with every step he took, leaving a trail of deep holes in the snow where his legs had just been. "Evening, Cal. Nice to see someone is clearing a path in this gawd awful snow."

"Second time this week," Cal grunted as he threw a shovelful of snow onto a mound higher than his own five feet eight inches. "I swear I'm in the mountain–building business."

"Buffalo must get more snow than any other city in the world," Jack commented.

"Ain't that the truth. But this winter's been the worst I've seen for many a year. I did think maybe, after that warm spell we had a few weeks back, it would ease up some."

"No such luck," Jack said as he gave a wave and continued on his way.

By the time he reached home, he was exhausted and leaned against the trunk of a tree in front of his house, contemplating how he would plow through the five–foot drifts in his driveway.

It would be much simpler if he could go in the front door, but that would never happen; Martha wouldn't allow it.

It had crossed his mind more than once that he'd married a woman just like his own mam, although it hadn't seemed so in the beginning. At first, she'd been as sweet and affectionate as a new puppy. But once established in her own home, shortly after John Patrick Mahoney was born, it became obvious that Martha was in charge of all domestic decisions, including the raising of little Johnny. And Jack, who was so busy trying to establish himself in the business world, allowed it to happen.

Jack had never lost touch with his Grandpa Mahoney and communicated by mail quite frequently. He was seven when his grandparents had left for Ireland, and he'd missed them desperately—especially his Grandma Gracia, who had showered him with her own special brand of love and affection.

When it became apparent that his mother wanted no part of her in-laws, it was Agnes Carter who helped him reach them by mail. The irony of this was not lost on him, because later she had done the same for Maggie. So through the years, he had kept his grandparents informed of family matters, which they greatly appreciated and returned in kind.

When he and Martha had come to Buffalo, Jack had written to his grandfather and explained his situation. It was only natural that the first job he sought out after they arrived in Buffalo was at the Gunderson Sawmill. After he'd worked there for a little over two years, his grandfather had encouraged him to go into business for himself. "The lumber business is not far afield from the cuttin' of it," he'd written. "Learn all you can about setting yourself up in a building, find a good location, and I will see to it that you have what you need to get started."

It had been quite difficult in the beginning, and he really appreciated the order and tranquility he came home to after so many harrowing days trying to establish himself. But his hours were long, and there was precious little time to spend with John Patrick. Martha said it was important that a baby maintain a strict schedule, so John Patrick was usually in bed when Jack left in the morning and asleep when he arrived home at night.

Who was he to argue? She planned marvelous meals, and they dined by candlelight each evening. Shades of the memory of his mother, Brigid Mahoney, while they still lived on Superior Avenue. There was no question that Martha did like the good life, and he was willing to work hard to see that she got it.

All of this fell apart when Johnny, at the tender age of five, died six days after contracting scarlet fever. Jack was devastated, but Martha was even worse off, having discovered only the month before that she was pregnant. She became a grief-ridden, bitter woman. Little Patricia was now two months old, and Martha ignored her almost completely. Once again, it reminded him of his mam, snapping at everyone after his father was killed.

No, there was no way he would ever go in that front door. It was bad enough that he was dog tired. He had no desire to listen to the tirade she would go into if he did that.

Jack began to scoop away the snow as he made his way up to the back door, surprised and relieved that Emiline had cleared the porch and steps. Bless her, bless her, bless her.

His entire body was inundated with sensual pleasure as he entered the back door into the pantry. Warmth embraced him like a woman's caress as he hung up his heavy coat, took off his boots and shoes, and slipped his cold feet into soft, woolen slippers. The aroma of pot roast and onions brought a rush of saliva to his mouth as his stomach growled, reminding him how hungry he was.

"That be you, Mistah Jack?" Emiline called from the kitchen.

"Yes, Emiline, and I'm afraid I brought a small lake in with me. If you bring me a mop, I'll make it disappear."

Unlike during the earlier years of gracious dining, before Johnny's death, Jack now sat alone at the kitchen table to eat his meal. Emiline, who had become a permanent daily figure in the household, was fixing a tray to take to Martha.

"Lawdy, Mistah Jack, the missus don't be eatin' enough to be keepin' a tiny sparrow goin'."

"We have to give her time, Emiline. Losing Johnny while carrying another child, and a difficult pregnancy at that, has taken its toll. Doc Porter says that time is the best healer, and we just have to be patient with her."

Emiline sighed. "Ah knows it, but it just be so worrisome. 'Specially since she seems to pay no mind to that sweet chile layin' there."

"You had quite a long night walking the floor with Patsy. You must be plumb worn out, Emiline. The two of you made quite a picture this morning before I left for work, you sound asleep in the big rocker with Patsy in your arms, sleeping like a kitten. How's her fever?"

"Seems the worst has passed. Ah don't know if she be catchin' a cold. Chilluns often as not get fevers for a passel of things. Ah do know it be too early for her to be teethin', though."

"Well, she's in good hands. And I thank you for it. Wash made it to the store today and said to tell you you'd best stay the night again. This weather is impossible."

Jack sat at the kitchen table, devouring the large portions of roast beef, little red potatoes, and sweet carrots as Emiline left to take a tray up to Martha.

Patsy slept peacefully in a bassinet next to his chair. This was the way it had been since she was born, for after Emiline left in the evening, having seen to his evening meal, he became both mother and father to the child. Martha had little interest in her newborn—or anything else, for that matter.

Jack tried hard to understand the depth of her grief. He, too, carried a heart broken with pain. But his life was full of things that needed tending to, and one of them was little Patsy. Martha had just given up. Occasionally he reached over and stroked the halo of golden ringlets surrounding his daughter's sweet, round face.

Jack noticed the mail sitting next to his plate and realized it must have been there since yesterday. But what with coming home last night to an overwrought wife and a sick child, he and Emiline had both had their hands full tending to their needs.

He shuffled through the pile of bills and came to an envelope that piqued his curiosity. It was postmarked Darby's Island, Ohio. When he recognized Maggie's handwriting, he put the other mail aside and opened it.

My dearest brother,

I received your letter telling me you would be happy to have Tim and me come and stay with you in Buffalo. I can't tell you how excited I was at the thought of it. I know you didn't seem to approve of our traveling in the winter. Your advice had been that we wait until spring. But I did explain my situation, and you can't know how deeply I needed to leave Herron's Point, especially after the death of dear Father Charles.

At any rate, we did cross over when there was a break in the weather and had every intention of calling you when we reached Erie, Pennsylvania. The problem was, we got lost in a blizzard and ended up in a place called Darby's Island. Two of the nicest people in the world, Gert and Hal Berning, have taken us in. The doctor here advised me to stay put until the baby comes, and I suppose it will be a little time after that before we'll be able to travel again.

I'm so looking forward to seeing all of you. Especially my little nephew, Johnny.

Your devoted sister,
Maggie

Jack held the letter in his hand and stared at the ivy-patterned paper on the kitchen wall. He had never told Maggie about Johnny's death. She had written the previous May, telling him she would be going away to school. Then her letter came at the end of November, explaining the horrible situation that had brought her to ask if she and Tim could come stay in Buffalo.

It's no wonder we've been out of touch, he thought. Poor Maggie was going through her own trial of fire at about the same time that he and Martha had lost little Johnny.

He'd have to write her a long letter explaining things. He knew she would not have her child until some time around April. Perhaps he'd take little Patsy and go visit next spring. He was familiar with Darby's Island. It wouldn't take long to get there on *The Mariner.*

CHAPTER SEVENTEEN
A New Home
Darby's Island—April 1909

Spring was definitely in the air. Maggie could feel it pulse through her veins as the delicate fragrance of lilac washed through the kitchen. A basket of ironing sat on the floor next to the stove waiting to be done, but it would just have to wait. This morning was too glorious to waste inside, and that aside, she couldn't wait to tell Gert her good news.

Little Maura sat on the kitchen floor, intent on stacking a pile of blocks, completely unaware of the change in seasons.

Maggie stooped down beside her, "Maura, let's put the blocks away, sweetheart. Mama's going to take you for a walk."

She began piling the blocks into a small cardboard box. Maura, imitating her mother, managed to put a few in, too.

"We'll stop by Auntie Gert's house. Perhaps she'll want to take a walk with us. Would you like that?" She scooped Maura up, giving her a big hug. The child squealed with delight.

Maggie pushed the pram to the corner and turned down Division Street, stopping along the tree-lined, cindered road to admire patches of violets, spring beauties, forget–me–nots, and jack–in–the–pulpit.

Maura, sitting upright in a pram she'd almost outgrown, her bonneted head tilted upward toward the budding trees, waved her arms at a pair of robins fluttering in the branches, intent on building a nest.

Maggie's heart soared with joy at the beauty of it all. She had come to love this little island she now called home.

As she continued the walk toward Gert's house, she recalled that day, three winters ago, when she and Tim had walked this same road, exhausted and cold, ending up on Gert and Hal's doorstep. How blessed they had been to be taken in by two such wonderful people. Their generosity and hospitality knew no bounds. After recovering from the astonishing story Tim told, relating the events of a harrowing two–day adventure, the couple opened their hearts and home, offering them the spare bedroom that had once been their sons'.

Given Maggie's condition, Gert would not allow her to lift a finger until she felt she had sufficiently recovered from exhaustion, and they then insisted the pair remain with them until some time after the baby was born. Hal, in the meantime, promised Tim employment at the quarry as soon as spring came and more workers would be needed.

With the help of Doctor Birch and Gert, Maura was born in Hal and Gert's house on April 16, 1907, around the same time Tim began work at the quarry. With the money they had brought with them, they purchased a small vacant house on Spruce Street, a side road near Gert and Hal's house on Division Street. It was just four rooms, but they were thrilled with the spaciousness of a house with more than one room.

Tim was completely happy doing the work he'd always done, doted on Maura, and adored Maggie. And Maggie, although quite busy with a new infant, could take all the dawdling time she wanted furnishing their new home. They had contacted Penelope, and all of their belongings had finally arrived at the end of May, with a promise from Penelope that they would visit as soon as Clifford's broken leg healed. That promise was kept the following September, and it was an exhilarating reunion.

Now, at eighteen, very soon to be nineteen, Maggie was happy and content. Her only sorrow was for her brother, Jack, who had come to visit the summer after Maura was born. It had been a bittersweet reunion. Her heart ached as he told her of little Johnny's death and the effect it had had on Martha. But seeing him, touching him, talking to him, and meeting her little niece, Patsy, for the first time had been quite a healing experience.

As she neared the little white cottage, she could see Gert busily sweeping the winter's deposit of leaves from the corners of the front porch.

Gert looked up as Maggie walked past the picket fence and turned into the stone walk.

"Well, I declare, look who's here! My favorite godchild."

She dropped her broom and rushed down the steps, taking Maura in her arms, smothering her cheeks with kisses.

Maggie watched with pleasure as Maura clung to her Auntie Gert's neck, then said, "We were just out for a walk on this beautiful day and wondered if you'd like to join us."

"What a splendid idea," Gert said, handing Maura back to her mother. "Just let me run in and get my shawl."

Maggie watched as Gert raced into the house and marveled at her good fortune to have made two such similar friends as Gert Berning and Penelope Orwell. Both were about the same age, both were so giving, and both had opened their homes to her in a time of need.

Their walk took them north on Division Street toward the quarry that was located at the far northwestern end of the island. Most of the population was located at the south end of the island, east to west along Water Street and all the little side streets along its three–mile stretch of shoreline. Maggie had commented early on that Herron's Point also had a Water Street and decided that the name must be indigenous to small towns facing water.

Division Street bisected the island for four miles from south to north. Altogether, there were 1,248 people on the island, most of whose livelihoods came from work at the limestone quarry. But there were some who found it profitable to farm large fields of grapes used to make wine on the mainland.

About halfway up Division Street, they paused.

"My goodness, would you look at that!" Gert exclaimed. "They've finally broken ground for the new school building."

Most of the crew laying the stone block foundation were unfamiliar faces from the mainland, but little Georgie Hawker— that's what Gert still called him from the days when he'd stop by as a young boy to see if she had any extra cookies she wouldn't be needing—stood by a huge mound of dirt, shovel in hand, and gave a yell. "Hey, Miss Gert, how's the world treating you?"

"Just fine, Georgie. And you?"

"The best," he grinned. "The missus just had our second boy yesterday. Eight pounds, nine ounces." His chest seemed to swell at the mention of it.

"Congratulations, young man. Seems we lost touch. Haven't seen you for a while."

"That's 'cause I moved to Conneaut when I got married. But I'll be working on the island till late summer, I imagine."

"Will the school be opening this fall, do you think?"

"The good Lord willin' and the weather man listenin'. That's what the school board's hoping."

"Well, you take care, now. And give my best to Laurie and that little one, will you?"

"I sure will. But I still can't get her to make those ginger cookies I used to love so much."

"Stop by, and I'll give you some."

"I was hoping you'd say that. You'll be seeing me soon. Maybe you can write down that recipe for Laura." With that, he waved and turned to scoop a shovelful of dirt onto the wagon beside him.

"I'm so happy about the new school," Maggie said as they continued their walk. "Maura will go there instead of that two-room schoolhouse on Berkley Road."

"They had no choice but to build it. The population of young ones coming of school age is booming. There are about two hundred children of all ages ready to occupy it next fall, provided it's done on time. But I'm told on Georgie's good authority that it will be."

"How in the world did that little school ever manage to accommodate so many children?" Maggie asked. "I know the high school children attend classes in the basement of Town Hall, but still."

"Most children around here quit going to school after the

third or fourth grade. A lot of the boys start working at the quarry before the age of twelve, and the girls stay home and help out. The ones who make it to high school are very few."

Gert stooped to pick up a very shiny stone, buffed it on her skirt, and commented with a satisfied grin, "Perfect for the fish tank."

As she slipped it into her dress pocket, she continued. "Seems there's been a shift in attitude about education around here ever since that new teacher, Geoffrey Harper, came from Boston. He's convinced many of the parents to keep the young ones in school. It's him that has pushed for this new building. He says that the world out there is very competitive, and children should get at least an eighth-grade education to be able to compete. You know, Maggie, many of the youngsters here grow up and leave the island. Georgie is just one example. My two sons did the same. But at least they did get their eighth-grade diplomas. Working in a quarry is not for everybody."

Maggie realized it hadn't been much different where she'd come from. Hadn't she quit school after the fourth grade? And hadn't Tim started working at the quarry when he was twelve? Well, she would have better for her Maura.

As they approached a black, wrought-iron fence along the right side of the road, Gert said, "Do you mind if we stop at the cemetery? I want to go in and say hello to my two angels. And Hal's mom and dad, too."

"Oh, Gert! You never mentioned any other children, just Bobby and Tommy. I'm so sorry."

"It's been years since they've been gone. Little Elizabeth was just three months old when we found her dead in her crib. And baby Eleanor, who was quite sickly when she was born, managed to live two weeks. I was devastated each time, but Bobby and Tommy were still very young and needed me. It's true, time is a great healer, but that doesn't mean you ever forget. I come and visit them quite often. Just to say hello and tell them I love them."

Maggie looked at her friend with admiration. She didn't know what she would do if anything ever happened to Maura. The pain and grief her child's conception had caused could never compare to the joy she had received from the moment she was born.

They stopped at the arched iron gate in the center of the fence. It stood wide open. Deciding to leave the pram there, Maggie lifted Maura out, and she and Gert each took one of her hands. Like a synchronized clock, they lifted her up and began to swing her back and forth as they walked down the pebbled walkway. Maura let out gleeful little yelps each time they lifted her.

For the most part, the gravestones on either side of the pathway were flat, set in the ground in neat, long rows. There was an occasional upright stone; these were of various shapes, but all seemed to be cut from limestone.

Directly ahead, at the back of the cemetery, was a white granite mausoleum with the name DARBY etched above the filigreed metal entrance. To the right and left of this structure, the headstones were quite large, varied in shape and color, and mostly of marble and granite. Another walkway ran parallel to the front of these, extending the width of the cemetery.

As they approached the mausoleum, Maggie decided that the intricate grillwork must be brass because of its long-neglected, dark green color. As she peeked inside the grill, she could smell the dank, pungent odor that filled the silent space untouched by sunlight. There were three tiers on either side, with four compartments on each one. Fourteen of these had brass plaques bearing the names of those entombed inside.

"Look at that, Gert! Ignatius Darby, born 1782, died 1836. Wife Agatha Darby, born 1794, died 1849. I didn't realize the history of the Darbys on the island went back that far."

"Oh my, yes," Gert replied as she picked up Maura, giving Maggie the freedom to look around. "Old Ignatius was just twenty-four when he bought this island from the Connecticut Land Company, back East. That was in 1806. His father was in banking back in Connecticut, but Ignatius and his brother Marcus moved into the Cleveland area. After sailing the lake, fishing, he purchased the island and went courting his many friends and acquaintances to settle here."

The appearance of a large dog brought an abrupt halt to the history lesson. Maura began to squirm to get down. "Homie, Homie," she called at the familiar sight of the Cartwrights' wayward dog.

Gert put her down as Homer bounced up to Maura, tail wagging, licking at her face. She squealed and clung to his neck to keep from falling. When a squirrel caught the dog's attention, he was off into the trees, chasing it. Maggie and Gert both laughed at the expression on Maura's face as she stood with open arms, bewildered and deserted.

Gert's family plot was in the far left corner of the cemetery. Maggie felt it was a very intimate moment for Gert, and she didn't want to intrude further, so she took Maura and walked along the rows of stones, reading the epitaphs, awestruck at the numbers of families, from infants to the aged, that had died within days of each other. Whole families wiped out. She knew it had to have been the influenza epidemic by the dates on the stones, for she had heard folks in Herron's Point talking about how it had taken so many of their family members in the late 1800s.

There were stones that told of fishermen drowned in the lake, and graves of young men, some of them mere boys, killed in action during the Civil War. The inscriptions on some of the stones touched her deeply, and as Gert and she left the cemetery behind, she decided she would come back someday to spend more time here.

"Maggie, have you heard from your mam lately?" Gert asked.

"Funny you should ask. I got a letter from her just yesterday. She's doing well and asked me to tell you what a fine person she thinks you are. You know, Gert, I can't thank you enough for insisting I write her."

"You have to admit you were pretty stubborn about it."

"I know. But you were aware of all the circumstances. I really didn't think she'd care what happened to me. It was Penelope that told her where I was. When I got that first letter from her, I was overwhelmed: begging my forgiveness and telling me how terribly she missed me and loved me. That was quite a shock. Mam was never given to big displays of emotion— unless she was angry, of course. We all knew to steer clear of her then. But this was a side of her I never would have expected."

"She's a pretty feisty lady, I admit."

"Yes, and I must say I had difficulty accepting her apology. After the way she'd treated me, I was quite resentful. It took all your prodding to make me realize that those kinds of feelings are not healthy. And she is my mam, after all. When she came to visit last summer, I was so thrilled to see her holding Maura, cooing and crooning lullabies. She held her constantly—when she wasn't cooking something, of course. The unbelievable part was the way she treated Tim. He could do no wrong. She couldn't have treated him better if he was her own son. And she really took a liking to you. She said I could count myself fortunate to have met up with such a wonderful friend. I can't thank you enough for making it all happen. Now, if I could just get my brother, Jack, and Mam to make their peace, everything would be perfect."

Gert smiled. "Well, the two of us will have to get to work on her the next time she visits."

"Oh, I don't think it's Mam that's the problem now. Jack is the one. I wrote and told him in detail about Mam's visit. His response was, 'She'd better not find her way to my doorstep.' I can't say I blame him. He really made such an effort to reconcile with Mam in the beginning, but Mam forbid even the mention of his name. Then with the death of his son and the problems he's been having with Martha, he's really a very unhappy man. His one ray of sunshine is his daughter, Patricia, but he seems to worry about her so much. I think he's afraid of losing her, too."

"Hopefully time will heal all his hurts. Such a nice young man. I enjoyed him immensely when he was here with you. And I must say, he does resemble your mam in looks. Who do you take after, Maggie?"

"My da, so they tell me."

"Well, there's no question your mam and da must have been one handsome couple."

"Thank you. I guess they were. My memory of my da is not so much what he looked like but the way he was. I was only five when he died, and I missed him desperately."

Maggie looked down at Gert, so plain with her mousy brown hair and pale blue eyes.

Gert doesn't realize what a beautiful person she is, Maggie thought. Always complimenting others and forgetting herself. She grows more so each time I see her. There are so many whose beauty fades with each meeting. Her beauty seems to grow and radiate from within.

Division Street ended at a long stretch of stony beach. Farther to the west, there was a large ship anchored at the long jetty that extended some two hundred feet into the lake.

Maggie and Gert stood watching the activity for a moment, and then Maggie turned to Gert. "My goodness, I almost forgot. I wanted you to be the first to know that Tim and I are expecting another baby."

Gert threw her arms around Maggie. "Oh, my dear," she said, "I'm so happy for you! And I'm sure this means a great deal to Tim. When will the big event take place?"

"Sometime in early October, I suspect." Maggie's face reflected an inner joy reserved only for expectant mothers, a joy that makes the plainest of women beautiful. In Maggie's case, her beauty was simply magnified.

The two women turned for home.

Gert knew there were plans to be made and knitting to be done. This adopted family of hers was going to give her another grandchild to love.

Herron's Point—April 1909

Whispering Pines Cemetery was on Quarry Road. At one time, it had been set apart from the rest of the town, accessible by a short side road at the bottom of Frontier Street and separated from the lake by a shallow wooded area. Now it was sandwiched between the quarry and the town and surrounded on the northern side by new housing that had sprung up because of work at the quarry.

Brigid was a frequent visitor there. Father Charles Scanlon was buried under a large yellow birch tree. His stone was the very best polished, silver–gray granite with a slight pinkish cast. Brigid had seen to all the arrangements. His epitaph read: *Charles Aloysius Scanlon, 1858–1906, Devoted Friend and Loving Spirit.*

Brigid's visits commonly brought her here on a Sunday, and she spent her time in conversation, just as she had on those many Sunday walks they'd had together. She generally began her reunion with her good friend by talking out loud, telling him of her week and the activities at Saint Michael's. Then she would grow silent, as though listening for a response, or perhaps she was in prayer. Her visits frequently lasted an hour.

What had brought her here this particular Tuesday was the exceptional weather. She wanted to clean up the winter's collection of leaves that clung in soggy clumps around his large stone and pull the pushy weeds that always seemed to crowd out the spring violets she had planted that very first spring. Brigid saw to it there were flowers for all seasons except winter.

She talked as she worked. "Saints preserve us, Chuck, 'tis a glorious day. And isn't yer tree a picture—covered in green buds. I was wantin' ta get here from the minute I awoke so I could share this day with yourself and me Patrick. Claire and the boarders didn't seem ta take notice of today's abundance, so busy with their lives they are. Although I shouldn't be complainin' about Claire, not with the way she keeps things runnin' at the house.

"And did I mention that I wrote Maggie last week? I'm ferever grateful fer finally listenin' to yer advice. But now 'tis Jack that weighs heavy on me mind. I must have been an idjit. What kind of mam throws her own son out like Monday's wash water? But I wasn't used to being thwarted. Not ever. It's lately I've been rethinkin' me ways. And now I realize that what yourself kept telling me is true. There is no problem fer which love is not the answer. And wasn't it yer up and dyin' on me that made me realize the patience you must have had with meself and me knowin' ways. Fer this I have ta be thankin' ya. Oh, now, would ya be lookin' at that! The violets are lovely. Such a deep purple they are."

Brigid stuffed the debris she had piled up beside her into a bag, got up, brushed off her skirt, and stood back to admire the beauty of the violet patch in front of Father Charles' stone. She was overcome by a sense of silent peace as she walked over to tend to the grave of her husband, Patrick, and to say hello.

Ennis, Ireland—April 1909

Holy Angels Cemetery was quite crowded as people thronged around the open grave of Gracia Mahoney. John Mahoney stooped to pick up the first handful of dirt to throw on the coffin, then stood to one side as the parade of mourners followed suit. He looked desolate, completely oblivious as the others slowly filed out of the cemetery to get into carriages or walk home.

One motorcar remained alongside the stretch of grass adjacent to the gravesite.

Liam and Fiona Harrigan stood at John's side, but try as she might to be strong for his sake, Fiona wailed with sorrow. John threw his arms around her, joining in the wailing. "Sure and it wasn't meant to be like this," he moaned through his sobs. "It was meself that wanted to go first. What good is life fer me now?"

Liam joined the circle, stroking the backs of his beloved wife and brother–in–law. "Shoosh, shoosh, now," he soothed, holding back his own tears. "Gracia wouldn't want ta be hearin' such things. I'm thinkin' not. Sure and hasn't she suffered enough without the two of you carryin' on so? She's finally at peace, now. And, oh, what a glorious day it must be fer her to finally be meetin' up again with her precious son, Paddy."

That thought seemed to have a calming effect on the two of them.

John pulled out a handkerchief, wiped his eyes, and blew his nose. "Ya best be getting' back to the house, Fiona. Before long, half the town will be at the front door again, and your wains will be expectin' directions as to how to feed them all. Liam can drive you back. I'll just stay a wee bit longer. The walk back'll do me good."

Fiona reached up and kissed her brother–in–law on the cheek. "God bless ya, Johnny Mahoney."

She continued weeping softly. Liam took her by the arm and led her to the car.

CHAPTER EIGHTEEN

A Fatal Accident

Darby's Island—1911–1912

"Watch you don't fall," Maggie said, looking up at Gert.

Tell–tale smudges of chocolate icing belied the clean spatula she held in one hand as she braced the ladder with the other. Gert teetered on tiptoe on the top rung, attaching the last of the yellow and green crepe paper streamers to the globe above the kitchen table.

"I just love birthday parties. Don't you?" she said, easing her way back down the rungs of the ladder. She then stood back with hands on hips and a satisfied grin to admire her efforts. "There! I think that looks quite festive."

"Gert, you're twice my age and half my size. Where do you get your energy and imagination? Little Kevin is just going to love it. And where did you ever get the idea for those paper hats you and the children made? They're adorable."

Gert folded the ladder and hauled it to the back porch. When she returned and closed the door, she shut out the raucous laughter of children at play.

"Bit nippy out there," she commented as she began to set the table.

Maggie stirred the applesauce. "It's hard to believe my baby is two years old already. He absolutely adores you, you know. Auntie Gert is his best friend in the whole world."

The aroma of roasting chicken and cinnamon filled the kitchen with warm, delicious comfort as the two friends stood at the back window watching Rosemarie divide her time between the swing and the sandbox and six tots between the ages of two and six.

"Look at her. Just like one of them, having the time of her life. I'm so glad she took the time to visit. Even though I told her it wasn't necessary that she come for Kevin's birthday, knowing her busy schedule and all, she still insisted she wasn't going to miss her godson's birthday, even if it meant missing the first week of classes. I know it's selfish of me to be glad she did, but it's been wonderful having her here. And she's a natural with the children."

Maggie paused and then spoke as though thinking out loud. "But I don't think having a family is in her plans. At least not yet. Not with two more years of college and then medical school."

"You have to admire her for trying to compete in this man's world," Gert sighed. "It's not going to be easy."

"Her father's a doctor. I'm sure he'll help her along."

Maggie went to the stove to check the chicken. "Looks like the bird is just about done. I hope Tim and Hal got off work on time. They should be here any minute, now."

Gert was busying herself mashing the potatoes when Hal walked in, his face ashen.

Something was wrong. That morning he'd said he would

,

stop off at the house after work to clean up for the party. But here he stood, his face grave, covered with the day's dust.

Maggie's cheerful smile faded the moment he faced her.

"Maggie, you'd best get over to the clinic. There's been an accident."

"Oh, my God, Tim!" Maggie screamed. She dropped the platter she'd gotten down for the chicken and raced through the house, out the front door, and down the road toward Everett Street.

Gert looked at Hal's haggard face. "Is it bad?" she asked.

"The worst," he answered.

Sitting heavily at the kitchen table, he cupped his face in his hands. "It was just awful. When the crane he was operating hit a soft spot, it tipped, and he was thrown under. Landed right on top of him. I don't think he's going to make it, Gert," he sobbed.

Gert pulled a chair next to his and began to rub his heaving shoulders in silence. There were no words to express the foreboding dread overwhelming her; she needed no answers as to how the accident had happened, but her spirit screamed out, "Why this wonderful young man?"

The minutes passed in a silence broken only by Hal's shuddering sighs. When shrieks of laughter from outside the kitchen pierced the room with another reality, Gert stiffened. There was a dinner waiting to be eaten and a little boy's birthday to be celebrated. She got up, automatically began cleaning up the broken shards of crockery, and said, "Hal, you're in no condition to eat right now. I think it would be a good thing if you went to Maggie. I'm sure she needs someone with her. I'll stay here. Rosemarie and I will take care that the children enjoy their party. They don't need to know anything just yet."

Hal looked up, his face bloated and smeared with grime. "I think that's best," he answered with a heavy sigh. After washing his face and hands at the kitchen sink, he dolefully walked out the front door.

The Christina Darby Clinic was located on the corner of Division and Everett Streets, just a block away from Water Street and the center of the community's commerce. Boswell Darby had donated the building, and after its completion in August 1901, dedicated it to the memory of his daughter Christina, who had died of influenza two years before, at the age of sixteen.

Prior to its opening, Dr. Phineas Wharton saw his patients at his home, or, just as often as not, made house calls when he wasn't fishing or working in his flower garden. After the clinic opened, Doctor Wharton was committed to regular office hours away from his house, which put a kink in the lifestyle he'd become so accustomed to. But because it served the people on the island so much better, he resigned himself to his new regime. It lasted six months. He died of a massive heart attack in March 1902. Dr. Phineas Wharton was replaced by Dr. Edwin Birch, who arrived with a flourish, bringing his family of fifteen to the island in May of the same year.

Edwin Birch was a doctor by profession, but his passion was growing grapes. To that end, he purchased a large tract of land on the eastern end of the island, and the family went to work tilling the soil and planting the vine cuttings he had brought with him. Eventually a house large enough to accommodate his brood would be built on the same tract of land. In the meantime, he settled his family in a very large Victorian house (originally owned by one of the deceased

Darbys) at the eastern end of Water Street.

It was Gunther Hornung who had dubbed Edwin Birch "Pops." Gunther owned Hornung's Grocery and Sundries at the corner of Water and Division Streets.

At least once a week, Edwin and the better half of his children (the two small ones at home with their mother and the three older ones working his land) would pull up to the front of the store. Gunther noticed there didn't appear to be any hierarchy concerning who drove the wagon. Edwin was always next to the driver, but whoever it was would jump out and tether the horse to the hitching post as the rest disembarked and paraded up the steps into the store.

He also enjoyed the interchange between siblings and father as they encouraged him to get this item and reminded him not to forget that. They all called him Pops. There were so many of them that, along with the other customers in the store, Gunther got the feeling that his business was booming—which indeed it was, when he tallied up their provisions. The rest of his customers also seemed to enjoy the watching, not minding the wait, as boxes of supplies were hauled out to the wagon. By the time Edwin reckoned up the bill, the rest of the crew were snuggled between boxes in the wagon bed, sucking on peppermint sticks, the driver waiting for its last passenger.

As they departed, comments were always made by the remaining customers. "What well–behaved children." "Such a nice–looking family." "My, my. How does he do it?"

Before he moved on to his next customer, Gunther would always shake his head in amazement and say, "That Pops Birch is some fella."

The name stuck.

Dr. Pops Birch stood beside Maggie's chair. "My dear girl, you must be exhausted. It's been three days, now, and you've hardly left this room. Why don't you let me take care of things? Go home and get some rest. I'll notify you if there's any change at all."

Maggie looked up with sunken eyes at the gentle face of the man who until three days ago had just been a slight acquaintance and said, "I suppose I should go home and take a bath and get a change of clothes. I must look a fright. I wouldn't want Tim to wake up and see me looking like this."

She had been clinging desperately to the hope that Tim would survive the devastating injuries caused by the falling crane that had crushed him under its weight. But in her heart of hearts, she knew there was little chance of that. His head injuries had caused him to remain comatose, but it was his broken back that was the reason they hadn't moved him to Mercy Hospital on the mainland for more extensive treatment. She knew she was going to lose her precious Tim.

She leaned over, looking at the handsome face that had not responded to her pleadings for the past three days, stroked his cheeks, and kissed him gently on the mouth. Her body felt like a rock as she rose to leave.

"I'll be back shortly, Pops," she mumbled, then collapsed into his arms.

The clinic was a one–story brick structure: waiting room, office, small surgery and lab, examination room, and two receiving rooms for those who needed special care. Tim was now in one and Maggie in the other.

Pops Birch covered Maggie's sleeping body with a blanket, his heart heavy with sorrow at the knowledge that this beautiful young girl, a mere twenty–one years of age, was soon to be a widow.

When she'd fainted in his arms, he'd taken her to the room next to Tim's. Realizing she was too exhausted to make the trip home, he felt perhaps it was best she sleep right here, where she would be close at hand when the time came, for he knew it would be soon.

He also thought it providential that she was now away from Tim. Her presence almost willed him to stay alive. He'd seen others do the same, clinging to their dying loved ones. By leaving the room, it made it easier, almost as though the dying one now had permission to depart.

Tim's lungs were beginning to fill with fluid. It wouldn't be long.

It was a crisp October morning, brilliant with sunshine. Maggie could hear the drone of Father Christopher Maxwell's concluding prayers as she watched a crimson leaf drift slowly into the open grave and settle on the casket of her beloved Tim.

This past week had been a nightmare of pain so unbearable, she had retreated to a place within herself that numbed her senses and helped block out the stark reality of life around her. When she heard the final "Amen" from the voices surrounding her, her knees buckled. She felt herself supported on either side by Hal and her brother, Jack, as they led her away from the place where a part of her heart would remain forever.

In the weeks that followed, Maggie moved through days in a zombielike state, so consumed by grief she took little notice of the activity around her. Her days were filled with the memory of Tim. Over and over, she relived that last morning she'd spent with him. That was the morning he'd picked up his lunch from the kitchen counter, taken her in his arms, kissed her passionately, looked in her eyes, and said, "I sure do love you, Maggie Ryan," then given her a quick peck on the forehead and was out the door.

Regardless of the weather, she made daily trips to the cemetery and lost herself in silent communication while staring at the brown mound of earth that covered her beloved Tim.

Many evenings, she would walk to the quarry and stand at the edge, looking down into the pit of inactivity below, almost as though Tim's spirit still wandered there. There had even been times when she'd thought of joining him, for her own life held no meaning now that he was gone.

After discussing the situation with her parents, Rosemarie decided that she would forgo this semester at the University of Buffalo and remain with Maggie. It was evident that Maura and Kevin needed someone to look after them, and obvious to all that Maggie was not up to the task. Gert had offered to take them. Brigid and Penelope, who had come for the funeral, had suggested the children go back to Herron's Point with them and stay for a while. But Rosemarie thought they should remain at home, where their mother could see them. Cognizant of the fact that Maggie felt her life was over, she sensed that the children's presence would soon make her aware that she had other reasons for living.

Maura, accustomed to a great deal of her father's affection, was especially affected by his death. Maggie had explained to both children that their daddy had gone to Heaven and would not be coming back, but their young minds couldn't fathom the concepts of death and forever.

It was Rosemarie who filled the void for the children, something she couldn't do for her dear friend. She soothed their tears, read them stories, played games, and sang little ditties as she went through the day, teaching them to sing along with her. After the first snow fell, they built a snowman and went sledding. Rosemarie readied the children for bed each evening. Then the three would cuddle together on the sofa as she read to them.

Maggie, who was always somewhere within earshot, knew that when Rosemarie was done, it would be up to her to tuck the children in and kiss them goodnight. Rosemarie had made that quite clear from the onset. Scooping Kevin up in her arms, Maggie would carry him off to his room, with little Maura tagging behind.

Kevin was an affectionate but quite demanding child who clung to his mother for love. Soothing him with kisses, she would hum a lullaby and stroke his hair until his eyes grew heavy and he was asleep. By the time she'd turn to Maura in the bed next to his, the child was was usually sound asleep.

Staring down at the little girl hugging her teddy bear and sucking her thumb, so peacefully lost in sleep, Maggie began to experience an emotion totally foreign to her nature. It began with the thought that had it not been for Maura, Tim would still be alive. Had it not been for Maura, she would have gone off to school, and she and Tim would still be back at Herron's Point, probably married by now.

Each evening this anger grew until it festered into rage. She found herself snapping at her daughter during the day for no reason at all.

This behavior did not go unnoticed by Rosemarie as she

and Gert made Maura and Kevin the center of all their Christmas plans. To Gert's delight, they spent hours in her kitchen, making cookies. Hal told them he needed their expert opinions as he led them through the woods, searching for just the right tree to chop down. Kevin, who didn't realize the importance of the coming event, was quite content to ride on Uncle Hal's shoulders, but Maura took the entire outing quite seriously.

When they came upon a scrawny Scotch pine, Maura's eyes grew wide. "Uncle Hal, can we have this one?"

There had been many trees Hal had considered along the way, but if Maura chose this one, then this one it would be.

Rosemarie showed the two children how to string popcorn and cranberries, and while Kevin napped, she and Maura made green and red paper chains.

Since everyone realized how difficult this holiday would be for Maggie, it was decided that Christmas would be celebrated at Gert and Hal's house.

Christmas Eve was spent decorating the tree in preparation for St. Nicholas's visit. Knowing the children would be anxious to see their gifts in the morning, it was decided they should spend the night and Christmas day there. Maggie remained at home.

When Rosemarie returned home on Christmas Eve, she found Maggie sitting in the dark and immediately went about lighting up the house.

"Maggie, I know how much you're hurting. I wish I could take some of the pain from you, but I can't. In four days I'll be gone, so for the children's sake, you're going to have to pull yourself together, dear. Your children miss their father, too. Especially Maura. Try to be a little more understanding with her,

Maggie."

Maggie looked at her friend through tortured eyes. "If it weren't for Maura, Tim would still be alive. I don't know how I can ever love that child again."

Rosemarie was incredulous. "Maggie, I can't believe I heard you say that! If it hadn't been for Maura, you and Tim wouldn't have had these last five years together. You wouldn't have Kevin. You wouldn't know Gert and Hal. And Tim absolutely adored Maura. You know that. He would be appalled to hear you speak the way you just did."

"I'm sorry, Rosemarie, but that's how I feel." Maggie got up and went off to her bedroom.

It is said that Christmas is for children because of the anticipation and the magical wonder and joy they experience. But it is all reciprocal. Everyone had a wonderful day—all but Maggie, who refused even to come to dinner.

Rosemarie bundled up the children at the end of the day. Hal gathered all their gifts, hitched up Ol' Gray, and took them home.

Maura, who was the first in the house, went running to her mother, who was sitting next to the window in the front room. "Mama, Mama, look at my beautiful new doll! I named her—"

Without acknowledging her child's presence, Maggie stood up and walked into her bedroom.

Rosemarie, close behind, immediately went to comfort Maura, whose eyes were brimming with tears.

"It's all right, Pumpkin. Mama doesn't feel well today. She'll hear all about your wonderful day tomorrow." Rosemarie would see that she did.

It had been an exhilarating and exhausting day for the children. Kevin fell asleep on the ride home, so Hal removed his coat, carried him in to his bed, deposited all the gifts in the parlor, and said goodbye to Rosemarie.

Rosemarie, quite upset with Maggie, went to her bedroom to speak with her. "Maggie, your children need you to tuck them in bed. Kevin is still fully dressed, and Maura is in there trying her best to take care of herself," she snapped. Then, in a voice almost pleading, she said, "She's had such a happy day. Please don't spoil it for her."

Maggie sighed heavily, got out of the chair next to her bed, and dutifully went to her children's room. She was surprised to find that Maura had removed Kevin's shoes and socks, had covered him with a quilt, and was just crawling into bed in her flannel nightgown—this serious little child, not quite five years old.

When Maggie approached her to cover her and turn out the light, Maura jumped up and threw her arms around her mother, crying, "Oh, Mama, please don't get sick and leave us like Papa did. We love you, Mama. Please, please don't go away!"

That simple gesture touched Maggie in a place she hadn't felt since Tim's death. All bitterness and anger were washed away. The two stood there clinging to each other as Maggie began sobbing uncontrollably, releasing tears she hadn't shed since the day of the funeral.

Maura kissed her mother's cheeks and stroked away her tears. "Don't cry, Mama. Kevin and I will help make you all better."

Maggie sat on the edge of the bed with Maura in her arms, rocking and quietly weeping. When Maura was asleep, she put her down, covered her, and looked down on the little girl with the silky brown hair and regal features, all gifts from the man who had fathered her.

Then she remembered what Tim used to say: "She has your ways, Maggie."

How could she have treated this sweet, innocent child so badly? Her recent behavior toward Maura brought back memories of the folks back in Herron's Point, especially her mam, and how they'd turned their backs on her for something for which she had been blameless.

Before Maggie turned out the light, she once again covered Kevin with the quilt he'd managed to push aside in his sleep, pondering the contrast between the two children. Kevin's black hair and big blue eyes reflected the faces of her mam and her brother, Jack.

She leaned down and kissed each one of her children on the forehead, turned out the light, and quietly closed the door.

Four days later, Rosemarie said her goodbyes to Gert and the children. Maura, who had become quite attached to Rosemarie, clung to her, begging her to stay. Gert distracted both children by offering them a hot cup of cocoa with a marshmallow on the top. That did it.

Hal drove the two friends down to the landing on Water Street, where Rosemarie was to catch the ferry to the mainland. He helped the two women down from the buggy and deposited Rosemarie's luggage on the dock next to a bench.

Rosemarie turned to Hal and embraced him. "Thank you so much for your friendship, Hal. Maggie is so very fortunate to have you and Gert in her life."

Hal returned the hug, gave Rosemarie an affectionate kiss on the cheek, and said, "It's been a pleasure knowing you, Rosemarie. And might I return the same sentiments?"

Maggie watched the two of them and realized she was indeed fortunate to have such friends, then said, "Hal, I appreciate your helping us with the luggage and all, but there's no need to wait around for me. I think I'll enjoy the walk back."

"Pretty nippy weather. Are you sure?"

"The walk will do me good."

Maggie and Rosemarie sat in silence on the cold bench facing the lake. No words were needed as they looked out at the frigid green water, watching the outline of a small ferryboat grow larger.

Time is the master of many events, Maggie mused. Five years ago, this entire lake was frozen over at this time of the year.

When the boat finally arrived in a huff, banging against the dock, splashing white foam everywhere, the two friends faced each other with tears in their eyes.

"I'll miss you sorely," Rosemarie said, "but we both know we must get on with our lives. Now, you take good care of those little ones—and yourself." She embraced Maggie fiercely.

"Oh, Rosemarie," was all Maggie got out before Rosemarie picked up her luggage, turned, and ran to the ferry.

CHAPTER NINETEEN

The Suitor

It had been three weeks since Rosemarie's departure. In the beginning, Maggie barely noticed her absence. Not that she didn't love her friend dearly, but her focus for the past several months had not been on those around her.

Gert had immediately taken up the slack, appearing bright and early each morning. After firing up the furnace to take off the night's chill, she'd check on Maggie, whose only solace from grief seemed to be sleep, then pack the children off to her house for the day.

Maggie awakened one morning to a cold house. She lay there shivering, trying to orient herself to the day. Then it came to her. Gert had told her that she and Hal would be leaving for Albany to visit their son, Bobby. For the life of her, she couldn't remember why, except that it had to do with some kind of surgery.

It had been months since she'd felt any real concern for anyone, and yesterday she'd barely acknowledged Gert's worrisome news. She immediately leapt from bed, wailing, "God help me, this has got to stop!"

All was quiet, and for a moment, Maggie panicked when she found the children's bedroom empty. Then she heard Maura's voice coming from the parlor and gave a sigh of relief. Both children were sitting on the floor, each wrapped in a blanket and stacking blocks.

Maura looked up, giving her mother a big grin. "Oh, Mama, you're up. Are you feeling all better?"

Maggie, relieved that her children were safe, said, "Yes, Maura, Mama's all better. But it's freezing in here. I have to go build a fire. I'll be right back to get you your breakfast."

Maura stood up, the blanket falling from her shoulders. She was fully clothed. "But we already had breakfast, Mama. And I changed Kevin's nappy and dressed him."

Maggie could see that Kevin was fully dressed, even though his shirt was buttoned wrong and his shoes were on the wrong feet. She marveled at her self-sufficient little daughter.

"What a sweetheart you are," she said giving Maura a hug, then shivered. "Brr, I've got to get that fire going."

As she passed through the kitchen, evidence of breakfast was everywhere. Breadcrumbs, plum preserves, and an open jar of her canned peaches sat on the counter. On the smeared kitchen table were glasses of partially drunk milk, bowls, and spoons, and with each step, her slippers stuck to a floor laced with sticky syrup.

Days passed. Gert and Hal returned with the good news. Bobby had come through gall bladder surgery just fine. He and his family were all doing quite well.

Spring arrived, followed by Maura's fifth birthday. There

would be no party, a painful reminder of Tim's accident, but Gert insisted she bake a cake and that she and Hal come over to help celebrate their godchild's birthday.

Maura, ever the little lady, sat primly at the table and thanked everyone for her gifts and for making her birthday a happy one. Maggie once again marveled at her self-reliant little girl.

Maggie's days were filled with the needs and demands of her children. They were the opiate needed during her waking hours to help dull the pain of a wounded spirit.

Doctor Pops Birch could see Maggie and her two children passing by his office window as he put on his coat to leave for home. He'd noticed them from time to time through these past months as Maggie, with the assistance of her little daughter, pushed the pram to Hornung's for supplies, and he'd wondered how she was faring. Those dreadful days she'd spent at the clinic were behind her, now, but she had left quite an impression on him.

There were other things on Maggie's mind besides provisions for the house this beautiful summer's afternoon. Lost in thought, she suddenly became aware of footsteps approaching from behind and turned around to see Pops Birch rushing to catch up. She waited and smiled as he fell into step.

"Hello there, Maggie. Been a while since I've talked to you," he said breathlessly. "And who, might I ask, is this lovely young creature you have next to you?"

Maura looked up and gave him a broad grin.

Maggie stopped walking. "Maura, say hello to the nice doctor, sweetheart."

"Hello, Dr. Pops," she said sweetly.

He and Maggie both laughed.

"And look at this strapping young fella," he said, stooping down to cup Kevin's chin in his hand.

Once again, Maggie directed her son to say hello.

Suddenly, Kevin became quite coy, put his head down, and let out a sound that could possibly be interpreted as hello.

"Looks like he's about outgrown that pram, wouldn't you say?" Pops Birch said as they continued to walk.

Again Maggie laughed. "Without a doubt. But the walk is just a bit too much for his short legs, and the pram also serves to help carry some of the groceries back to the house."

By this time, they had reached Hornung's Grocery and Sundries, and Pops Birch had still not asked. He looked at Maggie with concern. "So how are things going with you these days, Maggie?"

"Actually, not too bad. Of course, I've had lots of support from friends and family, but the time has come for me to find some kind of work to keep us going. I can't continue depending on others."

She paused, and then a thought struck her. "You wouldn't be needing someone to help out at the clinic, would you?"

"I always need someone to fill in if there's a patient recuperating at the clinic, but usually either Elsie Finch or Gladys Grumbacher does that for me. Anyway, that's not the kind of unsteady work I think you had in mind."

He paused in deep thought, then said, "You know, there just might be someone looking. Last week, the Darbys' maid ran off to the mainland with the Kennedy kid. Bernice Darby might be the answer. Let me look into it and get back to you."

Maggie was overwhelmed with gratitude as she thanked Pops Birch and said goodbye. Wasn't this the kind of work she had been trained for all her young life?

Bernice Darby sniffed haughtily and said, "You'll do. I'll expect you here at six tomorrow morning. Cook Thomas will see you get started."

With that, she got up and walked out of the room. Maggie had been dismissed.

Maggie stopped off at Gert's house to pick up the children. Excitedly, she discussed her interview with Gert over a cup of tea.

"Gert, I swear, one of her rooms is as big as my whole house. And I can just picture myself coming down that winding staircase feeling like a princess—even if I am only dusting the banister. Mam's house back in Herron's Point is quite large and beautiful, but this one's a downright palace. And can you imagine, only three people live in that great big, twenty–two room house!"

"So, tell me, what are to be your duties at this palatial estate?" Gert asked sardonically. She detested Bernice Darby and her haughty ways and was not a bit happy that Maggie, who she felt was worth ten Bernice Darbys, would now be subservient to her.

"Well, let's see. I have to help Cook Thomas with the cooking and washing up, I'm to serve all meals, make beds, change linen, and do all the light dusting. Oh, I forgot, polish the silver."

"My goodness, Maggie, that's sounds like a lot of working hours to me. When will you ever have time for your children—

and yourself?"

"It's not as bad as it sounds. After serving lunch and cleaning up, I'm free for the afternoon, until half past six. The Darbys dine at seven, and I should finish up around eight–thirty. I'll also have the second and fourth Sundays off."

Gert took a sip of tea, put her cup in its saucer with deliberation, and looked into Maggie's eyes. She paused, searching for the right words. "Maggie, Hal and I have been discussing your situation, and we would like you and the children to come and live with us. We have plenty of room here. I hate seeing you go to work for that woman. And you know I love the children as much as if they were my own grandchildren. Hal feels the same. That way, you won't have to go to work at all."

Maggie looked at Gert as though she'd hung the moon. She adored her. "I could never allow you to do that, Gert. You've already done so much. But my not working is now out of the question. However, since you did offer to watch the children if I got employment, perhaps it wouldn't be a bad idea if we moved in with you for a while, to see how things go. It would make it easier all around. That way, Maura and Kevin could remain in bed when I left early in the morning, and I could help you around the house in the afternoon. Of course, I'd expect to pay for our share of upkeep."

"Well, then it's settled, much as I hate to see you working for that venomous creature. Let's go get some of the things you and the children might be needing for the next few days."

When Maggie entered through the pantry into the kitchen, Cook Thomas looked up from a pot of oatmeal she'd been stirring, wiped her hands on her apron, and walked over to grab both of Maggie's hands and give them a squeeze.

"My, my," she said, holding Maggie at arm's length. "Master Henry's going to be real thrilled to see this new addition to the Darby staff. Come, sit yourself down, and I'll fix you some breakfast. Just call me Mary. And you are...?"

"Maggie Ryan," she answered. "But Cook—Mary, I don't think you're to wait on me. I'm here to help you fix the breakfast."

"Oh, posh, child. This bein' your first day and all, I think it best I put you at your ease before you begin."

Mary Thomas was tall and stout, but she moved around the large kitchen with purposeful grace.

"Here, have this nice bowl of fresh strawberries and cream and a hot cup of coffee while I set you straight on a few matters."

Maggie found she fit in quite easily at the Darby mansion. There wasn't a task she was asked to do that she hadn't done a hundred times over for her mam. And the flow of guests that filled the house were not a problem for her, after having served the boarders at home.

Henry Darby, having just graduated from Harvard Univversity, had come home for the summer to make plans for his future. He was impressed with the beautiful young maid who now graced the dining room at mealtime. He couldn't take his eyes off her and found every occasion to address her, just to look into her stunningly green eyes. There were also the occasional trips into the rooms she might be dusting, looking for some item or other, or to the kitchen, with the excuse that he was thirsty or needed a snack.

It didn't pass Cook Thomas by.

"Maggie, love, Master Henry has his eye on you. I wouldn't encourage it, though. He's a real mama's boy, that one. And mama would never approve of her precious son taking up with a servant, if you get my meaning. Just a word to the wise."

Henry's motives were a complete revelation to Maggie, and certainly she had no intentions of encouraging him. But Henry felt otherwise. He was totally besotted.

Maggie dried and put away the last pot, took off her apron and little lace cap, unpinned her long hair, and bid Mary good evening. She left for home by the pantry door.

It was a perfect summer evening. A balmy breeze swept in from the lake, caressing her senses with the fragrance of honeysuckle that climbed the trellised walkway leading to the carriage house in back, where Mary Thomas and her husband, Roger, lived in the apartment above.

Affected by an overwhelming melancholy, Maggie paused, then turned toward the front of the house and looked across the street to face the final moments of a brilliant sunset on the water, intoxicated by what her eyes drank in. She was reminded of her father's words: "The beauty of a sunset is Heaven's doorway. God's gift to us. Just a teasin' taste of the glories He has waitin' for us on the other side." She was overcome by a deep sense of peace.

Henry's voice startled her.

"Beautiful evening. Don't you agree?"

Maggie swung around, her arms crossed over her chest. "Oh! Mr. Darby, you startled me. Yes, it is quite beautiful. I do agree."

For a moment, Henry was speechless. The water's mist had curled wisps of ringlets around her lovely face, and the sun's fading rays framed a golden halo around her hair.

Finally, he spoke. "Not quite as beautiful as the young lady watching it. And the name is Henry, Maggie. You can call my father Mr. Darby, but please call me Henry."

"Oh, sir, I couldn't do that. After all, you're practically my employer."

"Well, then, as your employer, I insist." Henry smiled, but he spoke firmly.

Cook Thomas' words were fresh in Maggie's mind. But he seemed a nice sort. About her age, but somehow so much younger.

"I suppose there's no harm in calling you Henry, Henry. But I insist it's Master Darby when I'm in a working capacity at the house. Is that agreeable?"

"Most agreeable," he answered. "Now, let's watch that sunset's final hurrah."

The pair stood side by side, Henry quite aroused by the beautiful young woman beside him, Maggie quite content just to share nature's magnanimity with another.

Dusk washed away all color and covered their world in gray. Maggie turned. "I must get home, now. My little ones will be waiting for their bedtime story. It's my favorite time of the day."

"I'll walk along with you. I was headed for the marina when I saw you standing here. It's right on the way." He didn't tell her he'd been waiting for her to leave the house.

The two strolled the two blocks toward Division Street, oblivious to Bernice Darby's snooping eyes on the other side of her bedroom's lace curtains.

"Do you have a boat at the marina, Henry?" Maggie asked as

they walked.

"Sure do. She's my pride and joy. Named her *Serena* because she's given me so many hours of contentment. And what a beauty."

"What kind of beauty are you talking about?"

"Most people would just call her a sailboat, but she's really a long, sleek racing canoe rigged for sailing. While I was at Harvard, I spent some time sailing on the Atlantic with friends. That's how I fell in love with the sport.

"One Easter break, one of my friends who lived near Marblehead invited me to stay with him, and we spent the week sailing. There was a naval architect there by the name of W. Starling Burgess, and I hung around his shop for hours, watching a canoe under construction. That's when I knew I had to have my own. Paul Butler, a man working for him, designed and built my *Serena*. You can't imagine the planning, time, and pride he took in his work. What a craftsman he is! I envied him the joy he seemed to get from creating something with his own hands."

"It must be quite gratifying to do something you enjoy so much."

Maggie looked at Henry and smiled. She found his boyish enthusiasm comfortable. How long had it been since she'd talked with someone her own age?

"Truly is. There's nothing like it. I take her out on a good day and travel the lake, just *Serena* and me, and head for ports in Cleveland or Buffalo and others in between. Many times, I hunker down and stay overnight."

By this time, they had reached Ben's Marina, lakeside at the corner of Water and Division Streets. It was a three–level structure, the first being a restaurant and saloon with a floor covered in peanut shells, easily accessible from the street; the second–lower level a large deck overlooking the lake, scattered with wooden tables; and the next–lower level a long pier, lined on either side with a variety of lake craft. There was also a small bait shop and another cluster of rental rowboats to the west of the marina. These were available to the many avid fishermen who came during the summer season for the excellent fishing around the island.

Maggie stopped for a moment, expecting Henry to bid her goodbye.

He lingered.

"I would consider it a pleasure to show you my boat, Maggie."

In another life, Maggie would have loved to see his boat, but not this one.

"Another time, perhaps, but thank you for asking," she said. "I really do have to get home right now."

"Then I'll see you to your door."

Maggie became alarmed as she remembered Mary's advice. "No, really. That won't be necessary. You must have things to do. I shouldn't take up your time. Really!"

"Nothing that won't wait." Henry turned to walk alongside her.

Neither of them noticed the necks craning to see out the Emerald Diner's windows.

"Well, will you lookee here," said Luke Winters for the benefit of a handful of customers. "Mama ain't gonna like this. Seems Cinderella's reeled in her Prince Charming."

"Hush your mouth, Luke Winters," said Maisie, the waitress.

"You don't know anything about her. Sweet as she is pretty. Poor thing's still recovering from the loss of her husband. Henry Darby can't hold a candle to the one she's lost."

"I wouldn't mind getting' next to some of that myself," Byron Oaks whispered to Luke, out of Maisie's earshot.

Luke's chest swelled with air he intended to let out with gossip. "All's I know is, whatever Henry has in mind can't last. His mama won't allow it. Her Henry is just too good for the likes of us islanders."

Some heads nodded in agreement.

Luke went on. "Poor Henry. Never did fit in. And God knows he tried. Mind the time him and Dickie Rosen got in that tussle right in front of the marina?"

Most knew the story, but Byron Oaks spoke up. "I didn't live on the island back then. So tell me, what happened?"

Words Luke loved to hear. He spoke up for the benefit of all.

"As I recall, it was the summer after Henry's sister, Christina, died. He was about eleven at the time. He'd been away at some fancy boarding school that winter, and when he came home for summer vacation, Bernice Darby was still in the heavy grieving stage and paid little mind to Henry's coming and goings. That's when he really tried to become one of the gang. Most of the kids went along, but Dickie was used to running the pack, and Henry, spoiled as he was, wasn't about to be pushed around. At any rate, it started out with an in–the–face name calling. Then Henry threw the first punch, and it became a real brawl, with the rest of the kids egging them both on.

"Just happened Bernice Darby was coming out of the dressmaker's down on Water Street and saw her precious Henry rolling on the ground with Dickie on top of him. She marched over, pushed the kids aside, and grabbed Dickie by the ear. You could hear him yelping all the way down to Maple Street. The Rosens were no match for Bernice Darby.

"Needless to say, that was the end of Henry's popularity around here. The kiddos all called him mama's boy after that."

Maisie cleared away the dishes and wiped the counter in front of Byron Oaks. "Pay no mind to him," she said, then looked at Luke. "I swear, Luke Winters, you're worse than an old woman."

The couple walked in silence under a canopy of old maple trees that lined both sides of the street. Maggie breathed in the evening air heavy with the love songs of mating frogs in a pond somewhere nearby, accompanied by the crickets' stringed sonatas along the roadside. She longed for the man walking beside her to be Tim, but he wasn't.

She spoke. "So, what will your future plans be, now that you're a man of the world, Henry?"

Henry was slow to speak. "Banking, I guess. We have family in Hartford and Boston, all in the banking business. Father has me lined up to start in his cousin's bank in Boston this September." He sighed.

"You don't sound too enthusiastic about the prospect." Maggie looked over at his sober face.

"Oh, it'll be okay, I guess. I did fairly well in my studies, and Mother and Father have talked about my doing this ever since I can remember."

"Well, if you could have chosen your life's work, what would it be?"

"Promise you won't laugh?" Henry stopped walking and faced Maggie. Somehow, he knew she wouldn't. "I'd like to be a farmer."

"I understand that's a far stretch from banking, but if it's what you wanted to do, why didn't you tell your parents?"

"I did. I even lined up a great agricultural program at Purdue University, but you don't know my parents. They said that no son of theirs was going to end up a farmer. It was either do as they say or move out. As usual, I did what they wanted. It won't be a bad life, I suppose. But I truly love working with the soil. Most of the landscaping around our house, I designed and planted. There's just nothing like working with nature and getting your hands dirty. That's one of the reasons I love my boat so much. Being part of the elements."

They continued walking.

"How did you ever come to know that's what you wanted to do?" Maggie asked.

"Can't say exactly when I knew, but I know Pops Birch and his family had a big influence on me. I never had many friends here, being away at school all winter and Mother always watching over me in the summer. I guess my best friend was my sister, Christina. She'd spend hours reading to me and playing games to keep me entertained. Come to think of it, she never had too many friends here, either. But when I was almost eleven, she got the influenza and died. I was away at school when it happened. My parents brought me back for the funeral and then sent me back to school.

"Christmas vacation was awful. It was a terrible year for all of us. It seemed there was a big, empty hole in all of our lives. I suppose that's one of the reasons I didn't ever want to disappoint my parents after that. I tried to fit in with the guys around here, but that never did work out, so lots of times that next summer after Christina died, I would just go for walks.

"The following spring, before I'd even gotten out of school, Pops Birch and his family moved to the island. That following summer was one of the best I ever spent. At any rate, on one of my usual walks, I came across Ralph and Dexter Birch leaning against a big old elm tree, eating lunch. They'd been working in a large field, building rows and rows of some kind of arbors. Then along came Betsy, Hoover, and Willis, come to check up on their brothers. Willis was about my age, and we hit it off right away. Well, to make a long story short, I spent a lot of time with the Birch family that summer. Helped with planting vine cuttings and whatever else they were doing. I was never so happy. Pops Birch explained all about the grapes and how they were living, breathing things. He's a great guy.

"I looked forward to my summers after that, and I still spend as much time as I can working with the Birches in their fields, harvesting the early grapes and tending the few side crops they have. Mother gets upset with me when I come home so grimy, but doing that and sailing my boat are the only real pleasures I have in life."

Maggie wondered how Henry could be Bernice Darby's son. There wasn't an ounce of snobbery in him.

They reached Gert and Hal's house. Maura and Kevin were sitting on the porch steps, waiting. When they saw their mother, they came running down the walk, squealing with delight.

If there were ruts and potholes in the cindered road, Henry didn't notice. He was walking on air.

Only once had he even come the slightest bit close to feeling this way. That was the summer his mother's friend came to visit for two weeks and brought her fourteen–year–old daughter, Jenny, with her. He and Jenny became inseparable. He took her to the grape fields with him, they played games with the Birch children, and, before she left, he'd kissed her twice. He thought he would never forget her. He was in love. He never saw her again.

He wasn't completely inexperienced when it came to women. Twice the chaps at the dorm had talked him into going to town for some female companionship. The first time was quite exciting, of course. Although he'd never had sex with a woman and was quite shy about the whole thing, what's–her–name had put him at ease. He knew what to do; that seemed to come naturally. But Thelma—that was her name—showed him a few tricks he'd never have thought of. It was a real pleasurable evening.

The second time was not the same. The woman catering to his needs that night was much older, maybe even twenty–seven or twenty–eight. She seemed bored, and it was over quickly—but not so quickly that she didn't have time to remind him to put the money on the dresser.

After that, he hadn't cared much for that kind of female companionship. He'd also dated a number of young ladies during his college days, and though he didn't seem to have a problem attracting the ladies, he was always pretty much a loner.

With Maggie, it was different. She stirred in him something refreshing and comforting. Just looking into her beautiful green eyes gave him deep, arousing pleasure.

Ben's Marina buzzed with conversation: tourists dining and

swapping fish tales of the day's outings. The air was blue with smoke. Two sets of double doors facing the lake were open to the patrons who sat out on the deck, enjoying their quaff and the balmy evening. Dancing orange lanterns were strung on either side of the deck and continued along the right side to light up the pier below, where boats dipped and rose contentedly in the calm water.

Already, Henry missed Maggie's presence, and he knew he would invite her to join him here one evening.

He approached the bar area, where Ben was entertaining two customers with one of his humorous stories. Henry didn't realize until he'd climbed up on his stool to join them that the two men sitting to his left were Dickie Rosen and Luke Winters.

Each man grudgingly nodded acknowledgment of the other's presence. Henry ordered a beer and decided to move to a table on the deck, when Dickie turned to him with a smirk and said, "I understand you've got an eye on the prettiest girl on this island. Better watch it, Henry, or your mama will scratch her pretty green eyes out."

Henry bristled. It took all he had in him to put his drink on the bar, turn, and walk out.

Ben asked, "What was that all about?'

Luke Winters was only too happy to fill him in.

Henry knew he'd done the right thing. It would have given him great satisfaction to smash Dickie Rosen's face in, but ending up in a barroom brawl would serve no purpose. It was the way of these island folks to thrive on gossip, and that would be the last thing he'd want to fall on Maggie's ears.

He also felt sure that Maggie was completely oblivious to the fact that she was quite beautiful—something that was not lost on those around her, especially men, young and old alike. And there were many of these men, such as Luke Winters, who would jump at the opportunity to reel her in like the catch of the day. She deserved so much more than she had here.

He had about six more weeks to win her over.

When Maggie was working, Henry was quite discreet about his feelings toward her. She addressed him as Master Darby in response to his requests, and he made a point of staying out of her domain. But that didn't stop him from being available to walk her home on occasion, or to bump into her on the afternoons she did errands for Gert: not such a difficult thing in such a small village.

After about three weeks, he decided he had won her confidence enough to ask her to go sailing on her day off.

Maggie was quite taken aback. When was the last time she had been sailing? It was her sixteenth birthday, with Tim. That was over five years ago.

"I don't know if I can arrange it, Henry," she smiled. "I do have to consider the children, since I spend so little time with them."

"Bring them along," Henry responded without another thought. "We'll sail over to Henderson's Park on the mainland— make it a picnic."

"Oh, they would just love that! It sounds wonderful."

So the date was set for the last Sunday in August.

Maura and Kevin were ecstatic over the news, and Gert and Hal had not seen Maggie so excited in such a long time. They couldn't be happier for her.

"Maggie, are you just a little sweet on this man?" Gert asked as the two of them packed a picnic basket the morning of the outing.

Maggie looked almost shocked. "How can you ask such a question, Gert? For goodness' sake, no one can ever take the place of my Tim. He's really such a nice man, though, nothing like his mother, and it must have been quite difficult growing up on this island under her shadow. I think he's a bit lonely. He'll be leaving the island in a couple of weeks, and I'll probably never see him again."

She finished wrapping the chicken sandwiches in a napkin, stopped, and looked at Gert. "You know, I do enjoy his company. He's so interesting to talk to, and he loves that boat of his. It gives him so much pleasure; he just wants to share it with someone."

From what Gert had observed of Henry the few times she had been in his company, her instincts told her that this man did not just love his boat, and he was not going to leave the island without wanting to take Maggie with him.

She said nothing.

It was a glorious day. Henry had made all accommodations for Maura and Kevin's safety. Maggie marveled at his skill in handling the boat while the weather smiled on them with blue skies and a good wind as *Serena* cut through the water.

After about an hour's sail, they docked at the Henderson's Park marina and found the beach area to be quite crowded. Passing through the small clubhouse, they walked up a sloped walkway to the picnic area and considered themselves quite lucky to find a picnic table under a large oak tree. Henry whisked the children off to a large play area while Maggie busied herself setting out lunch.

Flashes of her last picnic on the icy lake with Tim, laughter over the enormous amount of food Penelope had packed for them, their excitement over their great adventure, the otters, the eagle, her last memory of Herron's Point, the storm, their igloo—all of it began to wash over her, flooding her memory with pain. She sat down on the bench and sobbed, overwhelmed with sorrow.

At some point, she heard distant laughter and realized that she had to pull herself together. She didn't want to spoil the day for Maura and Kevin—and, for that matter, Henry, who had been so kind to include them in this day. Slowly she rose, walked down to the lake, and cupped her hands for water to soothe her swollen eyes.

Maura came racing back to the table first, shouting, "I won! I won!" Kevin followed, grabbing on to her skirt to keep from falling, then Henry, who said, "These two are just too fast for me."

After a wonderful lunch, the children played with a ball, rolling it back and forth while Maggie and Henry sat at the table watching them as they talked.

All of a sudden, Henry stood and shouted, "Let's hit the water!"

Maggie and Maura headed for WOMEN, and Henry and Kevin, MEN. They found their spot on the beach and spread out a blanket. Maura and Kevin ran to the edge of the water with pails and shovels, while Henry and Maggie got comfortable on the blanket and leaned back to watch.

Henry slid his hand over and laid it on Maggie's.

She immediately withdrew.

Henry turned on his stomach and propped himself up to look in Maggie's eyes. "Maggie, surely you must know how I feel about you. In two weeks, I'll be gone, but I love you so much I can't imagine going without you."

Maggie sat upright and looked out toward the lake. "Oh, Henry, please don't say that," she said almost pleadingly. It was all she could do to hold back the tears she still had cupped in her heart. "I think of you as a friend. I can't tell you how much I've enjoyed having someone like you to talk to. You've made my days without Tim so much more tolerable. But please don't spoil it." Then she looked at him and smiled. "If it's any consolation, I would have found you to be quite attractive at another time, but my heart is still aching for the man I've loved for as long as I can remember."

Henry didn't show his disappointment and said, "I was hoping to take you with me as my wife when I left for Boston. But I'm a patient man, Maggie. I'll give you time to heal. I only hope this doesn't mean we can't still be friends in the meantime."

"I consider myself fortunate to have you as a friend, Henry. But that's all we can be, friends."

Henry knew he'd be going to Boston alone. "I can wait."

"And they pulled up to the dock, nice as you please, him carryin' one sleeping child, her the other. Must've been all of nine o'clock Sunday night," Myra Walters told Flo Pierson.

That's all it took. The barber shop buzzed, the beauty shop hummed, and Luke Winters was in his glory at the diner with the goings-on between Henry and Maggie.

Bernice Darby didn't mingle with the island people, but she did get her hair done every Saturday, so it took a week before she was privy to the by now grossly exaggerated news that her son was carrying on with the Ryan girl.

When Cook Thomas told Maggie that Mrs. Darby wanted to see her, Maggie was hopeful she might get a small raise in salary. She'd been there almost three months, and she knew Mrs. Darby was quite pleased with her work. Mary Thomas had told her so. "Said you were the best she'd ever hired," were her exact words.

Bernice sat stoically behind her desk as Maggie entered the library.

"Cook Thomas said you wished to speak to me," Maggie said softly.

Bernice looked her in the eye and said, "Here is a check for your services. We won't be needing them anymore." She handed her the check, stood up, and left the room.

Maggie had definitely been dismissed. It took her a few minutes to digest what had just taken place, and then she began to cry.

Gert was furious. "How dare she treat you like that? That pompous old twit! Who does she think she is?"

The two women sat at the kitchen table as Maggie wept.

"She's not worth your tears, Maggie. You're well rid of her and her old job. Here now, have a nice cup of tea."

Maggie decided to move back to her own house. Gert and Hal begged her to stay, but she insisted they'd done enough. Living with them, she'd managed to save a little money, and she could take in some ironing and do a little sewing. That way, she could spend more time with the children.

Maggie had tied a scarf around her head and was sweeping down the cobwebs from the corners of her neglected house when Maura came running in. "Mama, Mama, our Uncle Jack's here all the way from Buffalo!"

Maggie dropped the broom, ran, and threw her arms around him as he came in the front door. "Oh, Jack, it's so good you're here!" She smiled and caressed his cheek with her hand.

"Maggie, you look wonderful. You're even beautiful with that rag around your head and dirt on your nose."

Maggie blushed. "Come. Come sit down. Tell me all about Martha and little Patsy. And what brings you here, for Heaven's sake?" She couldn't contain her excitement as she watched her handsome brother settle himself in a chair, cross his legs, and smile up at her.

"Sit down, Maggie. I have some very good news for you."

Maggie was intrigued. "What kind of good news?"

"Well, I know you don't remember Grandmam and Grandpap Mahoney. They left for Ireland when you were just an infant. But do you remember me telling you that Grandmam Gracia died?"

"Oh, yes. I do remember you telling me that the summer I was pregnant with Kevin."

"Well, Grandpap and I have always stayed in touch, and six weeks ago, I got news that he had passed away."

"My goodness, Jack! I wouldn't call that good news."

"Well, no, not that part. He was an extraordinary man. Actually, Martha and Patsy and I went over there to visit him last year. We had a wonderful visit, and although he was quite old, he seemed in good health. But Aunt Fiona did say he'd never been the same since Grandmam Gracia died."

He paused as if recapturing some treasured moments of that visit, then said, "You are aware that he was quite a wealthy man?" He looked at Maggie.

"Oh, my Lord. He left me some money?"

"Well, I have to tell you that that 'some' is quite a sum. You now have two hundred thousand, five hundred and ninety-nine dollars in the First National Bank in Conneaut, Ohio. I deposited it there before I took the ferry over here. I also brought you two thousand in cash for your present needs."

He watched the blood drain from Maggie's face.

Jack spent the afternoon helping Maggie move furniture around. While she was preparing dinner, he spent his time on the front porch, getting reacquainted with his niece and nephew.

Henry was nonplussed as he came up the walk. He had no idea who the good-looking man on Maggie's front porch was, but he was quite relieved when Jack introduced himself as her brother.

Henry apologized profusely to Maggie for his mother's actions, but somehow none of that mattered to Maggie anymore.

She invited Henry to stay for dinner, and he and Jack hit it off very well.

After a pleasant evening together, Henry left for home.

Maggie and Jack sat together on the porch swing. "Nice fellow," Jack commented.

"Yes, very," was all Maggie had to say.

"Well, it's been a long day, my dear sister, and I have to be up early, so I think I'll turn in."

"I turned your bed down, Jack. Maura and Kevin are sharing tonight. Have a good sleep. I'll wake you in the morning and see you off."

He got up, kissed her on the forehead, and went in the house.

Maggie sat for quite a while, trying to sort out the day. It was hard to believe. She would never have to worry about money again. She could live in her house, raise her children, send them off to college, whatever. She could do it now.

Jack settled in bed, pleased that his news would make Maggie's life so much better.

But that Henry fella, Jack thought, he's the one for her.

It might take some time, but he had a feeling that Henry was up to the task. One look at his face when he looked at Maggie, and you knew he was madly in love.

Yes, Maggie, my love, you've a good life ahead of you.

They were both wrong.

CHAPTER TWENTY
Past Sins Revisited

These past six years with Helena had not gone well for Robert Arnaud, especially since her last miscarriage. All they did these days was snipe at each other, and the thought of spending his evenings with her had grown stale long ago. When she said she would be going back to Quebec for a prolonged stay with her family, he quickly agreed it would be for the best.

With Helena gone, he felt like a young colt let loose in a field of opportunity. After several weeks pursuing his pleasures—with the greatest discretion, of course—he began to grow restless with the senselessness of it all. He decided he needed a vacation away from the stresses of work, family, and social demands that had claimed him for so long.

Memories of his stay at Herron's Point kept popping into his head. Such a peaceful town; he'd been happy there. He wondered about Maggie Mahoney. Had she married that Tim fella? Perhaps not.

He called ahead to make arrangements for his stay and gave notice. He'd be gone for two weeks.

The train depot was a welcoming sight—in need of a little paint, but Zeb was there to greet him. Each thought the other hadn't changed one iota.

Robert embraced Zeb like an old friend and climbed up on the buckboard. As old Princess clip–clopped slowly down Broad Street, Zeb reminded him of the last time they had been together, the day he'd had to take him to the station and put him on the train.

"Thought it best to get you to the dining car. I asked the porter to pour as much coffee in you as he could."

Robert laughed. "You know, I barely remember getting home, that trip. That must have been some luncheon we had."

He leaned back to enjoy the view. "Still as pretty as a picture," he said. "Nothing seems to have changed at all."

Zeb spit and looked ahead, considering the man sitting next to him.

Either he's innocent of wrongdoing and knows nothing of the changes, which would make Mrs. Mahoney right, after all, or it just makes no difference to him. Pretty cool, this one.

Zeb drawled, "There's lots what doesn't meet the eye. I think you'll be findin' that out as you go along. Fer instance, this trip, I'll be droppin' ya off at MacPhearson's Hotel instead of Mahoney's boarding house."

"Yes. I was quite disappointed when I was told there was no room for me there. I was looking forward to sitting down at Mrs. Mahoney's table. I remember the last time you and I rode down this hill. When I told you where I would be staying, you said I was in for some real good eatin', and how right you were."

"Well, Mrs. Mahoney still owns the place, but she don't live there no more. She has a young woman run it for her, name of

Claire."

Zeb shifted his chaw, spit at a maple tree along the side of the road, and looked at Robert. "Truth be told, she'll never set a table like the missus, but she comes pretty close to it."

Robert looked surprised. "What happened? Did Mrs. Mahoney get sick? She seemed in very good health the last I saw her."

Robert's demeanor confounded Zeb. If he had done something wrong, he certainly didn't appear to be aware of it. Zeb didn't know how much he should say. Well, best he take him to Mrs. Mahoney. Let them have it out.

"Mrs. Mahoney has a piece of land facing the lake. Bought it about five years ago and built a restaurant there. People from all over these parts and even some from the States come just to eat there. She's changed the whole town into a regular tourist spot. I've never dined there personally," he put his nose in the air, "but havin' sat at her table for many years, I can understand why it's a popular place. Perhaps you'd like to stop off and see her first. I can take your bags up to the hotel."

"Splendid idea, Zeb. I knew Mrs. Mahoney was an ambitious one. Turns out she's a pretty smart business lady, too."

When they pulled up at The Elms restaurant, Robert commented, "Isn't this that Tim Ryan fella's property?"

"'Twas. But he sold it to Otto Klein's brother, Gunther, when he and Maggie went off across the lake. They ended up in a place called Darby's Island. Mrs. Mahoney bought it from him the following year, double the price he paid, cleared the lake front for a beach and bathing, and had this here restaurant built."

"My, there truly have been some changes." Robert climbed down from the buggy. "Well, Zeb, once again, thank you for tending to my needs. I'll be seeing you around town, I suspect."

"Yes sir, Mr. Arnaud, I 'spect you will."

As Zeb drove away, Robert stood looking at the sprawling one-story structure with its inviting green canvas marquee. Holly and other evergreens bordered the building, and geraniums and ivy spilled out of the window boxes under the windows on both sides of the entrance. Although most of the land had been cleared for the building, some of the wonderful old elm trees had been spared, giving the entire area an ambiance of peaceful contentment. Because of the lunch hour, the parking lot on the left side of the building was filled with automobiles and a few buggies. Beyond that, he could see a beach area filled with bathers.

As he stepped into the small reception area, an attractive young woman approached. "Will there be someone joining you, sir?" she asked with a smile.

"I won't be staying for lunch, but I would like to make a reservation for dinner this evening around seven."

"Certainly, sir. And the name?"

"Arnaud. Robert Arnaud. And miss, is Mrs. Mahoney around? I'm an old friend come back to visit."

"I believe she's in the kitchen, sir. I'll go tell her you're here."

She checked her book to make sure she'd written his name correctly and disappeared.

Robert looked into the dining area. Pewter chandeliers filled the room with soft light. There was a large stone fireplace that took up almost the entire wall on the left. Seascapes were perfectly arranged on the pale green damask walls. Tables were covered in white linen, crystal, silver, and fine china. The two waiters tending tables wore white shirts, gray vests, black pants, and extremely shiny black shoes. A baby grand piano in one corner boasted a huge bouquet of flowers. There was also a screened–in area facing the beach and lake that seemed to run the entire length of the dining room. Almost all the tables were filled.

No question, he thought. This is fine dining.

A waiter approached. "Will there be just one for lunch, sir?"

"Actually, I'm waiting to see Mrs. Mahoney. I was just admiring your dining room."

"It is rather nice, isn't it?" the waiter said as he headed toward the kitchen.

The pretty young thing returned. "I'm sorry, Mr. Arnaud. Mrs. Mahoney said she was done overseeing the luncheon menu and has gone to her apartment. Said she has a very bad headache."

"I'm sure she can take a minute to see me, but I'm afraid I don't know where her apartment is."

The receptionist paused. She'd gotten the feeling Mrs. Mahoney didn't want to see her visitor. But then how could that be? He was quite good–looking, and so charming.

"Just go out the door. Her apartment is to the right part of the building. Actually, it will be to your left as you leave. The entrance is at the side." She batted her lashes and smiled. "Will that be all, sir?"

"Thank you, yes. You've been most helpful."

Robert found his way to the side door and tapped lightly. When Brigid opened it, he gave her his most charming smile.

It was not returned.

"What do you want?" she spat at him.

"Mrs. Mahoney, don't you remember me? I'm Robert. From the shipping company. Remember?"

"Oh, and would I be likin' ta ferget? Yes, I remember you and yer charmin' ways only too well." She stood fast in the doorway.

Robert was completely baffled. She was not going to let him in. This was the lady who had clung to his every word. She had made it clear to him that he would always be welcome back. What was the matter with her?

"What have I done, dear lady? I thought you would be glad to see me."

"What have ya done?" she screamed. "What have ya done? Ya brought shame on me house, that's what ya done. Ya raped me poor sweet Mary Margaret and fathered her child. That's what ya done!" Her face was purple with rage. She slammed the door.

Robert stood frozen.

How can this be? How can she accuse me of such a terrible act?

He walked slowly toward MacPhearson's Hotel, overwhelmed.

It took him the best part of the afternoon to digest the information he had been given as he paced back and forth in his hotel room.

Was he capable of performing such an act? From past experience, a part of him knew the answer. He had been accused of many things he had no memory of, and all because of his inability to handle alcohol.

He recalled his wedding night—or, rather, his inability to remember it. It was a large social event with the reception at the

Clariton Hotel. Helena's family had come in from Quebec and taken rooms there, and he and Helena were to stay the night and go off to Paris for their honeymoon the next morning. During the reception, he'd shared a toast with just about everyone. No one had a better time than he did. He refused to believe what Helena later told him about his actions that night. It had taken days before she brought him to the realization that his behavior toward her own sister, in her hotel room, was demeaning and humiliating.

"She found you there, stark naked, in her bed!" she'd screamed.

Needless to say, the honeymoon had not been what he'd expected. But he dealt with Helena as he had his mother so many times before, explaining that he'd gotten the rooms mixed up, and it didn't take long for his charm and doting attention to win back her love and forgiveness.

But in the past six years, there'd been two other such incidents—which, added to the fact she'd had two miscarriages, pushed his wife further and further away. He found his charm no longer gained him absolution for his blatant indiscretions, and there were no words of consolation he could give that would make up for the loss of their last child. Now she was in Quebec.

There was still time to save his marriage. He'd go to Quebec to beg Helena's forgiveness. He'd win her back with the promise that he would never take another drink. Not one.

But Maggie! Sweet Maggie! How could he have hurt her like that? And there was a child—his child. He knew he would have to see her to make amends.

Zeb had said that she and Tim had moved to Darby's Island.

There were several boats for hire down at Kelly's Marina. Robert chose Dumpy Watson's because his little cruiser was the newest and looked the most comfortable.

Dumpy stood at the helm, Robert at his side, as they cut through extremely choppy water.

"You know, this Lake Erie can get mighty fierce," Dumpy said. "It can be downright treacherous. But to put your mind at ease, I want you to know that this ain't nothing to worry about."

Robert, quite familiar with the lake's moods himself, assured him he was not concerned.

"So you're headed for Darby's Island, eh? Not much call for folks going over there. Although I did take Mrs. Mahoney and Penelope and Clifford Benchly there about a year ago this coming October. They was going to a funeral for a local man, Tim Ryan."

Robert's ears pricked up. "Tim Ryan! Why, I knew him. He was just a young fella. What happened?"

"Terrible accident, I understand. Don't know the details, but I guess it happened at the quarry where he worked. Left that gorgeous wife of his widowed with two young ones to raise."

"Would that be Maggie Mahoney?"

"One and the same. Why? Did you know her?"

"Yes, I got to know her fairly well. I stayed at the Mahoney boarding house about six years ago. And you're right, she is a beauty. Charming girl."

"Huh," Dumpy snorted. "Not according to local folks. Got herself in a family way, she did. Her mother put her out, you know."

Robert winced.

"Then she had the nerve to have a regular wedding in the

church and act like it was nothing. Folks in our town don't take to loose women like that. But you gotta hand it to her mother. She kept her head held high. Done a lot for our town. Did you get a chance to eat in her restaurant?"

Robert knew it wasn't the choppy water that was making his stomach churn.

Oh, Maggie, what have I done?

Dumpy gave him a curious look, and Robert realized he was waiting for an answer. "No, sorry to say. I did have a reservation for last night, but I had to cancel. I hope I can find accommodations on the island."

"They have a fairly large hotel on Water Street. Shouldn't be a problem, since the summer tourists have about dwindled out."

Dumpy pulled up at the landing dock. "I'll pick you up here tomorrow morning about nine, like we talked about."

Dumpy moored the boat, put Robert's small valise on the pier, and pointed. "The hotel's up the road a piece. You can see the sign on that roof above them trees—Lakeside Hotel. Enjoy your visit."

He was just a dot on the water by the time Robert walked slowly up the small hill to Water Street and turned around to look.

It was too late to turn back. This was not a visit he was going to enjoy.

He found the hotel to be adequate, a fisherman's paradise, and sat on the edge of the bed to consider his next move.

This is a small community, he thought. Not much different than Herron's Point. I don't want to be inquiring after Maggie and her whereabouts. After what I heard on my way over, she's endured enough gossip in her young life. It's only three o'clock. I suppose their Town Hall is still open. Surely there's a directory there. That's what I'll do. And no telling if she has snoopy neighbors, so I should probably wait until after dark to call on her. Oh, Maggie, I just want to make things right!

Robert got the information he needed and spent late afternoon at Ben's Marina, having the best catfish dinner he'd ever eaten.

After dinner, he sat back and watched an intense competition between two men playing darts. A man by the name of Luke Winters pulled up a chair near him to agitate his two friends at the dartboard, and soon Robert found himself caught up in a spirited conversation with all of them. He spent the rest of the evening playing doubles with Luke Winters as his partner. They won—four out of seven.

When he looked out toward the lake, he could see the lights had been turned on. It was time to go.

Luke had to leave also, commenting on the fact that his wife kept him on a short leash, and he'd be in for it as it was. So the two of them left together.

Luke headed up Division Street, and Robert went back to the hotel to freshen up before he went to find Maggie. The pleasant afternoon he'd spent had helped relieve him of his purpose for being there, but it didn't disappear. It crept back like an anchor weighing heavy on his heart.

Maggie sat on the porch swing, perfectly content, watching Maura and Kevin play in the front yard.

Five days ago, she thought, I would have been sitting here worrying about the future. Jack's visit changed all that. It was wonderful to see him again, but the news he brought changed my whole life.

The burden of making the house livable again had actually been fun for her as she moved from room to room, cleaning, planning, and making a list of the things she needed to buy to make her home more attractive. As she sat, gently swinging back and forth, she made more plans: outside paint, flower boxes, screens for all over the house.

"Oh, mercy," she said softly to herself, "you can't spend it all at once."

She got up. "Maura! Kevin! Time to come in and get ready for bed."

Two young girls ran screaming down Division Street.

"There's a dead lady! There's a dead lady on the beach!"

Breathless, they ran into the town hall to find help.

Constable Woppy Nelson was sitting at his desk eating a sandwich from the diner when he heard the ruckus. He rushed into the hall. "Here, here. What's all the yellin' about?"

Marcie Pincus, from records department, had her hands full trying to calm the two hysterical children and hurried to him. "The children say there's a body on the beach. Poor things are scared witless."

"Keep these kids here and calm them down. I'll go check it out."

Everyone within earshot of the screaming followed Woppy.

Maggie's lifeless body was there, her neck broken and her clothing covered with grime.

Woppy had been constable on the island for the past seven years, and all he'd ever had to do was maintain the peace. The biggest crime he'd ever solved was a series of house break-ins by a delinquent teenager. He'd wrapped that up pretty quickly;

the family left the island. But murder? Incomprehensible!

He knew everyone that lived on the island would look to him to solve it. But how? There was no evidence. She was fully clothed. There were no signs that she had been sexually assaulted.

Why would anyone want to murder such a beautiful young woman? He knew her, just like he knew everyone else on the island. Seemed like a nice young thing. He'd heard the gossip about her and that young Darby lad, but he didn't pay much mind to petty gossip. But that's where he'd have to start, by questioning Henry Darby.

When he was told Henry had left the island the same morning Maggie's body had been found, he sent a telegram to the Boston police with the particulars and asked if they would seek him out and question him. They complied and got back to him on the matter by saying the man was overcome with grief at the news. He had seen the young lady the night before around nine o'clock to say goodbye, and she had been in good spirits. That was all they could tell him.

Woppy couldn't fathom the thought that anyone in the village would commit such an act of violence, and he considered the fact that a stranger to the island might have done it.

Everyone in the diner was buzzing with news of the murder. Most were of the mind that it had to be Henry Darby, spurned and angry at not getting his way. Spoiled rotten.

When Woppy asked if anyone was aware of a stranger in their midst the day of the murder, Luke Winters nervously spoke up. "Sure was. I remember this fella I met at Ben's. We played darts the whole afternoon. Kind of an uppity sort. He pronounced his name, Robert, the way a Frenchman would. But

I don't recall his last name. We parted about nine o'clock, and he headed back to the hotel. That's all I know about him. Except he was darned good with the darts."

Woppy checked at the hotel.

"Yes, there was a Robert Arnaud registered. He was the only one that left early yesterday morning, somewhere around nine. No, he left no forwarding address."

Woppy checked with the captain of the ferry.

"No, I brought no new people to or from the island that day. Tourist season is about over now."

That meant this Arnaud fella would have had to come by private boat. But who brought him, and from where? And why?

Woppy was at a dead end. He knew he would have to talk to the oldest child, something that went against his grain, but perhaps she could shed some light on the night of the murder. He decided it would be best to wait until after the funeral to do that.

It was Jenny DeMarco that broke the news to Gert and Hal. Jenny was at Hornung's for groceries when she'd heard that Maggie's body had been found. As Gert's neighbor, she was well acquainted with Maggie and her children. She was quite overcome herself, but she knew someone would have to go fetch Maggie's children, thinking they were probably still alone in the house. Gert would be the one to go get them. Oh, those poor young things!

As she approached Gert's back door, she could hear the chatter of young voices and was relieved they were already there. She asked Gert and Hal if they would please step outside for a moment. From the gravity of Jenny's expression, Gert knew not to question her request.

"I'm so glad the children are with you," Jenny said.

Gert was overcome with a sense of foreboding. "They came over looking for their mother," she replied. "It's not like Maggie to leave them like that, but I told them she'd probably run to the store to get something for their breakfast. Why, Jenny? Is there anything wrong?"

Jenny was finally able to muster the courage to tell them that Maggie's body had been found on the beach.

A deep groan came out of Hal. Gert began to scream and immediately covered her mouth so Maura and Kevin wouldn't hear her. Hal caught her as she fainted.

Family and friends came in waves for the funeral service. Jack arrived first on his boat, *The Mariner*. Rosemarie and her parents traveled from Buffalo and arrived by ferry. Dumpy Watson made two trips, first bringing Brigid, Penelope, Clifford, and Zeb, then Clara, Agnes, and the Baughmans. They all took rooms at the Lakeside Hotel.

Father Maxwell decided to hold the funeral service in the vacant lot next to Saint James Church, knowing that because of the nature of Maggie's death, probably everyone on the island would attend. The little clapboard building could hold at most fifty people. He was right. He set up his altar table and chairs in the field and made the service as brief as possible; then they all went to the cemetery, where again, he kept his prayers and comments brief.

Friends, neighbors, and mere acquaintances all gathered at Gert's house, overflowing into the yard. Gert had had little to do with the preparations. Jenny had seen to them all, and the islanders had been more than generous in supplying mounds of food.

Jack was the last to return from the cemetery, where he found his mother inconsolable. No matter what had passed between them, his heart went out to her. If he had any regrets over his neglect of Maggie, he had at least kept in touch sporadically. And though his mother's relationship with Maggie had recently changed, he was aware that her grief must be multiplied because of her treatment of Maggie before she left Herron's Point. He knew neither of them was responsible for Maggie's fate. What they were both guilty of was being too wrapped up in their own lives to have considered hers that much.

He walked up to Brigid and embraced her. They both wept.

After all but close friends and family left, it was decided through many tears, and with Jack's insistence, that it would be best for the children to return with him to Buffalo. He was young, and his large house needed more children to fill it. He also knew Patsy would be thrilled to have her cousin Maura as a companion, and perhaps having more activity around the house would help Martha out of her depression.

Kevin cried for his mother to return, but he was too young to realize that she wouldn't. Maura knew from her memory of her father's death just the year before that her mother had joined him. Her little heart was broken.

Before his return to Buffalo, Jack had been asked to stop off at the town hall with Maura so that Woppy could question her. Jack insisted he be present, which was agreeable to Woppy.

Maura sat primly on a straight–back chair in front of Woppy's desk, her hands folded in her lap. Jack sat behind her, against the wall, in the sparsely furnished room.

Woppy wasn't sure how to begin. "Maura, sweetheart, I was wondering if you remember anything about the night before your mother died." He was amazed at the composure of this young child.

"I don't remember too much, Mr. Woppy. Mama put us to bed, and she was just fine. I did get up for a drink of water and heard her out on the porch talking to Mr. Darby. He's such a nice man. He took us on a picnic one Sunday over at Henderson's Park. They were talking real nice, and I went back to bed. I fell asleep, but then I woke up when I heard my mother's voice. It sounded like she was at the end of the driveway, but she was loud. Mama never raises her voice like that. And I could hear a man's voice, but it was real low. I fell back asleep, and that's all I remember."

"Did you know what your mother was so upset about? Did you hear what she was saying?"

Maura considered this question for a moment. "No, I couldn't say. It was too far away for me to hear what they were talking about."

"Did you recognize the man's voice?"

"No. It was too far away. I told you."

"Do you know of anyone who would want to hurt your mother?"

"No." Maura began to cry. "My mama was nice to everybody." She jumped out of her chair and ran to her Uncle Jack.

Jack stood, picked her up in his arms, and said, "I think she's been through enough."

Woppy nodded. "I agree. I'm sorry I even had to question her. But I have no clues whatsoever to go on."

He walked over and patted Maura on the back as she buried her head in her uncle's shoulder and sobbed.

"You're a brave young lady, and thank you so much for talking to me."

Jack nodded, shook Woppy's hand, and left.

They were a sorry lot standing on the dock. The group from Herron's Point had left the day before, sometime in late afternoon. Rosemarie and her parents had stayed over one more night and had already gone by ferry earlier that morning. Brigid remained behind to stay with Gert and Hal for a few days.

Maura and Kevin clung to Gert's skirt as Brigid plied them with kisses, her face wet with tears.

Brigid turned to Jack. "Sure and be seein' they come ta visit next summer. And bring Martha and Patsy, too. Me life will nivver be the same after this day, I'm thinkin', but there is somethin' good come out of it all." She hugged Jack as fiercely as she had the day before.

Jack's emotions were raw. He'd lost his sister, gained back a mother, and taken on two children as wards in a matter of days. But he knew that somehow he had to keep his composure for the sake of the children.

He smiled down at her and assured her they would keep in touch. Then he turned to Gert and Hal. "I know how difficult this must be for the two of you, losing Maggie and the children you helped raise. But I promise you they will be back next summer."

What could they say? There were no words to explain how their lives had been torn asunder, that all they held dear was being ripped away from their daily existence. Yet they knew that what was being done would ultimately be the best for Maura and Kevin.

Hal shook Jack's hand, and Gert stretched up and kissed him on the cheek.

Then she knelt down, embraced Kevin, then Maura, saying, "Sweet girl, watch over your brother. I know how difficult this is for you, but if you act like a big girl and get on the boat without causing a fuss, your brother will do the same thing. That would make Auntie Gert so happy. Will you do that for me?"

After many tears, Maura hugged and kissed Gert and Hal and her grandmother, then took Kevin by one hand and Jack by the other and obediently boarded the small yacht. Jack weighed anchor and set sail. At some point, he looked back to the island and saw three desolate figures standing on the dock, still watching his departure. He looked at his niece and nephew sitting on the bench near the helm and thought, They may be orphaned, but they're not penniless.

CHAPTER TWENTY-ONE
New Beginnings

Kevin and Maura were awestruck. They'd never been in an automobile before. And there were so many of them everywhere. They gaped up at the tall buildings and became absorbed with all the people rushing here and there. This was a world they had never known existed.

The hubbub was soon left behind, and small stores and houses took its place. Jack approached a roadway framed on both sides with brick pillars. The brass plate embedded in the right pillar said GARDEN ESTATES. All the houses along the way were quite large.

Maura had seen only two such houses this size on the island, the Darby mansion and Pops Birch's house. She knew the Darby mansion was special, but wondered if all these houses were filled with as many children as the Birch house.

When they turned down Willow Lane and into the driveway, both children stared. We're going in here?

Jack had no qualms about going in the front entrance of this house. Since they'd moved, Martha now had a full-time, live-in maid. Emiline Washburn was still their cook.

As soon as they entered the foyer, Patsy ran to her father and wrapped her arms around his legs. Peeking around them, she gave a half smile to Maura and then a small, flapping wave with her hand.

Martha stood speechless for a moment, then, without so much as a nod to Maura, went to Kevin and scooped him up, kissing him on the cheek. He looked so much like her Johnny it was as though her son had been returned to her.

Martha wasn't unkind to Maura, just indifferent, as she had always been to her own daughter. She doted on Kevin.

Although the transition for the children was difficult in the beginning, after several months, the rhythm of family life seemed to fall into place. Maura and Patsy had become inseparable, and Jack was overwhelmed with Martha's transformation. Her depression was gone.

True to his word, Jack took time in early June to take his family, including Martha, to visit Brigid.

Brigid was overjoyed, taking as much time as possible to spend with her grandchildren and going out of her way to be nice to Martha. Jack was pleased.

She had reserved the third floor of the boarding house for all of them. Since Kurt Baughman had developed severe arthritis, he and Elsa had asked if they could have Brigid's old room on the first floor. That way, they didn't have to take the stairs. That worked out well for the summer rentals because the third floor could actually accommodate two families.

Jack's first trip back to Herron's Point had been filled with trepidation. How many years had it been? Twelve. He needn't have concerned himself. He was greeted passionately by the same boarders he'd left, all but Zeb, who, not to be left out, quickly made his acquaintance. He'd forgotten how much these people had meant to him.

As he walked around town, he observed the many changes that had occurred during his absence. He couldn't help notice all the ROOM TO LET signs in so many windows. The presence of numerous automobiles indicated to him that there were many tourists in town; he knew from experience that for the most part, the people in Herron's Point walked wherever they needed to go.

Water Street had been completely transformed. The Point was still there, with its freighters and barges anchored at their docks, but Kelly's Marina was three times as busy as he remembered, and the lake was dotted with pleasure craft and fishermen.

He strolled the boardwalk with its lampposts and benches, noticing people lolling along in their bathing suits. Carl Herron's statue still gazed out at the lake, but it was not quite as large as he'd remembered and was also a little greener around the edges. The park along the boardwalk was still dotted with picnic tables, swings, teeter totters, and slides, but the shrubbery that had once bordered the backs of the buildings on Commerce Street had disappeared, and a new feature had been added, giving the entire area a holiday atmosphere. A walkway had been constructed to approach the many shops along the periphery—souvenir shops, art stores, tackle shops, and concession stands. People along his way sunned themselves on blankets, and children played on the grassy turf.

Then there were the beach and bathhouse and his mother's

restaurant at the west end of Water Street. Leveling that beach had been the stroke of genius that had changed everything, and Brigid's fine cooking was the drawing card.

His mother was a woman to be reckoned with. He was proud of her. He realized that in many ways, Brigid was a changed woman. Maggie's death had done that. Those weeks after the funeral, she'd stayed on with Hal and Gert and had pushed Woppy to keep the investigation of her daughter's death ongoing. Woppy was only too happy to oblige, not wanting such a terrible tragedy to go unsolved while he was in charge. Unfortunately, all of his efforts wound up at the same dead end. Brigid returned home and consumed herself with her new plans. Work was her solace.

By week's end, everyone had had a grand time. Patsy, who had always been painfully shy, was beginning to show signs of asserting herself—Maura's doing. Kevin adored Martha. They all loved Grandma. And now it was time to leave.

Jack planned on stopping at Darby's Island to drop Maura and Patsy off at Gert and Hal's. They would spend the rest of the summer there. Martha insisted that Kevin was too young and should stay with her.

After her family had gone, Brigid took a walk up to the cemetery.

She approached her husband's grave. "Patrick, it would be so proud of yer family you'd be, I'm thinkin'. Jack is so successful. And was I tellin' yourself about Jack's new store? That makes four all tagether. And glory be ta God, those wee ones! I think I've been mentionin' more than once how much our Maura looks like her da, and more so as time passes, but she's got me Mary Margaret's ways, prim and proper, quiet and determined, and so bright! Ah, me heart aches at the thought of her. Nothing that Woppy fella or anyone else has done to find out what happened to her has turned out to give us any information. It seems we'll never know what happened to our sweet girl. Visitin' with all the others has been a real solace."

Then she turned to Father Charles. "It's like ya said, dear friend: Love surely is the answer to all problems. This past week is proof of that. I know me arrogance and pride pushed me family away, but God saw fit ta give them back ta me because of you. Me dear friend Chuck, how many times do I have ta keep thankin' ya fer showin' me the error of me ways and love ta me grievin' heart after me Mary Margaret was killed?"

Brigid pulled a few weeds and neatened the two gravestones, then returned to her restaurant with a grateful heart. She would look forward to the following summer.

CHAPTER TWENTY–TWO

Growing Up

Darby's Island and Buffalo—1923–1927

Gert took a batch of sugar cookies out of the oven and set them on top of the stove to cool.

"I can barely contain myself, I'm so excited. Just think, Hal, tomorrow this house will be filled with noise and activity— youth."

She poured herself a cup of tea and refilled Hal's cup.

Hal wrapped his hands around his cup, slowly sipped his tea, set it in the saucer, looked at Gert, and grinned. It did his heart good to see her so happy. It had been ten years since Maggie's death, and the first two were ones he'd rather forget. But time had passed, dulling the pain of the wrenching void that had overwhelmed them so.

Maggie was the daughter they'd never had, and Gert had mourned her loss quietly but deeply, as he had. Their only assuagement had been the summer visits Maura and Patsy made. Kevin came along one year, but he seemed more content to stay with his Aunt Martha rather than tag along with the two girls. Now their life was centered around those visits.

"I know how you feel," he said. "It sure will be good to see those two again. They're growing up, Gert. I couldn't get over how Maura had blossomed last year. She was always such a gangly youngster with that silky, flyaway hair. Now she's all filled out, almost as tall as me. But her hair, straight or not, is sleek and shiny. Reminds me of the color of mink. Patsy, on the other hand, always was a pretty little thing. Still is. She always outshone Maura in the looks department, but I think our Maura is coming into her own. She doesn't look like her mother, but she sure seems like her."

"Do you recall how timid and backward Patsy was the first year they stayed with us? She's come a long way from that. And it's all to Maura's credit, I think."

Gert sighed, and her eyes misted as memories of Maura as a small child filled her mind. "She's got her mother's disposition, without a doubt. Always quick to smile and wanting to please. But I think she's got a bit of her grandmother Mahoney in her, too. She's always been such a resourceful child."

Hal nodded. "You know, I think you're right." He spent a moment deep in thought, digesting this new revelation, and quickly added, "I never considered that before, but, yeah, you're right!"

Gert got up and handed Hal two cookies. "That will be it, mister! See to it you keep your hands out of the cookie jar. These are for the girls."

"Wonder what time of day they'll be coming in?" Hal mused.

"Midafternoon, I suspect. If I know Brigid, she'll set them down to a big breakfast, one that will probably hold them over till dinner. Then there's the last minute packing and all the fare–

thee–wells. The trip here takes a quite a few hours. So my guess is late afternoon. Past years, it's been that way—first week of June in Canada, then here. It does my heart good to see Jack and his mother coming so close. I find it consoling that he and Martha have taken the children there every year since Maggie died."

Maura loved the excitement of the lunch–hour activity in her grandmother's kitchen. As a child, she'd sat on a stool and watched. Now she pitched in where needed.

She was aware of the pride Brigid took in showing all her grandchildren off, but she knew that Brigid had always been partial to her for some reason. Probably because it was she who loved to spend time in the kitchen; Patsy and Kevin preferred the beach. Her grandmother had taught her a lot through the years, and Maura thought her an amazing woman.

When Brigid first opened her restaurant, she hired a number of people to help her. Mornings were spent making pies, cakes, and breads. She opened at eleven and did all the major cooking herself. She had an hour or two of rest before the dinner hour.

It was a much more demanding business than she'd anticipated. But work had become an opiate, easing the pain of regret for mistakes she'd made with her children. After Maggie's tragic death, she worked even harder than before, falling into bed each night dog tired.

When the business began to take off and she could no longer handle it all, she hired a chef, then two assistants, and later a girl who did nothing but pastries and salads. Now she simply oversaw the needs of the workers and checked that the presentation of the entrees was to her satisfaction before they were sent out to the dining room.

Having Maura in her kitchen was a joy she would never be able to express to the child. She reminded her so much of her Mary Margaret.

Maura removed her apron and said, "Grandma, since the lunch rush is over, I think I'll go out on the beach for a while."

"Go, child, go. Wasn't I tellin' ya not ta be spendin' yer time in here with me on your last day?"

"But I like being here, Grandma. Besides, it'll be a long time before I get to see you again."

Maura flashed her smile, and Brigid's heart melted.

"Don't be forgettin' ta remind your Uncle Jack ta have ya all here at seven sharp. I have a sumptuous feast planned."

"I won't forget."

Maura entered Brigid's apartment by the kitchen door. Before changing into her bathing suit, she walked to the picture window facing the lake, where she saw Patsy on the beach, surrounded by a bevy of young men vying for her attention.

Patsy had always been a little on the shy side, but Maura had noticed lately that her cousin could handle this kind of attention easily—unlike Maura, who felt nothing but discomfort around boys her age. Being taller than most of them, Maura found them to be rather silly. But Patsy was petite and soft, with eyes as blue as cornflowers and golden curls that framed an angelic face. Why wouldn't the boys fawn over her? And she seemed to like it.

Then she saw Kevin being chased by two girls with buckets of water.

There's another one, she thought. Not quite fourteen, but

already popular with the girls. Aunt Martha has spoiled him rotten.

Her Uncle Jack had explained the reason for that a long time ago, but Maura could never understand why Aunt Martha would prefer Kevin over her own daughter, even if he did look like her dead son, Johnny. But no question, he was growing up spoiled and self-centered and would soon be as handsome as his Uncle Jack.

Now in her bathing suit, Maura approached Patsy. All the boys just stared.

"I'm going for a swim, Patsy. Want to come in?"

"Naw, I don't think so. I went in earlier. I'll just stay here and get some sun." She rolled over on her stomach.

Maura caught up with Kevin, and the two of them spent the rest of the afternoon playing in the water.

Jack and Martha had rekindled a number of friendships from the old days and had plenty of visiting to occupy them for the week. In the evenings, the family ate at the boarding house.

Maura loved that. Each year there were always a few strange faces at the table, but she'd come to know the Bauchmans and Zeb and had become quite close to the elderly Carter sisters, who seemed to take such an interest in her.

She also spent some of her late afternoon time in the kitchen with Claire, talking as she watched her prepare the meal, helping if time permitted. She loved to hear Claire sing as she went about her work and sometimes joined in.

Some early evenings, she and Patsy would walk over to Aunt Penelope's house and visit for a while. They both loved Uncle Clifford. He was so funny. Once in a while, Maura would catch Penelope gazing at her with a strange, wistful look. She wondered about those moments and decided it was because she missed not having children of her own.

Tonight they would be dining at The Elms. Brigid had not exaggerated. It was a sumptuous feast with preferential treatment. She served a fine white wine, crusty French bread, lobster bisque, stuffed flounder, and asparagus vinaigrette, and there was a cart filled with a selection of French pastries.

This party had become the culmination of their visits for the past ten years, one in which Brigid actively participated. Because Penelope had a vested interest in Maggie's children, she remained close to them on their visits; she and Clifford were always included in the farewell dinners. Brigid had come to consider her one of her dearest friends. This had developed following Maggie's death.

Jack watched his mother with interest. She was no longer the young beauty she had once been, but she was a handsome woman, her raven hair streaked with silver. Her smile effervesced as she circulated among family and friends, interacting with each one on such a personal level—touching, hugging, making sure they wanted for nothing. She'd made her mistakes, but it was obvious she wanted to make amends. It warmed him to see his family together and his mother so happy.

Breakfasts were not served at The Elms, but the departure of Brigid's family was an exception. She cooked and served it herself, then walked with them to Kelly's Marina and watched as they sailed away on Jack's new yacht, *Sweet Maggie*.

Before Brigid went back to work, she walked to the cemetery. She had to tell the two special men in her life all about the past week's events.

After an overnight visit with Jack and Martha, Gert and the two girls walked them down to the dock the following afternoon and watched them depart for Buffalo with Kevin in tow.

Strolling back to the house, Maura turned to Gert and asked, "Aunt Gert, would you mind if we went to Pops Birch's house? I don't think Marietta and Joanie know we're here, yet, and we can't wait to see them."

"That's fine, child. But don't forget to be back by six. Uncle Hal will be hungry after a day's work, so we can't keep dinner waiting."

Marietta and Joanie were in the kitchen helping their mother with lunch dishes when they heard the girls at the back door. They ran out on the porch. Joanie grabbed Patsy and Marietta hugged Maura, the four of them jumping up and down in circles amidst whoops and hollers.

"Hey, what's all the racket?" The screen door slammed, and Michael came out to join them. He looked at Maura, then Patsy. "My, my, aren't you two growing up! So, how's the world treating you?"

Patsy batted her lashes and said, "Just fine, Mr. Birch. And you?"

"Hey, now, what's with the 'Mr.' stuff?"

Patsy pushed a curl away from her face and smiled coyly. "Well, after all, you are a man of the world now—big college man and all."

"True enough. But the name's Michael." He looked at Maura. "I've been in the fields all morning and was just going for a swim to cool off. Would you all like to join me?"

All the girls agreed they would.

Maura said, "We'll have to go get our suits, Patsy, and tell

Aunt Gert where we'll be." Then she looked at Michael. "I'm sure she won't mind, but she worries about us, you know. We'll just meet all of you there."

Of course Gert didn't mind. She knew the girls were excellent swimmers, but it had only been last year that she'd permitted them to swim in the quarry, due to the water being so deep. Like the other children on the island, they had learned to swim in the shallow water at the beach—under her supervision. But the older kids preferred the quarry, and for good reason. Unfettered by watchful adults, they could swing from a rope, jump or dive into the cool, pristine water, and swim with abandon.

Maura and Patsy walked toward the north end of Division Street and turned onto a path that led through the woods toward the quarry, Patsy chattering all the way.

"I wonder if Hank Braid and Skinny Oyler will be there? Remember last year how Skinny was showing off on the rope and did that humungous belly smacker? Knocked the breath right out of him. Then he came back to shore and acted like he'd tried to do it that way all along. Those two were such pests. I hope there're some cuter boys there today. Now, Michael, he's really cute. A little old for me, but cute. How old do you think he is, Maura?"

"I'm not sure, but he's finished his second year of college, so I guess he's about twenty, maybe twenty-one."

"There sure were a lot of kids in that family. How many still live at home, do you think? I never could keep track of them all."

"Mary told me she had eight brothers and six sisters. I know Dexter is the oldest. And he still lives here on the island, married with four children of his own. He runs the vineyards for his father. Mary said that most of the older brothers and sisters had gone away to school, but whether they had or not, they were gone, scattered all over northeastern Ohio. I think Michael is the oldest one left at home. Then there's Mary and Joanie and the two youngest, Timmy and Bert. But it's hard to tell with so many of them always coming back to visit. "

"Their mom looks pretty good for having all those kids, don't you think?"

"She sure seems to have a lot of energy. But I suppose after the first ones got bigger, she had a lot of help with the younger ones."

As they approached the clearing at the quarry, they could hear the laughter and splashing of a happy group.

"Hey, you two. It's about time you got here," Marietta said as she came running toward them, her hair dripping on her shoulders.

The three girls found a rock to sit on to watch the activity. It didn't take long for Skinny and Hank to spy Patsy, and soon there were five boys crowding around them with myriad questions for Patsy.

"How've you been doing? When did ya get here? What was school like last year? Gosh, you look great."

Maura knew Patsy would never go in the water. This was her idea of swimming.

She and Marietta dove into the water.

When Maura surfaced, she was face to face with Michael. "Hi, pipsqueak," he grinned. "Race you across the lake."

"You're on," Maura said as she treaded water.

"Since you're a girl, I'll let you start first," he said imperiously.

337

"I don't think so, Michael. We'll do it even-steven," she responded, just as imperiously.

"Okay, go!

They were off.

Maura was an excellent swimmer, and her slender body cut through the water with ease. When she reached the other side of the quarry, she saw Michael climbing up on a ledge of rock.

He extended his hand to help her up and said with a grin, "Not bad for a girl."

Maura smacked him on the arm. "Show off." She sat down to catch her breath.

"Ah, this sun feels so good." Michael leaned back on his two arms and lifted his face to the sky. "Isn't this great?"

Maura gave him a curious look. She had known Michael all her life, but it was as though she had never seen him before. He had an athlete's body, strong, straight features, and a shock of rusty brown hair. Until today, she would have described him as the one in his family with those big dimples that turned his face into sweetness when he smiled. He'd always been so much older, just another one of the bigger Birch kids.

"Michael, Patsy and I were wondering how old you were. Do you mind telling me?"

"I'll be twenty-one in November. Why do you ask?"

"I don't know. You always seemed so much older than that. Just wondering, I guess."

"And how old are you, young lady?"

"I was sixteen last April."

"My, my, you're getting old," he teased.

"What are you studying in college?" she asked, changing the subject.

"Well, I hope to be a veterinarian," he answered seriously. "But I still have four more years to go. I hope I can make it. Pops says I've got the stuff to do it, so we'll see."

Maura and Michael sat on the ledge of the quarry for well over an hour, talking and watching the swimmers on the other side. Maura was amazed that she could be so comfortable with anyone of the opposite sex other than her Uncle Jack. When they swam back, they didn't race. It was a leisurely swim with conversation all the way.

Patsy was still on shore holding court, and Maura suggested they should get back to the house to help Aunt Gert with dinner. Patsy grudgingly got up and followed, insisting the boys need not walk her home. She'd be back the next day.

"I saw you on the other side of the quarry with Michael. What was that all about?" Patsy asked as they walked through the woods.

"Oh, nothing, really. We had a race and ended up there. It was fun."

Patsy laughed. "So much fun you couldn't tear yourself away?"

"Oh, come on, Patsy. He's just a nice guy. We talked about everything—his school, his family—life. You should know. You spend enough time talking to all those boyfriends of yours."

"To tell you the truth, I don't have to talk too much. They do all the talking—about themselves. One has to outdo the other. And I pretty much just listen."

"Doesn't sound like much fun to me."

"Oh, but it is when you know they're doing it because they want to impress you. I like their attention."

"Well, I can understand why they do it. You certainly are the prettiest girl around."

"Thank you, Maura. But I think there is one prettier."

"And who would that be?"

"You, you big ninny."

Maura realized that Patsy had always looked up to her and followed her lead in everything since they'd been young children. She considered this compliment to be nothing more than Patsy's admiration for her.

The following day was a stormy one. Both girls lounged in their bedroom, reading and consuming the last of Aunt Gert's cookies. By mid–afternoon, the rain had relented.

"I'm going for a walk down to the lake," Maura said, sitting at the edge of her bed and looking at Patsy in the bed across from her. "Want to come with me?"

"Naw. I'll keep reading. I'm just getting into the good stuff."

"You and those romance novels. Don't you get tired of reading the same thing over and over again? It's all fluff and puff, no substance."

"Ah ha! You'd be surprised what little techniques I've picked up in the romance department. Not that I've ever had to use any of them. But someday I will. It's important to know how to handle the man in your life." She was dead serious.

"Patsy, I don't think you have a worry there. You're a natural."

Patsy turned on her stomach and propped her book on her pillow. "Have a nice walk."

Maura loved the fierce beauty of the lake after a storm. The sky was a blanket of gray with a hint of gold on the horizon that seemed to promise it would be right over.

She settled herself on a dock belonging to the Darby

mansion across the road. No one was living there anymore. Aunt Gert had said Bernice Darby couldn't stand being separated from her precious son, so they just up and moved to Boston—keeping all their interests in the island, however. Gert wouldn't tell her it was because some of the islanders felt that Henry Darby was responsible for her mother's death and wasn't welcome on the island anymore. Her mother's murder had never been solved.

Maura thought of her mother as she sat there, watching the waves swell and collapse, crashing against the rocky shore. The dock was high enough to protect her from a good drenching, but she managed to get misted from time to time. It didn't matter; the air was warm, and she was home.

Many times, her mother had brought her and Kevin down to sit and look at the water. Not in this spot, of course, but today her mother was very close to her. She still missed her. She loved her Uncle Jack and was grateful for all the things he'd done for her, and Aunt Martha was okay, but it had taken a few years for Maura to be able go to bed without crying in her pillow. She'd tried very hard to keep it to herself for Kevin's sake. He had been so little. But it hadn't taken Kevin long to attach himself to his Aunt Martha. She doted on his every move.

Maura got up and walked toward the large stone mansion. A FOR SALE sign was in the front yard, which caused her to wonder who the new tenants would be. Curiosity took her to the front porch, where she could peek into the windows.

Moving from window to window, she could see rooms big enough to cover her Aunt Gert's whole first floor. Cupping her eyes with her hands, she looked through the big oval glass in the front door. It revealed a large foyer and a spiral staircase at the far end.

"How grand," she whispered.

"Hey, there, missy. What are you up to?"

The gruff voice startled her. She swung around to confront a middle–aged man in coveralls standing at the bottom of the steps, holding a rake.

Maura ran down the steps. "Oh, sorry, mister. I didn't mean any harm. This is such a beautiful house, and it looked empty. I was just curious."

Roger Thomas knew who she was. He'd seen her around and watched her grow up summer after summer after her mother's death. Best to keep that subject closed.

When he realized he'd frightened her, he tried to put her at ease and chuckled. "No harm done. And it is a beautiful house, isn't it? Don't blame you at all for being curious."

He shifted his rake from one hand to the other. "My name's Thomas, Roger Thomas. My wife and I live in the carriage house in the back. The Darbys kept me on to look after the place till it's sold." He sighed. "But there's not much call for a mansion on this island."

Maura relaxed. He seemed like a nice man. "Maybe when I grow up, I'll just come back and buy it," Maura said jokingly. "Then you can stay and work for me."

They both laughed.

"My name's Maura Ryan. I'm staying with my Aunt Gert and Uncle Hal for the summer. You know them?"

"There's no one on this island I don't know. Been here all my life. They're great folks."

Roger started toward the back of the house, and Maura followed along to head back home. "You enjoying your summer here?" he asked.

"Just got here two days ago, but I love it here. This is my happy place."

The pair parted at the back yard.

"It was nice meeting you, Mr. Thomas. If I see you again, I'll surely say hello." Maura headed down the street toward her house.

Matt nodded with a smile and stood watching her until she was out of sight. What a charming young girl, he thought. Reminds me of her mother.

He went back to his raking.

Summer days unfolded like the petals of a flower, sweet and fragrant. By summer's end, Maura was in love.

Michael had won her heart in so many small ways. The way he cocked his head when he was thinking, his casual smile and wonderful sense of humor, his gentle voice, the tender care she'd seen him take of a wounded rabbit—all these things were part of the package that had been revealed to her as the days passed.

They rode their bikes all over the island, explored hidden paths, skipped stones on the water, swam in the quarry, and had a picnic. He took her to the fields and explained the art of growing grapes, then to the winery where his brother, Dexter, proudly showed her around. That was the day the three of them sat at a table under an old apple tree in the orchard next to the winery and sipped on a sweet white wine Dexter had named Icecap. The sun was shining, the sky was azure studded with white fluff, there was a gentle breeze, the locusts droned, birds chirped, and the company was perfect. Maura felt she had slipped into paradise.

It wasn't quite as easy slipping into the house before dinner to take a quick nap. She had to get rid of the buzz in her head. Gert caught her teetering to her room and was furious. She made it quite clear to Michael the next time she saw him that Maura was too young for that sort of thing, it was also against the law, and it had better not happen again. Michael was deeply apologetic and promised it wouldn't.

The day before the girls were to return to Buffalo, Michael asked Gert's permission to take Maura to dinner, and Gert reluctantly consented.

Maura was quite excited at actually going out on a real date and got out her pink dress and white sandals, the only dressy outfit she had brought with her.

Patsy fussed with Maura's hair, piling it up, trying to (according to her) put a little oomph in it. But the silky strands kept slipping down, so Patsy gave up, pulled it back into a long braid, and tied a pink ribbon on the end.

She stood back, admiring her work. "There. I think that shows off your beautiful face. And the ribbon matches your dress perfectly. Now put on these crystal earrings Mom gave me to finish it all off."

Michael picked her up promptly at six, and they walked hand in hand to Ben's Marina. It was the first time he'd actually held her hand, and it was thrilling.

Ben's was not too crowded, and they were seated immediately. Their preference was the deck.

Luke Winters was at the bar when they came in. Always with an eye for a pretty face, he watched the pair walk out on the deck to find a table, turned to Ben, and said, "Really hard to believe she's almost grown. She was just a tyke when her mother was killed. Pretty thing, but nothing compared to her mother. Maggie Ryan was the most beautiful woman I've ever seen."

"Sounds like you had a little crush on Maggie, Luke."

"A lot of good that would've done me. If I'd even looked at her sideways with Nancy around, she would have made my life a living hell. I swear she's the most jealous woman I know."

Ben knew Luke had given his wife plenty of cause to be jealous. He also wondered when Luke was home long enough for Nancy to make his life a living hell. He'd heard rumors, around the same time Maggie Ryan had been murdered, that Nancy had threatened to leave him. Luke seemed to have taken her threat seriously for about two years, but now he was back to hanging around his old haunts, doing what he'd always done. Ben figured that Nancy had just plain given up.

Maura and Michael sat out on the deck, soaking up the balm of the evening. Both ordered the catfish dinner and chattered on about the events of the summer—Patsy, Marietta, Joanie, anything, avoiding the most obvious subject. Tomorrow Maura would be gone.

When they'd both had their fill, Michael suggested they go sit on the pier by the water to watch the sunset. They sat at the very end, dangling their feet and looking toward the west to a large globe of brilliant orange. It began to work its magic, an artist with a palette of color saturating the lake and clouds with intense shades of pink, gold, silver, and crimson.

Maura sighed. "My mama loved the sunset. She always said it reminded her of her da. When she was a little girl, her da would say to her, 'Come on, little Maggie, let's take a walk down to the lake and watch God open his doorway.' Now the sunset reminds me of my mama."

Michael looked over at Maura's wistful face. It was the first time she had ever mentioned her mother. "You still miss her, don't you?"

"Desperately."

They sat in silence and watched the sun dip behind the horizon. Its masterpiece lingered a bit, but the door was now closed.

"Let's go for a walk," Michael suggested as he stood, extending his hand to help her up.

They strolled east on Water Street and turned down a side road abutting the Birch house, Maura following Michael's lead. Twilight was waning as they entered the orchard.

Until now, he had kept their conversation light and humorous. Now he turned to Maura, put his hands on her shoulders, gazed deeply into her eyes, then pulled her to him and held her, his cheek against hers.

Maura became limp. She could feel his hard, strong body against her, and she returned his embrace. This was a moment she had dreamed about often these past months.

He whispered in her ear, "Maura, I'm going to miss you. I love you." Then he kissed her fiercely.

When he finally released her, Maura cupped his face in her hands. "Michael, I love you, too. But I have to go back. And you have to leave for school next week. And—"

Michael put his finger on her lips, then kissed her again and again, draining the strength out of her.

She began to teeter. They sat on a bench, his arm around her, her head on his shoulder, listening to the symphony of nightfall.

Before they reached Gert's house, they stopped, embraced, and kissed again.

"You promise you'll write often?" he asked.

"Every day, if I can. And you write me. I'm really going to miss you. We'll see each other next June. It's going to seem like forever, but it'll get here."

They lingered on the porch. Michael held her hand tightly as they gazed into each other's eyes.

Finally Maura leaned up and kissed him on the cheek. "It's been a wonderful evening, Michael. I'd best be getting in."

Michael gave her hand a squeeze. He knew he had to go quickly. It was the only way. He turned and took the steps in one leap. "Don't forget, write," he called over his shoulder. "G'night."

She watched him sprint down the street. She was in the house by ten.

Gert looked up from her knitting. "Did you have a nice evening, dear?"

"Mm," Maura responded dreamily and went to her room.

Much as I hate to see her go, Gert thought, it's a good thing she's leaving tomorrow.

Gert was in the front of the house, weeding a bed of marigolds, when Jack came up the walk.

"You're early, Jack. I didn't expect you until this afternoon." She stood, removed her gloves, and brushed off her knees.

"I have to get Patsy back to pack. She's leaving for Cleveland tomorrow to start school there, you know." He looked around. "Where are the girls?"

"You just missed them. Joanie and Marietta Birch stopped

by on their bikes, and the four of them went off for a farewell ride. They shouldn't be gone long, though. They're all packed and ready for you."

She led him to the top porch step, and they sat down to wait. Hal came out on the porch, shook Jack's hand, and joined them.

"I'm glad they're not here just yet," Gert commented. "Maura told me about her quitting school and going to work for you. And about Patsy going off to Notre Dame Academy for girls. I asked some questions, but I'm not quite clear on it. How did this all come about? I thought Maura loved school."

"It actually started with Martha. You know how Patsy draws the boys to her. She's still quite innocent about all this attention, but there's no doubt she likes it. Martha felt she should go away to a private school for the next two years, and I had to agree it was a good idea. Of course Maura was included in these plans, but Maura didn't want to go. Then one day she came to me and said, 'Uncle Jack, I really would like to work in the office of one of your stores. I do like school, but I think I would learn much more about the business world if I worked for you.' Did you know she used to stop by my first lumber yard after school and help out the bookkeeper until dinnertime?"

"She's a bright one," Hal commented, nodding at the air. "Always was real quick with the numbers."

"She did mention something about that," Gert added. "But don't you think she should finish school first?"

"Yes, and I told her so. But she insisted that since Patsy would be away, she'd rather do this. I finally came to the conclusion that she was probably right. What she'd pick up in the next few years at the lumberyard would definitely prepare her for the business world much more than two extra years of high school. Then there's the fact that Harold Biner, my bookkeeper at Lumberyard One, will be retiring come January. I suspect that's what got her thinking about it all. Before he leaves, he'll have plenty of time to break her in. And I've no doubt she can do the job."

They saw the four girls rounding the corner on their bikes, and all stood up.

Gert looked at Jack. "You've done a grand job raising those two girls, Jack, so who am I to criticize? I'm sure it's all for the best."

She waved. "Hey, girls! Look who's here."

CHAPTER TWENTY-THREE

New Horizons

Maura threw herself into her work—six ten-hour days each week. She loved it. In her free time, she wrote to Michael and Patsy and lived for her return mail.

Patsy came home for the holidays, filling her in on all the details of the great parties the school had. It seemed the boys from Saint Vincent's School nearby were always invited. She'd met some really cute ones.

Michael wrote he was doing well at school, but each letter told her he missed her desperately. Her responses were much the same.

One thing Maura had not considered when she went to work for her Uncle Jack was that she would no longer have her summers free. Uncle Jack said she could have a week visiting her grandmother at Herron's Point and another with her Aunt Gert and Uncle Hal: two weeks. This began to register with her sometime during April, around her birthday. She was now seventeen.

She'd written to Michael explaining all this, telling him how much she was looking forward to seeing him. His return letter devastated her. He would not be able to be home that week in June. He would be working as an apprentice for a veterinarian near school, in Columbus, and also taking summer classes. He needed the work to help with his education and would continue the classes for the next three summers, so that he could graduate a year early.

The first week in June, Maura and Patsy spent their family time at Herron's Point, renewing old acquaintances. Maura still marveled at her Grandma Mahoney's endless energy.

Then on to Darby's Island, where she'd always felt she was coming home. Although she was showered with the love and affection of Gert and Hal, this year there was something missing.

She and Patsy stayed the week, then returned to Buffalo, where Maura went back to work while Patsy spent her summer with a whole new crowd of friends. Patsy was so busy socializing that she and Maura spent very little time together.

Michael had written to say he would have the last week in August free, and he planned on making the long trip to Buffalo to see her on Sunday of the week before he went on home—if it was all right with her.

She counted the days.

He called from Union Station around three in the afternoon to tell her he had arrived and wanted directions to her house.

"Stay right there, Michael. I'll pick you up outside at the main entrance," Maura said breathlessly. "It won't take more than fifteen minutes."

Michael sat on his suitcase and leaned against the building, looking at a large city that was, for the most part, deserted on a Sunday afternoon. What little traffic there was seemed to be centered around the station.

Maura drove up in a Model T Ford; a dog sat in the rumble seat, its ears flapping in the wind. She slammed on the brakes, the car chugged to a halt, and she jumped out. He stood as she ran and threw her arms around him. Aware of the passersby, he had to contain himself and kissed her affectionately but briefly. There would be time enough to show her how he really felt.

"Where'd you get the car? Borrow it from your Uncle Jack?" He walked around the black coupe, touching the shiny paint.

"Heavens, no!" She grinned proudly. "He drives an Oldsmobile. This one's mine. Got tired of taking the trolley to work, so I saved up. Bought it last week."

"And who is this?" he asked as he threw his valise in the rumble seat.

"This little cutie is Sadie," she answered as she held the dog's head between her hands and kissed her on the nose. Sadie gave a quick bark.

Michael took a moment to pet her. "Hey, Sadie girl, how ya doing?"

Maura handed him the crank. "Now, if you'll just give this beauty a few turns, we'll be on our way."

She knew she had to concentrate on the road. Driving was still rather a novelty, but it was so thrilling to actually have Michael sitting next to her—not just his words on a paper, but the real Michael.

She headed for Hadley Park before returning home. She had no intention of sharing him with anyone for the next few hours.

Sadie hopped out of the car and ran down toward the lake. They found a secluded spot on the slope of a hill facing the water and spread out a blanket.

Both were feeling rather awkward as they sat there, finding it difficult to pick up the rhythm of their relationship after a year's absence—even though by corresponding, they had shared their most intimate feelings during that time. For a few moments, they gazed at the swans and ducks that dotted the small lake, then Michael turned to her. "Maura, I've missed you."

She leaned toward him and stroked his face. He kissed her tenderly, and they both lay back on the blanket, facing each other. Tenderness turned into passion and heavy petting. Soon they were caught up in the need to consume each other.

It was all Michael could do to keep from taking the next step. He sat up.

Once again, they sat in silence.

A mallard came out of the water, followed by five ducklings. The last in line kept pecking at the one in front of it, tripping it as it waddled along. Sadie bounded over to greet mother and children, and mother lunged at her, pecking her nose. Sadie gave out a yip, turned tail, and ran up the hill toward Maura and Michael. They both laughed.

Michael leaned his elbows on his knees, supporting his head in his hands, staring at the lake. "What are we going to do, Maura? Seeing you for one day isn't enough. Maybe I should quit school and work with Victor at the winery. Then—"

She jumped up. "Michael Birch, don't you dare!"

She turned to him, one hand on her hip. "You've come too far and worked too hard to throw your dreams away. We're both young. We can wait. I don't want to hear another word about such nonsense."

She leaned over, gave the top of his head a quick peck, and pulled him up. "Guess we'd better head for the house. Aunt

Martha is having a family dinner party for you at six. She's having it early because she said you'd be starved after your long trip."

Michael shook the blanket and folded it.

"She's quite anxious to meet you," Maura said.

They walked toward the car hand in hand.

"That's right, I never did meet her. Your Uncle Jack I know from the island. I'd see him from time to time if I was tagging after Pops. The two of them seemed to hit it off, and they would stop to talk. He always put his hand on my head and mussed my hair. I hated that. Then he'd put his hand in his pocket and pull out a quarter and press it into my hand. I loved that part. I didn't come by many quarters back then."

Maura chuckled.

"What's so funny?"

"Oh, nothing, really. It's just that when I told Uncle Jack you'd be stopping by for the day, he told me a little story about the first time he ever saw you."

"And was I that funny?"

"It probably wasn't funny to you, but from an adult's point of view, I guess it was."

"Okay, what kind of fool did I make of myself?"

"I'm not sure whether it was the first or second year Uncle Jack came to pick us up, but he said you were around eleven, so I suppose I would have been about seven. That would make it the second year. Aunt Martha and Kevin almost always came with him to the island, but Aunt Martha never went out and mingled like Uncle Jack did, so I guess that's why you don't remember her. She always stayed close to the house."

"Come on, Maura! Just get on with it."

"Well, that year they came over the Labor Day weekend, so we all went to the big celebration at Parker's Pavilion. You were in the three-legged race with a bunch of boys your age. Uncle Jack said you and the boy you were tied to had a great lead, and that he would never forget the intense look of determination on your face, even after your knickers fell to your knees. You never even noticed, just kept running. The two of you crossed the finish line and had your moment of triumph, which came to a quick halt when you looked down to untie yourself. You pulled up your britches, and then, Uncle Jack said, 'The speed he'd used to win that race couldn't compare to the rapidity he mustered up to disappear from sight.'"

Maura pulled her car into the garage, and Sadie beat them to the back door.

"Golly, something sure smells good," Maura said as Sadie ran for her food dish. "Emiline, I'd like you to meet my friend Michael Birch." She looked at him proudly.

Emiline wiped her hands on her apron and took his hand in both of hers.

"Well, lawdy lawd, if it ain't Mistah Perfection in the flesh. I sure be hearin' some mighty good things 'bout you. Almost every day, I might add." She flashed a broad smile of perfect white teeth, stood back with hands on hips, and looked him up and down. "Mm hm."

Michael, slightly embarrassed, smiled back. "I think I've heard some pretty nice things about you, too, Emiline. Maura thinks the world of you. It's a pleasure to meet you."

Martha was taken by surprise when she came into the kitchen. "Well, my goodness, Maura. So this is your young man." Without waiting for an introduction, she extended her hand and said, "I'm so happy to meet you, Michael. I've been looking forward to it all day."

He smiled and shook her hand. "It's a pleasure."

She turned to Emiline. "Now don't forget, dinner is at six. And by the way, what did you decide for dessert?"

"I got me these scrumptious peaches at the market this morning, so I whipped up some peach cobbler. How's that sound? That and a dab of ice cream."

"Wonderful. What would I do without you?" Martha turned to leave. "Nice meeting you, Michael. I have to go change, now. See you at dinner."

"Can I help with anything?" Maura asked.

"No, chile, just run along. I think your Uncle Jack be in the study. And Patsy been asking 'bout you all afternoon."

Dr. Rosemarie Stewart and her fiancé, Dr. Alan Rowan, were also guests for dinner. Martha was in her element as hostess, making introductions and seeing that everyone was comfortable and had refreshments in her elegantly decorated living room.

Sadie made the rounds, seeing that everyone gave her the attention she deserved. Hadn't they all gathered there to pay her homage?

It had been easy for Rosemarie to keep in touch with Maggie's children, since she was going to medical school in Buffalo at the time of Maggie's death. Then she settled there to open her practice as a pediatrician. Maura felt closer to her than she did to her Aunt Martha. Aunt Rosemarie took her and Patsy on shopping trips, advised them on their choice of clothing, and always took them to a very fancy restaurant for their birthdays.

Although she'd tried, Rosemarie could never seem to get

that close to Kevin. But Jack had explained to her that Kevin had done wonders for Martha.

Dinner was to be promptly at six, but Kevin hadn't come home, so they waited.

"He knows he's to be home. I reminded him before he left," Martha said. "He and his friend Wally Stromp, who's a good year older, went to the country club for tennis, and Wally is to bring him home. Kevin's not quite fifteen, so we don't allow him to drive, yet. But that Wally!" She rolled her eyes. "Not too reliable. His parents have more money than brains, I suspect. He's got all the freedom in the world. And always causing a problem, you know. Poor Kevin is forever making excuses for him."

No, Aunt Martha, Maura thought. You're always making excuses for poor Kevin.

Emiline became quite adamant that dinner could wait no longer, so Martha acquiesced. "I guess we'll have to start without him."

Martha seated everyone in her very formal dining room. Jack sat at the head of the table, and she at the other end.

Michael thought she was charming, sitting there in her jade green dress and long string of pearls. She'd kept herself very trim, and he could see where Patsy got her good looks, except that Martha's hair was a darker ash blond and cut in a bob, quite chic.

Maura, Michael, and Patsy sat to her left, and Rosemarie, Alan, and an empty chair were to her right.

Their maid, Flora, served the salad.

Halfway through the rib roast, Kevin came breezing in in his white tennis shoes, white shorts, and a black and white polo shirt.

God, that kid is handsome, Rosemarie thought.

"Hi, folks. Sorry I'm late. But you know Wally."

Maura steamed to herself. He's got Wally to blame for everything. Why can't Aunt Martha see that? Wally is just a big dummy who does whatever Kevin says. If Kevin had wanted to be here on time, he would have made Wally take him home. She'd been around the two of them enough to know that Wally might be older, but Kevin ran the show.

He plopped in his chair and waited for Tina to put something in front of him. "Gosh, I'm starved."

Martha looked at him adoringly. "Kevin, I don't think you've ever met Maura's friend Michael Birch."

Kevin half stood and reached across the table to shake Michael's hand. "Hi, Mike. Nice meeting you." He sat back down and dug into his salad.

Dinner conversation was light and pleasant and for the most part directed toward Michael. Rosemarie had lots of questions about his studies. Patsy asked about Marietta and Joanie and talked about the island. Martha made it a point to mention Kevin's prowess on the tennis court.

Jack commented that he hated to see Michael go on the train in the morning. "I'd take you over in the yacht if I could, but Monday is my busiest day. If you stay over, I can take you back on Tuesday."

Michael thanked him for the offer but explained that he only had so much time and had to leave in the morning.

Maura and he would have preferred to spend the evening alone, but Martha took charge. She'd made reservations at the country club for an evening of dancing. "The band they hired is wonderful. It will be great fun."

Kevin had a party to go to. "Wally's picking me up at eight. Sorry."

Patsy had a date for the movies. "Randy is picking me up at seven–thirty. Gotta rush. Sorry."

"Well, there's still the six of us. And you two young people are just going to love this band. I guarantee it."

As a guest in the house, Michael felt obligated to accept. "Sounds like fun," he said with a smile.

Maura hadn't planned on sharing Michael. She wanted more time alone with him. When she said she would drive, Jack wouldn't hear of it and insisted they go with them. "There's plenty of room in the back seat of my Olds."

Rosemary and Alan would also drive, because they would just go home from there.

Michael and Maura sat close together in the cozy back seat and held hands. He hadn't mentioned it to her, but he'd taken a sleeper from Columbus at eleven the night before to make connections in Pittsburgh, where he had a two–hour layover. Somehow, he'd managed to get some sleep and stretch his legs along the way. The trip had been long and exhausting but worth every minute of it to finally get to see the love of his life. Time was so short. This wasn't the evening he'd looked forward to. Tomorrow morning, he'd be on his way back home. He whispered in Maura's ear. "I don't know how to dance. I've never done it."

She giggled, gave him a quick peck on the cheek, and whispered back, "It's okay. I'll show you how."

Michael was impressed as they drove up the winding driveway to a sprawling building nestled between trees and low hills. Inside, the place swelled with affluence: men in expensive suits and tuxedos with big cigars, women in the latest styles, feathers in their short, cropped hair, ropes of pearls and gemstones, short skirts, high heels—flappers.

"Great music," Michael commented as the waiter led them to their table.

"Just a young fella," Jack said. "I think his name's Eddie Duchin. There's no doubt in my mind he's going to go far with that band of his."

Maura was just about to sit down when she saw her friend Peggy waving to her from across the room.

"She wants me to come over. Come on, Michael, I'll introduce you to some friends of mine. We'll be right back, Uncle Jack."

There were six of them at the table.

"Michael, I'd like you to meet my friends. This is Peggy and her friends Jake, Sally, and Bob, and this is Millie and Jimmy."

The young men half stood and shook hands as Michael walked around the table saying, "Hello. Nice to meet you. It's a pleasure."

"Come join us." Peggy said as everyone started to make room.

"No, we really can't. We're with my Uncle Jack and Aunt Martha. My Aunt Rosemarie is with them. I don't get to see her too often, so we'd better get back."

"Too bad. Great meeting you, Michael," Peggy said.

"See you, Mike," Bob nodded.

"Hope to see you again, Mike," Jimmy added.

"Nice bunch of friends," Michael commented on the way back to the table.

When they returned, there were soft drinks waiting.

Rosemarie and Alan were dancing, and Jack and Martha were just about to join them.

"Come on, you two," Martha said over her shoulder. "Get out there and show them how it's done."

"We will, Aunt Martha. Give us a minute."

She turned to Michael. "Now, here's how it's done."

She traced a square on the tablecloth with her index finger. "You see? It's just a box. Take one foot across; slide the other over to meet it. That's one side of the box. Now forward with the same foot and slide the other to meet it. Back across using the opposite foot but doing the same thing, and then down again to where you started. That's the four–step. Here's another, called the three–step or waltz."

She explained the right, left–right, left–right–left movement.

"That can be fast or slow, depending on the tempo of the music. They're playing a waltz right now, so that would be the three–step. Try it under the table, Michael. Practice them both."

"I feel like a fool, but okay, here goes."

Maura sipped on her drink and grinned, watching the intense look on his face as he covertly moved his feet to the rhythm of the music.

With a look of triumph, he finally said, "I think I've got it."

By the time she'd convinced him to give it a whirl on the dance floor, the music had stopped, and the others joined them.

"How come you weren't out there dancing?" Martha asked.

"Oh, we'll get there, Aunt Martha. We were just talking. Catching up. But we will."

Rosemarie gave Maura a knowing smile, then turned to Michael. "After all the nice things I've heard about you, I'm certainly glad I finally got to spend some time with you."

"And you are everything Maura said you were. She loves you dearly, you know."

"Sorry I can't offer you anything stronger to drink," Jack said. "Prohibition sure has put a damper on everything. Every once in a while, someone will bring in a bottle of hooch and pass it around—under the table, of course. But we pretty well abide by the law, here."

"Not a problem. One of the guys at school brought some to the dorm one night, pretty potent stuff, and we all got sloshed. I was sick as a dog the next day, so I can't say that I much care for it. Now, a good glass of wine is another story."

"I've been meaning to ask you about that. It's been over five years since Prohibition took effect. How does your brother keep that winery going? Surely he has to obey the law."

"For the most part, he does. He manages to sneak through a few vats here and there if the weather has been favorable and he knows the grape will yield a superior wine. But we have quite a large apple orchard, too. So what with making grape juice, apple cider, and vinegar, he keeps pretty busy and does quite well marketing it. Not to mention the table grapes he ships off to market.

"Our winery is fairly close to the house, and the wine cellar under it is connected to the cellar under our house by a short tunnel. That makes one very large wine cellar, quite well stocked from the old days. Some of our oldest wines date back to 1908. Wine making has always been Pop's passion and hobby. He seems to have passed the passion on to Victor, but for him, it's a business. Perhaps someday that law will be repealed, and he can get back to it full time."

The band began to play "Alice Blue Gown."

Maura stood. "Come on, Michael. Let's dance, shall we?"

They stayed in one corner of the crowded floor and danced back and forth for several minutes.

"You don't have to stay in one spot," she told him. "You can change directions any time you want. See if you can get us over to the other side of the floor."

"You mean, like this?"

He was all over the place, with Maura gliding right along.

"Why, Michael Birch, I do believe you've got natural rhythm," Maura whispered in his ear. She rested her head on his shoulder and relaxed.

They remained on the floor and danced to "By the Light of the Silvery Moon." Michael, who'd begun throwing in a few innovative steps of his own, was quite enjoying himself when the tempo changed, so they went to sit down.

Martha approached. "Come on, Michael. Dance the Charleston with me. Jack doesn't want to dance."

"Oh, sorry, Mrs. Mahoney, I've never done the Charleston. Too fast for me."

She took him by the hand and pulled him to the floor. "Well, now, it's about time you learned. It's easy and so much fun. Just do what I do."

Maura watched with amusement as Michael crossed his hands on his undulating knees and then waved them in the air, following Martha's lead, keeping time with the music.

Rosemarie turned to Maura and said, "Alan has a very early call in the morning, and I have to be up pretty early myself, so we'd best be on our way." She hugged Maura. "I think you have a very special young man there. Take care you don't lose him. Love you, sweetie."

She turned to Jack and took his hand. "Thank Martha again for the wonderful evening. And don't forget, you're coming to dinner at my place next Saturday."

"Oh, that was so much fun," Martha said as she came puffing back to the table and plopped in her chair.

By the time the band played "Good Night Sweetheart," Michael considered himself a dancer. Perhaps not the best, but a dancer nonetheless. He held Maura close, pressing her cheek to his, hating to see this last dance end.

Jack dropped the others off at the back door. "I sure could go for another piece of that peach cobbler," he commented.

"Good idea," Martha said.

He went to park the car in the garage as the others went inside.

Sadie greeted them at the door. "Michael, would you be a dear and take Sadie for a quick run down the driveway?" Martha asked. "I want to go check on Patsy and Kevin."

Maura got out the remains of the peach cobbler, dished out four servings, and poured four glasses of milk.

Martha came down as Jack walked in the back door. "Patsy's sound asleep, but Kevin isn't in yet. Oh, dear, I hope nothing's happened to him."

"Now, Martha, calm down. It's not like it's the first time. It's barely eleven o'clock. Those parties sometimes run as late as twelve. Stop worrying."

The three of them had just sat down when Sadie came bounding in ahead of Michael and ran to the table, sniffing.

"That didn't take long," Martha commented.

"I think she was worried there wouldn't be anything left. Just tended to her business and led me back," Michael chuckled.

When Michael had taken the last bite of his cobbler and washed it down with the last of his milk, he pushed his chair back. "It's been a grand day, Mr. and Mrs. Mahoney. And I can't thank you enough for your hospitality. I have to be at the station at seven in the morning, so in case I don't see you, I'll say goodbye now. I hope to see you both again."

"You're welcome back any time, son." Jack stood and shook his hand. "Maura tells me she'll see you get to the station."

"Yes, sir."

Martha got up and gave him a kiss on the cheek. "I'm so happy I got to meet you, Michael. You know which room is yours? Maura, you did show him, didn't you?"

"Of course. We took his bag up there when we got here, so he could freshen up."

Maura started clearing the table. "I'll be up to say goodnight as soon as I clear up the dishes, Michael."

It couldn't have taken ten minutes to wash up the dishes. She tapped on his bedroom door. No answer. She opened it quietly and went in.

The light on the bedstand was on, and Michael lay on the bed, fully dressed and sound asleep. Her heart was full of love as she stood staring at his peaceful face.

She leaned over to kiss him, hoping he would awaken. He moaned and rolled over on his side. She covered him with a quilt, turned out the light, and tiptoed out, shutting the door quietly.

He's completely exhausted, she thought.

Maura was awakened by a heavy thump against her wall. The moonlight coming through her bedroom window allowed her to see the hands on her large alarm clock: half past three.

She knew it was Kevin. His bedroom was next to hers; she'd heard him before.

She lay there wondering if she should tell her Uncle Jack. Kevin needed a firm hand, or he would soon be out of control. Her thoughts then turned to Michael across the hall, and she drifted back asleep.

Maura was cooking eggs and bacon at six the next morning when Michael came into the kitchen.

"Mm, that coffee and bacon smell good," he said, setting his bag by the back door. "I hope some of that's for me."

"It's all for you. Sadie thinks I'm cooking it for her. She won't leave my side."

"Out of the way, Sadie. I want this young lady to myself," Michael said. He went to her, put his arms around her, and kissed her passionately. "I've been wanting to do that since before dinner last night. Not much chance, though. They kept us pretty busy. But all in all, it's been a wonderful visit."

They both heard sounds in the hall, and he immediately released her and sat at the table.

Tina walked in. "Oh, sorry, miss. I heard noises and came to check. Thought maybe Mr. Mahoney wanted an early breakfast."

"It's okay, Tina. You can go back to bed. Uncle Jack will be up at his usual time. Mr. Birch has to catch an early train."

Maura ate a piece of toast and watched Michael devour his breakfast. "You must have been worn out after all that dancing last night," she said. "It looked like you fell asleep the minute you hit the bed."

"Sorry about that. I thought I'd just lie there until you came up, and that's the last I remember."

He kissed her again before they got in the car, but they

couldn't linger. The train wasn't about to wait. Again at the station, he kissed her lightly, but held her close and looked in her eyes. "I'll miss you, Maura. I love you."

"Oh, I wish you didn't have to go!"

"Booooard. All aboard."

Michael gave her a quick peck and hopped on the train.

CHAPTER TWENTY-FOUR
The Entrepreneur

Jack had opened his first lumberyard with his grandfather's advice and financial assistance, but lumberyards two, three, and four he'd done on his own, and he was still looking into other possibilities for expansion.

He remembered what his grandfather had told him: "Location is everything." So Jack went in search of new housing developments in the growing city of Buffalo. He'd chosen wisely. Lumberyard number four was still floundering in its infancy, but he had no doubt it would soon stand on its own.

It had been Maura who suggested he add a line of hardware.

"After all, Uncle Jack, if people come in to buy lumber, they'll also need nails and other things, including tools."

Jack was never one to discount a good idea, and after giving it a great deal of thought, he added another building with a complete line of hardware to Lumberyard One. When that turned out to be successful, he did the same with his other three yards.

Maura hadn't counted on the workload that was dumped on the accounting department. As a result, inventory was more than quadrupled, there were dozens more order forms to be filled out, and contractors' invoices became a nightmare of itemization.

After Michael's visit, she threw herself into the task of revamping her office: the entire bookkeeping and filing systems. This took all her energy—sometimes twelve-hour days. At night, exhausted, she'd eat dinner and fall into bed. There was little time to dwell on missing Michael, but she did manage to find time to get a letter off to him and to Patsy at least twice a week, and Aunt Gert and Grandma Mahoney about once a month. She cut her Saturday hours to noon, however, so she could relax a little over the weekend.

There were offers to go out, which for the most part she turned down, but occasionally she would accept a date to a dinner dance at the club or to a movie with male friends her own age. But she wasn't much interested in keeping up with the latest trends of her peers, and for the most part, she found that these young men fell short of her Michael.

Early that December, Maura started to look forward to Christmas and seeing Patsy again. Some of her latest letters had hinted at a very special person in her life. She couldn't wait to hear all about it.

When Patsy came home for the holidays, everyone was quite taken with her new look. The long, curly hair was now bobbed, and she wore a bit of makeup. Martha was quite impressed that her daughter had taken such an interest in style, but Jack hated seeing his baby girl growing up.

When the two of them were in Maura's room, lying across

her bed, Patsy confided that she was in love.

"I met this fella at a Halloween dance this fall. This wasn't a school dance—you know, the kind with the chaperones all over the place. This was a charity affair, costumes and all, held at the Hilton Hotel. My friend Alma got permission to go because her mother was one of the ladies from the guild that was sponsoring it. So she asked me to go with her. Anyway, this skeleton asked me to dance—I was a witch—and we spent the rest of the night dancing and laughing. He said he'd call me, and he did. It all just went from there."

Her face glowed when she talked about him. Patsy had always been comfortable around the opposite sex and had had lots of beaus before this one—never any Maura had known her to take seriously, but obviously this one was different.

"What's his name? Where's he from? What does he plan to do when he graduates?"

"His name is Paul. Paul Johnston. He's in his final year at Case University. Studying to be an engineer. He comes from a small town in Illinois, somewhere north of Chicago. Evanston, I think it's called. His folks are quite wealthy. Mr. Johnston graduated from Case and wanted Paul to keep up the tradition. Oh, he's so handsome, Maura! And so smart. He's already had an offer with an engineering firm in Chicago for after he graduates. And guess what?" she said, almost in a whisper. "He's asked me to marry him before he goes there. Says he can't live without me."

"Uh oh, this is serious. But you have to finish school, Patsy. You know how your mom and dad feel about that."

"Well, we'll see. But in the meantime, keep this to yourself, will you?"

Her secret was safe, and everyone had a wonderful holiday. There were gifts galore.

Maura finished up her restructuring job at Store One about the time Patsy returned to school. Then Jack asked her if she would do the same for the other three stores.

"Of course I will, Uncle Jack. But first, I'll have to train someone to do my job here."

"Fine. Whatever it takes, because I feel it's imperative that all the stores maintain the same kind of system. I can't tell you how much I appreciate the splendid job you've done here."

Jack's plan was to bring in the head bookkeeper, Matt Gorsky, from Store Two in the Plymouth suburb, and Maura's assistant could take his place. That way she could train him. She was to do the same with bookkeepers from Stores Three and Four, her assistant going wherever needed. After reaching her goal, they would go back to their respective offices.

"Great idea," Maura said, but she wasn't prepared for Matt Gorsky.

When he sauntered into the office wearing a raccoon coat, pork pie hat, and big grin, her heart gave a leap. He had dimples just like Michael's and was about the same build. It wasn't his looks, exactly: light brown hair, more on the wavy side, a nice face, and perhaps a year or two older. But with his mannerisms, it was as if Michael had entered the room.

They hit it off from the beginning, but she wondered if this Matt person would take her seriously because of her age. She'd run up against this problem with some of the older help in her office, until they realized she was a hard one to keep up with and knew exactly what she was doing. She found Matt to be quick and attentive. He would master the job within the next two weeks.

At the end of week one, Matt asked her to go to dinner and a movie on Saturday evening. She accepted. She hadn't been this excited since Michael's visit the previous August.

Snow was always a part of a Buffalo winter, but there had been only one storm of any consequence so far, and fortunately it hadn't interfered with the Christmas holidays. But another showed up that Saturday afternoon.

Matt called. "Sorry, but there's no way I can make it through this pileup. I can't tell you how much I was looking forward to our date. Shall we try again for next Saturday?"

"I understand. Next Saturday will be fine."

She didn't tell him how disappointed she was. Now all she could do was look forward to seeing him on Monday.

The following week, they continued their tedious task of taking inventory, noting what was needed and what was being overstocked, discarding dead files and transferring items into three separate ledgers—lumber, hardware, and tools—making it much easier to keep track of stock.

It was a very busy week, and Maura noted how well they worked together as a team. They ate lunch at a table in the office every day, sharing thoughts and ideas.

Matt was shocked to find out she was only seventeen. "I thought you were much closer to my age." He was twenty–four.

At day's end, they lingered just a bit longer than necessary. Until then, Maura hadn't realized how lonely she'd been.

Matt showed up promptly at six the following Saturday, greeted by Sadie and Tina at the door. He gave Tina his best grin and stooped to scratch Sadie behind the ear.

"I'm here to pick up Maura," he said, stepping into the foyer, removing his hat, and stamping his feet.

"Come in, sir, and may I take your coat?"

"No, thanks. My feet are covered with snow. I'll just wait here."

Tina went to Maura's room. "Your young man is here, miss."

Matt watched as Maura followed Tina down the steps. She was wearing a short, black wool dress and black suede heels, with crystal earrings and necklace. Her silky hair was tied in a French knot. From the first time he'd seen her, he'd thought she was a good–looker, but coming down the steps, she looked absolutely regal.

She also noticed Matt. No raccoon coat tonight.

Hmm, she thought, a black Chesterfield topcoat. How distinguished.

"Hi, Matt. My, don't you look nice."

He helped her on with her coat, a gray Persian lamb. "You look stunning," he said. "What a beautiful coat."

'Why, thank you. Uncle Jack and Aunt Martha gave it to me for Christmas. I just love it."

Matt had chosen The Cloisters for dinner and dancing. He knew it was quite expensive, would probably cost him a week's salary, but it would be worth it. He figured Maura would expect something like this, being the niece of the owner and used to the better things in life.

That's what he wanted—the better things. He didn't intend to live on a bookkeeper's salary forever. His girlfriend, Loretta, didn't seem to mind, though. As long as she could make him happy—and she did a good job of that—she didn't seem to need much more. Loretta didn't have Maura's style and class, but she was desirable and so obliging. There was a lot to be said for a well-rounded, sumptuous body, so unlike Maura's tall, slender one—almost boyish. Not that he didn't like Maura. She was attractive, bright, and stimulating, mentally challenging him in all directions. Loretta hung on his every word. It had already been two weeks, and he was really missing her.

Even though Store Two was only twenty miles away, Mr. Mahoney had suggested Matt take a room close to Store One.

"At the company's expense, of course," he'd said matter-of-factly. "You'll be here for about three months, and with our unpredictable weather, I think it best you be close by. But I see no reason why you can't go home on weekends if the weather permits."

Matt would be leaving on Monday to take over his office. He hoped his clerk hadn't botched things up too badly in his absence. If he played his cards right, he could probably keep seeing Maura and keep Loretta, too.

His plan was to become manager of one of the stores, learn all there was to know about the business, and start a lumberyard of his own, probably somewhere around Erie, Pennsylvania. It didn't hurt to have an edge on that plan, and Maura was it.

Dinner was perfection, the music was heavenly, and Maura floated through the evening, dancing in the arms of a very desirable man. She felt warm and excited, and for the first time in many, many months did not think of Michael.

Matt saw her to the door, pressed her hand in his, and kissed her on the forehead. "It's been a grand evening. I hope we can see each other again," he said, looking intently into her eyes.

"Oh, I certainly hope so," she sighed. "Thank you so much

for a wonderful time." She squeezed his hand. "Good night, Matt."

After a week, Claude Kimmel was called in from Store Three with an attitude that announced itself the moment she shook his hand. Maura's reputation as a whiz with figures had preceded her, but he didn't care. No upstart was about to tell him how to do things. He had eighteen years of experience as a bookkeeper and was a crackerjack at what he did. Sure, he'd go along with the new system if he had to, but he felt the one he'd implemented in his store was probably every bit as good. He'd tried to tell Mr. Mahoney that, but to no avail. That rebuff hadn't sat well. But why two weeks of this, when he'd probably catch on in two days?

Maura ignored his contemptuous attitude as she set about explaining what had to be done. Soon they were in the thralls of doing inventory and transferring figures from the main ledger into the three others. He soon realized that it wasn't just the system he needed to learn, but the tedious work involved in changing it.

Matt called her several times, and on two occasions, he took her to the movies.

Although she still wrote to Michael, her memories of him seemed to be fading. He still had almost two and a half years before she could ever think of really spending time with him again. Right now, she looked forward to her phone calls and dates with Matt.

The last time they'd gone to the movies, he'd walked her to the door and kissed her passionately before she went inside. That memory was still fresh and new—and erotic. She thought of him often.

By the end of their two weeks together, Claude had actually become amicable. They shook hands and parted as friends.

Onward to Store Four.

Alice Whorrl was the next bookkeeper to learn the new system. In her mid–thirties, she was quite attractive, yet still unmarried. During one of their many conversations, she'd explained that she had to take care of her sick mother when she went home from work and had little time for a personal life, but there was a Mr. Foible whom she saw from time to time. He, too, had a mother who depended on him. Both mothers were quite demanding.

Maura and Alice got along famously. On March 27, Maura's mission was complete.

Although the end of March did not guarantee the absence of another snowstorm, today the snow was actually melting away. The roads were wet but clear. It was a very nice winter's day, sunny and calm, one of the few winter days on which the sky was actually blue—such a relief from the gray skies that constantly threatened. Maura felt free and giddy, relieved that a great burden had finally been lifted.

It was Saturday, and she decided to take a drive and visit Matt. He still called her frequently. The last time she'd seen him, they'd gone to the country club for dinner and dancing. He was a wonderful dancer. Martha and Jack highly approved of him and were happy to see her so happy.

At the end of the evening, he'd walked her to the door and kissed her more than once. Her feelings of arousal were quite strong, and she returned his kisses with passion.

"I care for you a great deal," Matt whispered in her ear. "I wish you didn't have to go in. It's early yet. We could go back to my place for a while."

Maura could have spent the night in his arms, but she was cautious and kept her emotions in check. "I'd love to, but that's too far. It's late, and I'm really tired. Perhaps another time."

They'd talked many times on the phone since, but the weather also made a statement.

Driving down the highway, she remembered that evening and thought, Perhaps I should have called him first. Oh, what the heck, it's early. Matt should be home now. I haven't seen him for weeks, and I have all day. Perhaps we can have lunch together.

She drove her little coupe up DeSoto Avenue, looking for his apartment building.

There it was—59.

She ran her finger down the six mailboxes in the hall to the one with the name Matt Gorsky typed neatly on the front. 2A.

She rapped softly on the door. No answer. She rapped again.

A young girl with very curly brown hair answered in her robe and slippers. "Yes?" she said as she yawned.

"Oh, sorry to disturb you. I must have the wrong apartment. I'm looking for a Matt Gorsky."

"No, you have the right apartment. What did you—"

"Maura?"

Maura was dumbfounded. She saw Matt across the room, standing in his robe in the doorway of what she supposed was the bedroom.

For a few seconds, she stood there with her mouth open, then turned and ran down the steps. Matt called down to her from his apartment door, but she kept on going. She got the picture.

By the time she'd gotten her car started, Matt had managed to throw some pants and a shirt on and get to the street. He yelled, waving his arms for her to stop, running after her in his bare feet, trying to jump on the running board. She looked through her rear view mirror and saw him finally give up, wearing a look of despair, shoulders slumped and arms at his side.

She kept on driving. How could she have been taken in like that? She wasn't sure whether it was her pride that was wounded or the fact that she cared so much for a person who had turned out to be someone she really didn't know, someone who had been lying to her from the very beginning.

Her body heaved with sobs, tears blinding her as she tried to drive. She pulled to the side of the road to let it all out.

With each memory of their relationship, she'd start sobbing anew. The first time they'd met, their first dinner date, working together, phone conversations, his touch, his kisses—all of it. She was such a blind fool.

An hour passed. Bankrupt of tears, she began her journey home. Anger started to seethe and boil, overtaking her with thoughts of bitter revenge. He was a sneaky, good-for-nothing liar. She'd fix him. She'd have him fired.

As she was passing a field of sheep, her car began to shimmy. Pulling over to the side of the road, she knew what she would find when she walked around to the right side of the car. A tire was flat. She stamped her foot, gritted her teeth, and let out a very loud, frustrated scream.

"Hey there, missy, that's a mighty loud sound comin' from a skinny young thing like you. You're about to scare my sheep into birthin' their lambs early."

The voice startled her, and she looked over at the man walking toward her, a big grin on his face. She hadn't seen him mending the fence up ahead.

She began to laugh. "Sorry, mister. It's just that I've had a very bad morning, and this was the last straw."

"Nothin' that can't be fixed," he said, looking at the tire and rubbing his chin. "Don't have an automobile myself. Been thinkin' about it, though. Let's just get out your tools, and we'll have this thing taken care of in no time flat. Whoops, it's the flat we have to fix."

They both laughed again.

"Name's Dunbar. Yours?" He held out a callused hand.

"Nice to meet you, Mr. Dunbar. I'm Maura. Maura Ryan." She shook his hand.

"Where's your spare?"

"That's the bad news. My spare is flat, too. I had a flat tire last week and used the spare. I was meaning to get the other one fixed and forgot. Too busy, I guess."

"Well, let's get out your tools, and we'll see what we can do."

They dug in the toolbox on the running board for a jack, tire iron, air pump, and patch kit. Dunbar jacked up the right front tire, removed it, and pulled out the inner tube.

Maura watched him work as he talked.

"Funny how things work out," he mused. "If I wasn't down there mendin' that fence, you'd be out here stranded. Don't know how bad your mornin's been, but I'd say you've had a bit of good luck with your bad. Ain't that the way life goes, though?"

"I suppose it is," Maura agreed.

"Same as yesterday and today. Who'd think, after that

gloomy cold we had yesterday, we'd end up with a bushelful of sunshine today? Yep, things is always changin'. Some for the good and some for the bad."

Maura watched him pull the inner tube out of the spare.

"Now, I'll just go back to the house with these." He hooked the two inner tubes on his arm. "Got to have a tub of water to check for the leaks."

"Shall I go with you?" she asked.

"No, little missy, you stay right here and enjoy this beautiful day. Watch the sheep, look at the sky, soak up the sunshine, drink it all in, and store it up. That's what I do. That way, when things ain't so good, I remember that there's always better."

He climbed over the fence and walked through the pasture toward his house, inner tubes, air pump, and patches in hand.

Maura leaned against the car and looked around. A very fat robin flew over and teetered on the fence. The roadside was dotted with patches of snow and tufts of green grass. Bright yellow dandelions found homes everywhere. Sheep grazed lazily in the field beyond.

She watched the diminishing figure of Dunbar moving toward the distant farmhouse. Smoke curled out of its chimney. There was sunshine overhead and a bright periwinkle sky sprinkled with wisps of downy clouds.

She was overcome with a sense of peace. It was a beautiful picture: a promising spring.

Forty-five minutes passed, and Dunbar returned with two inflated innertubes—three patches on one and two on the other. He also brought a brown paper bag and handed it to Maura. "Mable says I should bring this to you. Bread's still warm."

"Thank you, Mr. Dunbar. How thoughtful."

She dug into the most delicious ham sandwich she'd ever eaten as she watched Dunbar squeeze the inner tubes into the tires. She observed from his deeply lined, weathered face that life had not always been easy for him. Yet he seemed so pleasant, so appreciative of the world around him.

When he'd finished, he put the tools back and placed the spare in its rack behind the rumble seat, brushed his hands off, and said, "There you go, missy. All set."

"How can I ever thank you, Mr. Dunbar? You've been a godsend." She extended a five-dollar bill.

"No, no, missy. I don't want no money. As days go, this has been a good one, and I do what's needed. Glad to be of help."

Maura went with her impulse and gave him a hug and a kiss on the cheek. "Well, as you say, as days go, I'm sure glad you were with me on this one. Thanks again."

She continued her drive with a lighter heart, reaching into the brown bag for a maple twist Mrs. Dunbar had included. Mm, delicious!

That's when the practical, logical, sensible Maura took over. She'd grieved when first her father and then her mother had died. But Matt wasn't worth that kind of pain. She wouldn't spend another minute on him. And no, she wouldn't have him fired. He was too valuable an employee. Let him get on with his life—the miserable bounder. She'd get on with hers.

CHAPTER TWENTY–FIVE
Past Sins Revealed

Michael was becoming quite concerned. He'd had only one letter from Maura in the past two weeks, and lately her letters had been so detached. What could he do? He didn't want to lose her. Anxiously, he wrote to her.

My dearest love,

You've written lately of all the work you've been doing. I suppose that's why I haven't heard from you as often, and I really do understand. My schedule is also very demanding with classes, studying, and working at the clinic.

I miss you so much, but for the life of me, I can't figure out when I can find the time to come see you again. Not until next August—and that's so far away. I was wondering if after you completed your work for the four stores you might ask your Uncle Jack for some time off to come here and visit me. I have a female friend whose roommate had to go back home because of illness. She said you could stay with her in the dorm. Her housemother is willing to look the other way for a few days and a few dollars.

Please, please get back to me on this. I need so much to see you and hold you and kiss you.

I love you.
Michael

Maura had been busy at work in her own office for a week when she received Michael's letter. She picked up her mail when she came into the house Friday evening and went immediately to her bedroom to read it. She sat on her bed and wept.

Sweet Michael! How could she tell him she had been involved with someone else for the past three months? Three months she would rather forget.

Consumed with guilt, she didn't know how to reply.

Aunt Gert had described her relationship with Michael as an infatuation—puppy love—because she was so young. Perhaps she was right, but in Maura's mind, that was the way she would describe her relationship with Matt. She'd never fallen deeply in love with him, but she certainly had been attracted to his charm. He'd stirred feelings in her that she didn't know she had. She needed to see Michael as much as he needed to see her so she could sort out her feelings—to find out if Aunt Gert had been right about him also.

It took her two days to put the words on paper, but when she did, she felt better.

My dearest Michael,

I am sorry I've been remiss in writing as often as before, but I have been very busy. I know you have a tremendous workload also, and I can't imagine trying to keep that up for the next two and a half years. Yet you've always been faithful with your letters.

I guess the only way I can explain myself is to say that I was given a very large responsibility for someone so young. I love doing what I do, but it's difficult for me sometimes because of my age. There are many people who feel that the only reason I have my job is because of Uncle Jack. Which I suppose is partly true. But with the reorganization of four stores, I'm constantly trying to prove myself. There are some who would love to see me fall on my face, and it takes all I have in me to get the job done.

One of the best things that have come out of all of my work is that the worst is behind me, and I will now have Saturdays off. That means more time to write.

I love your idea of me coming to visit, but Uncle Jack will be out of town for the next two weeks, so I'll have to get back to you.

I hope all is well with you, and I'm really looking forward to seeing you in the very near future. I really do need to see you again.

All of my love,
Maura

She did not think it wise to upset him by telling him about Matt.

After Jack returned from his trip, he made his rounds of the other three stores and came back to report to Maura that the new system was working very well. "Matt Gorsky was asking about you. He said he's tried calling you a number of times, but you're never available. He was wondering if you were sick or something."

Maura shrugged. "He was getting too serious, so I decided to drop him. He's not my type."

She knew Matt was feeling her uncle out to see if she'd said anything. She was glad she hadn't. Things were better that way.

When she asked for time off to go see Michael, Jack said she had truly earned a vacation. "You go and relax. You need some fun back in your life."

She wrote Michael to tell him she would see him on the last Friday in April. "I'll send details later."

Maura's eighteenth birthday was April 16. Jack and Martha took her and Kevin to the country club. After socializing with friends there, they all had a wonderful dinner.

As self–absorbed as Kevin was, he always remembered Maura on her birthday by making her a special birthday card. He truly loved his sister, but he'd always found her too serious. His cousin Patsy was much more fun.

He gave Maura a peck on the cheek, said, "Happy Birthday, sis," and handed her the card, which read:

> *As sisters go I have to say*
> *You are the best*

Happy Birthday
Love, Kevin

He wasn't much of a poet, but the front of the card was quite creative. He'd painted garlands of flowers, butterflies, and bees. He actually was a very good artist, something he'd taken to when he was quite young, and it was one of the reasons he'd always made her a card. His bedroom was filled with pictures of houses that he'd painted. His plan was to become an architect.

Right now, he was looking around, hoping to see Wally, so he would have an excuse to spend time with his crowd. He'd already met up with a few of them sprinkled around the room. Elaine Parnell kept giving him the eye. She looked promising. But no Wally.

Jack and Martha handed Maura her gift, a long thin box—a string of pearls.

"Oh, Uncle Jack, Aunt Martha, thank you so much! They're beautiful."

"You deserve them and more," Jack said as she hugged him and went on to kiss Martha on the cheek. He looked at his watch. "Hmm, almost nine. Best we get going. I have a very early day tomorrow, and there's something I want to talk to you about, Maura, before I go to bed."

Maura couldn't imagine what that would be. She hoped it wasn't more work.

Kevin was relieved to see Wally come in with his parents and asked if he could stay behind and have them take him home.

"Why, of course, dear," Martha said. "Just make sure it's not too late. School tomorrow, remember." She patted him on the cheek.

He promised it would be early.

Jack dropped Martha and Maura off at the door. "You two go on in. I'll park the car and take Sadie for her run. Then I'll be up to talk to you, Maura."

She was propped up in bed reading when Jack came in the bedroom.

He looked at her with fatherly affection. "I can't believe our Maura is actually eighteen." He smiled, sat down on the edge of the bed, and took her hand. "But you've always been quite grown up and very special, ever since you were a very little girl. I suppose part of that came with losing your father and then your mother at such a young age. That had to be quite difficult for you. I know how hard it was for me when your mother died."

"I still think of them. Especially Mama. I don't suppose we'll ever know how it happened." She looked at him curiously. "Was there something you wanted to talk to me about?"

"Actually, yes, and it's about your mother."

"My mother?" She sat upright. "Have they found out who did it?"

"No, that's not it. It's about her money."

"Mama didn't have any money."

"Oh, but she did. She inherited quite a tidy sum from your great-grandfather a few weeks before she died."

Maura looked at him in amazement. "She did?"

"Yes, she did, and after her funeral, I had it put in a trust for you and Kevin, with the stipulation that each of you would get your share on your eighteenth birthday."

Maura's eyes widened. "You mean I'll have enough money to buy a nice car like yours?"

"More than that. Much more. Your mother left almost two

hundred and sixty thousand dollars. Half of which is Kevin's. But it has all been drawing interest for the past thirteen years. Your share comes close to two hundred thousand."

Maura gaped. "Two...hundred...thou...Oh, my goodness."

"I couldn't be happier for you, dear. My big concern is that with all that money, you won't need to work for me anymore."

"Now, Uncle Jack! Don't talk like that. What would I do if I didn't work? I love what I do."

"I was hoping you'd say that. But just think. Someday you'll get married and have a family, and you'll never have to worry about scrimping and scraping the way Martha and I had to do when we first got married. Money doesn't buy happiness, but it sure helps to keep it going."

He stood. "Well, I'll be off to bed. Five–thirty comes mighty early." He leaned and kissed her on the forehead. "Happy birthday, dear. Sweet dreams."

"Night, Uncle Jack. Love you."

Maura was so excited she couldn't sleep. Jack and Martha had retired around ten, and the house was very still. She heard Kevin come in around eleven.

Something has to be done with that brother of mine, she thought. He's not even sixteen, and he's becoming a real playboy.

She fell asleep trying to decide if she should say something to her uncle.

The trip to Columbus was long and tiring. One thing Maura had decided along the way was that if she'd had a photograph of Michael to look at while they were apart, she wouldn't be having this difficulty trying to remember his face. The dimples she remembered, but the nuances weren't there. He'd simply have to get his picture taken. However, when she got off the train, she had no problem recognizing him.

She threw herself in his arms and clung to him for what seemed to be a very long time. Michael held her face in both hands, kissed her softly, and groaned, "Oh, my God, I can't tell you how good you feel. Let's get out of here."

She met Ruth, Michael's friend, at the dorm and settled in her room. Mrs. Yorick, the housemother, set down all the rules and was adamant that she be in her room by ten p.m. If she wasn't, she wouldn't be welcome back the following night. Given the woman's robust looks, Maura decided she would never want to lock horns with her. She nodded; she would comply.

Michael took her to a charming, dimly lit Italian restaurant for dinner. They sat side by side in a booth and tried to satisfy their appetites for both food and each other.

The waitress gave them a knowing smile as she took away their half–filled plates of spaghetti. Ah, lovers, she thought.

It had been difficult for them to eat, kiss, fondle, and talk. But they got some of all of it in.

They'd taken a trolley to the restaurant, but it was spring, and the evening was quite balmy. Perfect for two lovers. They decided to walk back to the dorm, stopping along the way to hold each other and kiss. That was the only pause in their conversations. They had plenty to share.

They arrived at the dorm at ten minutes to ten. They lingered. Maura was in her room at ten on the dot. They still had Saturday and Sunday.

Michael met her the next morning at nine. They took the trolley downtown and had breakfast at Woolworth's Five and

Dime store, then spent the day in town, roaming through Woolworth's and some of the better stores.

Maura insisted on buying Michael a cashmere sweater at Lazarus. When he balked at her spending her money on him, she said, "Michael, I can afford it. I've got a job, remember. Uncle Jack pays me well, and I live at home. What else do I have to spend my money on?" She didn't, however, tell him about the small fortune she'd just received. She really didn't know why, except that it was hard for her to even imagine it herself.

Michael got his picture taken. A vendor on the corner of Maine and High Streets shouted out, "Hot dogs! Buy your hot dogs!" They each had two. Maura saw the capitol building, and Michael took her to see the clinic he worked in. She met Dr. Thaddeus Clifton, who gave her a tour of the building, introduced her to a few of the animal patients, and spoke very highly of Michael's work. Then they were off to the German Village, where they had dinner.

It was time to take the trolley back to the dorm. The closest they'd been to each other all day was holding hands. Neither of them could wait to get into the shadows of the trees in front of the dorm to embrace.

Sunday morning turned out to be a marvelously warm spring day. They ate a late breakfast at Herman's Drugstore on the corner by the dorm. Michael took her on a tour of the campus, where he kept meeting up with friends, proudly introducing her. He showed her the dorm where he lived. They would stop intermittently to sit down on benches scattered along the way, Michael with his arm around her, her head on his shoulder. They sat in silence.

For their last evening together, Michael had planned

something very special. Because it was Sunday, there wasn't much open. Downtown Columbus was dead. But there was a place he had in mind.

They rode the trolley to the Scioto River and walked along the waterfront until they came to a place called Catfish Charley's.

"Remember our first date?" Michael asked as they entered the smoke–filled restaurant.

From the aroma, there was no question that fish was cooking. A large grill behind a long counter was frying up at least a dozen pieces of fish.

The place was quite crowded and noisy. People were seated at the counter and at the tables that filled the room. They had to wait for a table and stood watching, fascinated by the skill of the waitresses carrying armfuls of plates heaped with fish, fries, coleslaw, and bread.

Maura looked around at the fishnets hanging from the ceiling, a large anchor leaning against the back wall, and an entire wall of pictures—of fishing boats, captains, and fishermen with their catch. She leaned over and said, "This place surely does have atmosphere. I can't believe you remembered our first catfish dinner together."

"I remember everything we've done together." He took her hand and squeezed it.

Two very portly customers with satisfied looks finally got up from a table in the back of the room, and they were seated.

The patrons were a familiar bunch, talking back and forth across the room, one table to another. Waitresses yelled out, "Where's my order?" "Ya forgot my slaw!" The cook shouted back, "I only have two hands!" or "What do you think I am, a machine?"

Maura and Michael loved every minute of it.

When their order came, they ate in silence, enjoying the panorama around them, soaking up the experience, knowing it would be their last evening together. They needed no conversation.

On their way back to the trolley stop, they leaned on a railing next to a dock. It was dark, and the moon cast a path of gold across the murky water. Two small boats moored at the dock dipped and swayed, creating a soothing lapping sound. It reminded both of them of Darby's Island.

Michael had his arm around Maura and turned her to face him. He stared at her intently for a second then said, "Maura, I'd planned to do this at the restaurant, but there was just no way. So I'm going to ask you now. Will you marry me?"

For a moment, she was at a loss for words. She hadn't expected this. But it only took her that moment to make up her mind. "Oh, Michael, you know I will."

They embraced. He kissed her long and hard. When he released her, he said, "Then stay. We can get married here. I'll find us a place. I'll work something out."

"Oh, that would be so wonderful, but I can't. It would be too difficult for you with your schedule and all. You're almost there, Michael. I would never want you to not finish school, and with me around, I'm afraid I would keep you from it. Besides, Uncle Jack is expecting me back. Patsy will be graduating in May, and after that, we'll be going to see Grandma Mahoney and Aunt Gert. There're just too many things in the way. But just think: only two more summers, and you'll be done. Can't we just plan to be married then? I know it seems like a long time, but it's only a year and a half. And we'll be married for a lifetime."

"Why do you always have to be so darn sensible? Don't you know how much I need you? Please stay."

Maura snuggled in his arms and murmured in his ear, "Sweet Michael, I love you, and as much as I'd love to stay, I'm willing to wait for you. Please do the same for me." She stepped back. "Tell you what: I'll set the date for August 1926. How's that?"

Michael gave up. He knew he'd never win out over her logical, responsible way of thinking. But that was part of why he'd fallen in love with her. He remembered how she'd always made sure that she and Patsy didn't keep their Aunt Gert waiting, how Patsy always looked to her for approval—and a good thing, too. Now, if it were Patsy he'd asked to marry him, she would see things quite differently. She lived in the moment, with her heart on her sleeve.

He gave her a big squeeze. "Okay, if that's the way you want it, I guess I have no choice but to wait."

He reached in his pocket. "I want you to wear this." He took her hand and slipped a ring on her finger. "I know it's not much, but it's all I could afford. It's your birthstone. Someday I'll get you something much better."

Maura looked at the silver band on her finger. The moonlight picked up the glint of a very small diamond. "Oh, I love it. Does this mean we're engaged?"

"Well, I guess. I expected to put it on your finger this week, when we got married. But since you've changed my plans, I see no reason why it can't be an engagement ring."

On the train ride back to Buffalo on Monday morning, Maura

stared longingly at Michael's picture. She knew how much she'd disappointed him and wished she could have stayed. She missed him already. But what if she married him and got pregnant? He'd probably quit school and work full time in the clinic.

It had crossed her mind that she had enough money to keep him in school, but he was too proud for that. That was one of the reasons she loved him. He had taken it upon himself to work his way through school rather than depend on his parents for support. She knew they'd helped him out from time to time, but for the most part, he'd done it on his own.

No, it was better this way. If he'd known how much she really didn't want to wait, he would have broken down all her resolution. It had taken everything in her to say no.

She twisted the ring on her finger and stared out the window at the passing, empty fields.

It was the first week in May when Tony Russo dropped dead in the lumber yard of a heart attack. Clyde Mersol came running into her office, out of breath. "Call a doctor! Call an ambulance!"

Startled, Maura looked up from her ledger. "What's the matter?"

"It's Tony. He was pulling some lumber down for a customer and just keeled over. I think he's dead. I couldn't get him to answer me. Just get help, will you?"

Dr. Reubin pronounced Tony dead when he arrived. The entire store was in shock. Tony's wife was contacted, and the doors were locked for the day. Four days later, the store was once again closed so that all the employees could attend the funeral.

The day after the funeral, Jack entered Maura's office and

sat down, something he did periodically just to pass time and talk about the business. He enjoyed discussing things with his niece because he knew that whatever was on his mind would go no further. Today he had a particular problem to discuss.

"I guess we have to hire someone to take over Tony's job as yard foreman. He'll be hard to replace. He was a good man. Been with me since I opened the store. I know Clyde expects to take over his job, since he worked under him in the yard, but he's only been here two months, doesn't know the stock, yet, and has a record of showing up late. There've been times when I thought about getting rid of him. But Tony would always say, 'Ah, he's okay. Not too quick, but he has a strong back.'"

Maura just nodded and listened.

"Maybe I should bring in someone from one of the other stores. Someone who has more knowledge of the yard."

Maura chewed on her pencil, thinking. "You know, there is someone here who knows every small detail of the business and is always on time."

"Who's that?"

"Wash. Lincoln Washburn. When anyone around here needs to know anything and there's no one else to ask, they go to Wash. He always has the answer. I know he's just the maintenance man, but I can't tell you how many times he's helped me out. He knows every nook and cranny, every crick and crack in this building. He knows when deliveries come and where they're stored. He knows what's on the shelves and in the yard. He's the first one here in the morning and the last one to leave at night. He deserves a chance at a better paying job. And I know he would do it every bit as well as Tony. Besides that, everyone seems to like him. I just love him to death."

"But, Maura, he's black! What would people think if I hired a black man as yard foreman? That's one of the most important jobs you can have in a place like this."

"And it's a job I think he could handle very well. So what do you care what people think, as long as the job gets done?"

"I just don't know. I'll have to give it some thought. But you're right. He's one of the most dependable workers I've ever had. Been with me from the beginning, same as Tony. That's when there were only four of us working here, and I took care of the yard myself. There wasn't anything I asked him to do that wasn't done well, and always with a smile."

It took Jack a few days to mull the problem over. He called Wash into his office the following Monday. "Sit down, Wash."

Wash held his cap in his hands and gingerly sat on the edge of the chair in front of Jack's desk. This was quite unusual for him, to be asked into his boss's office. He had no idea what he'd done wrong.

Jack put his feet up on his desk, leaned back in his chair and smiled. "How've things been going with you these days, Wash?"

"Good, Mistah Jack. No complaints."

"Your Emiline is one fine cook. I can't tell you how much she means to me and my family."

"Yessah. She thinks mighty highly on you all, too," he answered, twirling his cap

Jack finally got around to the business at hand. Wash left his office stunned but happy. He walked out into the yard. He knew he could do the job.

Clyde Mersol was irate. "I ain't workin' for no nigger." He quit.

There were others willing to take his place.

The rest of the store was nonplussed, but no one really blamed Jack for his choice. Everyone thought the world of Wash.

Martha was totally against the whole idea. "What will the people at the club say when they find out you hired a black man to oversee the work of others? He was doing just fine as a maintenance man. That is his place. Leave well enough alone."

She was totally embarrassed when the members of the country club started buzzing about the news. It was bad enough that they had an Irish name like Mahoney. Jack had been Catholic, but thank goodness she'd swayed him to join her at the First Presbyterian Church, where they were now members in good standing. Otherwise, they would never have been asked to join the country club.

Jack ignored her complaints. Things were moving along well at the store, Wash's new job made Emiline very happy, and who cared what the people at the club thought or said? It would all blow over, be forgotten when the next thing popped up.

Plans for the family trip to Cleveland for Patsy's graduation were totally sabotaged the following week. Mother Angela called around eleven on Tuesday evening from Notre Dame Academy to say that Patsy hadn't been in her bed at bed check.

She assured them there was no foul play, that Patsy was probably perfectly safe. She'd taken all of her clothes, and her roommate told them she was running off to get married. She was sorry things had worked out that way, but Patsy would receive her diploma in the mail. There was nothing else the school could do. It had been Patsy's choice to leave.

"I just called because I was sure you'd want to know—and God bless."

Martha was beside herself. "How could she do such a thing?" she screamed. "Running off two days before her graduation. Who is this boy? Why couldn't she tell us?"

On and on she ranted until the wee hours of the morning.

Jack listened and sympathized, quite upset himself. Finally, exhausted, they both managed to fall asleep around four.

Maura never said a word. It was up to Patsy to call and tell them everything. She wasn't really surprised that Patsy would do something like this. Maura was only happy she'd waited until she finished school.

Martha took the call from Patsy two days later. Bubbling with happiness, Patsy told her what she'd done. Martha tried to interject a few thoughts of her own, but Patsy kept babbling on.

She and Paul were in Chicago at the Drake Hotel. Paul would be going for orientation at Feltzer Engineering the next day. They thought they had found an apartment; that's what they were going to see about today. If that didn't work out, they could always stay with Paul's parents in Evanston until they found a place. They would be coming home—she wanted everyone to meet Paul, he was so wonderful—probably Saturday. He wouldn't be starting work for another week or so. "Byee."

"Of course, dear. We'll look forward to seeing you."

Martha sighed and hung up the phone. What else could she say? The deed was done. She shrugged and turned to Jack, who'd been trying to garner some information from his wife's periodic comments of "Uh huh" and "Oh, I see." Not much to go on. "You'll have to cancel our trip to Herron's Point," she informed him. "Patsy and what's–his–name are coming in on the four–thirty train this Saturday."

Emiline only worked Mondays through Fridays. This weekend was an exception. She was as excited about Patsy coming home as the rest of the family and planned to serve all her favorites.

Maura couldn't wait to see Patsy's handsome Romeo. It amused her to think of all the romance novels Patsy had read. She wondered if they were of any help on her wedding night.

Jack and Martha brought the newlyweds back from the train station around five in the afternoon. Kevin, Maura, and Emiline were all sitting on the veranda next to the driveway, waiting, as the car pulled in.

Patsy hopped out of the car, threw her arms around Emiline, plying her cheeks with kisses, then turned to Kevin and gave him a big hug. She and Maura rocked back and forth as they embraced, and Maura whispered in her ear, "You bad girl."

They both laughed.

Paul and Jack got the luggage out of the trunk and set it next to the veranda door.

"Everyone, I would like you to meet my husband, Paul Johnston," Patsy announced proudly.

After Maura shook his hand, she stood back as he gracefully met Emiline and Kevin. Tina came out to shake his hand, too. Of course, Sadie was in the midst of all the activity, racing from one to the other, accepting any crumb of attention she could get.

Maura observed that he was tall and lanky, with an angular face and a large Adam's apple that bobbed up and down as he talked. It was a nice, kind face, though, softened by his brown, curly hair. But handsome? No, she would never describe him as such. Patsy looked stunning.

Emiline left for the kitchen to prepare dinner. They were having fried chicken with mashed potatoes and gravy, warm apple pie, and ice cream. All of Patsy's favorites.

The week that followed was a busy one. Jack and Maura would return from work to find the house full of Patsy's friends either coming in or just leaving—lots of them former beaus with their new girlfriends. Maura would usually join them unless the crowd planned to be out late. Everyone liked Paul a lot. He was very bright and quick. Maura could see how Patsy would be attracted to him. She and Patsy had a number of private moments together. There was no question that Patsy was very much in love and extremely happy.

Patsy asked her about the ring on her finger.

"I'll be inviting you to my wedding a year from this August," Maura said, holding her hand in front of her and admiring her ring.

"Oh, Maura, I'm so happy for you!" Patsy covered her large diamond and emerald ring and gold band with her other hand. She could never gloat, not with Maura.

The house seemed empty after Paul and Patsy left. Kevin was out of school and always at the club playing tennis. Maura felt very lonely when she returned from work. She spent a great deal of time in the kitchen with Emiline, just talking and helping where she could.

She was especially disappointed that she didn't get her two–week vacation. She'd really been looking forward to seeing her Grandmother Mahoney, Uncle Hal, and Aunt Gert, but Jack had said he'd had to rearrange his entire schedule because of Patsy, and he'd try to set up their vacation for sometime in July.

"That's not too far away," he'd said with a patronizing smile, patting her on the head.

She'd been at work about six hours when the headache came. It was so fierce that she had to go into the restroom twice to throw up.

"Go home and go to bed. You must be coming down with something," Irene, her clerk, ordered. "I'll take care of things here."

It was all she could do to make it home and into the house. There was no one around. Even Sadie wasn't there to greet her. Emiline is probably taking her for a walk, she thought.

The kitchen was very warm, and the aroma of pot roast and onions filled the room. She ran to the sink and threw up again. After cleaning up after herself, she took a headache powder and slowly walked up the stairs to her bedroom.

Startled, Kevin jumped up from the edge of her bed, where he'd been sitting, reading her letters from Michael.

"What do you think you're doing, you little sneak?"

Kevin gave her a snide grin. "Pretty hot stuff, sis."

If she hadn't already had a headache, he'd have given her one. She shook with blood–red rage and screamed at the top of her lungs, "You slimy little sneak! How dare you! You have no business in my room. And you certainly don't have any right to go through my things. You're nothing but a despicable, spoiled brat!"

She grabbed the letters and stuffed them back in the box he'd taken them from.

Martha, having just come in from shopping, dropped her packages and followed the sound of screaming.

"Here, here, what's going on? Maura, you have no right to talk to your brother like that!"

"That's right, Aunt Martha. Take his side. You always do."

Martha had never seen Maura in such a state. In all the years she had been with her, she'd never spoken to her in that tone.

"Now, Maura, I'm sure Kevin has a good explanation for what he's done. Don't you, Kevin?" She looked at him standing there, the only one in the room who didn't seem upset.

She looked back at Maura. "I don't know what he's done, but I've never known him to be a sneak."

Kevin's handsome, angelic face smiled sheepishly at Martha. "Aunt Martha, I didn't mean any harm. Wally is supposed to pick me up just about now. We'd planned to take these two girls to the amusement park, and I only have a dollar twenty–five. No one was here, so I came in to see if Maura had any money. Sometimes when I pass her room, I see money lying on her dresser. Anyway, there was none, so I opened the top drawer of her dresser, thinking maybe she'd put some in there. That's where I throw all my stuff. Anyway, I saw this box and figured it might have money in it, but it was full of letters. I don't know why I took one out and read it. Just curious, I guess." He looked at Maura with hound–dog repentance. "I'm sorry, sis. I shouldn't have done it. It won't happen again."

"You creepy liar!" Maura screamed. "That box was buried under my camisoles and panties. And those letters were strewn all over my bed!"

At that moment, she could have strangled him gladly. "Aunt Martha—"

They all heard the horn honk.

"That's Wally," Kevin said, brushing past Maura and Martha. "Gotta go." He gave his aunt a pleading look.

"All right, Kevin. Here." She dug in the purse she was still holding and handed him a five–dollar bill. "Run along and have a good time."

"Thanks. You're a love." He gave her a peck on the cheek and raced down the steps.

Martha called after him. "Behave yourself, hear?"

She looked back at Maura, sitting on the edge of the bed holding her head. "You see, Maura? He really didn't mean any harm."

Maura looked up at her aunt through bloodshot eyes. Her head throbbed. She was so sick, and she'd come home to this.

"Aunt Martha, Kevin was lying. You really don't know him very well. In fact," she raised her voice, "you don't know him at all."

Martha had had just about enough. It was bad enough that the girl had been the cause of such embarrassment to her at the country club. Jack would never have promoted Wash to yard foreman if it hadn't been for her. Who did this high–handed girl think she was? Now she was angry. She shouted back, "I know very well who Kevin is! You're a fine one to talk. You're the one who doesn't know who she is."

"What do you—" Maura's face turned ashen and she ran to the bathroom.

Martha's voice trailed after her. "What's the matter, dear? Don't you feel well?"

She stood there wishing she could have bitten her tongue. Through the years, Maura had become as much a daughter to her as her own Patsy. She wouldn't hurt her for the world.

What's the matter with me? she thought. Why did I have to say that? If I know Maura, she won't let up until she has an explanation—in its entirety. Jack will be furious with me.

When Maura returned, her face was flushed, and she was shivering.

Martha was startled. "Oh, my dear, you look terrible. Here, get under the covers. I'll get you a quilt."

Quite concerned, she called the doctor.

She waited at the bottom of the steps as Dr. Riley came down with his black satchel. "Looks like she has that bug that's been going around. Must have had at least five others this past week with the same symptoms. Nasty but short-lived. Here, give her one of these every three hours. She'll be fine in a day or two."

For twenty-four hours, Maura slept in snips and starts between trips to the bathroom. First she was cold, then she was hot—covers on, covers off. Her headache slowly diminished, her fever broke, and by midday the next day, she fell into a deep, peaceful sleep.

Jack came home that evening and found Martha, who had finally mustered up the courage, sitting in his study waiting to talk with him about the confrontation the day before.

She broke down and cried as she related the event. "I'm so sorry. I don't know why I said what I did. If I could take it back, I would. You know I would never want to hurt her. It was just all those terrible things she said about Kevin, you know? I wasn't thinking. I'm truly sorry."

When it came to Martha, Jack was a patient man. She was the love of his life. He'd always overlooked her overindulgence of Kevin. Why wouldn't he? It was Kevin that had brought her back from the throes of depression and given her back to him. Martha was sometimes too concerned with her social standing, he knew that, and a bit too proud, but she was never mean.

Taking her hand, he smiled, accepting the fact that the family secret that had been withheld from Maura for all these years was finally in the open. He'd always thought that someday someone would tell her. He'd expected it would be someone from Herron's Point with a long memory and mean disposition, someone who found some sadistic pleasure in causing others discomfort.

"It's all right, Martha. I'll have a talk with her. She'd probably find out sooner or later, anyway, and perhaps under much worse circumstances. It won't be easy for her to accept at first, but she does have the right to know. She's a very sensible girl. She'll handle it like she handles everything else, logically and sensibly."

He patted her hand and went up to see Maura.

Maura was sitting up in bed taking nourishment when he walked in. Emiline had come to see her "sweet chile" three times that day and had finally convinced her to have some chicken noodle soup, toast, and tea.

"Well, young lady, you look a far sight better than that heap of bones I saw thrashing around in bed last night. Feeling better?"

Maura gave a wan smile. "Much better, Uncle Jack. I'll probably be able to go to work tomorrow."

"Don't even think about it. Irene is doing just fine." He sat in a chair and crossed his legs. "Everyone at work was asking about you. Wash told me to tell you hello."

She took a sip of tea, set the cup down and said, "That's nice."

There was a long pause.

Jack wasn't sure just how to broach the subject of yesterday's confrontation with Kevin and Martha.

Maura wanted to tell him about Kevin, and she, too, was having difficulty knowing how to begin. Finally she said, "You know, Uncle Jack, yesterday was not one of my best, and when I came home, sick as bejeesus, Kevin and I really got into it. I've been—"

"I know. Your Aunt Martha told me all about it. I can't tell you how sorry she is that she said what she did about you not knowing who you are."

Maura gave him a curious look. "She did? I was so sick I really don't remember everything that was said. I just remember how angry I was at Kevin. What he did yesterday was the last straw. I've been wanting to talk to you about him for a long time."

"That's interesting. Your Aunt Martha seemed to think you were more upset with her for what *she* said. She told me it upset you so much that you ran to the bathroom and threw up."

"Now that you mention it, I do remember her saying something about not really knowing who I am. What did she mean by that?"

Jack was sorry he'd even brought it up. Martha was so sure Maura was going to demand an explanation, and here was Maura telling him she didn't even remember. Now what should he do?

"Oh, I'm sure she didn't mean anything by it. She was just angry, that's all. You said such nasty things about Kevin, and in her eyes, Kevin didn't really mean any harm. You know how it is with her and Kevin."

"Yes, I do. That's the problem. It's one of the reasons I

haven't said anything before. But after yesterday...well. He is such a sneak and a liar, all the things I called him. He has Aunt Martha totally fooled with his charming lies. He doesn't always go where he says he's going. He and Wally both drink. I don't know where they find it, but they do. Kevin has come home drunk more than once. Sometimes he says he'll be in at a certain hour, and Aunt Martha takes him at his word. You're both sleeping when he comes in, but I hear him. His room is right next to mine. The next day, he tells her he got in long before he really did. Sometimes he sneaks out after everyone is in bed. I hear that, too. Uncle Jack, he's not even sixteen, and he's been at this for over a year. And you can't blame Wally, like Aunt Martha does if she catches him at something. Wally does whatever Kevin wants. I know that, too.

"Yesterday, I could have strangled him gladly. He must have spent a good part of the afternoon reading my letters. They were all over my bed. I surprised him, coming home so early, so he told Aunt Martha he was looking for money and that he only read one letter out of curiosity. Ate humble pie and apologized to me. Huh! He lied, Uncle Jack, gave her this long explanation of why he did what he did and convinced her, just like he always does."

Jack was shocked. He'd turned a blind eye to all of Kevin's comings and goings, feeling Martha knew Kevin well enough to handle him. "Well, that's quite enlightening. You should have spoken up sooner, Maura."

"It's not that I haven't wanted to." Her face grew quite serious. "So what did Aunt Martha really mean when she said I don't know who I am?"

Jack thought they had slid past that subject quite neatly. If he hadn't brought it up in the first place, it might have escaped her altogether. Now he knew she was going to pursue it until she got an explanation. That was Maura—no loose ends.

He looked down and talked to his hands. "It's nothing. Nothing at all."

"Yes, it is. Aunt Martha wouldn't have been concerned and sent you to talk to me about it if it was nothing. So tell me. What is it that I don't know about myself?"

"Well, Maura, there is just no easy way to tell you this other than to say that Tim Ryan wasn't your real father."

Maura put her hands to her face and gasped. "What do you mean he wasn't my real father?"

"What I mean is, your mother was raped, and you were the result of that rape. But no one could have been more of a father to you than Tim Ryan. He loved you like his own. None of this is your fault, understand, and it makes no difference who your real father is. We all love you just for being you."

Maura let out a long, whimpering wail. "Who is this man? How could he have hurt my beautiful mama that way?"

"I think you should talk to your Grandma Mahoney about that. She can tell you much more than I can."

He paused for a moment, then looked at Maura with tear-filled eyes. "I loved my sister dearly, and her pain was my pain, but the one wonderful thing that came out of all of it was you. Your mother loved you so much, and I can't thank her enough for giving you to me. I couldn't love you more if you were my own daughter. And think of it, Maura. I'm not your real father, either."

Maura began to weep.

Jack got up, set her tray on the floor, and took her in his

arms. "It's okay, sweetheart. Go ahead and cry. Sooner or later, you'd have found out anyway, and you do have every right to know about you heritage."

She finally lay back and buried her head in her pillow, weeping softly. Jack stayed, rubbing her back until she was silent and he knew she had fallen asleep.

By the following Monday, Maura had come to a decision. She went to Jack's office, where she found him talking on the phone. She waited in the chair across from his desk, watching him fiddle with a pencil as he talked.

When he finished, he put the receiver in its cradle and looked at his niece, her face pinched and pale. He leaned back in his chair and put his feet up on his desk, as he usually did. "Well, my dear, what can I do for you this beautiful June morning? Feeling better, I hope."

"Uncle Jack, I'm going to be leaving."

Jack sat upright. "Leaving? What do you mean?"

"I mean I'm going to leave my job here." She threw up her arms in despair. "I can't seem to concentrate on anything. All I can think about is that terrible man who's supposedly my father. I've got to find him and look at him face to face. Perhaps after I do that I can come back to work." She looked at her uncle and shrugged. "I don't know. But I have to leave and put my life back together."

"But why? You've lived all these years without him. Why do you have to find him now? He almost destroyed your mother's life. Don't let him do the same to yours."

"You don't understand. You can't know how deeply this has affected me. You, Aunt Martha, Aunt Gert, Uncle Hal, Grandma Mahoney—all of you thought you were protecting me, I know.

But now, just knowing that you knew all these years hurts me. I'm glad Aunt Martha finally said something. I can't imagine what it would be like if a stranger had told me. And then there's Mama and Papa. I keep thinking of them. I know I was young when they died, but my memories of both of them are quite vivid. Papa used to call me his little princess. He did love me, I know. And I could never think of anyone else being my papa. And Mama was so good, so loving. I just can't imagine what the two of them must have gone through because of me. They protected me from it all. You all did. But I'm a big girl, now, and I have to deal with it. I've decided I have to confront the man that hurt my mother and fathered me. I don't know why, but I do. I'm filled with anger and hatred toward him, and I don't like the feeling. Unless I see him face to face, I know it will never go away. I have to tell him how I feel and hopefully put closure on it all."

Jack looked at his niece with admiration. "I know you well enough to know you're not going to change your mind. You must do what you feel is right. I won't try to talk you out of it. Fortunately you now have the means to do it. When will you go?"

"If it's all right with you, I thought I would leave when we go to Herron's Point. We're all going there next week, anyway. I'll tie up things here with Irene before we go, and by the time you get back, she'll be all settled in at her job. I'll just stay on and talk to Grandma and find out more about this man. Perhaps I'll be back within the month, perhaps not. At this point, I really don't know which direction my life will take. All I do know is it sure took a detour."

"Seems like you've got this pretty much settled in your

mind. Next week won't be a problem."

Maura stood to leave. "Thank you for not giving me a hard time with this. It wasn't an easy decision. I've loved working here, and you know I love you and Aunt Martha, but I have to do this."

Jack got up, walked over, and gave her a hug. "Your going will leave a great big hole in this place. Not that Irene can't handle your job. You've trained her well. But that aside, everyone will miss you. You're a very special young lady. Home won't be the same with you gone. Emiline will be devastated."

He sighed as he opened the door for her. "First Patsy, then you. Maybe now I can concentrate on Kevin. From the things you've told me, he needs a lot of my attention."

CHAPTER TWENTY–SIX
Making Plans

Maura loved the hubbub in her grandmother's kitchen. Sometimes tempers flared, waiters became frustrated, the chef was running short of chops, the sauce burned, or someone dropped a dish. Through it all, Brigid kept her cool. It always amazed Maura that by the end of their shifts, each of the workers bid the others goodbye with a smile and went his or her separate way.

She noticed that her grandmother was slowing down a little, that she was no longer the petite dynamo she remembered from her early years. Her hair was completely white, now, but to Maura, she was still beautiful.

Brigid also spent less time overseeing things at the restaurant and more time working with Mary Murphy (now one of her closest friends) at Saint Michael's, helping Father DeSalle. If there was a family in need anywhere in Herron's Point, she and Mary saw that, if possible, that need was filled. Brigid no longer craved praise or looked for recognition, but found it completely gratifying to be of service. No child would go hungry or without shoes or a warm coat if she could help it.

Maura had asked Jack and Martha not to say anything to her grandmother regarding her new knowledge of her father. She would wait until the week was up and they had gone back to Buffalo. Then she could have a talk with Brigid without upsetting everyone's vacation. They'd agreed.

Jack spent most of the week with Kevin, playing tennis, fishing, and swimming, much to the chagrin of the girls in Herron's Point, who looked forward to Kevin's yearly visits. Jack did give him some time to have fun with his friends—and Kevin collected them wherever he went—but there was no question that Jack had his eye on the boy.

With each year's visit, Jack's admiration for his mother grew. The woman he had left so many years before no longer seemed to exist, at least not that part of her that demanded the world show her homage. She now reached out to others with a genuine concern. And it pleased him no end that she and Martha got along so famously. Martha hung on her every word and found Brigid to have a wonderful sense of humor.

Just as during all their other visits, they had a wonderful week. It was obvious to all that Kevin was quite pleased with his Uncle Jack's attention, checking with his schedule for the day's activities before he made plans of his own.

All but Maura left on Sunday. They planned to stop off on Darby's Island to spend a day with Gert and Hal before heading home. Brigid thought it strange that Maura was staying on another week, but was pleased that she was.

After Brigid had bid the rest of them goodbye, she walked up to the cemetery, as she was prone to do, and had a little talk with her two favorite men.

"There's somethin' afoot, I'm thinkin'. Our Maura's not quite herself this trip. Not that she's been a trouble, mind ya. She's pure pleasure ta me heart. And I sorely missed Patsy this trip, but she wrote ta say she and Paul will be comin' ta visit sometime in the fall. Jack says he's a fine young man. Ah, Patrick and Chuck, our girls are growin' up. But that's the way of things, I'm thinkin'. And our Kevin. Well! It seems Jack has taken him under his wing, and the boy is lovin' every minute of it."

She tidied up their graves and went back to her apartment to find Maura waiting.

"Grandma, could we take a walk down to the dock and sit? I just love being by the water."

"Certainly, child."

The dock was in the same place as the one Tim had built years before, but this one was a little wider. There were two benches, one on either side, facing the water. Sitting on the left, one could watch the swimmers on the beach and all the activity beyond. On the right, one could see the vastness of the lake and a wooded shoreline.

They sat on the right in silence for a few moments, watching a freighter fall off the edge of the horizon. Then Maura spoke.

"Grandma, I didn't want to say anything about this until the others left, but I was wondering if you could tell me who my father is."

Brigid stiffened. The very mention of Maura's father opened a wound that she had desperately tried to heal.

She looked at Maura. "Why would ya be askin' such a question, child? Tim Ryan was yer father from the day ya were born, don't ya know. And no better father could there be, I'm thinkin'."

Maura looked out at the lake and sighed. "Yes, I do know that. I loved him with all my heart. But I also know that he wasn't my real father."

Brigid's eyes were on Maura's face. "And who'd be tellin' ya such a thing?"

Maura explained the circumstances that had brought about the revelation of her heritage. "I'm glad I found out the secret all of you have been keeping from me. Just knowing that part of it makes me feel uncomfortable...terrible. Uncle Jack said I had every right to know, and that sooner or later, someone else would have told me anyway."

"Always stickin' up fer his Martha, he is. But knowin' the woman, I can't be believin' she meant any ill will. And I can't be thinkin' who else would be tellin'. No one in this town knew Tim Ryan wasn't yer father except meself, Penelope, and Clifford, the two Carter sisters, and Rosemarie and her parents. But there's none of us who'd want to be tellin' ya. Oh, then there's Gert and Hal on the island. But they'd nivver say anything either, I'm thinkin'. Of course, Jack and Martha knew."

"You have to admit that's a lot of people, Grandma. And now that I do know, I'm consumed with anger and malice for a man I don't even know. Uncle Jack said you were the one I should talk to. I don't know why, but I have to see this man face to face and tell him how I feel." Her face became pinched and her voice much louder. "I hate him for what he did to my mother."

She paused, then with a softer voice asked, "Do you think they'll ever find out who killed her?"

"Ah, me poor, sweet Mary Margaret." Brigid began to cry softly.

Maura slid over on the bench and put her arm around Brigid. "Oh, Grandma, I'm sorry. I didn't mean to upset you."

Brigid pulled away, tears streaming down her cheeks, and looked Maura squarely in the face. "It's me that's knowin' all about anger and hatred, child. I let it eat inta me soul. I drove yer mither and her darlin' Tim away from here with me willful anger."

"What do you mean?" Maura was incredulous.

"Tim Ryan was the son of a drunkard, and yer mither opposed me every step of the way when I tried to get her to stop seein' him. Ta my way of thinkin', he'd turn out just like his da. The man who raped yer mither was a charmin' man. A man of position and fortune who stayed with us for a considerable time. I thought I knew him quite well and could see he was sweet on me Mary Margaret. Now, *he* was someone I thought worthy of me beautiful daughter. When she told me she was in a family way, and how it happened, I didn't believe her. I truly thought she was coverin' fer Tim, since the man she accused of rapin' her was no longer around. I just couldn't accept the fact that he would ever do such a thing. How I could have been so blind, I'll nivver know. But I was. And filled with anger and hatred. I drove yer mither out of me house with me rage.

"I'll nivver ferget that fall and winter as long as I live. It was a time that changed me life ferever. I lost me daughter, and then I lost the dearest friend I had in the whole world. Before he died, he told me many times that I was wrong, but me with me knowin' ways always knew better. After he died, I realized he was right. By this time, yer mither and Tim had left Herron's Point. Fortunately, your mither had a fergivin' heart, and I came to know you and Kevin and yer father, Tim. No better man was ever born. I loved him like me own." Brigid sobbed.

Maura stared at her grandmother's heaving shoulders, trying to digest what she'd just been told. She reached over and wiped her tears with her handkerchief and put her arms around her. "It's okay, Grandma. It's been nineteen years. Nineteen! That was such a long time ago. Whatever mistakes you made in the past, you certainly have tried to make up for."

Then she held her grandmother at arm's length and smiled. "Look at you! A pillar of your community. Not only have you changed this town, but you're constantly doing works of charity. You're to be admired for all you do. And Grandma, I think you're just beautiful."

That last comment made Brigid sniffle and smile. She said, "None of it's enough to make up for the pain and suffering I caused me own daughter. I would undo it all if I could."

"Have you to the station in plenty of time for the ten–thirty, missy. Sure is a beautiful day for travelin'." Zeb gave Maura a tobacco–stained grin. "Where ya off to?" he asked as he chugged up Division Street with fierce intensity, chawing away, leaning forward with both hands gripping the wheel tightly, as though waiting for something to jump up in front of him at any given moment.

"I have to take care of some business in Toronto. Ever been there?"

Zeb stared doggedly at the road and said, "Nah. Always been meanin' to go, though. I knew a fella there by the name of Arnaud. He always said to look him up if I was ever in town."

Besides the fact that she thought it quite comical that Zeb could actually drive, chew, and talk at the same time, she was taken aback at the mention of the name Arnaud. But since Zeb had lived at the boarding house for years, it was only logical that he would know Robert Arnaud.

She had no intention of revealing the purpose of her mission. Still, she was curious as to what Zeb could tell her.

"Is he someone from these parts?" she asked.

"No, no, missy. He's too good for the likes of us. Stayed at the boarding house for quite a spell one year. That's how come I got to know him. His family back in Toronto owns the shippin' yard here. A real gentleman he is. Not that he didn't try to fit in, mind you. He just had so much polish and charm, he kinda stuck out from the likes of us. You know the kind. Good–lookin' in a foppy way. Had all the ladies oohin' and aahin' over him. Your grandma was one of 'em. Kinda sweet on your mama, too, as I recall. But she couldn't see him for dirt, she was so in love with your daddy."

Maura's heart had ached for her mother when Brigid had unfolded the details about her real father's visit that summer and all that had followed. Now she continued to fish for information. "That was a long time ago, wasn't it? Do you ever hear from him?"

"Nah. The last time I saw him was that summer, when I picked him up wanderin' in a vacant lot next to MacPhearson's Hotel. He'd been at the hotel for a goin'–away lunch with all the bigs at the shippin' yard, and he sure must've drank his, 'cause there was no way he knew what he was doin'. I had to put him on the train personal."

He practically slowed down to a halt so he could spit out the window, started up again, and said, "I'm a liar. I did see him once after that. And there's no way I should be forgettin' that one, 'cause it was two days before your mama was found dead."

He gave a sympathetic look toward Maura. "That was an awful thing. Her so beautiful, and you so young and all."

"I was young, Zeb, but I remember it all quite well. I'm over the pain of it, but it's something I'll never forget. So tell me, this Arnaud fella—was he still in town when my mama was killed?"

"Now that I don't know. I never did see him again after the day I picked him up at the station. And now that you mention it, it's mighty curious, 'cause he never asked me to take him back. I'd forgot all about him bein' here that time because of the news we got about your mama. But I do know he went to see your grandma."

She wondered why her grandma hadn't mentioned that visit. She'd told her everything else. But that was a period of Brigid's life when her thoughts would have been consumed with the tragic death of her daughter. Robert Arnaud would have been someone she wanted to forget.

Maura wondered about his visit.

Where did he go when he left here? she thought. Did he go to see my mother? And if he did, how did he get there, and did anyone on the island know he was there—if he was there? There were lots of unanswered questions.

During the entire train ride to Toronto, Maura rehearsed what she would say to the father she didn't know. She couldn't picture his face, but she knew she wouldn't like it.

The more she thought about the words she wanted to use to show him her contempt, the more agitated she became and the angrier she got. Part of her even began to believe that he was the man who had murdered her mother. Her mother had

had no enemies. He had to be the one. Why? She didn't know. But if he could rape, he could kill; those were her thoughts on it. Perhaps he felt he could go through life without being punished for his crimes, but he would know what she thought about him. She had to do this—not just for herself, but for her mother; life had been so unfair to her.

From when she was a small child, Maura remembered only that her mother was kind and gentle, never complaining. The loss of her husband had affected her deeply, but Maura always understood that side of Maggie because he had been her father, and she missed him, too.

When she got off the train at Union Station, she hailed a taxi and asked to go to the Windsor House on King Street. Her grandmother had told her it was a small, stylish hotel squeezed in between two other buildings. She had called ahead for reservations.

As she entered the small, well-appointed lobby, she was greeted with a big smile from the slightly balding desk clerk. "May I help you, young lady?"

After signing the register, she asked the clerk if he could direct her to the Alexandre & Arnaud Import–Export building.

He rubbed his chin. "Hm, let's see now. It's a short walk from here. I'm just trying to think of the best way to get you there."

He ended up drawing her a small map on a piece of hotel stationery. "There you are, young lady. I don't think you'll get lost. But if you do, just ask someone on the street. Everyone around here knows where they are."

She smiled. "I appreciate your time." She turned and then

waved the paper in her hand as the bellboy led her to the elevator. "And for this little map. Thank you so much."

"No trouble," the clerk answered as the elevator door opened.

Her room was quite pleasant—homey. She began to relax a little, but that was short-lived when she realized she had to call and make an appointment to meet this man.

After locating a telephone in the lobby, she dialed the number.

"Alexandre and Arnaud," a man's deep voice said on the other end.

"Why, yes, I was wondering if I could have an appointment to speak to a Mr. Robert Arnaud."

"May I ask in what regard you wish to speak to him?"

She had to think quickly. She hadn't expected that question.

"Yes...well...I have some very valuable furniture I want to ship to my sister in Paris. I was told to deal with Robert Arnaud about this matter."

"I'm sorry. He doesn't take care of those details. But I can put you in touch with Mr. Choppa, if you wish."

"No, I really need to speak to Mr. Arnaud. I was told by a close member of his family that I should speak to him directly. The legal details are quite complicated, and they said he would be the one to help me out."

"Well, fine, miss. Let me check his schedule."

Maura waited, relieved that she'd convinced the man on the other end to see it her way. She certainly couldn't tell him her real reason for the appointment.

The voice returned. "Actually, Mr. Arnaud is free around four-thirty this afternoon if that's agreeable with you."

"Wonderful. I'll be there." She'd expected to be put off until at least the following day.

"May I ask who's calling?"

"Uh, just tell him it's a friend of his mother's. I'll introduce myself when I see him."

"As you wish. Thank you for calling."

It was just a little past two, and Maura had had no lunch. She decided to go looking for that tea room on Bay Street her grandmother had told her about. She'd said she wasn't sure it was still there, hadn't been to Toronto for at least seven years, but if it was, she knew Maura would enjoy it.

Unfortunately, Monique's Tearoom was now a souvenir shop, but there was a delicatessen two buildings up.

As she ate her corned beef on rye and drank her tea, Maura again tried to relax, soaking in the austere ambience of the store. Customers sat at wooden tables. A long glass meat case was filled with a variety of meats, olives, pickles, some potato salad, and cole slaw, all of it sitting on a bed of crushed ice. The shelves on the wall behind the case held an odd assortment of dishes. Other than that, the rest of the walls were a stark white. A young girl worked at the counter below the shelves, making up the orders that the woman in the large, white apron took from customers. Long rolls of meats and briskets were hanging from hooks in the ceiling at the back of the store. A man wearing a yarmulke on the back of his head sat on a perch at the cash register by the door. There wasn't an attractive corner in the room. Even the plate glass window was without adornment except for the daily specials done on butcher paper that had been pasted somewhat randomly—blank on her side—meant to attract the passersby. Some of these were also scattered around the room.

She sniffed the pungent mixture of herbs and spices. Perhaps some garlic, maybe sesame, but definitely dill. There was a pickle barrel close by. The place was clean, and the sandwich was delicious. She watched the intercourse of customers laughing, sharing bits of their lives with each other, and wished Michael were sitting there with her.

She hadn't told him any of the latest developments in her life. It was so hard to put into words. Not that she couldn't or wouldn't. She just needed to see him face to face. It would be much easier to explain that way. Now that she wasn't working, she would make sure to be on the island when he came home in August. Just the thought of it was a great comfort to her.

Back in her room, she deliberately blocked the impending meeting from her mind by concentrating on getting dressed.

She took a leisurely bath, brushed her hair, and pulled it back into a long, thick braid that almost reached her waist. She attached a large white bow to the end of it. Ever since Patsy had cut her hair, Maura had wanted to do the same, but her hair was so silky, she knew it would be harder to maintain short. She had resigned herself; long hair it had to be.

She wore a pale blue middy dress with a wide, white collar, silk stockings on a pair of very long, shapely legs, and white and navy spectator pumps. Her only jewelry was the small engagement ring on her left hand. She looked in the full-length mirror on the bathroom door, satisfied she looked presentable, ready to take him on, well-prepared now to let the little drama she was about to create unfold as it would.

With map in hand, she walked for ten minutes on the side streets along the waterfront until she came to one called Arnaud

Court. It was a short street, one block long, housing two unimpressive red–brick buildings, two stories high, one on each side, each taking up the entire block. The building on the left had a large sign above the second floor, ALEXANDRE & ARNAUD, and a very large plate glass window with the same name painted in glittering gold and black letters at the far left corner on the first floor. There were a few other doors and many windows, but Maura felt that this entrance must be the one she should take.

She was right. The man with the telephone voice was sitting behind a large desk facing the window that sparkled, in a room starkly furnished with file cabinets along one wall and two straight–back chairs along the wall facing them. The man who stood to greet her was an older gentleman in a brown suit and white shirt with a slightly frayed collar.

"Yes, miss? May I help you?"

"I know I'm a few minutes early," she said, "but I wanted to be sure to find the place. I'm here to see Mr. Arnaud. I'm the one who called earlier, remember? "

"Oh, yes. I'll just go back and tell him you're here. Please have a seat." He motioned to one of the two empty chairs.

Maura waited, shuffling her feet on the cement floor, thinking to herself that the place needed a woman's touch. As she stared at the light gray walls, she began to decorate the room, as she had done with her own office. New paint, a few plants, some nice bright pictures, and definitely more comfortable chairs.

Her thoughts were interrupted.

"Miss, you can go back now. Mr. Arnaud is free to see you. Just go down the hallway to the door at the very end."

She walked past a number of doors with nameplates on them and recognized one: BERNARD CHOPPA—SHIPPING. She had kept her mind occupied with so many other things that when she reached for the doorknob of ROBERT ARNAUD—PRESIDENT, she panicked. After taking a few deep breaths to compose herself, she turned the knob and went in to face the man she detested—her father.

He was looking out the window, his back to her, as she entered a room that surprised her with its glaring contrast to the front office. She was greeted with thick carpeting, valuable paintings on salmon-colored walls, soft leather chairs, a huge hand-carved desk with gold-framed pictures on it, large tropical plants, and rich brown, damask draperies.

He turned.

They stood looking at each other for one awkward moment. His face turned ashen, and then he said, "Maura? Maura Ryan?"

She was incredulous. "I never gave you my name," she snapped. "How do you know who I am?"

"I can't believe you're..." He was at a loss as to what to do next. "You're here."

He ran over and stood behind a large, comfortable-looking chair. "Please have a seat."

She stood her ground. "I asked you a question, Mr. Arnaud. How do you know who I am?"

"My dear girl, for the past fourteen years, ever since I found out you existed, I have thought about you, wondered about you. I tried to imagine what you would be like, what you would look like. And here you are, the picture of my mother in her early years. I think if you look closely, you'll see you also look quite a bit like me. You've always been so much on my mind, there's no doubt I would have known you even if I saw you on the street."

Maura decided she'd better sit. Her legs were going to buckle if she didn't. She hadn't had any idea how this meeting was going to unfold, but she couldn't have imagined it would begin like this.

He was quite emotional. She looked at him long and hard. He was right. They had the same blue eyes, the same silky brown hair, and the same fine features. He was tall and slender, and she took him to be around forty years of age. This was her father!

"You're nothing but a contemptible, lowlife phony, Mr. Arnaud. First of all, I'm not your daughter, because I was not conceived out of love. I was conceived in violence. And if you thought about me so much, as you say you did, why didn't you ever try to contact me? I can't tell you how much I loathe you for what you did to my mother. And I am here to tell you so."

Robert pulled up a chair in front of her. He reached out to take her hand, but she pulled it away.

He looked at her pleadingly. "Maura, please believe me when I say I still have no knowledge of raping your mother. She was a beautiful young woman I could easily have loved. In my right mind, it would never have occurred to me to harm her. And I had no knowledge of you ever being born until I went back to Herron's Point to visit your grandmother. I didn't want to believe her when she first told me what I'd done. But there was part of me that knew it could be true, because I had a problem with alcohol back then. If I drank too much, I blacked out and did things I would never do otherwise. And I did get very drunk the day I left Herron's Point.

"After what your grandmother told me and sent me

stepping, I went to see your mother, just to make sure. She wasn't very happy to see me, either. It was obvious by the time she sent me away just how much she detested me for what I had done. And with good reason. She told me I was never to come near you, that the world thought you were Tim Ryan's daughter, and that I couldn't prove otherwise. So I left. But I will say this. It was a turning point in my life. I haven't touched alcohol since that day. It was an act that has saved my marriage. But my wife and I are childless, and since you're my only living flesh and blood, I have thought about you constantly."

It wasn't supposed to go like this. She was going to tell him what a contemptible, vile man she thought he was, then leave. Right now, she was without words.

He continued. "How did you find out about me? Did your mother finally tell you?"

She found it difficult to look at him and stared out the window as she spoke. "No, my mother couldn't tell me. She was murdered on the same night you went to see her." Then she glared at him. "They never found who did it, but after I was told all the details of my birth, I strongly suspected you had a hand in it. Not that I could ever prove it."

Now Robert was incredulous. The room was heavy with emotional silence. Finally, ignoring her accusation, he spoke softly. "I'm so sorry. I didn't know she was dead."

Maura sighed and got up to leave. Robert stood and walked her to the door. "Maura, I would be honored if you would let me take you to dinner. I'd really like to get to know you better."

She paused at the door and looked him square in the eye. "Mr. Arnaud, when I came here, I was consumed with hatred. What you did to my mother, in my eyes, was unforgivable, even though I know I wouldn't have a life if you hadn't raped her. I find now that I can forgive you, and I don't feel you have it in you to be a murderer. You have no idea what a weight has been lifted from me. But I have no desire to get to know you any better, so I won't have dinner with you. Tim Ryan was my father and always will be. He was the best. I'm sorry your life is so empty." She turned and left.

Robert watched his daughter walk down the hall and out the door, out of his life, as quickly as she'd entered it.

Maura went back to her hotel room and packed her bag. Everything had fallen into place so quickly, there was no reason to stay the night, so she caught the seven o'clock train back to Herron's Point.

Staring out the window of the train, she watched as fields of ripening corn and mown hay came and went. Daylight turned into dusk and then darkness, with an occasional small town revealing itself with welcoming lights. She dismissed thoughts of her meeting with her father.

She was glad she'd confronted him. Now there was no longer a need to feed an anger that had been consuming her these past months. It was a part of her life she'd just learn to live with.

She thought of her grandmother's words. "Maura, child, a wise man once told me that love is the answer to all problems. Try ta see the good in people. Be concentratin' on the blessings that surround ya, and don't be entertainin' ill thoughts. They have a way of takin' up residence and becomin' unwanted guests that control yer life."

She missed home and wondered if she'd been too hasty in

her decision to leave her job. She thought of Emiline and Sadie greeting her as she came in from work every evening. She missed Uncle Jack and his boundless energy, his sweet tenor voice singing as he got ready for work in the morning. She even missed Aunt Martha and Kevin.

Then she remembered that she wanted to be on Darby's Island in late August to see Michael. She missed him most of all. And she hadn't seen Aunt Gert and Uncle Hal in such a long time. These past few years, she'd traded her time with them for the adult world of responsibility—enjoying every bit of it. Kevin never could understand why she'd rather work than have fun. He always told her she was too serious. Perhaps by spending the rest of her summer on the island, she could recapture some of her youthful abandonment.

Three more weeks! She could hardly wait. She had never told Michael about the money she had received from her mother's trust. She would tell him that and so many other things when she saw him. She had been calling him long distance at least twice a week while she was still in Buffalo, ignoring his worries about the cost; she could well afford it. With each call, just hearing his voice rekindled her love for him. It was so much better than writing a letter.

Her return to Herron's Point was one of many tears and much healing. Brigid was not surprised that Robert had recognized her. She complimented Maura on the way she'd handled her problem, and they talked and shared many memories of Maggie. It was quite cathartic to now openly discuss the person that each of them had held so tightly locked in her heart.

By week's end, Maura left for Darby's Island.

CHAPTER TWENTY-SEVEN

The Reunion

She loved the rhythm of life on the island—unhurried, undemanding. And Hal and Gert were as relaxing as an old pair of slippers. Maura only hoped she and Michael would be that comfortable together when they were their age.

Having finished her first year of college, Marietta was now working on the mainland for the summer, so Maura only saw her in the evenings, when she returned from work. But Joanie was still available to share her days swimming at the quarry, riding bikes, fishing off the docks, or just whiling away the time with the young crowd at Ben's Marina.

The day before Michael's arrival, Pops Birch suggested to his wife, Katherine, that perhaps they should stay away and let Maura meet him at the dock. "From my understanding, the pair is completely taken with each other. You remember how that was, eh, Kate?" He gave her a sly wink.

She blushed.

The day was gray and overcast. But it could have been worse. It was warm, and the lake was calm. As far as Maura was concerned, it was a beautiful day.

The minute he stepped off the ferry, she ran to him and they embraced self–consciously, aware of those around them.

He grabbed his valise and wrapped his other arm around her waist. "Let's get out of here."

Everyone on the island knew Michael and greeted him with genuine warmth as he and Maura walked along Water Street. Some wanted to stop to talk, but Michael, as politely as possible, kept on walking.

They bypassed his house and headed for the orchard, where they could be alone. He embraced Maura and groaned with the pleasure of holding her in his arms, then kissed her passionately.

The rains came silently, dumping their moisture on everything below. At first, neither was aware of the downpour that was drenching them, but then Michael sighed. "Guess we'd better get to the house."

It was a week of tumultuous emotion for Maura. They spent every day together, mostly surrounded by family and friends, but each day, they found time to escape it all and go off alone. They made love with almost complete abandon.

Had it been up to Maura, there would have been no turning back, but as difficult as it was, Michael managed to restrain himself. He was determined to make it through one more year, just as Maura had suggested that night in Columbus. Then they would have the rest of their lives together.

They talked for hours, sharing their lives with each other. Michael talked about his classes, his work at the clinic, and his plans for opening a clinic of his own. Maura told him the reason she had left her job and went into great detail about her visit to Toronto and confronting her real father.

She didn't know why she was so apologetic when she told him about the money she had inherited. She supposed it was because she knew how hard he'd worked to put himself through school. She would have gladly given him what he needed to make the burden easier, but knew he'd be too proud to accept it.

"Now you know why I can afford to call you so often," she told him. "I love hearing your voice. It's the next best thing to having you next to me."

Their last day together was spent with thirty–two members of the Birch family. Most had come from the mainland to see Michael and bid him goodbye.

Kate and the girls set up a large picnic table in the back yard, where they feasted on fresh sweet corn, sliced tomatoes, string beans, fried potatoes, and hamburgers, finishing off with apple pie and homemade ice cream. All were products of their farm.

That's when Maura and Michael announced the plans for their wedding.

Marietta and Joanie were elated when Maura asked them to be bridesmaids, and as the oldest member of the family, Victor said he considered being the best man an honor. The rest of the family gathered around Maura and embraced her into the fold. Pops and Kate were very pleased. They now had another addition to their family.

With Michael missing, Maura felt a tremendous void in her life. Her entire summer was gone, and she was at a loss for something to do. She had no work to go to. Marietta and Joanie were both off to business college in Erie. The summer crowd was gone.

She found herself regretting having left Buffalo and was considering going back. As much as she loved Uncle Hal and Aunt Gert, she missed her family—even Kevin. She took to taking afternoon walks along the lake. There was something soothing about being near the water.

It was one of those special golden autumn days that she walked along Water Street. Locusts droned. The air was warm, and the lake lapped peacefully against the shoreline. Leaves drifted silently to the ground, carpeting the earth in a quilt of crimson and gold. It seemed as though life was slowing down, getting ready to sleep.

She found herself in front of the Darby mansion. She saw the same FOR SALE sign in the front yard that had been there the day she went peeking in the windows, just a little the worse for wear.

She'd passed it many times since she'd returned, but today she stood and stared at it—thinking long and hard. She went around the back to the carriage house to look for Roger Thomas and found him clearing the vegetable garden.

"Hi there, Mr. Thomas. Remember me?" She gave him her best smile.

Roger Thomas stood, holding a handful of tomato vines, and stretched to get the kinks out. "Well, hello there, missy. How's the world been treating you?"

"Very well, Mr. Thomas. And you?"

"Not bad. A little rheumatism here and there. But overall, not bad at all."

They stood looking at each other for a moment, then he

said, "I see you and that Michael Birch are quite the item around here. Watched you a number of times passing by, holding hands. He's a fine young man."

"I think so. Michael and I are to be married next August. That's why I'm here."

"You came to see him while he was home, I take it."

"Well, that too, but I mean that's why I'm here in your backyard. I was wondering if you could show me the house. I was thinking perhaps I might be interested in buying it."

"Whoa there, missy. I know it's been sitting here empty for near on ten years, but that don't mean the Darbys ain't holding out for a good price. That's why it's still theirs. They can afford to wait."

He rubbed his chin and looked at her hard. He knew she was Maggie Ryan's daughter, the one who had worked as a maid in this very house.

"Now, where would a young thing like yourself be getting that kind of money?"

"Well, Mr. Thomas, I do have my resources. And if the price is a fair one, I'm sure I would be able to handle it." She looked wistfully toward the house. "For some reason, this house has always intrigued me. I'd love to see it from the inside."

Roger Thomas had shown the house to many people, making sure they saw all its flaws. There was that one couple that came back for the third time, ready to buy, but the husband took deathly ill, and they had to renege on the deal. So far, he'd managed to steer the rest of the people away, realizing that if someone did buy the place, he and Mary would have to leave the home they'd lived in since they'd been married. He was in no hurry to see it sold.

"Now, why would you be wanting a house here on the island? After you and Michael are married, won't the two of you have to find a place where he can do his animal doctoring?"

"Michael is planning to set up a clinic right across the way on the mainland after he graduates. There's a desperate need for a veterinarian in that area because of all the farmland. He loves the island so much—with his family here and all. And I feel the same way. He seems to think it would be no problem ferrying back and forth—at least in the summer. Perhaps we can find a place on the mainland that will serve as his office that we can also live in during the winter months.

"We talked about it a lot while he was here. Pops and Kate said we could live with them until we build a house of our own. Aunt Gert and Uncle Hal offered us their place as well. But this would be perfect. I have a whole year with nothing to do but get a home ready for my Michael."

Roger knew he was not about to squelch this young lady's enthusiasm. He sighed. "Just let me go wash my hands and get the key."

When he returned, his wife was with him. "I don't believe you've ever met my wife, missy. Mary, this is Maura Ryan. Maggie Ryan's daughter."

"Oh, my. Oh, my." Mary's eyes misted as she grabbed Maura's hand with both of hers and shook it heartily. "Your mama was such a love. Took me near a year to get over her tragic demise. But look at you. All grown up and everything."

Maura swallowed the lump in her throat. "I'd almost forgotten about that, but my mama did work here, didn't she? I do remember a man that lived here, though. I think mama called him Henry. He was such a nice man. Took us on a picnic one time." She paused and looked down at her feet. "That was so long ago."

Mary gave her a little hug. "Come on, Roger. Let's show this special young lady the house."

They took her in through the front door, their footsteps and voices echoing in the large, empty, marbled foyer. Mary noticed Maura's eyes widen at the spiral staircase at the far end. "Your mama loved that staircase. She said it always made her feel like someone special when she came down it."

They moved from room to room. Dust and grime revealed the years of neglect. Many rooms, such as the dining room, still contained very large pieces of old furniture. Wallpaper and paint were peeling everywhere. The third–floor rooms had brown stains in the ceiling from obvious leaks, and a broken window pane in one of the rooms gave access to a family of sparrows that had found safe haven there.

Maura remained relatively quite while on the tour, and Roger felt she had seen enough to discourage her from any further interest.

Once outside, her first comment was, "The oak woodwork is in wonderful condition, and the crown moldings and chandeliers are just magnificent." She chewed on her lip. "It sure needs a lot of attention, though."

Roger's hopes were up.

"How much are the Darbys asking, Mr. Thomas?"

When he quoted her the price, he expected that would completely deter her.

But Maura was no one's fool when it came to business. She knew the going rate in real estate. Although expensive, this was a real bargain.

"You get in touch with Mr. Darby and tell him he has a buyer if he'll knock off two thousand for a new roof. There's more needs done, but that can be taken care of room by room."

Roger's hopes were dashed.

"Also, Mr. Thomas, I would be pleased if you and Mary would remain here. I can't do it alone. I'm going to need all the help I can get."

Now Roger's hopes swooped back up into high gear. He didn't care where she got the money, just as long as he and Mary were part of the deal. "I'll get in touch with Mr. Darby today, missy. Stop back tomorrow, and we'll talk."

When Maura returned to tell Gert and Hal of her new venture, she found them both sitting at the kitchen table in silence—quite sober.

"What's wrong, Aunt Gert?"

"It's bad news, I'm afraid. Your Uncle Hal was told today that they'll be closing the quarry. He's known for some time that this was coming, but the day has finally arrived. One more week, and there will be no more work for dozens of men."

She looked up at Maura and then over at Hal with heartfelt pain on her face. "What will all those families do? Where will everyone go?"

It was so like her aunt to worry about everyone.

"Oh, that is bad," Maura said. She stood behind Hal and rubbed his shoulders.

Hal said, "Well, we're not as bad off as most of the young people around here. We do have some savings. And our house. If bad comes to worse, we can always go live with our son Bobby. Every time they come to visit, he asks us to come live with them."

He looked at Gert, knowing full well that was never going to happen if she could help it. She would never want to leave her beloved island. "What's troubling to me," he said, "is what will become of all the folks without work. They'll have to leave. What will happen to the island then?"

Maura sat down between the two of them. "This is a wonderful island, full of so much potential. Sure, people will leave, but others will come and buy summer homes. This is a paradise for young children. I should know; I spent my summers here. Perhaps you could even start a summer camp for children. And then there's all the land. Lots of room for more vineyards and wineries." She took Hal's hand and smiled. "Things are always changing—and not always for the worse."

He looked at her with admiration. "How did a young thing like you ever get so smart?"

She blushed, then said, "Actually, I have some news of my own. And a job offer for both of you."

"A what?!" Gert said in astonishment.

"I'm going to buy the Darby mansion."

"You're what?" Now it was Hal's turn to be amazed.

"That's right. The Darby mansion. I don't mean to make light of your problem, but this couldn't have happened at a more opportune time—because, let me tell you, it surely needs a firm, loving hand. I was hoping the two of you could move in with me and help me put it back together."

She looked at their gaping faces. "There's plenty of room. And I'm hoping that through the years, Michael and I will fill it with children. But there will always be room for the two of you."

The pair sat in stunned silence as Maura continued to talk, first to one, then the other.

"Aunt Gert, it's so big, I can't possibly keep the place clean by myself. And Uncle Hal, there's so much work to be done fixing it up. I've already asked Roger and Mary Thomas to stay on. She'll be more than happy to do the cooking." She looked at Hal. "And you and Mr. Thomas will be hard put to get Humpty Dumpty back together."

They all laughed.

Hal gave her a quizzical look. "That bad, huh?"

"Uh huh, that bad."

Henry Darby put the phone back in its cradle on the desk and swiveled his chair around to look out the plate glass window. From his vantage point on the fourteenth floor of the Second National Savings and Trust building, he would usually take in the five blocks of hubbub in the streets below and Boston Harbor beyond. But not today. Today all he could see was Maggie's beautiful face: bittersweet memories of a time long ago, when he'd found his first true love.

Little Maura. She'd been such a lanky little thing with that long, wispy hair. Sweet child, though. Smiled just like her mother.

He'd taken care of his parents' finances for the past five years, since his father had had his stroke, and had all but forgotten the house on Darby's Island. Normally he would send Keith Bartlow to handle a small matter such as this, but he wanted to go himself. He had to see Maggie's daughter.

Maura's appointment at the Farmer's Bank in Conneaut was for eleven. She made sure she was there early and waited on a bench outside the bank with Hal and Roger.

Henry Darby pulled up at the curb in front of them at exactly eleven. Maura hadn't imagined that he would be the one to take care of the sale, but she recognized him immediately.

"Mr. Darby, how wonderful to see you again," she said as she gave him a little hug and a peck on the cheek, then stepped back and smiled. "You probably don't remember me, but I have some very good memories of you."

It took Henry a moment to respond to such an open display of esteem. He took both of her hands in his and stood back. "I remember you very well. But my, just look at you. You've become quite a lovely young woman. And you still have your mother's smile."

He shook hands with Hal and Roger, and the four of them went into the bank.

Roger gaped when Maura wrote a check for the full amount of the house.

Henry had agreed to take not two thousand, but five thousand off the selling price.

"I haven't been back to that house since the day I left for Boston, but I can imagine it must be falling down with neglect on the inside," he commented. "And I couldn't be happier that it is now in the capable hands of such a wonderful young lady."

He didn't tell her that he would have given the house to her if it had been his to give. Although he'd been happily married for the past fourteen years, his love for Maggie had not died with her.

He took the three of them to lunch at The Tavern, a charming country inn. He wanted to spend a little more time with the daughter of the woman he had loved so deeply—a delight, so open and effervescent. And what an astute mind!

When he dropped them off at the pier where they would catch the ferry back to the island, he said to Maura, "It's been a wonderful afternoon. I'm so happy our paths crossed again. And if you're ever in Boston with that new husband of yours, please don't hesitate to come and visit me. I truly mean that."

Once again, Maura kissed him on the cheek. "Thank you for everything, Mr. Darby. You're just as nice as I remembered."

In order to move in, it was imperative that they prepare three major rooms of the big house—the kitchen and two bedrooms. The five of them rolled up their sleeves and got to work, spending the next month scrubbing and scouring, scraping and peeling, mending and patching.

Gert and Maura went into fits of coughing, then laughter, as they watched the curtains and draperies crumble into dust when they took them off the windows. There were enough pieces of bedroom furniture in the eight bedrooms to fill two quite comfortably, and although Bernice Darby had taken all of her valuable china, crystal, and silver with her, the kitchen cupboards and pantry shelves were still filled with dishes, pots, pans, and other essentials.

Jack took a week off in October, and he and Martha came over to help out. He'd congratulated Maura over the phone for investing her money in real estate.

The day they arrived was one for celebrating, as far as Maura was concerned. She met them at the marina, thrilled to see her aunt and uncle again.

"Next best thing to gold," Jack said as they stood outside looking at the house. "You did well picking this beauty."

She took them in through the pantry, and they were quite impressed with the kitchen.

"You still have a way to go," Jack commented after they'd taken a tour of the house. "But when you're done, you'll have a fine showplace. One to be proud of."

Mary and Gert prepared a wonderful meal, and they all sat around the kitchen table, feasting on pot roast with little potatoes and carrots, cole slaw, homemade bread, and chocolate cake—and lots of conversation and laughter.

The next day, they all got to work.

"What in the world do people do with two parlors?" Maura wondered out loud as she and Jack put the finishing touches of trim around one of the parlor walls.

She stood up, holding her paintbrush in mid–air, wagging it like a finger. "I know what I'm going to do with one of them. It will make a perfect playroom for the children. What do you think, Uncle Jack?"

"Sounds good to me. You're not planning to have a brood of fifteen, like Pops and Kate, are you?" he asked jokingly, then got back to concentrating on avoiding smearing paint on the oak woodwork.

Maura laughed. "You never can tell," she said, quite seriously.

"You sound like you might be considering it."

"Oh, Uncle Jack!" She dabbed a spot of paint on his nose.

They worked in silence for a while, concentrating on the fine detail of trimming, and then she asked, "How's Kevin been behaving?"

"Very well, actually. Getting great marks in school. He's really settled down. Hardly sees Wally at all anymore. Of course, you know your Aunt Martha's thoughts on the matter. He's perfect."

"Oh, I'm so happy to hear that."

Martha measured the tall casement windows on the first floor. After a long discussion, they decided on a pale cream brocade of some sort. She promised she would have the draperies made and shipped over. The rest of the house could wait. Blinds would suffice for now.

By week's end, they had the two parlors and the dining room cleaned and shining with new paint. The library door was left closed. It would be Michael's domain and his to do after he moved in. The large guest bathroom had been scrubbed down, but there was some plumbing work still to be done. It would have to wait until spring, when they could get to Erie to buy the necessary plumbing supplies.

The draperies arrived by mid–December. Gert had made curtains in a colorful floral print for the kitchen dining area, which added the final touch to a very welcoming and cheerful room. The spiral staircase was polished, its thick, burgundy runner cleaned and swept. Windows glistened, chandeliers sparkled, and the marble foyer and oak floors were scrubbed and waxed to a pristine shine.

They were quite impressed with all they had accomplished, and Maura's weekly conversations with Michael were full of the details concerning their progress.

Because it had been a rather mild winter, Gert and Hal were going to visit their son for Christmas. Maura decided to take off for Buffalo. She called to tell them she'd be arriving at five–thirty on the twenty–first.

Kevin was at the depot to meet her. She was surprised to

see how much he had matured in the six months since she'd last seen him. His physique had taken on a manly form, and the shadow on his face showed he now had to shave daily.

After they embraced, she held him at arm's length and said, "My Lord, you've turned into a handsome devil," then gave him another squeeze. "Oh, it's so good to see you again, Kevin. I'm so glad to be home."

They rode to the house under gray skies. The absence of snow gave the landscape in the business district a lackluster look of soot and grime, but Maura's heart was full of joy. She was home again.

"I understand from Uncle Jack that you're doing quite well at school," she said as they drove along rutted roads.

"Yeah, well, with you and Patsy gone, I have Uncle Jack's undivided attention. And let me tell you, he's one tough taskmaster. Not like Aunt Martha. She was easy. He's really put a kink in my social life."

"He only wants what's best for you."

"I know that. But I hardly see my friends anymore. Wally's out of school, so he's practically out of the picture except when I see him at the country club for special occasions. I'm not allowed out during the week." He gave her a stern look, imitating his Uncle Jack. "Have to crack those books, mister."

She laughed.

"In the beginning," Kevin continued, "I tried to get Aunt Martha on my side, but for some reason, she'd just say, 'Whatever your Uncle Jack says.' What a switch. I could always wrap her around my little finger."

Maura was relieved he wasn't aware that she was the reason for her aunt and uncle's change of attitude.

"If you want to know the truth, I kinda like it. Uncle Jack is really a swell guy. Last summer, he taught me to play golf. The weekends I don't have a party to go to, he takes me bowling, or we just spend time together."

They pulled into the garage, and Maura ran ahead while Kevin got her luggage. She was greeted at the door by the aroma of roasting chicken and sage, then yips of joy from Sadie, who slathered her face with dog kisses when she stooped down to pet her. Whoops and hollers came from Emiline, who almost squeezed the breath out of her with her embrace. "Oh, my baby's home!"

Not knowing Patsy would be there made for a big surprise when she came bouncing into the kitchen, followed by Paul, Martha, and Jack. More hugs and kisses made Maura feel totally loved.

She was greeted by yet another surprise when she went into the living room and saw her grandmother Mahoney sitting in a big wing chair by the fireplace.

"Oh, Grandma, this is just a perfect Christmas," Maura said as she stooped to kiss her. Then she sat down on the floor at her grandmother's feet and looked at the tree with its glittering lights and the green garland and red bows on the staircase. "This is so wonderful."

Patsy, Kevin, and Maura spent the next three days together, shopping and wrapping gifts. Christmas Day was as it had always been, with gifts galore heaped under the tree. But the best gift of all for Maura was having her grandmother there.

On Christmas evening, they were sitting around the dining room table after a sumptuous dinner, sipping a sweet liqueur and talking, when Brigid brought up the subject of Maura's impending wedding.

She said to Maura, "Tis your thoughts I'll be needin', love, but after much cogitating about the matter, I'd be considerin' it a great honor if you'd be lettin' me put on the whole affair as me weddin' gift ta ya."

"Oh, Grandma, I couldn't expect you to do that. Just the cost alone! And you're such a busy lady. I can't imagine you spending that much time away from your business."

"Posh, child. I had no thoughts of a weddin' on Darby's Island. No, no. The weddin' would be in Herron's Point at Saint Michael's. Your Michael should like that. And don't I have all you'd be needin' fer the reception?"

"But there are so many people that would have to get there. Where would they stay? I think it would be too difficult for you to make all those arrangements. It's too much to expect from you."

"Maura, love, I want ta do this fer yer mither's sake. It's something I should have done fer her and didn't. There won't only be the pleasure of the doin' but the thought that I can make up in small measure the things I was so remiss about in the past."

Maura could see this meant a great deal to her grandmother, and it was all she could do to keep the tears from spilling out. "Oh, Grandma, I think it's not only a wonderful wedding gift, but a thoughtful one. Thank you so much."

"Thank *you*, child."

Kevin spoke up. "I think it's a swell idea. I don't know anyone on Darby, but I sure have a collection of pretty young things I know at Herron's Point."

Everyone laughed.

Before she and Paul took the train to Chicago the next day, Patsy made Maura promise she would come to Chicago to shop for her wedding dress. Paul had to get back to work, and they planned to spend New Year's at his parents' house. Maura accompanied Jack and her grandmother to Toronto, where Brigid caught the train to Herron's Point.

Before she boarded the train, Brigid shed a few tears as she hugged Maura. "Now, don't be fergttin' to be in touch. We have lots ta be considerin' before that big day arrives."

The next few days, Martha took Maura on the rounds of furniture stores and antique shops, where they picked up a number of odd chairs, a beautiful Turkish rug for the parlor, and two oil paintings. Jack said he would haul it all over to the island before they went to visit Brigid in June.

New Year's Eve, they all went to the country club for dinner and dancing. Maura met up with a number of old friends, and Kevin kicked up his heels in grand style, but he obediently rode back to the house with them instead of hanging on with the younger crowd.

The day Maura was to leave, a snowstorm threatened. Somehow it managed to blow over, leaving just a dusting of snow in its wake. Maura was relieved. There was no compelling reason for her to get back, but she was getting anxious to return to her new home.

As they drove to the station, Jack wanted to know what she planned to do with her car. "It shouldn't just sit there idle," he said.

"There's not much use for one on the island. Uncle Hal has one he takes to the mainland on the ferry. If I need to, I can use his. Just give it to Kevin. He'll be graduating in June. No reason he shouldn't be driving it."

The second week in June, Maura made the trip to Chicago, as promised. When she got off the train, she was greeted by a happy Patsy, who embraced her fiercely. With tears of joy spilling down her cheeks, she said, "Oh, Maura, I can't tell you how much I've looked forward to this. It's like old times, us being together."

During the week she stayed with Patsy and Paul, they took her to the beach, went for bike rides in Rogers Park, played gin rummy, dined in, dined out, and talked till the wee hours of the morning. She'd come to grow very fond of Paul. Patsy had chosen wisely.

Patsy dragged Maura in and out of every dress store on Michigan Avenue and State Street looking for "the one." And they found it in Marshall Field's. They also found gowns for Patsy and her two bridesmaids there.

Once again, it was a tearful Patsy who bid Maura goodbye at the train depot. "I can't wait until August. Only two more months," she said excitedly as Maura boarded the train. "Take care, and see you then."

Maura hugged her, thanking her profusely for the wonderful week. She continued to wave down from her window as the train pulled away.

Gert and Hal had settled in nicely. Their little house had been rented out for the summer, and Hal tended to the maintenance at Maura's new house. He and Roger had hired a crew to take care of the roof repairs and were now painting the outside of the house a buff color with dark green trim. Gert insisted on doing all the cleaning, and she and Mary were like the Bobbsy twins in the kitchen. They all still ate there. When Mary suggested that Maura, Gert, and Hal move to the dining room for meals because it was only fitting, Maura spoke up. "I suppose the dining room will get used for parties and such. But I just love this kitchen. Much more homey. Don't you feel that way, Aunt Gert?" Gert agreed.

Marietta and Joanie were now home for the summer and spent a great deal of time at the mansion, helping Maura with washing and painting the extra bedrooms. The day they tried on their dresses, they were quite excited. "Oh, they're beautiful!" Marietta commented. Joanie's fit perfectly, but Marietta was just a bit of a thing. Hers had to be taken in at the waist and altered for length.

When Marietta and Joanie weren't around, Maura loved working in the yard. One day, after coming in from planting a flat of petunias and some geraniums, she commented to Gert, "Whoever did the landscaping here must have done a great deal of planning. I wouldn't change a thing. And Roger has kept it all in such trim shape. I just love planting flowers and working in the dirt, don't you, Aunt Gert?"

With three weeks to go before the wedding, Maura decided she would go over the yard and flowerbeds one more time. She wanted Michael to be impressed as he came up the walk to enter their new home.

After spending the entire day trimming, pulling weeds, and digging in dirt, she was completely overheated. Putting her gardening tools in the shed, she wiped the sweat off her face with the back of her hand and decided to go sit on the dock across the way and put her feet in the water to cool down. Her bath could come later.

The cooling effect of the water relaxed her as she leaned back on her elbows and lifted her face to the sky. That's when she realized she was looking up at the face of Luke Winters. She hadn't heard him approach, probably because she was swishing her feet back and forth. But there he was.

"Mr. Winters, you surprised me. Where on earth did you come from?" she said, sitting upright.

"Sorry, Maura. Didn't mean to startle you. Saw you sitting out here and decided to come join you to talk. Mind if I sit?"

"Of course not. Take off your shoes and get your feet wet. It's wonderful."

Not that they were good friends, but Luke Winters had become a very familiar and friendly face throughout the years she'd spent on the island. He seemed to go out of his way to speak to her as she passed by. But they'd never had any conversation longer than "Hello," "Nice day," or similar greetings. She couldn't imagine why he was here.

As he proceeded to take off his shoes and sit next to her, he said, "I've been wanting to talk to you for some time. Seeing you sitting out here seemed to be the perfect opportunity, so I grabbed it."

"That's curious, Mr. Winters. Why would you need to talk to me?"

She looked into his angular face, remembering how good–looking he had once been. Time had not been kind to Luke, and he looked well beyond his fifty–some years. His once–blond hair had become almost nonexistent, and his formerly muscular body was now shrunken and stooped.

"Well, this is not an easy thing for me to talk about. But since the doc told me I have a bad ticker, I've been pondering some things I feel need tending to. This surely is one of them. I think you need to know about your mama."

Maura sucked in her breath. "My mama!"

Luke looked out at the calm lake, his face drawn, lacking any animation when he began talking to the horizon.

"From the time your mama came to this island, I thought she was the most beautiful woman I'd ever laid eyes on. Not that it mattered, her married and all. Me too, for that matter. I used to watch her sometimes when she'd be shopping or walking you and your little brother around the island. Just saying hello to her made me all kinda goosebumpy, ya know. Then your daddy died and she was alone. I can't tell you how many times I wanted to go to her and comfort her. But me being married and all, and a jealous wife to boot—well, I knew I'd best not."

He looked at Maura. "You'd have to know my wife, June, to know what I mean. We got married when we were seventeen because we thought it was the thing to do. After she suffered three miscarriages, she kind of pushed me away, and I had an affair with an old girlfriend. When June got wind of it, the girlfriend moved to the mainland, and I suffered the consequences. June eventually forgave me, and we finally had a child. A boy named Mark. He was just about your age."

Once again, he looked out toward the lake and sighed. "I know this is a long explanation, but I feel you have to understand why I haven't spoken up until now." Then he looked down at his feet in the water and swished them back and forth. "You know, this really is relaxing," he said, looking at Maura with a half smile.

He continued. "After Mark was born, I thought June and I was going to have a good life together, but she gave all her attention to the boy and harped at me all the time. 'Where were you? What took you so long? You never do anything for me.' On and on, every day, she'd harp. I tell you, it was enough to drive a man to drink. There were times when she'd threaten to leave and go to her family on the mainland if I didn't straighten out. But I didn't know what I was doing that was so wrong. I truly did try to please her, and I could never figure her out. I suppose she never really forgave me for that affair I had, but it was Mark that kept us together, and I didn't want her to take him away from me. So I kept trying, even though I spent most of my time trying to stay out of her way."

Maura looked at the man next to her, his face strained with pain, struggling for words. Why was he rambling on about his life in such intimate detail?

"What in the world does all of this have to do with my mama?"

"I can't tell you how hard this is for me, Maura, but it's the only way I know how to make you understand why I took so long telling you this. That's what I'm trying to get to."

Luke reached down into the lake and cupped up a handful of water to cool his sweaty face, then continued. "The night your mama died, June sent me over to the Burkes' place with some of her grape jelly. She and Louise Burke were great friends and were always sharing, giving back and forth. Anyway, the Burkes lived at the other end of your street at that time, and on my way back, I saw your mama out in her driveway, arguing with a man. I couldn't hear exactly what they were saying, because his voice was low, but I could tell by your mama's tone that it wasn't something she'd want me to intrude on, so I just stayed back and waited in the shadows. It was only a minute or so, and then the man left. Since it was so dark, I wasn't sure who he was, but I think he was a man I had met earlier in the day. Man by the name of Arnaud.

"Anyway, I waited for a minute, expecting your mama to go back into the house. But she didn't. Even from where I was standing, I could tell she was crying as she ran for Division Street, in the direction of the quarry. I don't know what possessed me to follow her. I just felt I wanted to somehow comfort her. She had quite a head start on me, and I just followed a ways behind. I figured she'd be turning around any minute to go back to the house, and I would be there when she passed me by. But that's not what happened.

"She just kept on running until she came to the edge of the quarry. As I got nearer, I could hear her weeping and sobbing, just standing there looking into the abyss. I didn't know how to approach, so I started to whistle. Figured she'd think I was just out for a stroll. But my whistling startled her so much she swung around, lost her footing, slipped off the edge, and fell into the quarry. I was so shocked, I just stood there for a minute. Then when I finally got my wits together, I had to find my way down into the quarry to see if I could help her.

"Well, ever since that end of the quarry was worked out, people used it for a garbage dump. And there she was, lying in it. I could see right off that she was dead. Her neck was off to the side—broken. I can't tell you how long I stood there bawling my head off, not knowing what to do. I couldn't just leave her there, but if I went to tell someone, I knew June would probably think the worst of me being where I was and leave me for sure. Then I decided that if I carried her body to the beach, someone would find her first thing in the morning, and I'd be free and clear."

Luke choked up and began to cry.

Maura was so overwhelmed with what she'd just heard that she simply stared at him, incredulous.

He looked pleadingly into her face, tears streaming down his cheeks and off the end of his nose. His voice quivered as he said, "I know I was a coward. It was a dumb thing to do. I should have done the manly thing right off. But I didn't. It never dawned on me there'd be an investigation into a murder."

At that point he stopped, pulled out a handkerchief, and blew his nose. Maura stared at him, stunned.

Regaining some composure, he went on. "I can't tell you what I went through for months. I knew that if anyone got accused of murdering her, I would have no choice but to speak up. I had to act like I knew nothing, but the worst part was knowing that if it hadn't been for me, she'd still be alive." Once again, his voice broke and he whined, "I've lived with that sorrow all these years."

Side by side, each sat covered in a heavy coat of silence.

Finally, Maura recovered sufficiently to say, "All these years, I've wondered who the person was that murdered my mama. Once, I even suspected someone."

She didn't know whether to hate the man next to her or feel sorry for him. Picking up her shoes and stockings, she stood to leave.

Luke followed suit.

When they reached the road, she turned to him. "I suppose I should thank you for telling me that awful story. It's some small comfort after all these years to know that my mama wasn't brutally murdered."

"I know I should have spoken up a long time ago, but thank you for listening to me today. At least that part of my burden is lifted."

"What's done is done, Mr. Winters. We can't change it. I hope you can find some peace in your life."

Gert was drinking a cup of coffee as Maura entered the kitchen.

"Aunt Gert, how well do you know Luke Winters?"

Phone calls between Herron's Point and Darby's Island were frequent. Brigid kept Maura informed on all her activities, and Maura was quite pleased with her reports.

Keeping in touch with Michael was her other priority. By the second week in August, he was winding up his classes and packing up his things.

"I've packed up my books and the bulk of my belongings, Maura. They should arrive at the end of the week. Can you believe it? It's almost over. I can't wait to see you."

"Oh, Michael, you should be so proud of yourself and what you've accomplished. I only wish I could come with your parents to see you graduate, but that's impossible. I'm leaving for Herron's Point that day. I didn't realize when we set the date for the wedding that we'd be cutting it so close. You'll just make it home in time to get ready to leave for Herron's Point."

CHAPTER TWENTY-EIGHT
The Circle is Complete
A Wedding

Anyone entering The Elms after the middle of July could see the sign posted on the door.

THE ELMS WILL BE CLOSED ALL DAY SATURDAY, AUGUST 19.

The clientele was now informed. Brigid intended the wedding of her granddaughter to be an event the likes of which the town had never seen. They had driven her Mary Margaret away with their judgmental gossip and scorn, and she was fully aware of the role she had played in that. This was her chance to make it up to her daughter. Her Maura would have a wedding befitting the best that would ever come out of this town.

Phyllis Cortland and Brigid were nodding acquaintances in June. By August, they'd become good friends, spending time together after shop hours planning the flowers to be ordered and shipped in from Toronto for the occasion. Phyllis, who owned Budding Blossoms, helped Brigid design the bouquets, the setting for the restaurant, and the placement of flowers in the church for the day of the wedding.

Antonio Donofrio, Brigid's head chef, would make the cakes to her specifications.

"Just remember, Antonio," she said, "I want the groom's fruitcake ta be made with brandy. I prefer that over rum. And be sure 'tis cut and boxed for the guests before the wedding. Put pretty pink ribbons on the boxes. That should look nice on the table next to the bride's cake, I'm thinkin'. I want the bride's cake ta be white. I'll leave the decorations up ta yourself. I know you'll be doin' a nice job. Just don't be fergitten' ta put in the glass ring."

She would have loved to do all this herself, but there wouldn't be time in her busy schedule at the last minute. She also asked Antonio if he would ask his cousin Mario to play the violin during the reception. He had a group of three—himself, an accordian player, and a bass fiddle player—that did quite a bit of entertaining at the hotel on different occasions. Mario met with Brigid, and the contract was set.

Michael's brother, Victor, had shipped over eight cases of his best wines. That and a Champagne punch would be sufficient, to her way of thinking. It was the menu for a sitdown dinner at the reception that she considered crucial. After much consideration, she decided they would start with a creamy lobster bisque, followed by her own special crab salad. The entrée would be Chateaubriand of beef with parsley potatoes, glazed carrots, mushrooms— and of course cake.

She'd informed Father DeSalle of the wedding way back in May. Most weddings were held during the morning hours, but he'd agreed to hold the ceremony on Saturday afternoon at five o'clock because of the large numbers of people who'd be arriving from the States on Saturday morning. He assured her that the banns for Maura Ryan and Michael Birch would be announced three consecutive Sundays before the wedding.

In the past eighteen years, Saint Michael's had undergone numerous changes as a result of Father DeSalle's dogged persistence. A badly needed parish house had been built in the empty lot behind the church, and the church itself had been razed and rebuilt. Both buildings were quite handsome, done in limestone from the quarry, with flagstone walkways. The builders had kept the beautiful oak doors and the four stained-glass windows, two on either side. But above the oak doors, they had added a very large, round, stained-glass window with the figure of Christ praying in the garden. The church now had a choir loft and organ, and seating could easily accommodate two hundred parishioners.

Claire Conroy was a member of the choir. Brigid felt a little twinge in her heart when she remembered how many times Maggie had commented on how she loved to listen to Claire's beautiful voice as she went about the boarding house, singing while doing her chores. Brigid had to admit that she enjoyed it, too. She asked Claire if she would be the soloist at Maura's wedding.

"Oh, my goodness, I'd be honored," Claire responded with heartfelt enthusiasm. They chose the music.

Jim Villani, the local printer, designed the invitations, beautifully done in gold lettering embossed on a special white linen paper. Those were sent out by mid July to a select group.

Back in June, Brigid had approached Allen Dorsett, manager

of MacPhearson's Hotel. He was only too happy to reserve seven rooms for the Birch family on Friday, the 18th of August, and all twenty rooms in the hotel for Saturday, the 19th. She had written Maura to get the head count before doing this, and Maura had replied, "Michael, his parents, and three of his brothers and their wives will be coming on Friday. But you'd better reserve another two rooms for their seven children. On Saturday, reserve them all. I just hope there's enough room. The entire Birch family, with spouses and children, comes to fifty-three."

Penelope and Clifford assured Brigid they would be happy to take the overflow if there turned out to be a problem. But Gert and Hal, as well as Mary and Roger Thomas, were definitely invited to stay with them.

Rosemarie was delighted at the news of Maura's wedding, and quite early on, she'd invited Maura to stay with her parents, the Stuarts. Rosemarie and Alan were planning to stop off at Darby's Island to pick up her, Gert and Hal, and Mary and Roger Thomas. They would be coming over in Alan's new cabin cruiser on Wednesday.

Jack, Martha, and Kevin would be staying on the third floor of the boarding house, where Emiline and Lincoln Washburn would have the beautiful front room on the second floor. All of the regular boarders would be invited to the wedding: Clara and Agnes, Kurt and Elsa, Claire, and Zeb. They were all looking forward to the coming event.

Mary Murphy had offered her home if it was needed, and it was. Patsy was to be Maura's matron of honor, so it was decided that she and Paul would stay with Mary, since it was right next to the Stuarts' house. Maura would want Patsy close by the day of the wedding.

Brigid would have loved to have Maura with her those last few days, but her apartment was too small to accommodate anyone but herself. But she'd be seeing her and the rest of her precious family. That was all that mattered. Jack had written to tell her he would be bringing a wonderful surprise, which had her curiosity piqued. Now that she'd taken care of all the out–of–town guests, she only hoped she hadn't forgotten anyone or anything.

Two weeks before the wedding, the restaurant had an unusually busy luncheon crowd. It took everyone in the kitchen, including Brigid, to keep up with the orders. When they finally had time to take a breather, she and Antonio sat down to have a cup of coffee.

"How are the plans fer the cake comin'?" Brigid asked.

"Oh, I've got a picture in my head. I think I'm going—"

It was the word "picture" that grabbed Brigid's attention. She got up, untied her apron, threw it on the table, and marched out and up to Commerce Street. She'd forgotten to get a photographer.

There would have to be a photo of the wedding party for the families. And the newspaper! Of course! She would want *The Point* to have a photograph of the bride, with all the details of the wedding. Harold Bixby, the local photographer, said he'd be happy to handle the assignment.

A reunion of old friends took place the day of Maura's arrival, the Wednesday before the wedding. Maura, Gert and Hal, Clifford and Penelope, Drs. Rosemarie and Alan Rowan, Dr. Mark Stuart and his wife, Sarah, the Murphys, Mary and Roger

Thomas, and Brigid sat at a long table on the screened porch of the restaurant, eating lunch.

Yelps and squeals of laughter filtered in from the beach, and a balmy breeze wafted in, caressing Brigid's cheek. Powder puffs dotted an azure sky that looked down on a serene lake dotted with colorful sails and one large coal barge in the distance.

It gave Brigid a sense of drifting. She couldn't remember when she'd felt more joy. Picking at her salmon salad, she looked out at the dining room with a judicious eye, making sure all the patrons were taken care of properly, then watched her granddaughter's face glow as she happily responded to the animated conversation centered on her impending wedding.

Sara Stuart, sitting next to Brigid, leaned toward her and commented, "These warm cinnamon rolls are absolutely delicious. And this salmon! What else do you have in here? I make a salmon salad myself, but I've never tasted one like this before."

Brigid smiled. "I'll give ya the recipe. Remind me ta be writin' it down for ya before ya leave."

Settling in at the Stuarts', Rosemarie showed Maura to her room. She leaned against the door frame and watched as Maura began to unpack. "I can't believe you're all grown up and ready to get married," she said wistfully. "I remember when I took care of you after your father died. You were always such a sweet, serious child. Your mother would be so very proud of you, Maura."

"I hope so. I've been thinking of her a great deal these past months, wishing she could be here to see me get married."

Rosemarie sighed. "I know. I think of her often myself. She was like a sister to me. But somehow I think she'll be here in spirit, looking down on you with that beautiful smile of hers, giving you her blessing."

In order to lighten the mood, Maura asked, "Aunt Rosemarie, would you like to see my wedding gown?"

"Would I? My goodness, yes!"

Friday came around, extremely hot and overcast, threatening rain. The waves in the lake were quite agitated.

Maura couldn't wait for Michael's arrival. It had been almost a year since she'd seen him, and the anticipation was intense. In the early afternoon, she was watching for him from the porch of the boarding house when she saw *Sweet Maggie* pulling into the dock down at Kelly's Marina.

She ran to greet her family and saw that Jack was distraught. He jumped down to moor the boat while Kevin stayed onboard to help with the lines. She surmised that their trip over from Buffalo had been a rough one.

Jack gave her a quick glance. "Hi. Just give me a minute." He pulled and yanked as the boat dipped and swayed, banging against the dock. "The only thing I can say is I'm glad we started out early," he grunted as he secured the lines. "There's a storm coming for sure."

Wiping his hands on his pants, he rubbed his tired eyes and looked at Maura with concern. "I hope the others don't have any trouble getting here. Lake Erie's got to be one of the worst for traveling in bad weather."

Then he gave Maura a big hug. "Good to see you, sweetheart. Ready for your big day?"

Maura's heart sank, but the unsettling news about the impending storm did not diminish her happiness at seeing the family she had been away from for so long.

Wash got off the boat, his black face ashy. "Lawdee, it be good to stand on solid ground. Mighty good seeing you, Miss Maura."

He reached up to help Martha, who groaned as her knees buckled slightly when she hit the dock.

"My goodness, I seem to have lost my sea legs." She held out her arms to Maura and smiled. "But it's worth it all just to see you again, dear." She embraced Maura and kissed her on the cheek.

Emiline appeared to have weathered the trip fairly well. She landed gracefully on her feet, grabbed Maura, and wrapped her in her arms, swaying back and forth. "My baby, can't tell you how I be missin' you."

Kevin and an older man Maura had never seen before handed down the luggage and hopped off the boat.

"Hey, sis. Good to see you." He gave her a peck on the cheek.

The stranger stood there with an impish grin.

Jack spoke. "Maura, I would like you to meet your Great-Uncle Edward."

Maura looked at her great-uncle with consternation. "How do you do?" she said. "But..." She looked at her Uncle Jack to explain.

Jack laughed. "Eddie here came into the lumberyard looking for employment a few months back. When he told me his last name was Walsh, I told him my mother's last name was Walsh, and wouldn't you know, after a bit of back and forth, it turned out she's his sister. Can you believe the luck?"

Maura turned to take in the man in front of her. He had a broad face, snow-white, wavy hair, and twinkling blue eyes. He appeared to be her height and somewhere around her grandmother's age, or perhaps a bit older. "Oh, my goodness! Uncle Edward, this is wonderful. Does Grandma know you're coming? She hasn't said a word to me about a brother."

He gave her a grin that revealed a missing front tooth. "No, 'tis yer Uncle Jack's idea we should be surprisin' herself. 'Tis truly excited I am ta be tyin' up with me family again. And what a pleasure ta be meetin' such a pretty colleen as yourself."

"Thank you, Uncle Edward. But why have you stayed out of touch?"

"'Tis well over forty years since I've seen me wee sister, so I'm thinkin' me story's a pretty long one." He looked at the threatening sky and the others, who were patiently waiting. "Perhaps another time. We'd best be movin' on."

Maura saw Zeb coming down the road, intent on getting to the shipping yard. She waved him down. "Zeb, do you think you could get all this luggage in the car and take the two ladies up to the boarding house?"

"Glad to oblige," he said. He got out of the car, came around, and opened the back door. "Hop in, ladies." After loading the luggage wherever it would fit, he looked at the pile still left, rubbed his chin, and spit tobacco into the water. "I'll come back to get the rest."

The others trudged the three blocks to the boarding house to settle in.

Emiline and Wash were agape at the beautiful room they were given. When they'd been left to unpack, Wash turned to Emiline and said, "You knows I be full of misgivin's 'bout this trip from the beginning, but, no, y'all had to be seein' your baby married off. I's 'spectin' we be put in with the servants. But no, they's treatin' us just like white folk, Emmy. Feels kinda strange. Oh, well! Guess we might's well enjoy what we can."

Emiline was looking out the window as he spoke. "Lawdy, lawd, Wash. Come looka here. Now ain't this a picture to carry back home?"

Kevin seemed genuinely happy to see his sister and put his free arm around her as the five of them climbed to the third floor, loaded down with luggage. "You excited, sis?" he asked.

"I'm about to bust," she said in all seriousness. "I only hope everyone gets here safely." Jack's report on the conditions of the lake worried her.

She headed directly to the staircase at the far end of the center hall of the large apartment and climbed to the roof as the rest settled in. Outside on the widow's walk, hot wind grabbed at her long hair, blowing it in all directions.

She leaned on the rail overlooking the lake. The only ship in sight yawed, struggling to keep its course through huge waves that peaked and crashed, pounding the shoreline with sprays of white foam. Black clouds, heavy with rain, were rolling in fast. One lone swimmer, his towel streaming behind him like a striped tail, was running up from the beach toward home before the rains came.

A jagged streak of lightning that seemed to penetrate the lake was followed by a thunderclap that opened up the heavens. Rain poured down in torrents. Maura raced down the steps to escape the storm's fury.

She was truly worried. Father DeSalle wanted them at the church that evening for a quick rehearsal.

What if they don't get here? she thought.

And they didn't.

Jack called Brigid to tell her he was in town, but the weather being what it was, he would wait until Saturday morning to come see her and bring along her surprise. Maura called the Stuarts to say she'd stay over with her Uncle Jack because of the storm. She called the Birch house on the island, but the line was dead. She'd talked to Michael for almost an hour on Thursday, after he'd gotten in from Columbus, and he'd made it quite clear he couldn't wait to get there.

Dinner at the boarding house was always served at six o'clock. Wash and Emiline were seated at the dining room table with the rest of the boarders. Emiline had cooked and served people all of her adult life, and it was all she could do to stifle the urge to get up and help, but she decided to sit back and enjoy being waited on. This was an experience she and Wash had never had in all their born days. Agnes and Clara were so gracious, making them both feel very much at ease. Zeb was curious about Wash's job, asking all kinds of questions. Even Kurt had a few of his own. There was never a lull in the dinner conversation.

As Maura readied for bed, she was hopeful the weather would be clearer the next day. There was nothing to worry about, was there? Nevertheless, she slept fitfully on the sofa.

Morning came and the sunshine with it. After breakfast, Maura didn't go with Jack and the rest, although she wanted to see her grandmother's face when she was reunited with her long–lost brother. Instead, she went out on the porch once again to watch for Michael.

The lake's mood had changed dramatically, like that of a bratty child whose tantrum had subsided because it had finally gotten its way. It flaunted its serene smugness at a cloudless blue sky. Maura breathed in the moist, sweet scent of grass and nicotiana, so prevalent in the area. The day was much cooler, a relief from the intense heat they'd been having.

What a beautiful day for a wedding, she thought. Please, Lord, get the Birch family here safely.

She made numerous calls to the island with no success and waited until after one o'clock, with no sign of any member of the Birch family. She had to get back to the Stuarts'. Her dress needed pressing, and she had to wash her hair. There were so many last–minute details she had to deal with. She called Allen Dorsett at the hotel, asking him to inform her the minute the Birch party arrived. Then she called Zeb.

Five boats ferried the entire Birch family over from the island— where, because of the storm, they had gathered en masse, some the day before and some that morning. Michael was completely on edge. He'd almost been ready to jump in and swim when Pops Birch had decided they should wait and all leave together. "Safety in numbers, you know. No chance of losing each other."

Had it been up to Michael, he would have left the day before, storm or no storm. It was Pops who'd deterred him. "I understand your feelings, son, but the whole idea is to get there. This storm will blow over. You'll see. And we'll be there in plenty of time for the wedding."

Maura had asked Zeb if he would mind watching out for Michael and his family. "No problem, missy. Glad to."

When the five boats came into the marina, Zeb had no problem guessing who'd be on them. Michael jumped off first, hoping to see Maura. Zeb, all business, approached and held out his hand. "I'd be Zebadiah Chadwick, here to meet ya. Folks 'round these parts call me Zeb. I'd take it kindly if you did the same."

Michael shook his hand. "Good to meet you, Zeb. From what Maura tells me, you're one of the people who stay at the boarding house."

"Yep. Been there near on thirty years, now. Knew your intended's mama back when I first moved in. Shame about her. Beautiful girl. But I must say, you picked a winner in her daughter. Sometimes I can see her mama in her when she smiles at me. A lot pluckier, though."

Zeb offered to drive the folks to the hotel, but they chose to walk and stretch their legs once they were told it was a mere two blocks away.

Passersby stood and gazed with curiosity at the large group of strangers laughing and talking as they walked up the hill.

Seven trips, and Zeb managed to deliver all the luggage. Michael thanked him profusely for his assistance, offering to pay for his services.

Zeb frowned and waved the money away, shaking his head. "'Twas my pleasure to be of help," he drawled. "Lookin' forward to seein' you all at the church. One of the biggest events we've had in these parts back far as I can remember." He spit out the window and leaned over the steering wheel, ready to drive away.

"I wonder if you could do just one more thing for me," Michael said, leaning toward the car window.

Zeb nodded. "Ask away."

"I don't know where Maura is staying. Would you happen to know, and if you do, could you take me there?"

"Sure 'nuff. Right up the hill here. Long as you don't take too long. Hop in."

He continued to talk as they headed up Division Street. "I got to wind up some work at the shippin' yard and get back to get all dressed up for that weddin' of yours. First new suit I've had since my mama's funeral. Clara Carter made me buy it. Didn't she just take me over to Bauchman's and pick it out for me! She can be mighty bossy sometimes." He gave Michael a knowing look. "She was my old school marm, you know." He pulled into the Stuarts' driveway.

Jack jumped out. "Can you wait? I won't be long. I just want to see Maura to let her know I'm here."

"No problem," Zeb said as he got out and leaned against the car door, stuffing another chaw in his mouth.

Patsy answered his knock. "Michael! How well you look!"

Michael grabbed her and gave her a quick hug. "Good to see you, Patsy. It's been a long time. You look as pretty as ever." He looked into the house. "Where's Maura? Can I see her for a minute?"

Patsy put her hands on her hips and didn't budge. "At this moment, she's taking a bath. But you can't see her anyway. Don't you know it's bad luck for the groom to see the bride before the wedding?"

Michael's face fell. "I just want to see her to tell her we're all here," he pleaded.

"She knows. The hotel called just a minute before you got here. I can't tell you how relieved she is that you're here safely. But you'd best get back and get ready. I'll tell her you were here." She smiled and closed the door.

Within minutes, Patsy heard another knock at the door and expected it to be an insistent Michael. But it was Phyllis Cortland standing there, holding a wreath of gardenias.

"I brought Maura's headdress."

"Oh, it's absolutely gorgeous! Thank you so much. Maura will be thrilled."

"I certainly hope so. If not, it will be her grandmother I'll have to answer to. She's put her heart and soul into this wedding. Now I have to get to the church with the rest of the flowers for the bridal party. Lots to do. Been working since yesterday on this wedding. I hope it's as lovely as I think it will be. Tell Maura I wish her the best."

Patsy picked up the garland and went upstairs just as Maura came into the bedroom in her robe.

"Look what just came, Maura." She didn't bother to tell her about Michael.

"Oh, it's wonderful!" Maura leaned over to smell the blossoms. "Don't you just love the fragrance?"

"Um! Might as well get started on that hair of yours. That's going to take a good half hour or so."

Rosemarie came in and sat on the edge of the bed, watching in awe as Patsy brushed Maura's hair skillfully, pulling it all up and carefully braiding it. She then twisted the braids on top of Maura's head and attached them with hairpins. "Now let's see if the garland fits." She placed it on Maura's forehead above her eyebrows. It fit perfectly around her crown of braids. "Wonderful!" Patsy said as she removed it. "Now, why don't you just take a rest or finish up what you have to do, while I go next door to get ready. Then Rosemarie and I will come back to help you with your gown and all."

Maura welcomed the time alone and leaned back on the chaise, trying to relax. She hadn't slept well the night before and had spent a very anxious morning waiting for Michael.

The minute she'd walked in the Stuarts' door, she'd been fawned over, with Sarah Stuart insisting she eat something and Rosemarie following her to her room to have some girl talk. And Patsy! Where did she get all that energy and enthusiasm? Maura only wished it were contagious, but all she could muster up was a gnawing ache in the pit of her stomach. She hoped she wouldn't get sick during the ceremony. Maybe she and Michael should have eloped, like Patsy and Paul. Quick and over! All this fussing and attention were just too much. Try as she would, she couldn't relax.

Patsy bounced back into the bedroom half an hour later, waving a wide-brimmed, white straw hat with a streaming, mauve-colored ribbon. She was dressed in a calf-length, pink silk chemise with capped sleeves. Her satin shoes had been dyed the same color. "I'm back. How do I look?" she asked, twirling around.

Maura sat upright. "Oh, Patsy, you look beautiful! That dress is stunning on you. Remember the fun we had in Chicago when we bought the dresses? I wanted you to pick the lace one, and you insisted this one was better. When we asked the salesgirl to settle it, she agreed with you. I'm glad you won that argument. It's perfect."

Rosemarie came in, dressed in a fashionable, sea-foam green linen suit.

"And look at you, Dr. Rosemarie Rowan," Patsy said. "You look good enough to be going to a wedding." She laughed and turned to Maura. "Okay, cuz, your turn."

Maura's gown was quite simple. It, too, was a chemise with capped sleeves—white satin, ankle-length. Her white satin pumps were patterned with tiny seed pearls.

Patsy fastened a Belgian lace veil around Maura's braids with combs. The veil draped softly around her shoulders and tapered to her ankles. "Now for the headpiece," Patsy said as she placed the garland of gardenias on Maura's head.

She and Rosemarie stood back in silence for a moment.

"What?" Maura asked, looking down. "Is something wrong?"

Rosemarie's eyes brimmed with tears. "You look absolutely beautiful, Maura."

Patsy went over and hugged her cousin, then stood back again. "You look wonderful," she sighed.

"Thank you both for all your help, but I sure wish this were all over. I'm so nervous. I'll probably stumble down the aisle."

Patsy put two fingers against her cheek and circled Maura. "Let me think. As your matron of honor, it's my duty to check on every last detail." She faced her in all seriousness. "Do you have on something old?"

"Why, I believe so. I'm wearing the pearls I got for my eighteenth birthday. Does that count?"

Patsy sighed. "Oh, I suppose they'll do. I know you have on something new, so the next things are something borrowed and something blue."

"I do have on something blue. You should know. You're the one who gave me the blue garters. Remember? But no, I haven't borrowed anything."

Rosemarie spoke up. "I have just the thing. Wait a minute." She left the room and returned quickly. "These pearl earrings should do the trick. They're not only borrowed; they're really old."

Maura put them on.

"All right!" Patsy said. "Now that I'm satisfied everything is perfect, let's go to a wedding."

Kevin and Peter, Michael's younger brother, made a handsome pair of ushers in their black tuxedos and white carnation boutonnieres. They each took their job quite seriously, greeting the wedding guests and escorting them to their seats—Birch family on the right, Mahoney family on the left. Father DeSalle had also told them, "Leave the first pew open for the bridal party. The second is for immediate family. After that, wherever they choose." Most had chosen seats by the aisle, so they could see the bride. Emiline and Wash were considered family and sat in the second pew, along with Brigid, Eddie, and Martha. Jack would join them later.

Everyone had come decked out in his or her finest, and Kevin stood in the back, observing that the women's hats gave the illusion of a field of colorful flowers. But none of them could equal the white pedestaled urns, one on either side of the altar. Each contained a magnificent fern and trailing ivy. Long spikes of delicate, bell–shaped pink foxglove and feathery spikes of deep purple heather were nested in each fern.

Soft organ music filled the church with a medley of hymns while Jack paced back and forth at the rear of the church, waiting for the bride to appear. A very nervous Michael and his brother, Victor, waited in the sacristy for orders from Father DeSalle.

Maura and Patsy had been told to go to the recreation hall in the basement of the church to join the rest of the bridal party. They were greeted with a reception of oohs and aahs.

"Oh, here you are," Phyllis Cortland said with relief. "You

both look wonderful. Maura, you make a beautiful bride."

Little Emily came running up to Maura. "Auntie Maura, look what I get to carry!" She held up a basket of pink rose petals. She was adorable in her pink and white taffeta pinafore with its puffed sleeves and full, knee–length skirt. She wore a large pink ribbon on top of her head, white patent leather shoes, and lacy white stockings.

Maura cupped her face in her hands. "You look good enough to eat," she said, then gave her a kiss on the forehead.

Little Kenny was about to bust his buttons in his first pair of long trousers. He felt quite the little man in his black pants and shoes, white shirt, deep burgandy and gray brocade vest, and black bow tie. Not to be ignored, he said, "Aunt Maura, I'm going to carry this pillow with rings on it." He held it up for her to see.

"Oh, Kenny, you look so handsome. I love your vest." She gave him a kiss, too.

Marietta's and Joanie's outfits were identical to Patsy's except for the color—burgundy.

After five minutes of instruction on how to walk and where to go, Phyllis began fluttering around, lining them up, making sure all the hats were pinned on and everyone had their flowers. The matron of honor and the bridesmaids were each given a small bouquet of white roses and trailing green ivy. Maura's bouquet was fabulous: a long spray of dark green palm leaves and trailing ivy embedded with white trumpet lilies, pink rosebuds, and heart–shaped caladium leaves, which showed off their lacy patterns of pink, white, green, and burgundy.

They formed a procession and ascended the steps to the back of the church.

When Jack saw Maura, he choked up. "Maura, you look like

a Greek goddess." He had to clear his throat. "You look—"

"Uncle Jack, I'm terrified. I don't think I'll be able to walk down the aisle."

Jack held out his arm. "You just hang on to your ol' Uncle Jack. He'll get you there." As she hooked her arm in his, he patted her hand.

They all stood quietly waiting. They could hear the bells announcing that the Mass was to begin. Father DeSalle followed the two altar boys out to the altar and stood, solemnly facing the congregation. Everyone stood and turned toward the back of the church. He gave a nod, and the organist blasted out Mendelssohn's "Wedding March." Little Emily turned to look back at Maura, putting her hand over her mouth to stifle a giggle. Then she flipped back her long piped curls and put on a very serious face, and she and Kenny proceeded to enter the church.

Maura's knees were shaking as she and Jack followed the procession. She wondered if she was going to be able to hold herself up. When she saw Michael, so handsome in his black tuxedo, standing by the altar with his dimpled grin, their eyes locked. She looked radiant as she smiled openly at him the rest of the way down the aisle.

There were a few in the church, including Martha, who wondered why everything was spoken in Latin. And why did the priest have his back to them? He faced them during the readings and sermon, which were in English and all about marriage and family, but then everything resumed as before. And why all this up and down stuff, and why so long? The rest, accustomed to it all, took the Mass in stride.

After Communion and before the wedding vows, everyone

sat down and listened as Claire sang "Ave Maria." It was chilling. Brigid, who was clinging to her brother as though he was going to fly out of her life if she didn't, had to let go to wipe her eyes. She was not alone.

Once again, Father DeSalle faced the congregation as Maura and Michael joined him. He began. "We are gathered here together to join..."

He reached the conclusion: "I now pronounce you man and wife." He turned to Michael. "You may kiss the bride."

Maura and Michael timidly kissed, and the congregation applauded as the organ struck up and they jubilantly walked out of the church, followed by the wedding party. Once outside, Michael embraced Maura, so happy to have her near. That was short lived as the wedding guests descended upon them, pelting them with rice and showering them with congratulations.

The wedding party stayed behind for pictures while the rest either walked or drove to the restaurant.

The guests entered the dining room through a trellised archway dripping with ivy and gardenias. In the center of each table, a candle–lit hurricane lantern surrounded by beds of ivy and colorful anemones welcomed them. Potted palms were placed aesthetically here and there. The French doors to the screened–in porch were wide open.

A table for the wedding cakes, Champagne punch, and hors d'oeuvres sat in the left–hand corner of the room. The groom's cake had been boxed, and each box was tied with a pink ribbon, just as Brigid had ordered. These were stacked next to a beautiful five–tiered cake with white buttercream frosting. Each tier was edged with a live vine of tiny ivy leaves. The top tier had an arch of ivy, under which the wax figures of a bride and groom stood. Live pink rosebuds were placed around each tier. The Champagne punch and platters of clams on the half shell, caviar, crackers, an assortment of other spreads, chocolates, and nuts sat on the other side of the cake.

In the right–hand corner was a table laden with the wedding gifts the guests had dropped off earlier. In the center of the room was the long table reserved for the wedding party, covered with a white cloth and the low spray of evergreens and pink and white roses that ran the length of the table.

Since this would be an evening affair, Brigid had had a fairly large platform built to put on the floor in front of the fireplace for dancing after dinner. Mario wore a perpetual grin, playing his violin, filling the room with atmosphere. Two waiters stood ready to assist the guests. Brigid radiated happiness, traveling from table to table with her brother in tow, making introductions and small talk.

At one point she asked Mario to play one of her favorite songs, "Fascinatin' Rhythm." He continued circulating about the room, filling requests as everyone socialized while waiting for the wedding party. They arrived shortly after seven, accompanied by Father DeSalle. Once again, they were greeted by applause.

Everyone was in a festive mood. Mario and his two associates (who would play later for the dancing) began to play "It Had to Be You" as the wedding party slowly made its way to the head table. There were now four waiters standing on the sidelines, ready and waiting for Brigid to give the word to pour the wine. There were toasts to be made to the bride and groom.

As best man, Victor went first. He held up his glass and faced the newlyweds. "To my little brother, Michael—who, I might add, is not so little—and his beautiful bride, Maura, I offer you my best wishes for a happy life together. Maura, you bring your charm and intelligence as a gift to our family. We are all happy to have you in our fold. And Michael, just remember, when it comes to having a family, you don't have to compete with Pops."

Everyone laughed and took a sip or two of wine.

Patsy stood, holding her glass. "To the sweetest, greatest friend I could ever have, and to the wonderful man she has chosen to share her life with. I wish all the best for both of you." She was visibly shaken with emotion, tears streaming down her cheeks. She took a sip of wine and hugged Maura.

Eddie was sitting next to Brigid, close to the wedding table. He stood, held up his glass, and looked out into the room. "I"d like ta be givin' a toast ta the new couple, if ya don't mind. I can't be tellin' ya what it means ta me ta be here tonight. I'll be thankin' all of ya fer the kindnesses showered on me." He turned to Maura and Michael, and, in typical poetic Irish style, gave a blessing. "May there always be work for yer hands ta do. May yer purse always hold a coin or two. May the sun always shine on yer windowpane. May a rainbow be certain ta follow each rain. May the hand of a friend always be near ya. May God fill yer hearts with gladness ta cheer ya."

A few "Hear, hears" came from the room as they all drank up, and Father DeSalle stood to give the blessing before they ate.

Michael and Maura held hands under the table. That was the best they could do for now. They had not had one minute to themselves, and though quite pleased with all that Brigid had done to make their wedding such a wonderful event, they restrained themselves from publicly showing their desperate need for just each other.

They both looked forward to leaving soon after the meal to go back to Michael's room at the hotel for the night. The following morning, they would go to Darby's Island, where they would have the house to themselves. Gert, Hal, Mary, and Roger would remain with Penelope and Clifford for an extended stay while the newlyweds honeymooned.

Mario again circled the room. "Makin' Whoopee," "Tea for Two," "The Man I Love"—there was no end to his repertoire. The four waiters came out laden with trays of lobster bisque and began to serve the meal.

Brigid's heart was full. The wedding had turned out to be everything she'd hoped it would be. She was touched to see how deeply Maura and Michael loved each other. It would be a good marriage. And the reunion with her brother was that special something that intensified her great happiness. She'd had more than her share of bitterness, anger, resentment, and sorrow in her lifetime—all of it her own doing—but God had turned it around when she'd finally cooperated, just as her good friend Father Charles had said. She realized she was truly blessed.

She could hear the murmuring of conversations and pockets of laughter as she looked around the room at her many friends and Maura's new family. Their animated faces revealed pleasure in each other's company and the meal they were being served.

Slowly, the room took on a golden glow. The sun was setting. Brigid got up and went to the porch to look out. There it was: gold and silver mixed with lavender. Pink and blue to the east, progressing to the west with fingers of magenta, fiery crimson, and brilliant orange saturating the clouds. The sun once again put on a brilliant display, silently filling the sky with its splendor.

Brigid was overcome with peace. She sensed their presence—Mary Margaret, Tim, Patrick, Charles, yes, even John and Gracia. They had all come to give Maura their blessing.

Oh, Patrick and Chuck, won't we be havin' a lot ta talk about tomorrow, I'm thinkin'.

About Mary Alice Baluck
In Her Own Words

When you live 92 years, your frame of reference becomes quite broad. And if you had a father who told stories and tall tales around the dinner table in your childhood, as I had, then you might understand where my imagination came from.

I was born in Youngstown, Ohio, to very loving parents. I married my handsome high school sweetheart at age 20, and we had six great kids. At age 33, I was given the opportunity to go to Youngstown State University, and I grabbed it. With the help of my family and the constant encouragement of my oldest daughter, Linda, I was able to finish in seven years, and at age 40, I graduated with a B.A. in Education and a minor in English. I then taught junior high school English for 24 years and retired in 1991.

My husband passed away in 1999, and although I had always written short stories and poetry as a pastime, I had never seriously thought of writing and publishing anything until he died. That is when I began using my frame of reference, which was rich in personalities and lifestyles. These were my "golden years," and they were just that: golden.

I now reside at the Blackburn Retirement Home, an outstanding place that has allowed me to use all of their technology to spend my hours writing. Enjoy my first brain child, *Heaven's Doorway.* There's more to come.

Website: https://www.dldbooks.com/marybaluck/

To comment on the book or to contact me, you may write to my daughter, Linda Pompeii: lapompeii@gmail.com

Made in the USA
Middletown, DE
13 July 2020

12642081R00268